THE ASYLUM THREAD

A DAN RENO NOVEL

DAVE STANTON

LaSalle Davis Books

THE ASYLUM THREAD
Copyright © 2022 Dave Stanton
All rights reserved.

This book is a work of fiction. Names, characters, places and incidents are either products of the author's imagination or used fictitiously. Any resemblance to actual events, locales, or persons, living or dead, is entirely coincidental. No part of this publication can be reproduced or transmitted in any form or by any means, electronic or mechanical, without permission in writing from the author or publisher.

Cover art by *Heidi Gabbert*

ISBN: 978-1-64713-950-6
LaSalle Davis Books – San Jose, California

ALSO BY DAVE STANTON

Stateline

Dying for the Highlife

Speed Metal Blues

Dark Ice

Hard Prejudice

The Doomsday Girl

Right Cross

FOR MORE INFORMATION, VISIT DAVE STANTON'S WEBSITE:

DanRenoNovels.com

For my friend of forty years, adrenaline junkie and skier extraordinaire, Ron Regan

1

CANDI AND I DIDN'T talk much as we drove across the high-desert flats. Ahead of us, I could see midday storm clouds resting low on the horizon. The parched grasslands stretched to the east, waiting patiently. It was late October, and it hadn't rained since early spring.

"Looks like weather," I said, glancing at her, but she seemed alone with her thoughts. I turned my eyes back to the ribbon of asphalt splitting the cracked earth. The buzz of my tires was loud as we reeled in the miles to the airport in Reno.

When we reached the departure terminal, I lifted Candi's suitcase from my truck bed. She waited on the walkway, gazing away. I took her in my arms, but she pulled away after a brief moment.

"You'll be fine, I know it," I said.

"I will," she whispered, but there was little conviction in her voice. Then she walked to the terminal doors, her eyes studying the ground, as if she was afraid to raise her head and look toward the future. I waved at her, but she didn't look back. She went through the glass doors and disappeared.

I climbed into my cab and stared out at the afternoon. After a minute, I noticed I was blocking cars that were trying to drop off passengers, and I maneuvered from the curb and drove away. I headed south automatically, back toward South Lake Tahoe and my empty home.

Raindrops started pelting my windshield outside of Washoe City, and sleet was coming down hard as I climbed the grade over Spooner Pass. I steered through the slush accumulating on the sweeping turns, wondering what I would do with the rest of the day, or for that matter, the rest of the month.

Candi's troubles had started four months back, when she miscarried. After her initial grief, she seemed to have quickly recovered, or at least that's what she led me to believe. But then she became fixated on getting pregnant again. At first, I was all too happy to oblige her amorous agenda, for I viewed Candi as the sexiest woman I'd ever known, and our lovemaking had always been passionate and exuberant. I didn't think it was possible I could get enough of her. But after two months of fervent couplings, her obsession with becoming impregnated started to concern me.

She began going through pregnancy kits, testing herself daily, even though the directions said to wait until a period was missed. She started researching fertility drugs and treatments. She asked that I get my sperm count checked.

Finally, she said, "I think something's wrong with me."

"I don't know why you'd think that," I replied. "Your doctor said you're fine."

She stared at me sullenly. "I know my own body."

"You can't rush these things," I said. "Hell, three months from now you'll probably be pregnant, so why not just let nature take its course?"

"Three months?" she said, her lips trembling. Her eyes were pinched at the brow, and for a moment I didn't know if she would burst into tears or leap up and attack me. But instead, she turned and walked to the front door. "I need to call my mother," she said.

I stood and rubbed my temples as she left the house. I was at a loss; Candi had always been stable. Even during my most difficult cases, when

I was threatened with imprisonment or worse, Candi had been like a rock, never burdening me with panic or fear or questions I couldn't answer. To see her become illogical was somewhat of a shock. Although I knew a miscarriage could play havoc with a woman's emotions, I thought it would be a relatively short-term matter, not something that would take months to resolve.

I sat on the couch and through the window watched Candi pace on the deck, speaking into her cell phone. Candi and I had lived together for over two years and were engaged to be married. I loved her and was ready for us to start a family. I'd seen how composed she was during crises, and believed she was a rare woman. But my assumption that I knew everything about her was clearly illusory. So was the notion that I could comprehend the intricacies of any woman.

Regardless, to see her melt down, and that's the best way I could describe it, was surprising and perplexing. It also served as a reminder that sanity can be both relative and impermanent.

When Candi came back into the house and told me she wanted to go stay with her mother in Houston for an indeterminate amount of time, my initial instinct was to protest. But I stayed silent for a long moment, then said, "If you think that's best."

. . .

When I came off the grade, it was snowing at lake level. I counter-steered as I slid sideways on an icy patch, until my tires bit into a shoulder and re-gained traction. Checking my speed, I drove along the stretch of Highway 50 that hugged the eastern shoreline of Lake Tahoe. Through the pines, I could see the lake was gray and roiling with whitecaps. In my headlights, the snowflakes swirled in a hypnotic dance. Ten minutes later, I reached Stateline, Nevada. The tops of the casino hotels were obscured by the wintery haze that had descended upon the city.

I crossed the state line into California, my tires spitting snow. I had no plans or purpose for the remainder of the day. Without thinking, I turned into the parking lot for Whiskey Dick's, the bar closest to my house. As I walked into the joint, a little voice in my head reminded me to moderate. I wasn't in the mood to listen.

Inside, the bar was noisy and more crowded than I expected. I immediately thought it must a birthday party or maybe a company celebration. I took a seat on the only empty stool at the far corner and looked down the bar at the patrons. They were a misshapen bunch. The couple next to me were in their twenties and covered in tattoos offset with every sort of facial jewelry; nose rings, nose bones, lip studs, brow studs, ear hoops, and other bits of hardware I couldn't identify. Beside them sat a wispy man. He wore a pink silk shirt and had lank blonde hair. On second glance, maybe it was a woman. On the next stool, an obese fellow with huge fleshy arms slurped noisily from a straw. To his right, a curly-haired midget sat on a phonebook and sipped some green concoction from a snifter.

The bartender finished making a flurry of drinks and came over. "Jack and Coke?" she asked.

"Please. Busy today, huh, Pam?"

"An hour ago, it was dead. Next thing I know, it's a damn looney bin. Like a bus from a freak show pulled up."

"Maybe you'll make some good tips."

"I already have, compared to the usual cheapskates that bless me with their presence."

"Hey, last time I was here, I left you two bucks."

"Yeah, you're quite the high roller." She set my drink in front of me and hurried to the taps to pour pitchers for a group of ski bros that just walked in. I took a sip and winced. It was at least a double. I'd definitely leave her a good tip.

. . .

It was late afternoon when my cell rang. It had stopped snowing, and the sun had burned through the clouds. Shafts of light beamed through the slats on the front window, piercing the barroom gloom. I looked at my phone and saw a local number I didn't recognize. I was sitting next to the fat man. Two drinks ago, I'd struck up a conversation with him and the dwarf. They were visiting from New York. The big dude was a sports journalist, his pal a movie critic. They came out west to tour the brothels of Nevada. I was enjoying our barstool banter, and disconnected the call.

It rang again, and I glared at it, then pressed the Receive button. "Who is it and what do you want?" I said.

"Wake up on the wrong side of the bed today?" It was Sheriff Marcus Grier.

"I don't remember."

"Good grief, are you drunk?"

"That's a rather personal question."

"Where are you?"

"Whiskey Dick's, if it's any of your business."

"Get a coffee and sober up. I need to talk to you."

"My calendar's open tomorrow."

"Mine's not. Tonight, Dan."

"Is that an order?"

"I'll call you back in an hour."

I set the phone down and looked wistfully at my half-full highball. As a private investigator in a small town, I needed to maintain my relationship with the local authorities. In South Lake Tahoe, that meant keeping Marcus Grier on my side. We'd been through a lot together, including his shooting of a corrupt district attorney who tried to jail me on a trumped up manslaughter charge. I was crouched next to Grier when he pulled the trigger on his .38 and ended the D.A.'s life. I also testified that the shooting was strictly in self-defense. After the hearing, I patted Grier on the back, and said, "Now we're partners in crime, eh?" I don't think he appreciated the remark. I also didn't get the impression he felt he owed me.

I left the bar and walked over to the 7-11 in the adjacent strip mall. The air was damp and a brilliant rainbow stretched across the ridgeline on the north side of Lake Tahoe. I bought a tall coffee, then went next door to a taqueria and ordered a burrito. Give me five drinks, a large coffee, a burrito, and I can conquer the world.

Provisioned as such, I began walking home. The snow on the streets was rapidly melting and little rivers were running across the pavement and into the gutters. I drank my coffee and tried to enjoy the remainder of my afternoon buzz. I had no idea what Grier wanted. He sounded a little wound up, but he usually did. Maybe he had a case for me, a referral. I hadn't worked a decent case for months. I'd spent much of my time tending bar at Zeke's Pit over the summer, but it was now the slow season, and I'd left the job for those who needed the money more than I did. Not to say I didn't need the steady paycheck, but my last case provided a nice buffer. Which was now nearly gone, I reminded myself.

I ate while I walked, carefree for the moment. Whatever Candi was dealing with, surely it would be temporary. Thinking otherwise would do nothing but turn me into a mental basket case. As for Grier, it sounded like he had a problem. That didn't make it *my* problem. Unless I had a damn good reason to make it so.

The sun was falling behind the mountains by the time I approached my house. The twilight skies were a wild dreamscape of broken white and gray clouds backlit with red light and interspersed with blue sky. I paused and took in the view. Then, just as I stepped onto my driveway, my cell rang again. It was the same number as before.

"Marcus?"

"Yeah."

"What number are you calling from?"

"A payphone. Don't worry about it."

"All right. What's up?"

"Let's meet somewhere."

"Fine, come on over."

"Is Candi there?"

"No, she's out of town."

The line went silent, then he said, "I guess that's okay. I'll be there in a few minutes."

It was six-thirty when Grier parked at my curb. He was driving a silver Subaru wagon, not the squad car he often drove home. I met him at my front door and he followed me inside. He wore street clothes—blue jeans, white tennis shoes, and a gray polo shirt stretched tightly across his thick belly. We sat at my kitchen table.

"How's biz?" he asked.

I shrugged. "Hit or miss."

"You free for the next week or two?"

I stared back at him. His skin looked like polished walnut under the glare of light from above. He leaned back and crossed his big arms.

"Why?"

"I could use your help on something," he said, his fingers tapping his arms. He shifted his weight and the chair creaked.

When I didn't respond, he said, "Did you read about the rape case a month ago? The high school girl?"

"I saw something about it in the local paper."

"What I'm about to tell you, it's between us and us alone, understand?"

"Sure."

"The attacked girl was sixteen. She was a close friend of my daughter's. We arrested Justin Palatine the next day. The evidence was all there. He's the rapist. It should have been an easy conviction."

"Who's the D.A. now?" I asked, feeling no need to remind Grier of his role in the demise of the previous district attorney.

"Tim Cook."

"Cook? I thought he moved away last year."

"He moved back when he heard his old job was open."

I rubbed my chin with my fist. I'd met Tim Cook before, and believed him to be hard working and ethical. But I didn't think he was a top-notch attorney. He rarely had to prosecute serious crimes.

"So what happened?"

Grier's lips tightened and seemed to become flat against his face. "We got our asses handed to us, that's what happened. Justin Palatine chose to defend himself, without a lawyer. And the jury found him not guilty."

"How so?"

"It was one of the craziest things I've ever seen. It's usually a disaster for anyone who goes to trial without counsel. But this guy…" Grier squeezed his eyes shut and I could almost see his head vibrate.

"What?"

"It's like he was some kind of evil genius. In all the time I've spent in courtrooms, I've never seen anything like it. Palatine had a legal answer for everything, I mean, every point Cook made, he countered brilliantly. But Cook fought hard, and I thought we still should have got a guilty verdict."

"You're sure Palatine didn't have a background in law?"

"We checked him out thoroughly. He has a bachelor's degree—in freaking computer science. That's it. He didn't even take a business law course in college. He must have been self-taught. "

"Not many guys could pull that off."

"You're right, but there's more to it. Palatine is handsome, I guess, in a boyish way. He has this harmless, innocent demeanor to him. It's all an act, but a couple of women in the jury couldn't take their eyes off him, like they were mesmerized. I wouldn't be surprised if one of them jumped in the sack with him as soon as he walked free."

"So a guilty man beats the charges. Wouldn't be the first time."

Grier's eyes bulged, and his dark skin flushed and turned nearly purple. "A couple other things," he said, his voice a low rasp. "One of the issues that screwed us had to do with evidence I got from his car. He claimed lack of probable cause and an illegal search. The judge agreed."

"So you're on the hook, huh?"

"The county D.A. in Placerville blew a gasket when Palatine walked. He called me and Cook down to Placerville and reamed us a new one. Cook offered his resignation, but the D.A. seemed more pissed at me."

"That's unfortunate."

"Honestly, I don't give a shit what that politician thinks. I've got bigger problems," he said, his voice tailing off.

"Like what?"

"I promised my daughter the rapist would be sent to prison."

"I see."

"And she relayed it to the family of the victim."

"Oh…"

"So not only am I pathetic and incompetent, but I'm also a liar."

"That's a little harsh."

"My daughter won't even look at me anymore."

I waited for him to continue, but his eyes were staring at where his meaty fists sat clenched on the table. After a silent minute, I said, "What do you want from me, Marcus?"

"We want Justin Palatine off the streets," he said.

"Who's 'we'?"

"Cook and me." Grier lifted his head and blinked his bloodshot eyes.

"So, what, you want to hire me to dig up the dirt on this guy?"

"I don't think that would do much good."

"What then?" I said, feeling my eyes narrow.

"We want him off the streets," he said, slowly enunciating the words. "One way or another. Either in jail, or…"

"Are you serious?"

"We'll pay your expenses."

"That's it?"

"It's all we can afford."

"Have you lost your mind?" I said, standing. Then I smiled. "This is a prank, right?"

"I'm dead serious," Grier said, his voice a low rumble. "We can't have a violent predator like Palatine running free." Grier shook his head. "No, sir. Not him, not on my watch."

"Your watch? Where is Palatine now? Is he a local?"

"No. His home address is in San Jose."

I walked over to where a fifth of whiskey sat next to my sink. Then I turned and faced Grier. "Spell it out then, Marcus. What exactly are you proposing?"

"Palatine needs to go down for the count. Like I said, jailed or otherwise. I need you to arrange it."

"How do you expect me to do that?"

"It's right in your wheelhouse, Dan, and you know it."

"I do?"

"That's right. I can't think of anyone more capable than you and Cody Gibbons."

"Gibbons?" I cocked my head. "How did he get involved?"

"Palatine lives in San Jose. So does Gibbons. You can team up with your old buddy."

I put my hands on my hips and stared at the floor, shaking my head.

"Look," I said. "I'm sorry for what you're going through. But I don't think I can help you."

"I figured as much," Grier replied, as if my denying his request was a petty and selfish act.

"You figured right."

"That's why Cook and me want to offer you another incentive."

"Which is?"

"You help bring down Justin Palatine, we'll grant you a degree of immunity in South Lake Tahoe for any future violations."

"You mean, like a get out of jail free card?"

"Something like that, yeah. With some restrictions, of course."

I resisted the temptation to roll my eyes. "Like what?"

"I mean, you can't just murder someone."

"Every killing I've ever been involved in has been an act of self-defense," I said, my voice rising. "And you know it."

"Yes, but that hasn't always been obvious, has it?"

Grier was referring to the events of last April, when a man tried to stab me. I dodged his knife thrust and hit him with a right cross. The punch was well executed, but he must have had a weak chin, because the blow shouldn't have killed him. But it did, and I was accused of manslaughter and had to risk my life to prove my innocence.

"You mean more like a 'benefit of the doubt' card," I said.

"I think that's a good way to put it."

"You willing to put it in writing?"

"You know I can't do that," Grier said.

"And what about Cook? Am I supposed to take your word he's on board?"

"He is."

"Assuming I'm interested, I'd need to hear it from him, in person."

"He'd prefer not to be directly involved."

"Then we're done here."

"You really want to make this difficult, don't you?"

"Give me a fucking break, Marcus. You're asking me to conduct an under-the-table investigation, for free, with the end result being the incarceration or death of a man your justice department couldn't convict. In return, you're offering nothing tangible, just a loosely worded verbal commitment that you'll take it easy on me down the road. And let me add, only as long as it's perfectly convenient for you."

Grier's face dropped, his eyes round with indignation. "I thought we had a relationship," he said.

"A relationship is a two-way street, Sheriff."

Grier sat hunched over the table, leaning on his elbows. Then he sighed and said, "All right, I'll call Cook and tell him to come over."

"I got to take a leak," I said. When Grier started punching numbers on his cell, I went down the hall and ducked into my office. I grabbed a solid-state recording device from my desk drawer, yanked up my shirt, and taped it to the center of my chest. Then I went into the bathroom, flushed the toilet, and pushed the record button. The battery would last for two hours.

When I returned to the table, Grier said, "He'll be here in five minutes."

"Fine," I said. "You want a drink?"

"I'd like five or six, but I've got enough troubles without driving home drunk."

. . .

It had been two years since I'd seen Tim Cook. I remembered him as a slim man with hollow cheeks and a thin mustache from a bygone era. The other thing I recalled was the polyester sheen of his suit, which looked like he picked it up on sale at a discount department store. I was also aware that Cook became nearly destitute after his wife began cancer treatments and his insurance coverage ran dry.

I heard Cook's vehicle before I looked through the front window and saw him park. He drove an older model Chevy Blazer. The muffler was shot, the pipes probably rusted through, and it sounded like a wounded cow in its death throes. When he shut off the ignition, the motor backfired and belched a plume of white smoke.

I looked at Grier and tried to repress a smile. He was stone-faced. We walked out to the porch and watched Cook climb out of his rig. He was wearing a tan-colored three-piece suit that may have once been in style, but if it ever was, the fashion world quickly reconsidered. But at least he no longer sported his 1930s mustache.

Cook followed us inside, and we all sat at the kitchen table. "I understand Sheriff Grier has explained everything to you," he said.

"He has," I said. "But just to make sure we're all on the same page, I'd like to hear it from you."

Cook drew a breath, his chest expanding, and he shot a glance at Grier. Then he rested his dark eyes on me.

"Justin Palatine raped a sixteen-year-old girl, and he would have killed her too, if she hadn't escaped. These types of criminals are always serial; he'll do it again."

"I believe you," I said.

"It was my responsibility to convict him. I failed, and that's on me."

I waited for Cook to continue, but he just stared at me. After the pause became awkward, he asked if I had any questions.

I almost laughed. "Oh, just a couple, I think. You two are proposing I deliver some sort of vigilante justice, right?"

"No," Cook said quickly. "We are not asking you to do anything illegal. We'd simply like you to apply your, ah, creative talents to the situation."

"And the bottom line is you want to see Justin Palatine incarcerated. Correct?"

"I want this monster put out of business," Cook said. "I'll leave it at that."

"One way or another, huh?"

Both Cook and Grier nodded silently.

"Are you hiring me to act as an agent for South Lake Tahoe PD?" I asked.

"Where did you get that idea?" Grier said, eyebrows raised.

"I don't know, Marcus. It's not every day I get asked by a D.A. and a sheriff to take down a suspect that was found innocent."

"Well, we can't deputize you."

"Mr. Cook, I understand you can't pay me for my time. So how do you propose to compensate me?"

"You have a history of violent acts in this town. You seem to feel that the ends justify the means. But that's not the way the law works. Help us achieve our goal with Palatine, and we will afford you increased leniency."

"I'm sorry, I need something more specific than that," I said.

"Let's put it this way, Mr. Reno," Cook replied. "We think you're one of the good guys. As long as your motivations remain as such, we won't hassle you when you veer into the gray area."

I sat with my arms crossed and shifted my eyes to Grier. "We mean it, Dan," he said.

"It needs to apply to Cody Gibbons, too."

"That's a stretch," Cook said.

"It's got to be a package deal."

"All right," Grier said. "Gibbons is included. Just try to contain him somewhat."

"He always has pure motivations," I said.

"Can you get started tomorrow?" Cook asked.

I could hear the clock on my wall ticking. It sounded unnaturally loud, as if it was laboring mightily. "Bring me the arrest report and the trial transcript," I said.

• • •

As soon as Grier and Cook drove away, I saved our recorded conversation on my notebook PC, then sent the file to a cloud backup service. How far could I trust Grier and Cook? The main issue was that they were criminal justice system employees, and their job security was tied to arrests and convictions. Based on the circumstances at any moment, they might revert to that baseline. If they suddenly got a case of collective amnesia, or simply chose to ignore our verbal agreement, I would send them a copy of the recording. Cook's offer was past borderline; it was outside the law. He and Grier would shit a brick if they knew I'd recorded our conversation. They would do anything to prevent its release, as it would likely end their careers.

I sat on my couch and wondered if Grier or Cook could have an ulterior motive. If so, I couldn't imagine what it would be. I'd known Grier for almost five years, had gone to his home for BBQ parties, and had drinks with him on numerous occasions. He had shared stories of when he was a big city cop in the Deep South, and told me how he decided to escape the racism and depravity by moving his family to a small, tourism-centric town on the California-Nevada border. I knew his wife and daughters, and knew that Grier had at one time considered becoming a pastor. I'd also had frequent dealings with him during various investigations. Some were messy, violent affairs that tested our relationship. Although our bond had become strained at times, I knew he still thought of me as an ally. Bottom line, I trusted Grier as much as I could ever trust a cop. More so, I considered him a friend.

Cook was a different story. I'd only met him once before, and my initial impression was that he was a straight shooter. His reputation in South Lake Tahoe was that of an honest government employee serving the law-abiding citizenry. He also handled his wife's illness and subsequent death with dignity and fortitude. That alone earned him a degree of respect. Basically, I had no reason to suspect Cook of chicanery.

So why would these men be willing to put their careers at risk by enlisting me to put Justin Palatine out of commission?

Cook must have been humiliated to be beaten in court by a rapist with no formal legal training. And Grier, after making promises he couldn't keep, looked like a chump to his family and friends. Both of their reputations were surely diminished in the eyes of their colleagues. Revenge seemed like an obvious motive. But I also thought that Cook and Grier were genuinely good and moral people, and were truly alarmed at seeing Justin Palatine walk free to do as he pleased wherever he went. If I viewed it in that light, it was a noble act on their part.

I put on my coat and walked outside. The fall night had turned frigid, and I suspected more early-season snow was coming. I stood on the deck, hands in my pockets, blowing puffs of vapor into the darkness. Maybe a week or two away would be a good thing. It would keep my mind off Candi, and keep me out of Whiskey Dick's. I reached out and flattened my palm against the trunk of the huge pine in my front yard. The tree stretched into the sky like a spired monolith, impervious to storms or drought or the shaking of the earth. When I stepped back far enough to see its top, the needles seemed to be touching the stars.

I went back inside and sat in front of the television, but left the volume muted. Finally, my eyes grew heavy. "What a strange day," I said, before lying down to sleep.

2

THE NEXT MORNING I was sitting at my picnic bench and drinking coffee when Grier pulled up in his cruiser. He handed me two manila folders without comment, nodded, and returned to his car. I sat in the cold sunlight and watched him drive away, then opened one of the folders.

Justin Palatine had been arrested a little before midnight on the same night as the alleged rape. His Mercedes SUV was pulled over by Marcus Grier in the parking lot of a grocery store in the center of town. He was charged with multiple crimes, including rape, kidnapping, and assault.

According to his victim, he had grabbed her off a quiet street at eight P.M. that night. She had been walking home from a friend's house. This occurred about a mile from where I lived.

While being wrestled into his car, she had lost consciousness. It was later determined, based on bruising, that he had knocked her out by a strike to the neck with the edge of his hand. I knew this move as a carotid chop. It's banned from mixed martial arts because it can potentially kill the recipient.

Palatine then drove her to a dirt road three miles away, near the intersection of Pioneer Trail and Al Tahoe Boulevard. He drove up the unpaved track for a few hundred yards until he apparently felt safely remote. This is where he choked and beat her, while raping her. At some point, probably after he thought she was too weakened to escape, she managed to deliver a disabling kick to his crotch. Then she fled into the trees and made it to Pioneer Trail, naked and bleeding. A local man in a pickup truck spotted her promptly. He took her to the emergency clinic in Stateline.

I read through the details, gall rising in my throat. Then I flipped the page and found myself presented with photos of the victim and her injuries. The picture on the first page showed a close-up of her face. She had a pronounced bruise on her neck, and one of her eyes was blackened and shut. Her ear on the same side looked puffy, probably from repeated slaps. Her lips were cut in multiple places and grotesquely swollen. But the thing that struck me most was the expression of innocent hurt in her single open eye. If I didn't know better, I would have guessed she was ten-years-old, not sixteen.

I felt like a lump of rancid stew had thudded into my gut. I quickly closed the folder and stood, sucking in the brisk morning air. After a minute I picked up the folders, went inside the house, and put on my hiking boots.

I unlocked the gate in my back fence and headed down an overgrown trail toward the center of the large swath of meadowland that ran behind my house. When I reached the creek that split the meadow, I turned southeast. Pioneer Trail was less than a mile away.

I paced along the path, kicking up dust. The field grass was brown and matted. Tangles of deadfall were interspersed with pines, fir, and smaller trees. A few patches of snow remained in the depths of the shadows.

I told myself I needed to examine the crime scene, but while that's something I always do in an investigation, in this case it wasn't a priority. I continued along regardless, promising myself I'd return to the folders when I got back home.

Without thinking why, I broke into a jog. I tried to focus my thoughts and recreate the peace I sometimes felt when I was deep in the forest and alone with the natural elements. I breathed deeply and smelled the change of the season coming, the air musty with the scent of decaying undergrowth. The first snow had already come, and more would follow, falling from the sky as if by divine order, coating the land in a cleansing white.

It may have been peace I sought, but my facial skin felt tight against the bone, my upper lip raised in a scowl. The lump in my stomach was rising into my throat like a flood of venom begging for release. I ran faster.

This wasn't my first case involving sexual assault. But it wasn't something I dealt with on a regular basis. Even if it was, I doubted I could get used to it. The nature of the crime was beyond simply violent, degenerate, or cruel. The act indicated a depravity of the soul, a horrible failure of humanity. I believed the perpetrators of such crimes may well have entered this world with the blood of the devil pulsing in their breast.

When I reached Pioneer Trail, I caught my breath while waiting for a few cars to pass, then I jogged across the road and followed it to the left. After a couple of minutes, near Al Tahoe Boulevard, I saw a fire road that led into a thick stand of pines. I turned onto the dirt track and hiked up a mild grade, looking for a likely stopping point. I followed the rutted path around a couple of bends, and continued into the woods until I reached a flat spot where the trail widened slightly.

I turned in a slow 360. I was surrounded by tall trees and invisible to the cars I could hear rushing by about a quarter-mile away. This was the likely spot where the rape took place, and must have been where she eventually escaped from her abductor.

I studied the hillside scrub, trying to find evidence of the exact path the victim used to flee. Soon enough, I spotted a few broken branches and matted twigs. I walked into the brush, and ten feet off the fire road, I saw strands of brown hair dangling from the bark of a pine trunk. I pulled the hair from the tree and into my palm. As evidence, it was meaningless, for Justin Palatine had already avoided prosecution and double jeopardy rendered him immune from repeated charges. I looked at the hair and imagined the girl running blindly through the undergrowth, no doubt scraping herself bloody, in a mad panic to escape the evil that had invaded her life.

I gently folded the strands and placed them into my zippered coat pocket. It was pointless, I told myself, but I did it anyway.

Stepping carefully, I saw just enough signs of passage to be fairly certain I was following the path the young girl took to the main road. It would have been much easier to walk down the fire road back to Pioneer Trail, but I'm always compelled to walk in the footsteps of both victims and perpetrators.

I didn't jog back home, but walked with a steady sense of purpose. I would spend the rest of the day immersed in the arrest report and trial transcripts. I would take the emotion out of the equation and concentrate on absorbing every last detail. Most importantly, I wanted to learn as much as I could about Justin Palatine.

. . .

It was late afternoon when I finished pouring over the documents. I had scrawled numerous questions, most which were answered by the time I'd read all the pages.

- Palatine had worn a mask during the attack. This prevented the victim from making a 100% identification.
- There was not a single eyewitness to the abduction or the rape.
- An APB went out at 10:20 P.M. for a gray Mercedes SUV. Grier was alerted via a cellular app. He left his house shortly afterward and began driving up and down Lake Tahoe Boulevard, checking parking lots.
- The victim had memorized Palatine's license plate digits, but these digits were for a Mercedes SUV registered to a different owner in Southern California. Tim Cook claimed that Palatine replaced his actual plates with these illegitimate plates.
- When Grier pulled over Palatine's 2017 Mercedes SUV, the license plates were the correct version. Cook claimed that Palatine had

reinstalled the correct plates after the attack (The alternate plates have not been found. It is assumed Palatine discarded them).

- When Palatine was arrested, his clothes were very different from those the victim described. The clothes Palatine wore during the attack were never found, probably discarded along with the phony license plates.

- The victim's DNA was found in Palatine's SUV. But the search of the vehicle was declared illegal, since neither the license plate nor the suspect were a match for the victim's description. Thus probable cause was not warranted.

- Since the jury never knew about the DNA evidence, Palatine's mistaken identity defense was believable.

- Palatine had worn condoms during the attack, and his DNA was not found on the victim.

- Palatine is employed as a systems analyst for a large Silicon Valley software company. He's been employed there for eight years. He portrayed himself as a solid citizen.

- Palatine had been arrested in San Jose a year ago for rape, but the charges were dropped.

- Palatine is thirty-nine years old and single.

I got up from the old metal army-surplus desk in my spare bedroom office and stood looking out the window. Clouds had replaced the morning sun and it was overcast, the skies bleached of color. I neatly stacked the folders and put them in my file cabinet. Then I set out on foot to pick up my truck from Whiskey Dick's.

The neighborhood was quiet. Each house, whether it was a small cabin, an older tract-style house painted blue or green, or a contemporary wood-sided chalet, seemed its own island of tranquility. The lots were irregular, some large and some small, and all were shaded by old growth pines. Most had trimmed shrubs and lawns recently mowed. Cars were parked in driveways and not on the street.

I paced along, hoping to enjoy the serenity emanating from this slice of mountain suburbia. I was fortunate to live here, a place where visitors came from far away to bask in the scenic splendor of the alpine lake. I enjoyed breathing the clean, pine-scented air, and hiking in the summer and skiing the same trails in the winter. All things considered, living here made me feel fortunate to be alive.

I tried to not think about my new case as I walked. I wanted to relegate it to a corner of my mind that would activate only with my permission. Of course, whenever I made an effort to control my thoughts that way, it had the opposite effect; I could think only of what I wished to force from my head.

The DNA found in Justin Palatine's vehicle was critical to the prosecution. It was the sole piece of smoking gun evidence. Without it, there wasn't enough for a conviction. Palatine had done a damn good job of not leaving any other evidence.

In the trial transcript, Cook argued that the search of Palatine's car was legal because not only did probable cause exist, but by California statute, Palatine's arrest, on its own merit, allowed the search to be conducted legally.

Palatine countered by claiming probable cause was based only on the make and model of his vehicle, which was insufficient grounds. He then argued that his arrest was made after the search, and could not retroactively create search justification. And he reinforced the argument by ascertaining that his arrest was made without adequate foundation, since there was no obvious evidence found, given that DNA is microscopic. And further, he accused Grier of making the arrest solely as an after-the-fact effort to legitimize the search.

Unfortunately, the judge upheld Palatine's position. Although I found Palatine's argument more nuanced and intelligent than Cook's, I would have hoped the judge could have found rationale to side with the prosecution. But it was Cook's job to provide that rationale, and he didn't cite any precedents to bolster his argument.

I sighed and kicked a pinecone down the street. I could only assume that Cook did the best job he could, and never figured to be outclassed in court by someone with no formal legal training. Cook would probably feel the shame for years to come.

As for the judge, I'd stood before him last spring. He was a man about sixty who lived in a fancy home in Tahoe Keys. He had a year-round suntan and a full head of silver hair and owned a luxury yacht that he used to host dinner parties on the lake. I'd once seen him playing tennis with a woman about half his age, and it wasn't his daughter. He was paid a full-time salary for what was actually a part-time job. When he assigned bail for my case, he seemed to arbitrarily pick a number. He chose $200,000, which meant I had to pay $20,000 for a bond. It didn't matter that the charges against me were eventually dropped; bail bonds aren't refundable, so I was out twenty grand.

But neither Cook nor the judge were relevant to my investigation. I needed to focus on Justin Palatine, and so far the only things I'd learned about him, besides his age and occupation, were that he was highly intelligent, a meticulous planner, and a violent predator with a predilection for young girls.

I reached Whiskey Dick's and walked up to my Nissan pickup truck. It bore numerous battle scars and needed a wash. But the tires were new, and it ran well. I backed out of the parking lot and bounced off the curb onto Highway 50. I drove for two blocks and turned into the gym, which had been renamed again, and was now called the Tahoe Fitness Club. It had changed names so many times that I stopped paying attention. Inside, it was always the same.

I rode an elliptical trainer for twenty minutes, then circuit trained with weights for an hour, alternating bench press, back machine, leg press and the leg extension machine. I did eight circuits, and by the time I moved to the speed bag, my limbs felt like rubber.

Drenched in sweat, I drove home and showered before heading out to Zeke's Pit. It was near dinnertime, but there were only a half-dozen cars parked against the bumper logs in front of the restaurant. I went through the saloon-style doors and into the lounge.

Zak Papas was behind the bar talking with Liz, the long-term bartender. Zak's curly hair was dyed green and he wore round spectacles on his rotund face. Zak was fifty pounds heavier than when I first met him, but that was when he was on a cocaine diet. He'd been clean and sober for over a year, but still had an addictive personality. So when he went cold turkey on booze and blow, his replacement was food.

Liz, on the other hand, was a slender brunette who was partial to half-shirts and never wore a bra. Her nipples were always visibly pointy, and she was a favorite among local men.

"Hey, Dan," Zak said. "I've got a new drink for you to try." He put a copper mug on the bar.

"What is it?"

"It's a blood orange and pomegranate syrup Moscow Mule."

"How about a draught beer?"

"Come on, Liz just made it. We need a taster."

Liz grabbed my forearm. "I think you'll like it," she said, leaning so close one of her nipples almost bumped my forehead.

"All right." I picked up the mug, which was garnished with orange slices and a sprig of mint. I tasted it and thought about giving an honest appraisal, then decided against it. "Not bad," I said.

"It all started with the Moscow Mule, which is vodka and ginger beer with a slice of lime," Zak said. "Now the variations are trendy as hell. The bar will be packed this season, I guarantee it."

"That's great," I said. Zak always felt obliged to update me on his business, even though he'd paid back most of the twenty grand I fronted him after two years of cocaine binges left him deep in debt.

"I'm starving," I said. "Can you bring me some BBQ chicken?"

"Sure thing, boss," Zak said, and left for the kitchen. He was the head chef of the best BBQ joint in town, and probably in the Western Hemisphere, if anyone asked me.

"How's Candi?" Liz asked.

"Just fine."

"She's one cute lady," Liz said, and for a moment I wondered if she had any lingering emotions over our single drunken tryst, back before I'd met Candi. And then it occurred to me that she might actually be attracted to Candi, for Liz was definitely an adventurous type. I shook my head and took another sip of the odd-tasting concoction, then asked Liz to pour me a beer.

"Need to make a phone call," I said, as she set a foaming pint on the bar. I left my stool and sat at a small table in a darkened corner next to the wood stove. I hadn't talked to Cody Gibbons for a month or so, and I had no idea what he might be doing at the moment. He didn't keep regular hours.

"Dirty Double Crossin'?"

"What's the haps, Cody?"

I heard a female voice in the background. "Hold on a second," he said. A door thudded shut, and a moment later, he said. "Sorry, I had to find a safe place to talk."

"Where are you?"

"At home."

"And that's not safe?"

"Uh, no, not exactly." I waited for him to continue. "No, I'm just going for a walk," he called out. "Be back in a few."

"Man, I can't believe this. Check it out. Last week I get a call from this bar owner over in Campbell. Place called Khartoum."

"I remember that joint," I said.

"Yeah, so they have karaoke night every Thursday. A guy brings his karaoke box, or whatever it's called, and people get up and sing. You'd be amazed how many people go for this shit. And some of them are really great singers, I mean like, professional."

"What, singing's your new hobby?"

"Huh? I can't sing worth beans. Where the hell did you get that idea?"

"Who knows, you're always full of surprises."

"Whatever. Anyway, the place is packed every Thursday, and the bar is raking it in. Until these three dudes start showing up and acting like assholes. Like, they take over the microphone and won't let anybody else sing."

"Well, are they good singers at least?"

"What the hell does that matter? Christ, Dirt," Cody laughed. "Sometimes I wonder about you. So get this—the owner asked me to show up last Thursday and play bouncer. He tells me the minute these dickheads start misbehaving, he wants me to throw them out in such a way that they never come back."

"Why doesn't he just hire a regular bouncer?"

"Because for the most part, he doesn't need one. It's not a rowdy place, you know? But he said these wannabe rock stars need some serious discouragement. So I show up there last Thursday, and the place is getting crowded, and the owner has a table reserved for me right near the karaoke machine. So I'm well-positioned to take care of business when the time comes."

"Very convenient."

"Right, but next the owner brings over this broad, and my first thought was, it's got to be a practical joke. I mean, her clothes are painted on, and she's got a body that's got every person, both men and women, staring with their jaws hanging open. She looked like a Triple-X queen making a promotional appearance."

"Let me guess, this was a prepayment to you."

"Nice thought, but no. The owner says he doesn't want to arouse suspicion that I'm there to stomp ass, so he called an escort service and hired me a date for the night. So we could sit at the table together and be incognito."

"But instead everyone there is staring at you."

"Exactly. Even the singers were tweaked, because no one's paying attention to them, they're all scoping the porno diva. And I'm just laughing.

Then the three amigos walk in. You could tell right away, they had the look."

"What look is that?"

"Like if anyone messes with them, they'll start something. Asswipe number one is a tall punk wearing a Forty-Niner shirt. He grabs the mic and tells the karaoke jock to play Stairway to Heaven. And let me tell you, Robert Plant, he ain't. When he finishes the song, he tells the jock to play some AC/DC. At this point I stand up and say, 'Sit down, pal. It ain't your turn.' He looks at me, and his two buddies stand up, and he says, "You think you can take all three of us? You better take your slut and get the fuck out of here."

"This guy got a death wish?"

"Who knows? He's probably not playing with a full deck. But I'm not going to put my hands on him unless he starts it. So I say, "The Niners are a great team, what happened to you?" For a second there was this weird silence, then a few people started laughing. Next thing I know, he comes at me with a big right hook. I blocked it and hit him with a straight right, flush in the center of his face. His nose starts gushing blood, and he drops to his knees. Then his two comrades jump me. I drilled the first with a punch to the gut, and he hit the floor, but the second guy got behind me and put me in a choke hold. He had his legs wrapped around my waist, so I took him out the back door to that brick walkway."

"I know where it is."

"I ran backwards and slammed him into a steel column, but he didn't let go. So I did it again, and this time his head smacked it good. He fell off me, out cold. Then I go back inside and grab Mr. Forty-Niner by his stringy blond hair and drag him outside. I dumped him on his unconscious buddy, then went back for number three, who was still curled up on the carpet. I grabbed him by the ankle and started dragging him toward the back door, but before we got there, he puked big time, spewing his guts all over the place. By this time the bar owner is right there, and he's pissed, because his bar now reeks of vomit and people started clearing out."

"Just another uneventful Thursday night, huh?"

"So I get number three out the door and pile him in a heap with the other two shitbags. And a sorrier sight you've never seen, these three white trash a-holes, bleeding, moaning, covered in puke and blood. So I address the tall dude with the busted nose, because he's the most conscious of them all. I tell him, 'You're eighty-sixed permanently from here, and that includes your lame buddies too, got it?'"

"I take it he begged for forgiveness?"

"No, you're giving him too much credit. He says, 'We'll find you and fuck you up, man.' And that sort of attitude, I find a little offensive. So I yanked him to his feet and kicked him in the nuts. And before I dropped him, he pissed his pants, a big dark stain on his crotch and running down his legs. And a bunch of people are watching, and he knows it. He didn't have much to say after that."

"Sounds like a job well done."

"Yeah, not bad, but as I'm headed to my truck, I hear this clacking sound, and it's Miss Triple-X running up on her heels. She grabs my arm and says, 'I've been looking for you all my life.'"

"That's a rather suggestive comment."

"It suggests she's a nut case, but I've always got to learn the hard way. So I helped her into my truck and we drove to my place. We're not there for ten minutes before she goes into the bathroom and comes out naked except for her high heels. Then she gave me the most outrageous lap dance I've ever had. But the whole time I'm thinking, what's the catch?"

"Because there's always a catch," I said.

"Yeah, but this one I'd never run into. We go into my bedroom, and I'm ready for a real workout, but she starts asking me to hit her. I'm like, what, spank your ass? She says, no, I mean smack me good, on the ass, the face, the legs, and don't hold back. So I give her a couple little pats on the butt, and she jumps up and says, 'no, like this,' and she winds up and slaps my shoulder as hard as she can. I push her back and say, 'What the hell's the matter with you?'"

"She's into S and M?"

"Maybe, but she doesn't have whips and chains or any of that crap. She's just into pain. Said she can't get off without it."

"Got to hand it to you, Cody. You're a magnet for this type of thing."

"You mean, damaged women?"

"You said it, not me."

"Anyway, she says she wants to train me to please her, but I've never hit a woman, and I'm not about to start. As soon as we hang up I'm gonna tell her she needs to hit the road."

"Hmm, good timing. I was hoping you could put me up for a few nights."

"Really? What for?"

"I've got some work in San Jose."

"Perfect, just the excuse I was looking for. I'll tell her it's a work thing. When you gonna be here?"

. . .

When I returned home, I spent two hours plugging Justin Palatine's name into people-search engines. These sites, for a fee, provide a variety of publically available information on any individual. I learned Palatine owned a house in Santa Clara, and there was no record of a current mortgage, so he may have owned it free and clear. The SUV he drove was a 2017 Mercedes GLS 450, a car that sold new for about eighty grand. A social media scan showed he had a Facebook page, but it appeared inactive; no posts, no photos, no updates of any sort. The data on his arrest in 2020 was minimal and valueless. His employment record told me nothing I didn't already know. As for relatives, it listed dozens, but I couldn't tell which ones were truly related to him.

I printed all the reports and placed them in a thickening folder. Then I threw my clothes into a suitcase and dumped my gear bag onto the bed. I checked my Beretta .40 caliber pistol, made sure all three 11-round clips were full, then opened a small zippered bag and picked through an assortment of audio bugs, magnets, and Velcro fasteners. In another bag were plenty of zip ties long enough to bind wrists and ankles. I also carried binoculars, a gold badge with a black leather backing, a camera with a telephoto lens, and of course, my old, weighted sap, which I'd named Goodnight, Irene.

By three P.M. I'd secured my gear, along with the case folder, in the locked steel box mounted behind my cab. I tossed my suitcase in the truck bed and bungeed it behind the fender well. Then I backed out of my driveway and began the four-hour drive to San Jose.

The heavy cloud cover dissipated as I left town, leaving white streaks in the afternoon skies. I drove past the gas station in Myers and began climbing the corkscrew toward Echo Summit. Granite walls lined the narrow passage to my right, and higher up I could see darkened recesses where waterfalls ran when the snow thawed. Then the tight bends eased and I accelerated into the sweeping curves carved out of the dense white fir and sugar pine forest.

As always, I looked forward to meeting Cody Gibbons with a measure of trepidation. He'd been my friend since before his father kicked him out of the house at age fifteen. Back then, he lived in various places, sometimes on the streets, and sometimes he stayed with me at my mother's house. We often worked odd jobs together, usually heavy physical labor. Even though he'd not reached his adult height of six-five, and at 230 pounds was at least fifty pounds lighter than his eventual weight, he had phenomenal physical strength. I once watched him pick up an old, rusted iron engine block that must have weighed four hundred pounds. He stuck his fingers in the head ports, deadlifted it, and carried it sixty feet to a rubbish pile. I wrestled in high school, and I was 185 pounds of pure muscle. I thought I was pretty damn tough, and I wasn't about to let my buddy outdo me. I walked over to the engine and tried to lift it. I tried three times and never got it off the ground.

When he was still a teenager, Cody became involved with an established organized crime family in San Jose, and started showing up with wads of cash in his pockets. After a couple of months, he had a disagreement with the patriarch's son, who Cody described as a big mouth weasel. Their debate was resolved when Cody smashed the son's face through a windshield.

As for Cody's adult life, he lasted for seven years as a cop with SJPD before he was forced out in a corruption scandal. Many in San Jose's criminal justice system thought Cody would likely relocate after leaving the force. Truly that would be the prudent thing to do, they thought, for he had made numerous enemies. But they didn't know that he'd also enlisted many quiet allies, both from the fringes of the system, and in the mainstream. When he started his career as a private investigator, he knew who his friends were.

And friends he needed, because Cody's track record as a P.I. included an ongoing series of incidents that could have resulted in serious jail time, or worse. He'd shot dead a Mexican drug enforcer who kidnapped him, point-blank shotgun blasted a devil worshipper who planned to rape and sacrifice a young lady Cody liked, set explosives and blew up the house and inhabitants of a racist gang that threatened my life, shot a rapist thug in the spine and paralyzed him, killed two members of the Russian mob in a shootout, and extorted the district attorney in Placerville, prompting him to drop a bogus manslaughter charge against me.

Some viewed Cody Gibbons as nothing more than a reckless vigilante hiding behind an eternal claim of self-defense, but that ignored the unique blend of intelligence and insight he brought to the job. He was an outstanding investigator because he instinctively understood that criminals think differently than law-abiding citizens, and often behave in ways most people would consider illogical. He knew that some criminals think they are above the law, many think they are too smart or lucky to get caught, and others are desperate or unintelligent and behave stupidly. It was obvious to him that while there is honor among thieves, it is at best a convenient ethic. And he believed that most criminals subconsciously know their day of reckoning will come, and when it does, they must choose whether to be caged, or to go out in a blaze of glory.

Regardless, Cody went about his business with a cocksure smile and a Falstaffian belief that a few drinks could cure any problem. He'd saved my life on three occasions, and we'd had more good times than I could remember. I'd long ago stopped judging him, for my track record was far from perfect. But if I was to pass judgment, I'd say Cody was the most loyal friend a man could have.

I drove past the old Kyburz Lodge, one of my favorite roadhouses in my hard-drinking days, then descended through the curves for half an hour before reaching the county seat in Placerville. Highway 50 straightened after that, leading through the foothills and into Sacramento. I slowed for the typical traffic, grumbling and finally conceding that Sacramento had grown to the point that its freeway gridlock was as bad as L.A.'s or San Francisco's.

I drove on, and the sun was setting as I came over a rolling hill and saw the lights of Santa Clara County. A few minutes later, I could just make out the brown court building jutting up on West Hedding Street. It was where my father used to work, and a few blocks from where he was shot and killed.

It was a little after seven when I parked in front of Cody's house in central San Jose. His neighborhood was a mix of homes remodeled in various styles, along with some that had not been updated since the tract was built in the early 1950s. His house was among the latter. The lot was large, with a detached garage in the back and a huge elm out front.

I knocked on the door, waited, then knocked again. I was tempted to just walk inside, but I wasn't entirely sure he'd sent his recent love interest on her way. When he didn't come to the door, I began calling him on my cell, but stopped when I smelled barbeque smoke. I walked over to his driveway, pushed open the gate, and went into the backyard.

Cody was sitting at a glass table next to the lawn. On the table was a bottle of tequila and an ice bucket. A few feet away, a gas barbeque was smoking.

"Dirty!" he exclaimed, smiling and waving a lit cigarette in my direction. He still called me by the nickname he made up years ago. It was short for Dirty Double Crossin' Dan, and it originated from a night at the bars when he claimed I left with a woman he was hitting on. I doubted that actually happened, but the nickname stuck regardless, at least in his mind.

"What's cooking?" I asked. Smoke was beginning to billow from beneath the barbeque lid.

"Steaks, of course. Tend to the grill while I mix you a drink." He rattled ice into a glass. "I squeezed a bunch of fresh limes."

I lifted the lid, fanned at a plume of smoke, turned the heat down, and flipped the T-bones on the barbeque. Cody handed me a glass. "It's my special margarita recipe," he said.

I took a long sip. "Marcus Grier called me yesterday," I said. Then I recounted Grier's proposal, and the details of the crime and the trial.

"I got to give you credit, Dirt, you've outdone yourself."

"What's that supposed to mean?"

Cody shook his head and laughed. "I used to think I had a patent on crazy shit. But this deal is way off the reservation. Has Grier lost his mind?"

"You think I should blow him off?"

Cody rubbed his red stubble and tossed an errant ice cube onto the grass. "It's a thought."

"Look, I want to find out what Justin Palatine has been up to, what makes him tick."

"And then?" Cody asked, one eyebrow raised.

"I don't know. Cross that bridge when I come to it."

Cody drained his drink, the ice cubes clicking against his teeth, and stared off as if he was thinking about something outside our conversation. Then he turned back toward me, smiling broadly. "I'm free tomorrow, so why not?" he said.

3

SANTA CLARA COUNTY, ALSO known as Silicon Valley, is a patchwork of cities with varying attributes, but one common theme—they are all modern day boomtowns, based on exorbitant real estate valuations. San Jose is the largest city, and has something resembling a big city downtown, but lacks real skyscrapers; its proximity to the airport limits building heights to thirty stories. Santa Clara boasts a respected university, a huge theme park, and a stadium the San Francisco Forty-Niners call home. Cupertino, with two-thirds of its residents of Asian descent, has a large number of affluent Taiwanese immigrants who came to Northern California for the personal computer boom. Sunnyvale is not much more than a mix of three bedroom-two bath homes and business parks, and Campbell is the same minus the commercial buildings. Moving north, the peninsula cities of Los Altos and Palo Alto offer a degree of charm and sophistication that the cities in the heart of the valley lack.

Justin Palatine's listed address was for a residential avenue in Santa Clara, right off El Camino Real. Ten minutes after leaving Cody's house, we turned onto the street. All the houses were cookie-cutter, with two-car garages out front and the main house set back behind a lawn and shrubs. Each house had a section of roof that extended outward and shaded the front door. Next to the door were windows looking out over the avenue.

I imagined the neighborhood looked very similar to when it was built during the post-WWII boom.

I drove slowly, looking for a suitable place to park.

"There's his rig," Cody said, pointing to a gray Mercedes SUV parked in a driveway. I pulled over and parked three houses down on the opposite side of the street.

"Ten A.M., Tuesday morning. I thought he had a regular job."

"Maybe he took the day off," Cody mumbled. We both stared at the house. Blue shutters aside the windows contrasted the off-white stucco. The lawn was patchy and overgrown bushes partially hid the front door. The street was still and quiet.

"What do you want to do?" Cody said, after a minute.

"Tail him."

Cody grunted. "Let me see your case file."

I got out of my truck and removed the folder from the gear box. "Here you go," I said.

While Cody read the contents, I sat watching the house. I imagined the neighborhood was a mix of retirees who hadn't cashed out yet and younger working couples whose combined income allowed them to afford the mortgage payments. I wondered if any of the residents had the slightest idea that their neighbor, a man who appeared relatively normal, got his kicks by raping and maybe murdering young women.

Twenty minutes later, Cody put down the file. "You know who the investigating cops were on the San Jose rape charge a year ago?"

"No."

"Let's find out." He tapped on his cell. "Hello, Hilda," he said. After five minutes of flirtatious conversation, he hung up.

"Who's Hilda?" I asked.

"A desk clerk at SJPD. The detectives were Charlie Dunning and Rigo Hernandez."

"You know them?"

"I know Dunning. He's an old school cop. A straight arrow, I think."

"You friendly with him?"

"He steered clear of me, mostly."

"How about Hernandez?"

"Don't know him. He must have come aboard after I left."

"Think they'd talk to us?"

"Worth a try," Cody said, tapping his phone.

· · ·

At noon, we parked at the Fairmont Hotel on Market Street. The hotel was a centerpiece of San Jose's efforts to create a vital downtown. The building's elegant entrance promised refined luxury, and the lobby didn't disappoint. It was a huge expanse, the floors tiled in white marble, and it opened up to a sunken lounge with at least fifty tables. Men wore either suits or fashionable casual attire, and women milled about in business dress and modestly sassy outfits.

We walked into the restaurant next to the lobby and spotted Dunning and Hernandez waiting. They both wore sport coats and slacks, no ties. Cody and I were decidedly underdressed, but I doubted Cody cared, nor did I.

"Gentlemen," Cody said. The hostess led us to a corner table in back. I sensed the detectives had prearranged it, for it was removed from the other tables, the lighting less bright.

We sat across from them. Dunning had a meaty, florid face. He was in his fifties, his body thickening, a man built for power, not speed. Hernandez was younger and slender, and his copper skin looked like it had never seen a razor. But his dark eyes were sharp and watchful.

"Men, my partner, Dan Reno," Cody said.

"You got some history with Russ Landers if I'm not mistaken," Dunning said.

I shrugged. "I don't think he likes me."

"But he's out to pasture now, so who cares, right?" Cody said.

"I don't care if you don't," Dunning replied. "That bastard was as crooked as they come."

"He's the main reason I left the force," Cody said. "If not for him, I might still be there."

"I understand you've done well in the private sector." A small smile appeared on Dunning's lips.

"It has its ups and downs," Cody said.

We studied the expensive menu for a minute, and a waiter took our order. As soon as he left, Dunning said, "What do you know about Justin Palatine?"

"He beat and raped a woman in South Lake Tahoe a month ago," I said. "He got off on a technicality. But there's no doubt he did it."

"We think he's a serial predator," Cody said.

"You're right," Hernandez said. His eyes were flat, betraying nothing.

"Can you tell us what happened in San Jose?" I asked.

"All right," Dunning said slowly, as if considering our motivations and potential implications. Then he tapped the table with his blunt fingers a few times.

"Palatine was accused of raping a maid he'd hired to clean his house. She was eighteen years old and spoke limited English. She fled the house and called the police right away. We work sex crimes and caught the case."

"I took her statement," Hernandez said. "We took her to the hospital for a rape kit, and Palatine's DNA was all over her. She was beat up pretty bad."

"We arrested him that night," Dunning said. "At first, Palatine claimed it was consensual. We didn't buy that for a second. Our D.A. charged him with the whole gamut—rape, sodomy, false imprisonment, assault. It would have been an easy conviction."

"But by the next afternoon, the charges were dropped," Hernandez said.

"Why?"

"She was paid off," Dunning said. "She wouldn't say it because she signed a nondisclosure agreement, but we checked her bank account."

"One million dollars," Hernandez said. "It was sent from a dummy corporation hidden by layers of transactions. We couldn't determine who actually sent the money."

"You have any guesses?" I asked.

"More than a guess," Hernandez said.

When neither detective elaborated, Cody said, "Who?"

"Palatine's older brother is Jerrod," Dunning said.

I looked at them and turned my palms upward.

"Jerrod Palatine is the CEO of Digicloud. He's a multi-billionaire."

"And that's where Justin works," I said.

"Right," Dunning said. "We think Jerrod arranged the payoff for two reasons: One, to save his brother's ass, and two, and maybe this was just as important to him, to keep his company from being tarnished by scandal."

The waiter brought our lunch. We ate in silence for a minute, then I said, "Palatine represented himself at trial in Tahoe. He doesn't have any legal training that we could find, but he ate our D.A. alive. Any thoughts on that?"

"Yeah," Dunning said, wiping his mouth. "The guy's a fucking genius. Him and his brother are both at the top of the Mensa charts for IQ. I mean, upper one tenth of one percent."

"Let me ask you a question," Hernandez said, his enunciation slow and deliberate. "What is your purpose in investigating Justin Palatine?"

"It's really not something I can talk about."

Hernandez studied me, his eyes narrowed. "You know, I come from El Salvador, and many of my relatives still live there. In 2012, my country had the world's highest murder rate. But rape is also a terrible problem there and is far more frequent than murder. Everyone in El Salvador knows a woman, or many women, who have been raped. It got so bad that the fathers and brothers of victims formed a gang and began hunting down and killing rapists. This type of lawlessness happens when the police cannot protect the civilians."

The table became silent until Cody said, "Even in the highly civilized USA, the police can't always protect you."

"That is an unfortunate reality," Hernandez said.

I looked at Dunning, and he nodded in agreement, his lips down-turned above his clenched jaw.

"I think we're looking at this through the same lens," I said.

. . .

We drove back to Justin Palatine's house. It was two P.M., and the sun was invisible in the colorless skies. The Mercedes SUV was still parked in the driveway. A woman in jeans was pushing a wheelchair down the sidewalk. The person in the chair was hidden under an umbrella and had legs like sticks.

"Screw this," I said. "Let's come back after dark." I started my truck.

"Where we headed?" Cody asked, lighting a cigarette.

"Back to your house. I want to research the Palatine family, and this company, Digicloud."

"They're big. That's about all I know."

I drove along, navigating through Santa Clara, passing sites where large apartment complexes were under construction, next to seemingly endless office buildings and retail stores of every variety. In the year I was born, all of it had been orchard land. The personal computer revolution had transformed Santa Clara County's economy into one that was larger than all but the world's top twenty countries.

But as we drove, I kept noticing something I'd never seen before in Silicon Valley. Everywhere a patch of open dirt bordered the roadways, tents and lean-tos had been erected. Trash overflowed from these dwellings onto the streets, sometimes causing cars to swerve into another lane. Every so often, I spotted a man in filthy clothes scavenging about, tending to a stolen shopping cart or working on a bicycle rigged to pull a wagon.

It was as if the poorest and most desperate class of people had swelled to the point that they could no longer remain in the shadows.

"What's up with this?" I said, pointing at a center divide where a dozen tents were pitched on a ten-foot-wide dirt strip.

"It's the Bay Area's latest crisis," Cody said. "Rents have got too expensive. More and more people have been forced to the streets."

"I thought it was mostly schizophrenics, drunks, and meth heads."

"Sure, you got your schizos, wet brains, and tweakers, along with lifelong scumbags who just don't want to work. Then you add in people who are recently unemployed, and can no longer afford housing. Some of them are trying to improve their situation, and eventually will. Either that or they'll catch a bus to somewhere cheaper to live."

"So they account for all this trash?" I said, looking at a ragged tent on an unpaved triangle at a freeway entrance. Plastic bags and paper wrappers were everywhere, and blew into the air as cars passed by.

"Nobody really knows the breakdown between the mentally deranged, the addicts, and those just in a temporary bind. The local bureaucrats are trying to figure it out. In the meantime, people are bitching like crazy."

"Can't say I blame them."

"Me neither. It pisses me off to see this, I mean, it's fuckin' hard on the eyes." Cody flicked his cigarette into the slipstream. "There was an article in the paper the other day, talking about our failure to house the psychos. They used to all stay at Agnews State Hospital, the insane asylum. But they closed that joint years ago."

"They better figure out a solution."

"One of my old buddies from the force says they should make street living illegal. Give people an option: we'll put a roof over your head, but you got to sober up and work. If not, you go to jail."

"Easy as that, huh?"

Cody sighed. "They got to do something."

. . .

When we got to Cody's house, I set up my computer on his kitchen table and began collecting information on the Palatine family. Because Jerrod Palatine was the founder of a large, publicly traded corporation, there was an abundance of surface-level data available.

Jerrod Palatine was fifty years old and had founded Digicloud when he was twenty-four, back before the dot-com crash. Venture capital was readily available at that time, and not only did Digicloud survive the crash, it grew and then expanded exponentially after a series of acquisitions. Palatine was considered one of Northern California's top executives, a true visionary in the technology space.

I read through the details of the acquisitions and Digicloud's metamorphosis into a huge corporation. Jerrod Palatine was widely praised for positioning his company to take advantage of the world's transition to cloud-based data management as well as digital commerce.

I skimmed forward to a brief section on his personal life. His parents were born in Italy, and moved to the United States in 1959. His father, Anthony, once owned and ran a mortuary in San Jose. Jerrod was born ten years after Anthony and Marcia Palatine moved to the U.S. He was granted a scholarship to Harvard and earned a master's degree in business administration in just three years. He married while in college and divorced ten years later.

I spent a few minutes looking for Justin Palatine on the Internet and came up empty. I then continued researching Jerrod Palatine and his company, searching for anything that might shed light on Jerrod's relationship with his much younger brother. I looked for lawsuits filed against Digicloud and found nothing atypical. I ran Jerrod's name through a public record search and saw no indication he'd ever been sued or had anything worse than a traffic ticket on his record.

"How goes it?" Cody asked, coming from his spare bedroom office.

"Nothing so far. Jerrod Palatine seems to have covered his tracks pretty well."

"I'm sure he did. Paying off a rape victim is not something he'd want publicized."

"I'd like to talk to someone who works there," I said, standing. "Or worked there. I'll try LinkedIn."

"You got a paid subscription?"

"No."

"Then you can find names, but no contact information."

I started typing, but Cody said, "Try this instead—type 'disgruntled employee' into Google. You can find chat rooms where people bitch about their former employers."

Cody left me alone, and I spent two solid hours on LinkedIn, making a list of Digicloud employees, including salespeople, software engineers, human resource managers, marketing directors, and a handful of those with a vice president title. I limited the list to those who worked at the San Jose headquarters.

I also took Cody's advice and ended up at a site called Fucked-Company.com. It seemed to be a popular forum for recently terminated employees to vent their grievances. Some of the posts were pretty funny. A woman called her ex-boss a 'needle-dick wannabe,' who was barely qualified to scrub toilets. Another post made fun of a Facebook vice president for buying a Harley-Davidson motorcycle, and claimed he was a yuppie nerd who could barely keep balance on two wheels.

The skies had started to darken when I found a string about Digicloud. A salesman had been terminated a few weeks ago. He wrote that the sales VP was a pompous jackass who couldn't sell his way out of a wet paper bag, and Digicloud's products were inflexible and only attractive to a narrow band of customers, none of which he was assigned. When another salesperson responded in defense, the ranting ex-employee retorted that Digicloud executives are all cowering sycophants serving Jerrod Palatine, who is a heartless son of a bitch with the personality of a snake.

The ex-employee was named Bob Crowley. I found his phone number on a people-finder site and called him.

"Your dime," a voice said.

"Is this Bob Crowley?"

"Whatever you got for sale, bite me," he said.

"Don't hang up, please. This is Dan Reno, private investigations."

"Investigator?" He paused, then said, "Let me guess, you work for Digicloud. So go ream yourself."

"No, I'm actually investigating them."

"No shit? Why? Because the place is full of douchebags?"

"That's one reason. How about we meet up and chat about it?"

"I'm just heading out for happy hour at Boswell's."

"I'll meet you there, okay?"

. . .

Boswell's was a small bar tucked away in a shadowy nook in an open-air shopping mall less than two miles from Cody's house. We walked into the dark hideaway, and while Cody headed to a table offering free bar food, I surveyed the clientele. Mostly white collar, a mix of men and women. Not a dive or a trendy spot, but more likely an established watering hole for middle-aged regulars.

Bob Crowley was parked in the middle of the bar. He was wearing flip-flops, jeans, and a yellow Hawaiian shirt. He was a good-sized fellow, and looked perfectly comfortable perched on a stool and sucking on what appeared to be a vodka-cranberry. The broad cowlick jutting from his thick brown hair made me guess he'd risen from an afternoon nap right before I called, thrown his clothes on, and rushed to the bar to make the happy hour drink specials. His complexion was ruddy, and when he looked at me, his eyes were unnaturally large behind thick spectacles.

"Bob, Dan Reno." I threw a ten on the bar and caught the bartender's eye. "One more for Mr. Crowley," I said.

Crowley grinned. "Right on, brother."

Once the bartender mixed him a fresh drink, we moved to a table next to a platform just big enough for a drum set and a pair of guitar amps. Cody joined us with a plate piled with cold cuts and crackers.

"Hey, man," Crowley said. "I'm looking for work, and the P.I. thing sounds pretty interesting. I mean, you guys make a good living?"

"It's not exactly a steady paycheck," I said.

"Well, neither is sales, when you're on commission. Especially if you get rat-fucked on your territory."

"That's what happened at Digicloud?"

"Big time. They got a few sales guys making over five hundred grand a year, because they have the big accounts. Then guys like me get stuck with a bunch of bullshit prospects."

"Tough gig."

"Story of my life. So, why are you investigating them?"

"I'm looking into Justin Palatine, the younger brother of the CEO. You ever meet him?"

"No, I never saw him. I used to walk by a cube with his nameplate, but he was never there."

"You think maybe his big brother put him on the payroll and let him skate?" Cody asked.

Crowley took a long drink from his cocktail. "If Jerrod Palatine wanted to, I'm sure he would. He's a prima donna like that. Kind of like a dictator. I never had to deal with him, which was fine with me."

"You don't trust executive types?" Cody said.

"Not him. Everyone thought he was an asshole."

"Most bigshot bosses are pricks, right?" I said. "What was different about Palatine?"

Crowley stirred his drink and raised an eyebrow. "He had a strange obsession with the Roman Empire. If you look at all of Digicloud's products and application suites, they're all named after stuff from ancient Rome. You can check it out on their website. Like, the main software is

Colosseum, and the add-ons are Rubicon, Romulus, Caesar, Cassius, and so on."

"What's the problem with that?" I asked.

"Jerrod Palatine would call meetings with the various departments, marketing, product development, sales, whatever. He'd have people fly in from all over the world. Everybody would go to his big meeting room, which was like a shrine to ancient Rome. It had Corinthian columns and red velvet curtains and this huge freaking wall painting of gladiators and slaves and all sorts of shit. He'd stand in front of everyone, lecturing about how we should strive to serve the glory of Digicloud. He'd say how lucky we were to live in modern times, and how Rome was built by slaves captured during conquests. Nobody dared ask him a question of any sort, because that would just make his babble go on longer. After a couple hours, people were dying to run out of there."

"Sounds like a whack-job egomaniac," Cody said.

"He was demented, man, it was all about him. He liked to compare himself to various emperors. He also said that Palatine Hill was the first settlement of Rome, like back before Christ, and his family name goes back that far. It was kind of creepy. I'm actually relieved to get out of that bughouse."

"You ever hear anything about Justin Palatine getting busted for rape?" I asked.

"No," Crowley said. "Is that for real?"

"I'm gonna get a drink," Cody said, standing. "You want something?"

"Yeah, get me a beer, and another vodka for Bob."

Cody left for the bar. "You know anyone at Digicloud that worked with Justin?" I said.

"I think he was in cloud services. I don't know any of those propeller heads."

"Who's the VP of that division?"

"Ah, that would be Ron Donaldson. We all called him Ronald Mc-Donald. There were some guys that used to call DoorDash and deliver

McDonald's happy meals to his desk, just to dis him. He's a major techno-weenie. Made himself a fortune in stock options, the lucky bastard. I heard he bought himself a five million dollar spread in Los Gatos. Probably thought that would help him get laid. He's one of those nerds with zero game."

"Did Justin report to him?"

"Either to him, or to a director, I don't know."

"Hmm. Did you know anybody who knew Justin at all?"

Crowley shook his head. "Not really. Like I said, I never saw him in the office. Honestly, I don't even know what he looks like."

Cody came back with the drinks, and Crowley went to the men's room. When he returned, I said, "Do me a favor, Bob. Don't tell anyone about our conversation."

"And don't post anything about it online, right?" Cody added.

• • •

At seven P.M., the rush hour traffic had not yet abated, and it took us fifteen minutes to make the short drive to Cody's house. Cody left my truck and climbed into his red Dodge diesel rig, then followed me to Justin Palatine's street. We parked within a hundred yards of each other, in between pools of light beaming down from streetlamps. We waited for a minute, watching Palatine's tract house. His SUV was still parked in the driveway.

Cody called my cell. "Looks pretty quiet," he said. "Why wait?"

"All right. Text me if you see anything."

I switched off the dome light in my cab so it wouldn't turn on when I opened the door. Then I quick-stepped across the street, staying in the shadows. I hustled over to the Mercedes, which had been backed into the driveway, and slid on my back underneath the rear of the vehicle. I held a penlight in my teeth and found a spot on the frame next to the gas tank. I cleaned the spot with an acetone-soaked rag, then attached a magnetized tracking device. It was linked to an app on my phone and would alert me when the vehicle became mobile. The app would then track its movement, allowing me to see in real time where the vehicle went.

As soon as I pushed myself from beneath the SUV, a motion-activated security light above the garage door flashed on. I cursed and ran back to my truck. I hadn't spotted the light; it was well hidden, but that was no excuse. It was shoddy work on my part.

A moment later, the front door opened. A man stepped onto the porch. He wore dark jeans and a long-sleeved black shirt. He looked up and down the street, then walked out to the sidewalk. It was Justin Palatine.

I slid lower in my seat and studied him. He had an average build, medium-length brown hair, and indistinctive features. Nothing about him stood out. Aside from a somewhat boyish face, he looked very ordinary.

He stood on the sidewalk for another thirty seconds or so, slowly looking around. His gaze fell directly on my truck, and then on Cody's more noticeable red vehicle. He didn't show any sign of alarm or concern.

As soon as he went back into the house, I called Cody. "I think he spotted us," I said.

"That doesn't change our plans."

"Not for the moment, anyway. But that light was hidden. It was tucked up under the gutter."

"So?"

"Most people put up security lights to deter robbers or vandals. They want the lights visible."

Cody grunted. "What's that tell us about Palatine?"

"I'm not sure."

At that moment, Palatine came back outside, and this time he was wearing a black baseball cap. He climbed into his SUV, pulled onto the street, and drove past us. I ducked down before the glare of the headlights panned over my windshield.

I waited a minute for Cody to call me. "All right, I got him," he said.

"The app's working fine?"

"Yeah, I see the blinking red arrow. He's on El Camino. I'll keep within a mile of him."

"All right."

Cody hung a U-turn and drove down the street. As soon as he disappeared, I put on a ski mask and latex gloves, then jogged to Palatine's house. I stayed to the side of the driveway and tried the wood-plank gate to the side yard. It was locked, so I scaled the fence in a quick motion and dropped down onto the concrete walkway leading to his backyard.

I tried the side door to the house, but it was secured by a firm bolt lock that would be nearly impossible for me to pick. I moved to the backyard and tugged briefly on a sliding glass door before spotting the slide bolt on the inner base. I checked two windows looking out on the backyard. Both were covered by blinds, and dual locks made them impenetrable, unless I chose to break the glass.

On the opposite side yard, there was a bathroom window about twenty inches square. It was secured only by a standard single locking mechanism. I stuck a slide lock tool into the frame and ten seconds later, the window opened. After a considerable amount of shimmying, I was able to wedge my upper body through the opening, scraping the hell out of my forearms and shoulders in the process. Then I pushed myself forward and let my weight drag me inside until I could hold myself up on the toilet seat. A moment later, I lowered my legs inside, hopped to a standing position, and stepped into the hallway.

I walked to the front room. The furnishings were modern and appeared relatively new. The room was clean, the carpet recently vacuumed, the glass coffee table free of crumbs or smudges. On it rested two remote controls. A large television was mounted on the wall and a cable box and DVD player sat on a shelf below it.

Next to the cable box was a separate device, small and round and immediately visible because of glowing red and green LED lights. It was a security camera, recording any movement in the room. I turned it to face the wall and did the same to a second unit mounted on an adjacent wall.

Moving swiftly, I reached beneath the couch facing the television and stuck a listening bug onto the wooden frame. Then I lay on my back, pushed up the end of the couch, and found a suitable spot to wedge a larger, cone-shaped receiving module.

After glancing around the kitchen, which was gleaming and modern and in stark contrast to the home's exterior, I went back down the hallway to the bedrooms.

The first door, opposite the bathroom, was locked, but the mechanism was an inexpensive variety available at retail hardware stores. It took only ten seconds to pick it.

When I scanned the bedroom with my penlight, my first impression was that the room was unnaturally large. Then I realized that the wall to the adjoining bedroom had been knocked down, resulting in a single, larger rectangular room roughly twenty by twelve feet. There was a round table in the center of what was originally bedroom number one. Set in the far corner of the former second bedroom was a modular desk unit. On it were two large computer screens, a notebook PC attached to a docking station, and a big, upright desktop computer in a black, louvered case. Its faceplate was made of transparent plastic, and I could see three separate fans inside, illuminated by a number of pulsing red and blue lights.

I studied the jumbles of wires running around the setup, searching for an external hard drive or a smaller USB flash drive. Seeing nothing, I opened the single drawer in the unit. Other than a scattering of pens, there was nothing but a checkbook, a roll of stamps, some printer cartridges, and a few blank pads of paper.

I tapped the Enter key on the notebook, and the screen flashed to life with a password prompt. I tried the same with the full-sized keyboard, and one of the monitors came alive, also requiring a password. It was exactly what I expected, but I scowled anyway.

Turning away from the computers, I went to the sliding closet doors near where I had entered the room. I pushed one open and saw a dozen or so jackets hanging in a shallow closet. Beneath the jackets were six boxes, stacked two-high. I checked the pockets of every coat, found nothing but lint, then began pulling the boxes out and checking their contents. I did so carefully, for I didn't want to leave any obvious sign that an intruder had been here. Before leaving, I planned to return the two living room cameras to their original position. If he checked his video feed or simply had an eye for detail, Justin Palatine would know regardless, but I hoped to not alert him, at least not yet.

The first box was jammed full of computer cables, surge protectors, and a mishmash of small electronic parts and pieces that I assumed were old and obsolete. Unfortunately, there wasn't anything that potentially contained data. No old cell phones, tablets, flash drives, or anything similar.

The remaining boxes were filled with filing folders and stacks of papers. It would probably take more than an hour to adequately view the contents. And that was assuming I knew what I was looking for, which I didn't. At this point, I was simply hoping to find something I could use against Justin Palatine.

Cody would text me when it appeared Palatine was headed back home, so I'd have time to exit. With that in mind, I flipped on the light switch in the room, and began on the first box.

The contents were all related to Digicloud. Thick documents described specifications for data center computer systems. There were also printed email trails of discussions with colleagues, mostly pertaining to hardware and software compatibility challenges. I removed a single page that listed a dozen email addresses for Digicloud employees. I doubted it would be helpful, but I folded it and stuck it in my pocket.

The second box contained ten years of Justin Palatine's tax returns. He reported a consistent six-figure income from Digicloud, dating back to when he was twenty-two years old. I looked at his deductions, hoping to find something unusual, but it all looked very standard. I took photos of the first few pages of his most recent Form 1040s, then moved to the third box.

It was heavy with paperwork related to his home purchase. He had bought the house six years ago for $800,000. The original loan included a first and second mortgage, but after three years, he paid off the balance. I couldn't find any indication of how he came up with the money; the payment was over seven hundred grand. He didn't make enough to have saved anything near that amount. I spent ten minutes eyeballing the pages, then reopened the previous box. Nothing in his tax returns reported a spike in income or a windfall of any sort.

I lugged the fourth box from the closet. It was heavier than the others. Inside were a dozen large, hardback books. All were non-fiction works on the Roman Empire.

Just as I shoved the box back into the closet, I heard a distinct clicking sound from the front of the house. I froze for an instant, straining to hear. Someone had stuck a key in the front door lock. A moment later I heard the door knob turn.

I stood, turned off the light, and silently slid the closet door shut. There was no way it could have been Justin Palatine, because Cody would have texted me. That left a few other possibilities, none of them good. I peeked into the hallway just in time to see the front door open. I darted into the bathroom, stepped onto the toilet seat, and began pushing myself out the window.

Just as I'd wedged my torso through the window frame, the bathroom light clicked on, and someone wrapped their arms around my legs.

"Get back here," a deep voice said. I felt the man hook his fingers in my rear belt loop. I tried to lunge forward, but had little leverage from my position. For a moment I resisted the force trying to pull me back into the bathroom. Then I decided on a second option.

"Okay," I said, narrowing my shoulders. The man continued tugging on my belt loop, and as soon as my upper body came free of the window, I kicked with my feet, breaking his grip on my legs. But my feet slid off the toilet and I fell back toward the man. He caught me and wrapped me in a bear hug, but I drilled him with a hard elbow to the ribs, then broke his nose with a left-handed snap punch.

We fell in a tangle. He tried to put me in a choke-hold, but I grabbed his arm and hit him with another elbow to the midsection. I heard his breath leave him in a whoosh. Then I spun to face him and came down hard with my right fist. I felt my knuckles bruise as they slammed into his chin. His eyes went dull.

He wasn't out cold, but he was dazed. I turned him onto his stomach and zip-tied his right wrist to his left ankle. His shirtsleeve was pushed up, revealing a large tattoo on his shoulder. A knife and an eagle were intertwined with the words, Death before Dishonor, and in the center, on a small globe, were the letters USMC.

I checked his pockets, removed his wallet, and took a picture of his driver's license. As I went down the hall toward the front door, I heard him groan and curse.

When I stepped onto the front porch, I saw a black Chevy truck parked in the driveway. I looked up and down the street before snapping a picture of the license plate. A moment later I ran to where my pickup was parked and took off.

My phone buzzed as I weaved through the surrounding residential grid. I hit my brakes at a Stop sign and saw Cody's text message. *Looks like he's headed back*, it read.

I'm driving. Meet at your house, I replied.

. . .

Cody and I sat across from each other at his kitchen table. "Sounds like a private security service," he said.

I dabbed at a cut on my elbow with an alcohol soaked napkin. "He had cameras in his living room. They probably sent an alert to an alarm company."

"That's not how typical residential security systems work," Cody said, standing. He grabbed a whiskey bottle from the counter and set it on the table, along with two shot glasses.

"I know," I said. "I have one at home. Costs fifty bucks a month."

"And it won't send an alert unless a door lock has been breached, right?"

"Yeah," I said, watching Cody pour the whiskey.

"That means he probably has a more advanced system. The motion detector was activated when he left the house, and set to alert a security guard."

"Pretty quick response," I said. "I wasn't even there half an hour."

"Why would this guy have a system like that? Must be expensive."

"Paranoia?"

Cody pushed a shot glass at me. "It means he has something to hide."

"Like what? His career as a rapist?"

Cody stared into the amber fluid suspended between his thumb and forefinger. Then he turned his eyes toward me. "He might have souvenirs stashed away."

I tapped my fingers on the table. "I don't know. He's probably too smart for that."

"It ain't about brains, Dirt," Cody said, gunning his shot. "It's about the sick craving these perverts have. They'll save little mementos from each rape. Then they can pull them out and relive the attack. It's the only way they can get off."

"You saw this when you were with the force?"

"Yeah, once. The suspect hid his trophies under a false floorboard. He kept driver's licenses and panties. The son of a bitch couldn't help himself. When we found his stash, he knew he was facing the death sentence, because he'd killed two of his victims, and one was in Texas. We cut him a deal in exchange for full disclosure. He avoided the needle."

I sipped from my glass. "Sure would be nice to take his house apart, but I don't see how."

"Not without a warrant, and we're not even cops."

"Maybe we could talk to Dunning and Hernandez. You think they could get a warrant, based on what happened in Tahoe?"

"It's a stretch," Cody said, rolling his empty glass between his fingers.

"Worth a try, don't you think? They seemed sympathetic."

"I doubt a judge would approve it."

I swallowed the remains of my whiskey and pushed the glass at Cody. "All right," I said. "Where did Justin go?"

"Nowhere," Cody replied. "He didn't stop anywhere, just drove around."

"That doesn't make sense."

"Look," Cody said, angling his phone so I could see the map on the screen. "He took San Tomas to the freeway, then ended up on Southwest Expressway. He hung a U-turn and drove up and down Southwest, then drove back home. That's it."

"The guy sits at home all day, then drives around aimlessly?"

"Maybe he was looking for a lonely girl wandering the streets."

I leaned forward and rested my jaw on my fist. "Pour me another, would you?"

"Hoping the bourbon will bring about a revelation?" Cody said, half a smile on his big mug.

"Sure, why not?" I replied.

4

IT MAY HAVE BEEN a whiskey vision I hoped for, but when I woke in the morning, I'd not gained any clarity or wisdom. My head was still a jumble of questions, and I wasn't sure what to do next. I sat up on Cody's couch and rubbed the sleep from my eyes. I hadn't found anything useful during my search of Palatine's house, and tracking his vehicle had gone nowhere. The only thing I knew for certain was that I didn't want to contemplate my next moves until at least two cups of strong coffee.

I went into the kitchen and started a pot. Before it finished brewing, Cody appeared from the hallway and sat at the kitchen table. He wore gray sweat pants and a black T-shirt with the Oakland Raiders logo on the front.

"You still a Raider fan after they moved to Vegas?" I asked. He grunted, moved to the couch, and turned on the television. He switched the channel to a local news broadcast.

"I'm thinking of canceling my newspaper subscription," he said. "The paper never gets here until after nine. And it costs around a thousand bucks a year."

"The Internet's putting the papers out of business. They probably can't afford a decent paperboy."

"He's not a boy. He's some middle-aged man driving a Toyota. I guess he likes sleeping in."

"Look at this," I said, pointing at the screen. Cody turned up the sound. A reporter was interviewing a man in front of a pile of charred debris. The man's hair was matted, twigs clung to his beard, and his layers of clothing looked caked with grime.

"I was asleep in my tent," he said, gesturing behind him, his eyes jittery. "Then it was on fire. I never saw nothing, just fire. A minute later, here comes this truck with a hose, spraying ice water. I was soaked, freezing cold, with nowhere to go."

"Were you using a stove in your tent?" the reporter asked.

"No, man, I never cook or smoke in there. Somebody lit me up. All my stuff, burnt and gone."

The camera panned away to show about two hundred yards of blackened, sodden rubbish stretching along the side of a road. The camera went back to the man, who had started crying. The reporter ended the segment by saying, "Live from Southwest Expressway in San Jose."

"What the..." I said.

"I drove by there last night," Cody said. "Saw the tents."

"After Justin Palatine drove by."

"That's right."

"Let's get over there, see if we can find a witness."

"What about breakfast?"

"We'll get fast food. Come on, let's roll."

. . .

We took my truck to Southwest Expressway. The section we were looking for was the last quarter-mile leading to a freeway on-ramp. When we got there, we saw a single SJPD squad car parked off the road. I pulled in behind it. The skies were overcast, and the ground was muddy in places. It was in the fifties, but felt colder. The road shoulder was about fifteen feet wide and shadowed by a variety of trees. A chain-link fence separated the strip of land from railroad tracks running alongside it.

"Imagine sleeping here," Cody said. "Cars whooshing by, the train rumbling and blasting its horn. Must make for a nice night's sleep."

We started forward and spotted a woman near the fence picking through a shopping cart. The cart's wheels were deep in mud next to a charred tree trunk. The ground was covered in ash, metal poles, and what looked like the remnants of a gas stove.

"Excuse me, ma'am," I said. "Were you here when the fire happened?"

She glanced at me, then returned to rummaging through her cart. I couldn't guess at her age or race. Her facial skin looked like crumpled paper. Then it occurred to me that the network of wrinkles on her cheeks could have been layers of cracked dirt. Her hair fell over her face in a matted tangle of black and gray snakes, almost as if dreadlocked. "Ma'am," I repeated, stepping closer.

Her head snapped up, her eyes like milky blue marbles bouncing in oversized sockets. "Hallowed be my name, by Lord, take it in vain and perish!" she shouted.

"Excuse me?"

"If you are the rapture, I will strike you down, Jesus be my witness."

"I'd just like to ask you a question, if you don't mind."

"Be gone, Satan! Or feel the wrath!" She stood straight and raised her arms as if preparing for combat.

"Have a nice day," Cody said. "Come on, Dirt."

We moved farther down the strip, stepping around portions of tents that hadn't fully burned and hung like limp rags from leaning poles. Then we saw two patrolmen standing near the road, speaking to a lone, disheveled figure.

"Let's avoid the cops if we can," I said. Cody nodded, and we turned back toward my truck. A moment later, I spotted a man on the other side of the chain-link fence. He was sitting on a stump near the railroad tracks and smoking a hand-rolled cigarette. We walked over to the fence.

"How's it going, man?" I called out.

He turned and squinted at us. He was bearded and his clothes were dirty, but he didn't look as ragged as some street people.

"What up?" he said.

"Were you here last night? Did you see how the fire got started?"

He blew a stream of smoke into the cold morning, then stood and walked to us. When he got close, I was surprised to see he looked like a teenager.

"Yeah, I was camped here. I saw it all. Spare me ten bucks and I'll tell you about it."

I opened my wallet, found a ten, and stuck it through the fence. He pocketed it, then said, "My tent was down near the freeway. I was sitting outside about ten, having a beer and a smoke. Then from down the street comes this black truck. There was a guy in the bed with what looked like a big water gun, like a super soaker. But it was full of gasoline. The truck slows down and he lets it rip, spraying every tent. I saw it happening, and before they got to me, I grabbed my beers and hiked the fence. I could smell the gas."

He paused and spit a stray piece of tobacco onto the ground. "Then what?" Cody said.

"A second truck, looked like the same kind, comes real quick. There's a guy in the bed with, I shit you not, a flamethrower. He torched all the poor fuckers in their tents. I saw it. The thing was throwing fire like thirty feet. People were screaming and running around like chickens. This one lady I know caught fire and all her hair burnt off."

"Were any other cars around?" I asked.

"No, it gets pretty quiet here at night. Then, here comes a third truck. Except this time, the guy must have had a barrel of ice water and a pump, because he starts blasting everyone with freezing water, and it was bitch cold last night. He put out all the fires, but left everyone soaked with nowhere to go."

"Did you see a gray Mercedes SUV?"

"Not that I remember."

"What about these black trucks?" Cody said. "Were they all the same make?"

"Yeah, they were all black and looked the same. Big trucks, with four doors."

"Fords? Chevys?" I asked.

"I don't know."

"But they just came one after the other? Gas, fire, then water?"

"That's right."

I looked at Cody, eyebrows raised. "Reminds me of the old Pat Benetar song, *Fire and Ice*," he said.

The teenager glared at Cody. "Is that supposed to be funny?"

"Did you get a good look at any of the drivers or the guys in the bed?" I asked.

"No, it was too dark to see much," he said. "There's no streetlamps out here."

"What time did the police come?"

"I don't know. I boogied over to the shelter over on Fourth Street. They usually have an open bed or two."

I heard footsteps and turned to see the two uniforms approaching.

"Later, dudes," the kid said, and hustled away.

"What are you doing here?" said one of the cops. He was tall with a narrow face and pocked skin.

"I know a homeless guy and I think he was sleeping here," I said. "I saw the news this morning and came to see if he was all right."

"You find him?" asked the other cop, a younger, athletic looking fellow.

"Nope," I replied. "Any idea how the fire started?"

"It's an ongoing investigation."

"Right. You think it might be arson?"

"These people make their own fires, cook their own food," the taller cop said.

"Yeah," I said.

"This is a crime scene," the other cop said. "We'll need you to move on."

"No problem," Cody said. We walked back to my truck and drove away.

. . .

Fifteen minutes later, we were eating breakfast at the old Bill of Fare Restaurant, after Cody rejected my suggestion for drive-through fast food. The Bill of Fare was tucked behind a Texaco gas station, and was one of a handful of businesses that had remained unchanged during Santa Clara County's transformation from a sleepy community to a technology epicenter.

"You believe the kid's story?" Cody said, shoveling a forkful of scrambled eggs into his mouth.

"Seems farfetched," I said, sipping coffee. "But I didn't get a sense he was bullshitting us."

"If he was, he's got a hell of an imagination."

We ate without speaking for a minute amid the hubbub and clatter of the dining room.

"Three trucks?" I said, wiping my mouth. "If you wanted to screw someone over, I can think of easier ways."

"It wasn't targeted at an individual. It was targeted at a group." Cody set down his fork and knife. "It was a statement. It was meant to attract attention, to strike fear into the hearts of the homeless."

"Someone's sending a message? Like, get off the streets or else?"

"Something like that. Look, Northern California has a homeless crisis. It's not only an eyesore, it's a health hazard. Everyone's saying we need to fix this, but it's just getting worse. The politicians seem helpless."

I leaned on my elbows and stared at a spot on the table. "A vigilante strike force, targeting the homeless." I raised my eyes. "It's hard to believe."

"Why?"

"Criminals are usually motivated by money. There's no money in this, just risk."

"I don't think money has anything to do with Justin Palatine's rapes."

"Rapists are a different story."

"So are vigilantes."

I cut a strip of bacon in half and placed both pieces on a triangle of toast. "There was a black, full-size Chevy pickup parked at Justin Palatine's house. It was driven by the guy who caught me there. The guy with a Marine Corps tattoo."

"You should have put a tracker on his rig."

"Hindsight's twenty-twenty." I raised my coffee cup, but it was empty.

. . .

As we drove back to Cody's house, I considered what motivated some of the worst criminals I've dealt with during my career. My comment that money usually drives criminal acts was a lazy assertion, for it ignored many aspects of psychopathic behavior.

I once saw a man murder his rich nephew in an attempt to rob him. The man was fresh out of prison and broke after losing his fortune. He couldn't accept living as a pauper, and was motivated by the desire to reclaim his wealth. In another case, a devil worshiper was involved in many crimes, including the kidnapping of a young woman for a satanic ritual, during which she'd be raped and murdered. What prompted him to attempt such an atrocity? He was on a quest to pay back humanity for his horrible childhood; it had nothing to do with money. And then there was the young man who murdered two of his womanizing father's latest conquests, before killing his dad. His motivation? He felt deprived of his father's affection.

Obviously, the arson perpetrated on the homeless people camped off Southwest Expressway was a well-planned crime involving a number of conspirators. I could fathom a couple of theories on the motive, but it was pointless unless I knew Justin Palatine was involved. Was it coincidental that he drove up and down the street within two hours of the crime? Palatine was a violent sexual deviant, and the indiscriminate burning of ragtag dwellings had nothing to do with sex. If Palatine was complicit, what could his motivation be?

When we reached Cody's house, I sat at the kitchen table and opened my computer. "Our best lead is the security company," I said. "If I could get Palatine's credit card records, maybe we can find out who they are."

"So call Grier. This is his gig, so tell him to get on it."

I smiled. "I'm sure he'll love taking orders from me."

"Tell him I said hello, too."

"All right. You're one of his favorite people."

"No shit?" Cody sat across from me. "What about the bugs? Any hits yet?"

I checked the app on my phone. The listening devices I'd placed at Palatine's house would download their recorded content at four-hour intervals, as long as voices were detected. Typically, this meant listening to hours of whatever was on the television. But there were no downloads yet.

"That's strange," I said.

"What?"

"No response on the bugs. No TV, nothing."

"When Palatine got home, he would have found the security guard and freed him. They had to have said something, right?"

"Yeah, but the bathroom was too far from either of the bugs I placed."

"So what, the security guard takes off, and Palatine sits there in silence?" Cody tapped his fingers on the table.

"Not everyone watches TV all the time."

"I bet they swept the place," Cody said.

"Could be," I said after a moment. "We'll see if any downloads come through later today."

"Fine," Cody said, rising from his chair. "I got some other stuff to take care of." He walked down the hallway.

I watched him go into his bedroom, then I called Marcus Grier's cell.

"Dan."

"Morning, Marcus. I need you to run a license plate, and I need three months of Justin Palatine's credit card records."

"You're in San Jose?"

"Yes. Cody Gibbons says hi."

"He does, huh? Are you with him?"

"Yup."

"Just keep things in control, understand?"

"What does that mean?"

"Don't commit any felonies, to start."

"How soon can you get me the info?"

"Give me an hour," Grier said, and hung up.

I reached into my backpack and found the sheet of paper I'd taken from Palatine's house. I sat looking at the ten email addresses, all of which included the full names of the recipients. One of the names stood out: Lonnie Fijak. I knew the name from high school.

Lonnie had been a teenage motocross sensation. He began riding professionally when he was fifteen years old. He achieved celebrity status at our school and somehow managed to graduate while juggling his schedule on the pro circuit. But things didn't go so well for Lonnie after high school. Flush with money and a degree of fame, Lonnie found willing women and cocaine readily available. By the time he was twenty-four, his career was circling the drain, and he was a full-time addict.

I'd heard he'd gone broke and hit his rock bottom in a room in San Francisco's Tenderloin, where he'd been holed up smoking rock cocaine with a prostitute. The situation turned bad when her pimp arrived to rob Lonnie, who escaped by jumping out a second story window stark naked.

He found a cop, but was arrested for possession, as he was whacked out of his mind and still clutching a vial of crack. It was his third bust in six months, and he was facing a year in lockup. This prompted him to seek treatment, as it was the only way to avoid jail time.

I didn't know what happened to Lonnie Fijak after that, but I assumed his rehab must have been successful, because I couldn't imagine he'd be employed at a major corporation if he hadn't gotten sober. I ran a people search, found his cell number, and tapped it into my dial pad.

"Hi, Lonnie here."

"Hi Lonnie, it's Dan Reno. Remember me from Oakbrook?"

"Wow, Dan Reno? Yeah, I remember you. You used to hang out with the big dude, Yeti."

"Huh?"

"That's what we used to call him. He was the biggest guy at Oakbrook."

"Oh, Cody Gibbons."

"Right. With his wild hair and beard."

"I'm still friends with him. We work together."

"Really? Doing what?"

"We're private investigators. That's why I'm calling you."

The line went silent, then he said, "About what?"

"A guy that works at Digicloud. Justin Palatine."

I heard him draw a breath. "What about him?"

"How well do you know him?"

"Not at all, to be honest."

"Come on, you worked with him, right?"

"I'm sitting here in a cube, you know? With people everywhere."

"How about I buy you lunch?"

"All right," he said, after a pause.

. . .

We met at noon at a small, uncrowded Mexican restaurant in Los Gatos. It was a ten-mile drive from Digicloud's Santa Clara headquarters.

"Is the food good here?" I asked him, while we waited to be seated.

"I don't know. I just wanted to go somewhere away from the company."

"Why's that?"

Lonnie had an angular face, all cheekbones and jaw. He looked at me with yellowish-brown eyes that seemed too small for his diamond-shaped sockets, as if years of drug abuse had caused the eyeballs to recede into his skull. "I don't need anybody from Digicloud seeing me with you," he said.

"You mean, because I'm an investigator?"

He swiped his lank hair off his forehead with a big knuckle. "Right."

We sat at a table next to a blue and white tile sculpture. Lonnie was a shade under six feet and knobby bones jutted from his elbows and wrists. His frame could easily carry an extra fifty pounds, but he looked naturally wiry.

"What's to hide?" I asked.

"Nothing, really. But we got some suspicious types working there."

"Suspicious of what? Just a bunch of people doing their jobs, right?"

"It's part of the company culture," he said, holding a tortilla chip by the edges. "People get fired for weird reasons."

"Like what?"

Lonnie scraped his shoes against the clay floor. "Anything that might be seen as disloyal."

"Well, if someone's doing something against the company's best interest, that would be cause for termination, right?"

"It's more than that," he said, now staring at me. "I mean, if you make a negative comment about higher ups, you could get shit-canned. I've seen it happen."

"You mean higher ups like Jerrod Palatine?"

"Especially him. If you're even suspected of disrespecting him, you might be walked out the door."

"That is weird," I said.

"Look, if someone saw me with you, and figured out you're a private detective, all they'd need to do is report it to HR, and I'd get the third degree."

"Sounds paranoid."

"You know," Lonnie said, "That's a good way to describe it. Digicloud has a paranoid culture."

"But paranoid about what? What do they have to hide?"

Lonnie raised his hand, palm upwards. "Besides the usual trade secrets, I have no idea."

The waitress brought our lunch. After she left, I said, "What can you tell me about Justin Palatine?"

"Not much. I never even met him. He works from his house mostly, I think, or at our data centers."

"Is there anybody at Digicloud who knows Justin well? Anybody that's friendly with him?"

Lonnie bit into a taco and chewed slowly. When he swallowed, his big Adam's apple bobbed in his throat. "Only one guy I can think of. His boss, Ron Donaldson. They're pretty tight, I heard."

. . .

Our conversation after that shifted to a casual chat about people we'd known in school. Toward the end of lunch, Lonnie confided that he'd just got his ten-year chip from A.A., and was proud to be a lead meeting speaker on a regular basis. "It's all about knowing yourself," he said. "I know if I took one drink, within an hour or two I'd be ripped out of my skull on booze and coke and shacked up with a hooker. One drink, and I flush my life down the toilet."

When we left the restaurant, the hazy sky had lightened and was tiger-striped with blue. I could see the pines atop the Santa Cruz Mountains etched against the sky. I looked down the trendy main drag of Los Gatos, at the Teslas, Audis, and Maseratis lining the curb outside the restaurants and shops. It was all paid for with technology money. To that end, Digicloud was certainly a contributor, but I couldn't imagine how that might be relevant in my investigation of Justin Palatine.

As I got on the freeway and headed back toward Cody's house, I felt an unexpected rush of nostalgia. Back when I lived here, I'd driven this stretch of Highway 17 often. It made me remember my old car and hungover times in a lonely apartment I'd rented. I also thought back to local people I'd known, some wealthy, some poor, some jailed, some dead. Then I thought about my old boss, Rick Wenger. I smiled and laughed dryly. Wenger was an eccentric teetotaler and on a good day, a marginally competent investigator. He was also the most money-obsessed person I'd ever met. While I knew him, he made a small fortune in the stock market, then lost most of it. He actually offered to serve as my financial advisor, and was offended when I declined. I wondered if he regretted leaving Silicon Valley for the East Coast. If he stayed here, he surely could have found many rich clients. He probably felt he left a vast financial opportunity on the table. That's how Wenger looked at things.

It was 1:30 when I pulled into Cody's driveway. I let myself in and saw he was on a phone call in his back office. I'd just sat at the kitchen table and opened my computer when Marcus Grier called.

"The license plate you gave me is registered to a company, Hadrian Transport in San Jose."

"What's their address?"

"It's a P.O. Box."

"Are there any names attached?"

"Nope."

"All right," I said. "What about the credit card records?"

"I'm looking at them."

"Email them to me."

"Sorry, can't do that. I can mail you hard copies if you want."

"Fine, but I need to go over them now. I'm looking for payments to a security company."

"Okay," he said. "I'll start with July. I see grocery stores, a car repair shop, fast food, and other miscellaneous purchases. Nothing that looks like a security company."

"Any payment to Hadrian Transport?"

"Not in July. Let me check the August and September statements." I waited a minute until he said, "No. Nothing that looks like security at all."

"Do you see anything that looks suspicious? What are the biggest payments?"

"He paid eleven hundred to Cartex auto repair. Everything else is small, a couple hundred here and there."

I bumped my fist against my chin. "Mail it all to me. I'll give you Cody's address."

After we hung up, I went into my photo gallery and found the driver's license belonging to the man who pulled me from Justin Palatine's window. His name was Mark Costa. He was thirty years old and had an apartment address in Sunnyvale. I plugged his name into a people search site and found a match. He had served in the Marine Corps for five years and was honorably discharged two years ago. His most recent employer was Obsidian Security Services in Mountain View.

"Getting close to happy hour," Cody said, glancing at his watch as he walked into the room.

"It's only two o'clock. Grier called me back. The pickup is registered to Hadrian Transport. No names, just a P.O. Box. He also got Palatine's credit card history. No payments to a security company, or anything else that looks suspicious."

"Google Hadrian Transport."

"All right," I said, typing. A moment later, I said, "If they exist, they don't have a website, or any other Internet presence."

"Nothing but dead ends, huh?"

"Palatine's a clever boy, whatever he's up to," I said, standing. "Let's go for a spin."

"Where to?"

"I got the home address for the security guard that showed up at Palatine's house."

"You know what I always say."

"What's that?"

"When all else fails, put your hands on somebody." Cody flexed his shoulders and rolled his neck.

"Let's roll," I said.

We got into my truck and ten minutes later parked in front of an apartment complex within walking distance of downtown Sunnyvale's restaurant row. Fortunately, it was an open complex; there was no lobby, and all the front doors were accessible from the street.

A minute later, we stood in front of unit 152. I raised my fist to knock, and said, "If he opens the door, I'm gonna bull rush him."

"Okay, chief," Cody replied.

I rapped on the door. I was ready to knock again when a very pregnant blonde woman opened the door. She stood with her hand on her belly, looking at me with impatient eyes.

"Excuse me, ma'am. I'm looking for Mark Costa."

"I'm sorry, you have the wrong address."

"He doesn't live here?"

"No, he certainly doesn't. I have no idea who he is."

"Sorry to bother you, then. How long have you been here, if you don't mind me asking?"

"About a year."

"Have a nice day," I said, as she closed the door.

"Let's drive through the parking lot," Cody said. "Maybe we'll see a black Chevy."

"You think she was lying?"

"Who knows?"

We drove around to the rear of the complex and slowly proceeded down a row of covered stalls. The pavement at each stall was stenciled with an apartment number. Parked at number 152 was a silver Acura. I snapped a photo of its license plate, then we drove to the end of the row and continued around the corner to another long strip of parking spots. There was no black Chevy pickup.

"I'll have Grier run the license plate," I said, then paused, staring at my phone. "Palatine's on the move." I held my phone so Cody could see it. A red arrow showed the Mercedes SUV had just taken the on-ramp to 880 northbound.

We were on the other side of the valley. I drove to the 101 freeway entrance and accelerated into the flow of traffic. If Palatine continued north, we wouldn't be too far behind him.

When we reached 880, Palatine was still moving and was already in Milpitas. We were five miles south of his vehicle. Cody held my phone and a few minutes later said, "He took the Stevenson Boulevard exit in Fremont. He's heading toward the bay."

When we exited on Stevenson, I turned left and we entered an industrial zone bordering a broad network of salt ponds. The buildings were long, white, single-story, and all built by a developer as a unified project. A flock of seagulls was swarming over the flats a hundred yards out. The parking lots were half-full and a few cars drove past us. The sporadic signs in front of the buildings identified a data center, a concrete company, and an automotive parts depot.

"Right here," Cody said. "This is where he should be."

I pulled to the curb and peered at a building with a glass front door but no street facing windows. No cars were parked out front and no signage identifying the resident. The structure was about a hundred feet long.

"Wait here," I said, and walked to the front door. The windows were opaque and the door was locked. I looked for a ringer, then rapped on the door with my knuckles. After a minute I returned to my truck.

"Let's try the back," I said, turning into a driveway. I followed it behind the building and saw six steel roll-up loading doors.

"He must be in there," Cody said.

"The garbage bin," I said, pointing at a single Dumpster against the cinder brick wall separating the building from its neighbor. "Ready to do some diving?"

"And rob you of all the fun? I'll be lookout."

I parked and stared into the bin. It was about five feet tall and held mostly broken wooden pallets. I pushed aside some of the pieces and grabbed a few scraps of paper. One was a receipt from a welding supply store. Other than that, I saw nothing of interest.

I handed the receipt to Cody, who gave it a cursory glance. "We should talk to the neighbors," he said.

The building sharing the lot was the same size but had windows and a sign identifying it as a medical equipment manufacturer. I parked and went into a small lobby where a young receptionist sat reading a paperback book.

"Hello," I said, forcing a smile. "I'm trying to reach the company next door." I pointed to the left. "Do you know if they're open?"

She shrugged. "I thought it was vacant. I've never seen any cars or people there."

"I see."

"Sorry I can't help you," she said, and lowered her eyes to her book.

Cody was smoking a cigarette and listening to a country music station when I returned.

"I think we need to stake this joint out after dark," I said. "Got any plans tonight?"

"Actually, yes," he said. "Hilda just called me." He pulled on his lip and stared out the windshield.

"Hilda from SJPD?"

"Yeah. I owe her one." He squeezed his eyes shut, then opened them wide.

"What's the deal?" I asked.

"The deal? She'll want to go out for drinks, then come back to my place for a night of exercise."

"Sounds right up your alley."

"Last time we met she brought a bindle of flake and told me her life story. She has daddy issues, uncle issues, brother issues, you name it. They all abused her as a little girl. I mean, I feel bad being with her, like I'm taking advantage of her messed up head. But I got to tell you, she's a sex fiend, a complete nympho."

"Just your type, you mean."

"You might want to get a hotel room tonight. Unless you want to hang around for sloppy seconds."

"No, thanks. She'll probably look like she was mugged after you get done with her."

"What? I take exception to that. She'll be in a heightened erotic state, I guarantee you."

"I'll pass all the same," I said, pulling from the curb.

We drove back to the freeway and headed south through the early rush hour traffic. Half an hour later we took the Hamilton Avenue exit in San Jose. I pointed at a squalid community of tents erected in a small basin next to the off-ramp. It took another ten minutes to get to Cody's house, and I counted twenty panhandlers with cardboard signs.

"You'd think it's the great depression," I said.

"It's not," Cody replied. "Unemployment is at an all-time low."

"Ironic."

"The economy booms, rents skyrocket, and look what happens. Nobody saw it coming. But in hindsight it's pretty obvious."

We went inside and Cody went to his back office. With two hours to kill before sunset, I sat in front of my computer and typed *Palatine* into the search bar. I didn't know what I was looking for, but I wanted to see what I might find if I probed deeply into the search engine.

An hour later, I was ready to give up when I found a reference to Jerrod and Justin's father, Anthony Palatine. An archival site that chronicled local news from the 1970s noted that Palatine Family Mortuary closed in 1971 after owner Anthony Palatine became ill and was hospitalized at Agnews State Hospital. I couldn't find any further details.

I went to Cody's microwave and reheated a cup of coffee. My familiarity with Agnews was limited to a general knowledge that it had been a nut house before closing many years ago. Had Anthony Palatine lost his marbles? I didn't think people ended up at Agnews unless they had serious mental illness.

Jerrod Palatine was born in 1970, so he was only a year old when his father was hospitalized. But Justin was born in 1980. Was he conceived at Agnews? Or, maybe Anthony had been released by then.

A quick online search revealed that Agnews discontinued its care for mentally ill patients in 1972, but continued housing and treating people with developmental disabilities until 2011, when the property was sold. The site is now the corporate headquarters for a large technology company.

It didn't sound like Anthony Palatine had developmental disabilities. After all, he'd been the owner of a medium-sized business. I could only assume he'd had some sort of mental breakdown. It must have been severe, and perhaps permanent, for him to be institutionalized, assuming Agnews treated only patients requiring full-time care.

I rubbed my jaw. Why should I care about what occurred forty or fifty years ago? How could these events possibly benefit my investigation of Justin Palatine? I wasn't interested in investing myself in irrelevant family history. Why waste the time and energy?

Because you don't know what you don't know, chided a small voice in my head. It was a lesson taught to me by my father's friend, an old school investigator who gave me my first job. For him, investigations were all about work ethic. He believed most private detectives were lazy and lacked the discipline, creativity, and persistence to crack tough cases. I sat still for a minute, remembering his words, immersed in my past. And then my mind traveled back to when I was a child, to my father's presence. Relentless and driven by an unforgiving code, he was an unstoppable force. At least that's how I always remember my dad. The sentiment persists in my head, though a point-blank shotgun blast had indeed stopped him.

I turned my attention back to my computer. If Anthony Palatine was still alive, he'd be in his mid-eighties. He was probably dead, given that he'd been sick enough to be treated at an insane asylum. Regardless, I wondered if he ever knew that his youngest son was a rapist, and quite possibly a murderer.

I entered Anthony Palatine into a people finder site. It didn't take long to discover that he died in 1985, at age forty-nine. There was no cause of death listed. Other than a list of his immediate family members, there wasn't any other information about him. This wasn't surprising, given that 1985 was long before digital databases were ubiquitous.

"How about the mother?" I muttered, and entered Marcia Palatine. Apparently she was still kicking, for there was no indication otherwise, and she'd been cited for a traffic violation just two years ago. Her address was in Saratoga, a quaint town on the west side of the valley.

I jotted down the address and closed my computer. The skies outside were darkening, and when I walked to the window, I could see a band of pink and orange haze on the horizon. I put on my coat and went down the hallway and into the room where Cody was sitting at his desk.

"I'm gonna go see what goes on after hours in Fremont," I said.

Cody looked at his watch. "You'll be going against traffic."

"According to the app, Justin is still there. At least, his Mercedes is."

"Call me if anything interesting happens."

"I wouldn't want to interrupt your romantic evening," I said.

"How considerate of you," he replied.

. . .

Driving north, it took less than half an hour to arrive at the industrial zone off Stevenson Boulevard. It was a little after six and full dark. I turned my lights off and drove past the building where I assumed Justin Palatine's vehicle was still parked inside. If his Mercedes had moved, I would have known, unless he'd discovered my tracking device and removed it. I considered it unlikely, but I reminded myself that Palatine was a highly intelligent criminal, and everything I'd learned about him suggested he had secrets to keep. Plus, he was no doubt on high alert since I'd broken into his house.

The building was dark and looked empty. I parked my truck around the corner, but close enough to reach it in a thirty-second sprint. Then I strode to the rear of the structure and walked along the opposite side of a cinderblock wall. A variety of trees grew along the barricade, and I found an oak with a low branch that served as a convenient ladder. I stepped up and pushed myself to the top of the cinderblocks. Partially hidden by the branches and leaves, it was an adequate position for surveillance. What it lacked in comfort, it countered by offering a clear view of all six of the metal roll-up doors.

I stood for an hour, leaning against the tree trunk. Behind me was an empty parking lot in front of another white building. I felt no impatience, for I was resigned to wait for hours if necessary. I let my mind wander where it may, and I began thinking about Candi. And just at that moment, my cell chirped. It was her.

"Hello," I said, voice lowered.

"Hi, Dan. What are you up to?"

"About fourteen feet. I'm standing on a fence."

"Huh? Where are you?"

"San Jose."

"Why?"

"Marcus Grier asked for my help on something."

"Oh."

"How are you doing, Candi?"

"A little better, I think. My mom's had two miscarriages. She's helping me understand what I'm going through."

"That's good," I said.

"She also has a therapist I've made an appointment with."

"Okay. That should help, right?"

"It's all about knowing that my feelings are normal and natural, and the pain will go away in time."

"I'm sorry I couldn't be more helpful," I said. "I mean, I..."

"Don't feel that way, Dan. There's no way you could know what I'm going through."

"I guess not."

"I think I'll be coming home in about a week," she said, just as one of the roll-up doors began opening.

"Candi, I've got to run. I'm on a stakeout."

"Oh. Sorry for interrupting you."

"I'll call you later," I said, cradling the phone between my cheek and shoulder as I began lowering myself.

"Have fun out there," she said, but her cheer sounded awkward and artificial.

I jumped to the ground, ran to my pickup, and drove around the corner so I could see the driveway where the vehicle would exit. I saw headlights flash, and then a black Chevy four-door truck turned onto the street. I couldn't tell how many occupants were in the vehicle.

Headlights off, I followed the truck. There were no other cars in the area, and I had to stay well behind to avoid detection. Once we got onto 880 southbound, the moderate traffic made it easier to follow safely.

The truck continued south on 880 for fifteen minutes, then took the overpass onto U.S. Route 101. I followed it around a sweeping cloverleaf, and a minute later it exited on South 28th Street in northeast San Jose.

We were in a rough part of town, a stone's throw away from a notorious Vietnamese gang neighborhood, and about a mile from San Jose's worst barrios. Before I moved to South Lake Tahoe, my investigations took me here on a regular basis.

When the truck hung a U-turn, I turned onto a side street and waited before reconvening the tail. A minute later we were on Story Road, where I'd once followed a subject into a bar and ended up in the middle of a gang brawl. The truck again turned around, as if the driver was lost. Then it took the on-ramp back onto 101, only to exit again. This time, we drove past a homeless encampment built along a different on-ramp. It was a relatively large camp; I estimated about seventy people occupied the dozens of tents and makeshift shelters.

Driving at twenty miles per hour, I watched the pickup as it passed the roadside shantytown. It slowed almost to a halt, then accelerated and got back on the freeway. Instead of following, I doubled back and entered a trailer home park. A chain-link fence topped with barbwire separated the mobile home neighborhood from the encampment.

I parked and stood peering through the fence. The stench of unwashed clothes and urine made me step back. From the closest tent, I could hear a man arguing with a woman. A moment later, the man pushed open the flap and stepped outside. He was holding a glass pipe to his mouth. He flicked a lighter and took a deep drag, his eyes toward the sky. When he exhaled, he dropped his head and saw me staring at him.

"What you lookin' at, motherfucker?" He might have once been an athlete, but he was twenty pounds underweight and missing a few teeth.

"Not much," I said.

"Then get the fuck out of here, clown, 'less you want me to come over that fence."

"I think I'll do that," I said. "The stink of this place could knock a buzzard off a shit wagon."

"Go fuck yourself, funny man."

I turned and walked farther down the fence line, until I was roughly at the midpoint of the camp. That left me looking at a shelter made of cardboard and hanging carpets. The night was dark, the camp lit up garishly as cars drove past. I leaned against a tree and checked my watch. It was 8:30, and I planned to wait until midnight if necessary. From my position I had a clear view of the street.

After a few minutes, I went to my truck and got my camera. It had much better zoom-in capability than my phone. I returned to the fence and waited.

It was 10:30 when they came. I could smell the gasoline before I saw the first black pickup roll by. A man standing in the bed had a sprayer of some sort, and the upper portion of a barrel was visible. Standing straight, he doused the tents and lean-tos as if he was applying weed killer to an overgrown field. He wore a dark mask, but I snapped photos anyway, hoping I might get something useful. But the truck's windows were tinted, and I couldn't see the passengers or driver.

A few seconds later, I saw the flash as fire erupted. I trained my camera on the road and watched the second truck appear. The man in the bed held a flamethrower at his waist, and was torching every shelter as the pickup rolled slowly along. I clicked away, but he wore the same type of mask as the man who sprayed the accelerant.

The third truck arrived shortly afterward, and by this time the encampment was in chaos, people yelling and running around. The man who swore at me was on fire from head to toe. He staggered onto the pavement and howled in agony until he collapsed. A woman ran after the second truck, shrieking profanities. The truck stopped and the man in the bed waited until she got close enough, then he let her have it with the flamethrower. She went up like a Roman candle and ran in circles, screaming, until she plunged over the railing on the opposite side of the road.

With every tent and lean-to ablaze, the stunned occupants scrambled about, trying futilely to put out the gasoline-fueled flames. The third truck, its bed sitting low over the tires, waited until the flames mostly burnt themselves out, then the hose man opened up with a water cannon.

I watched him take aim at different people, soaking them. By the time he reached where I stood, I'd moved behind a tree to avoid an icy blast.

"Have a nice evening, dirt bags!" he yelled, as the truck neared the end of the on-ramp. A moment later it accelerated onto the freeway and was gone.

I heard someone behind me, and then more voices as people emerged from their trailers.

"My god, what happened?" a bearded, middle-aged man in a bathrobe asked me.

"Someone drove by and lit the place up. Some of the campers probably burned to death. Please call nine-one-one."

"The fire's out. Caltrans owns the land. They'll probably send a cleanup crew tomorrow."

"People are dead," I said. "And others need medical attention. Please make the call."

"We've been trying to get the county to oust these lowlifes for over a year. Looks like someone took care of it for us. You want to call the authorities, do it yourself."

I went to my truck, climbed into the cab, and dialed 911 on my cell. After I reported the incident, a woman said a firetruck and patrol cars were on their way.

The firetruck arrived five minutes later, but the fire had already died. I watched the firemen cover the body of the burnt man and tend to a few of the homeless people who appeared to have sustained minor burns. After that they milled about and conversed with the campers, many who were soaking wet. I assumed they were waiting for an ambulance. The night was getting colder.

I continued to wait, expecting SJPD to show up at any moment, but they never did. I found that perplexing, for a violent crime had been committed, and at least one person died. As a standard policy, the police always prioritize violent crimes. I kept waiting for the wail of sirens. At midnight, I gave up and drove away.

5

IT WAS RAINING WHEN I woke the next morning. I'd spent the night at an old motor lodge on the El Camino. By the time I'd shaved and dressed, it was nine A.M. Huddled in my hooded coat, I walked through the steady rain to the diner next door. I took a seat at the counter and ordered breakfast. Three seats down, a man sat, and I felt his eyes on me. It took a minute to place his face. His name was Buck Kierdorf, and he was a detective at SJPD. He was an old ally of ex-police captain Russ Landers, who at one point had aspirations to become San Jose's Chief of Police. Those aspirations were blown apart when Cody and I uncovered Landers' dalliances with the sister of a terrorist who planted explosives at a San Jose high-rise apartment building. Ultimately, Landers was forced to resign. I never knew what exact charges led to his dismissal, but I knew he was waist-deep in dirty money.

Kierdorf was at least six-foot-five, and weighed close to two-fifty. He had wide shoulders and no fat around his midsection. His head was shaped like a football, and beneath his permanently furrowed brow, his close-set eyes looked pitiless. When I first met him, I had a distinct impression he was a cop who hoped the job would provide a socially acceptable outlet for whatever turmoil raged in his malformed head. Looking at him now reconfirmed the notion. I imagined he spent his waking hours plotting how to ram a railroad tie up the ass of whoever opposed him.

"What are you doing in San Jose, Reno?"

"It's *Reno*, as in no problemo."

"Whatever. Answer the question, please."

"Visiting friends," I replied, sipping from my cup.

"Like who, Cody Gibbons?"

My phone beeped, and I pulled it from my jacket. There was a reminder alert from my tracking app, showing Justin Palatine's SUV leaving the Fremont building at one A.M., and arriving at his Santa Clara home twenty minutes later.

"You got a problem with your hearing?" Kierdorf said.

"No, I hear just fine."

"You better watch your ass, Reno," he said, again mispronouncing my name. "Cody Gibbons is at the top of my shit list. You can tell him I said that."

"What have you got against Gibbons?"

Kierdorf smiled with half his mouth, exposing stained teeth. "His track record speaks for itself."

I motioned to the waitress, who was talking to a cook through a cutout in the back wall. The cook handed her two plates.

"Make my order to go, please," I said.

"You're not enjoying my company, huh?" Kierdorf said, his eyes boring into me.

"That's a polite way to put it."

· · ·

By the time I started driving to Cody's house, the rain had stopped. The morning skies were gray, the clouds low over the valley. I bounced through potholes, muddy water splashing from my wheel wells. I wondered where the homeless population went when the weather turned inclement. They were probably wet and miserable. I guessed they were used to it.

I didn't see any cars parked in front of Cody's house, so I assumed his date had departed. I picked up his newspaper, shook water from the plastic bag, and banged on the front door. Cody let me in. His face was freshly shaved, his hair wet and combed.

"Have you watched the news this morning?" I asked.

"No, why?"

"They pulled another fire and ice last night, over near Story Road. I witnessed it."

"Really?"

"Big time. About seventy people were there. A couple got roasted."

"Did the trucks come from the Fremont building?"

"I'm pretty sure. I followed one of the trucks at around 7:30. It was on a scouting mission. It drove past a roadside encampment, real slow, then took off. Three hours later, three more trucks show up. It was just like the kid we interviewed said. First truck sprays down the area with gas, then the next truck lights them up with a flamethrower. And after the fires die down, a third truck hits them with cold water."

"Did the cops come?"

"I waited for an hour and a half. A fire engine arrived within five minutes, but I never saw any police."

Cody sat at the kitchen table and opened the newspaper. "It probably happened too late to make the paper," he said, turning the pages. "Turn on the TV."

I found a local news station. We watched for fifteen minutes before the newscaster made a brief mention of a fire at a homeless encampment. There was no reporter on the scene, and almost no details were provided.

"Hilda said something funny last night," Cody said, scratching his head.

"What?"

"I told her about the fire and ice on Southwest Expressway. She knew about it. She said she didn't think SJPD was very interested in investigating."

I widened my eyes. "I saw two people get torched last night. I doubt either survived. We're talking homicide."

"She said the local uniforms thought the Southwest incident was funny, and one detective said, 'Well, somebody had to do it.'"

"That somebody is Justin Palatine and his crew."

"He may be on his way to becoming a folk hero."

"I think SJPD will change their tune when they see those dead bodies."

Cody pulled on his ear. "You have to consider *who* got killed."

"You mean, no big deal, just a couple of homeless derelicts bite the dust?"

"That's how a lot of people will see it."

"It's a massive failure by our government. California has higher taxes than any other state. We should be able to house these people, somehow."

"It's a bureaucratic nightmare."

"So the fire and ice routine is a convenient solution?"

Cody shrugged. "Let me put it this way. I don't think SJPD will bend over backwards to bust Palatine for it."

I stood and put my hands in my back pockets. "I've got to find an angle on that son of a bitch."

. . .

At eleven A.M. I left Cody's house and drove south across Santa Clara Valley. Saratoga was a small, old-money city nestled at the base of the Santa Cruz Mountains. West of Saratoga, if one was inclined to hike, forty miles of rugged switchback trails led to the Pacific Ocean.

Marcia Palatine lived in a senior care facility off Big Basin Way, downtown Saratoga's main drag. It was a single Victorian building, painted yellow and set back off the road, deep in shadows cast by tall pines.

I opened the front door and stepped into the lobby. The woman sitting behind the counter had her hair in a bun and wore a blue nurse's smock.

"Hello," I said. "I'm wondering if I could speak with Marcia Palatine."

She raised an eyebrow. "I'm sorry, that would have to be prearranged."

"Why?"

She tapped a pen on her desk. "It's our visitation policy."

I smiled. "Well, could you let her know she has a visitor?"

She sighed and rested her eyes on mine. "She has late stage dementia. We don't just allow anyone to walk in and visit, for obvious reasons."

"Oh," I said. "I'm sorry, I didn't know."

"Why do you want to talk to her?"

"I'm writing a book on Silicon Valley's most successful companies. I wanted to speak with her regarding her son, Jerrod. He's the CEO of Digicloud."

"Yes, we are all aware of that."

"Well, I won't take any more of your time," I said, and turned to leave.

"Wait. If you like, you could probably talk with Mr. De Carvalho. He's been her best friend."

"Would he know about the Palatine family?"

"I imagine so. Before she declined, Mrs. Palatine and he were very close."

"Well, thank you. I'd be happy to speak with him, if he's up to it."

"I think he'd enjoy the company. He's been lonely since Mrs. Palatine is no longer herself. Please take a seat and I'll call him."

I retreated to a chair against the wall, moved my miniature recorder from my backpack to my shirt pocket, and pressed the Record button. After a minute on the phone and another five minutes of silent waiting, the nurse led me through a doorway to a large common room. The walls were natural wood, and a fire crackled in a stone fireplace at the far end, where two elderly folks sat staring into the flames.

A man in a wheelchair by a window watched as we approached. His legs were covered by a plaid blanket, and he wore a heavy corduroy shirt.

"Hello, sir," I said, reaching out to shake hands. "I'm Dave Edwards."

He slowly extended his arm, his hand gently shaking. His bony fingers were purplish and cold.

"Pleased to meet you," he said. "Arthur De Carvalho. Please call me Art."

I sat opposite him, rested my arms on the small table between us, and watched the nurse walk away. "I understand you know Marcia Palatine," I said.

"Yes, I know her quite well. You may find this odd, but I considered her a soul mate. I think it would be fair to say I loved her."

"Why would I find that odd?"

"I'm eighty-seven years old, and never married. And to think, it's only at my age that I finally found a woman to love. Just in time for both of us to depart this earth." He looked at me with fallen eyes and tried to smile. The bags under his sockets were dark and sagged to where his hanging jowls were streaked with red veins. His entire face looked like it had surrendered to gravity.

"Better late than never, I suppose," I said.

"True enough, young man."

I set a notepad on the table, even though I was recording our conversation. "I'm interested in learning about the Palatine's family history."

Arthur De Carvalho pushed his thick-rimmed spectacles higher on his nose. "I spent my career as a reporter, first at the Chicago Tribune, and then at the San Francisco Chronicle. A good reporter needs to not only be a good writer, but just as importantly, a good listener. When Marcia talked, I listened to every word."

"Did she talk about her late husband?"

"She did. A sad story, really."

"I'm all ears."

"Anthony Palatine was a mortician and a businessman. He was quite successful too, until he started losing his mind."

"How so?"

"He was diagnosed with schizophrenia at age thirty, and ended up living at the Agnews asylum for a year. But when Agnews stopped caring for schizophrenics, he returned home to Marcia. He died almost fifteen years later. He had wandered onto a freeway under the belief that he could stop traffic. He was struck by a car and killed."

"So Marcia cared for him all those years?"

"She said drugs controlled his schizophrenia, but made him feel dead inside. In his last few years he stopped taking the pills, and his delusions became more severe."

"What kind of delusions?"

"Anthony thought he was born in 63 B.C. as Gaius Octavius, later known as Augustus Caesar, first Emperor of Rome. He claimed he was reincarnated and reborn as Anthony Palatine in 1935."

"Seriously?"

"Yes. They call it schizophrenia with grandiose delusions. Paranoid schizophrenia, which is based on negative thoughts, is far more common. Grandiosity in schizophrenics is based on optimism, and is somewhat rare."

"You seem to know a lot about it," I said.

"I may be physically feeble, but my mind still functions well. When Marcia told me about it, I read up on the subject. I read for two hours every day. I believe one should always be learning."

"Did Marcia ever mention how her husband's disorder impacted their children?"

"It was a difficult situation for her, obviously. Her first son, Jerrod, was fifteen when Anthony died. He was very close to his father, and he believed in reincarnation. More so, he believed his father truly was Augustus Caesar reborn."

"Did Marcia believe that?"

"Of course not. Before Alzheimer's diminished her mental functioning, she was a very bright and logical thinker."

"Jerrod named all of Digicloud's products after people and places from ancient Rome. From what I've heard, he's obsessed by it."

"Given his upbringing, I suppose that makes sense."

"How about the younger son, Justin?"

"He was just five when his father passed on. From that point, Jerrod became somewhat of a surrogate father, but he left for Harvard shortly after his father's death."

"I see." I paused and considered my next question. "Do Jerrod and Justin visit their mother often?"

Arthur folded his hands in his lap. "No, never. Jerrod pays for Marcia's care, but neither of her sons ever come here. She told me once that they blame her for Anthony's death."

"Why?"

"They accused her of both forcing and not forcing Anthony to take his pills. Either way, it was her fault. Despite all the sacrifices she made in caring for him, in the end they simply needed someone to blame."

. . .

"I got you lunch," I said to Cody when I arrived back at his house. I set a bag full of Mexican food on the kitchen table.

"You got hot sauce, right?" he said, poking through the bag.

I sat at the table and unwrapped a taco. "I visited Palatine's mother at a rest home, but she has late stage dementia. I ended up talking to a guy who was her friend."

"What'd he have to say?"

"Her late husband, Anthony Palatine, was bat shit crazy. He believed he was a reincarnated Roman emperor."

"That's a new one."

"I'm thinking, maybe Jerrod has similar thoughts, given his obsession with the Roman Empire."

"The apple don't fall far from the tree, huh?"

"Anthony Palatine was schizophrenic with delusions of grandeur. When he stopped taking his pills, he walked onto a freeway. He thought he could stop traffic."

"How'd that work out?"

"Take a guess."

Cody went to the refrigerator and returned with two cans of beer. "Jerrod Palatine may be very smart and have an overinflated sense of self-worth, but he's not schizophrenic," he said. "There's no way, given his responsibilities."

"I think that's a safe assumption," I said. "But that doesn't mean he's not delusional."

"What kind of delusions you got in mind?" Cody sat and slid a beer in front of me.

I clicked my fingernail on the pull tab. "Maybe he's reaching beyond his role as a businessman. Maybe he thinks he can fix society's problems."

"You think he's behind fire and ice?"

"I think it's clear Justin is involved. But I don't think it's his brain child. I don't think he gives a shit about the homeless problem. He's got other motives driving him."

"Like planning his next rape?"

"Yup."

"So you think Justin is taking orders from Jerrod?"

"Something like that. When their father died, Jerrod was fifteen and Justin was only five years old. Jerrod became Justin's surrogate father from that point. I think that dynamic is still at play."

Cody sipped from his can, then tilted it and took a big slug. "Hate to tell you, I don't see how any of this will help you take down Justin Palatine."

"What if I got pictures of him participating in a fire and ice?"

"I already told you, SJPD is letting it happen, man."

I shook my head. "I find it hard to believe they can ignore murder."

"That's because you don't live here, and you don't have to see, on a daily basis, how the homeless have turned San Jose into a cesspool. And the local government is helpless, or pretends to be."

"You're serious?"

"You saw for yourself, Dan. The police didn't even show up off Story Road."

I opened my beer and sipped at the foam. Then I threw my head back and drained the entire can.

"Thirsty?" Cody asked.

"Do you think SJPD knows Jerrod Palatine is pulling the strings?"

"I don't know."

I grabbed another taco from the bag. "I forgot to tell you, I saw one of your old friends this morning at breakfast. Remember Buck Kierdorf?"

"That asshole? How could I forget such a charmer?"

"He told me I better watch my ass, and you're on top of his shit list. I believe those were his exact words."

"This just came out of the blue?"

"Yeah. I was in a diner on El Camino, over near De Anza Boulevard. I'm sitting at the counter, and next thing I know, he's staring at me with his beady eyes."

Cody set down his burrito and looked out his front window. After a long moment, I said, "What?"

"When I was on the force, Kierdorf used to do scut work for Landers."

"Kierdorf kept his job even after Landers was eighty-sixed, huh?"

"Buck's a man of special talents."

"Such as?"

"He's a ringer. They bring him into cases on an 'as needed' basis."

"You mean, when some extracurricular persuasion is needed?"

"One time he broke the legs of a drug dealer who wasn't cooperating. Good ole Bucky boy is the type that enjoys it."

"You think he's somehow involved in fire and ice?"

"I don't know. But I don't think it's coincidental that he showed up at that diner."

"Look, as far as SJPD knows, we're interested in Justin for rape and nothing more. Those detectives we had lunch with seemed fine with it. So what's Kierdorf's angle?"

"I wouldn't be surprised if Jerrod Palatine recently made a large donation to the San Jose Police Foundation. It's a legal, non-profit organization set up to accept donations. Or bribes."

"You're thinking the Palatines have SJPD in their back pocket?"

"I'd bet on it."

I rubbed my forehead with the heel of my hand. "Could Hilda confirm it?"

Cody sighed. "I suppose."

. . .

I spent the afternoon downloading the photos from the previous night onto my PC. Looking at the images on a relatively large screen, I was hoping to see something helpful. But the pictures I took of the black trucks revealed nothing. The men in the cargo beds wore similar masks and black coats, and I couldn't see anything through the tinted windows. The only thing potentially useful was the license plate numbers.

After texting the plates to Marcus Grier, I left Cody's house on foot and began walking aimlessly. My mind felt like it was stuck in low gear. The more I learned about Justin Palatine, the more I doubted my current efforts would get me anywhere. If I persisted, I was sure I could learn more about him and his strange family relationships, but to what purpose? I already knew he was a rapist, and that he would strike again. But I had no idea when, and I didn't have endless weeks to keep him under surveillance. And even if I did, I'd already concluded that he'd discovered and deactivated the bugs I'd planted at his house. That meant he would be doubly careful.

But the attack on the encampments I'd witnessed was not the work of a cautious man. It was an egregious crime, one meant to send a wave of fear over the local homeless population. Ordinarily, it was the sort of crime that would be a top priority for law enforcement. Did Justin feel safe knowing SJPD would not treat it in this manner? Was he confident the authorities wouldn't investigate the arson and murder committed by the men in the black trucks?

It almost seemed too outrageous to consider. The crimes begged for publicity, and I expected to soon see front page reports in the local newspaper. It was the kind of story reporters crave; violent, sensational, and politically charged. SJPD would be under pressure to make arrests. Unless there was a different dynamic at play.

I spotted a ratty tennis ball in the gutter and booted it down the street. I rarely give credence to so-called conspiracy theories, because eventually one or more of the conspirators would talk and reveal the conspiracy. It's simply human nature. People are social animals and need to communicate continuously. Secrets can be kept by individuals, but rarely by groups, especially those large in number. Given the right motivation, or even without it, someone always talks.

I know a man in Utah who despises large institutions. He thinks the individuals running governments and mega-corporations always act solely in their own interest, and should never be trusted. More so, he believes, lock, stock, and barrel, that an elite group of the world's most wealthy and powerful individuals aspire to assert control and dominance over all people. Some people call them globalists, others refer to them as the *Illuminati*. Their aim is to create a new world order, one that will rule the planet under a single totalitarian government.

If you ask this man about vaccines, he'll say they are tainted with drugs to render people more pliable. Ditto for airplane condensation trails and fluoridated water. Ask him about the events of September 11, 2001, and he'll claim the U.S. government was complicit in a plot to murder three thousand American civilians. He insists the assassination of JFK was done by the CIA, and that Bill and Hillary Clinton ordered the murder of over fifty political adversaries. The Sandy Hook shooting was staged, world leaders have irrefutable and detailed evidence of alien visits, and the rise of ISIS was a CIA plot to wreak havoc against the Muslim world. Pick a subject, and he'll find a conspiracy behind it.

So, did I think it possible that SJPD had decided that the fire and ice crimes would go unsolved? If so, the mayor of San Jose was likely involved. Was that too absurd a notion? Would that constitute a conspiracy too preposterous to exist?

No, I told myself, as I walked through the afternoon chill, hands deep in my coat pockets. I'd seen enough corruption at a local level to know what was within the bandwidth of most city governments. SJPD could definitely de-prioritize the investigation if they were motivated to do so. Maybe the mayor, feeling the pressure to clean up the streets, told the police to lay low. If so, it would be difficult to prove. The police could assign a couple of trusted detectives with a wink and nod agreement. Failure to act is much more difficult to prove than the opposite. Maybe put a detective like Buck Kierdorf on the case. Sadistic and without the slightest ethics, he'd be the perfect choice.

I reached Leigh Avenue and stood for a minute watching the traffic whoosh by. There was no trash strewn about, and no panhandlers on the corners. It looked like the San Jose where I'd been raised, back before the technology revolution gained full steam. A rush of bittersweet memories took hold in my head, harkening a more innocent time, a time that ended when my father was murdered by a man who slept in the weeds on the bank of the Guadalupe River.

At that moment, if someone had asked me my opinion about the homeless problem, I might be ashamed of my answer.

6

WHEN JUSTIN PALATINE RECALLED his childhood, his thoughts always coalesced to a single image: a terrified five-year-old boy cowering under a small table, his knees touching his chin, arms wrapped around his legs. He would remain in that position while glassware crashed around him and his parents' shouting rose to a cacophonous crescendo. He wouldn't move for minutes after the chaos subsided, fearful that he might fall victim to his mother's or father's wrath.

Justin didn't know why his parents fought, but he was certain it had something to do with him. He believed he was a burden, an unwanted albatross to those who should have loved him. There was no way for him to understand that his father's mental disease had spiraled out of control. His young mind could only assume that he was the main reason his parents hated each other.

Justin Palatine's recollection of his father was like a fuzzy nightmare. He couldn't recall any of the man's physical attributes; he didn't know if Anthony Palatine was short or tall, handsome or homely. The only lasting impression Justin had was an intense feeling of fear and resentment. Over time, Justin's mind filled in the blanks, and his impression morphed into a caricature. He saw his father as a hunchbacked man with the face of an ogre and a violent temper. This man was evil and planned to devour Justin alive. It was only a matter of time.

On the day Anthony Palatine died, Justin remembered the change in his mother. The lines on her forehead eased, and her skin looked fresh and bright. The happy glow in her eyes made Justin sure that something wonderful had happened. Without his father around, there would be no more fighting, no more chaos. The ogre was dead.

Shortly after the funeral, fifteen-year-old Jerrod came into Justin's bedroom.

"You understand our dad has died, right?"

Justin stared at his brother with round eyes. "Yes."

"Do you know what that means?"

"What?" Justin whispered.

"The money has run out. Mom will need to work. You and me will be on our own. You think you can handle it?"

Justin was silent.

"The blood of Roman emperors runs in your veins," Jerrod said. "You have strength you could never imagine."

. . .

Six months later, a man named Earl moved into the Palatine home and shared a bedroom with Justin's mother. Earl was swarthy and barrel-chested and always wore white, short-sleeve, button-down shirts. He worked as an insurance claims adjustor and spent most of his time visiting sites in the Bay Area. He would frequently stop in at the house during his daily travels.

Justin once opened his mother's door when he heard strange sounds early one evening. He saw Earl's naked body on top of his mother's, and he was grunting as if he was an animal in pain. His body moved up and down rhythmically, his hairy back slick with sweat. Before Justin could close the door, Earl's head turned, and they locked eyes. Justin ran to his room and hid beneath his blankets until he fell into a tortured sleep.

It was shortly after Jerrod left for Harvard that Justin was first molested by Earl. Justin had just turned seven years old. He was alone in the house with Earl and was forced to do things he didn't think possible for a little boy. Earl's face was clean-shaven, but his cheeks felt like sandpaper. His skin smelled stale and slightly rotten, as if his body hair prevented his odor from escaping. Tufts of hair sprouted from his shoulders and from between his buttocks. The only words he ever uttered were, *"When in Rome…"*

Over the next three years, Earl brought many strange men into the house. It happened mostly in the summer, during the day when Justin was left alone at home while his mother was working. Earl made Justin swear he would never speak of what occurred during those afternoons. Earl said he knew Justin enjoyed it, and besides, it was the only way Justin could earn his keep.

Once, when he was eight years old, Justin tried to talk to his mother about Earl. Marcia Palatine listened stone-faced, her expression unchanging. If anything Justin said concerned her, she never conceded it. Instead, she said they needed Earl's money to make ends meet. It was as simple as that.

At school, Justin was shunned by his fellow students, who considered him odd at best, while his teachers were truly disturbed by things he said. Friendless and having discovered his reading comprehension was far greater than his peers, he spent long hours in the library, reading every book he could find on ancient Roman history. He hoped he might learn things that would enable him to make sense of the world.

When he was home, Justin spent most of his time alone in his room. Sometimes he would crawl under his bed and lie awake staring. His father was dead, his brother gone, and his mother ignored him. He couldn't have been more alone if he was the last person on earth. That would have been preferable to his current situation, for he existed only to serve the perverse needs of others.

His childhood had been one continual act of betrayal. His father, a raving lunatic, had betrayed him. And in the absence of his father, his mother had further betrayed him. And Earl, well, Earl's betrayal was from a different dimension. He was a demon from a sordid underworld, a place where little boys were punished for their mere existence, punished by grown men with horrible and relentless appetites.

Before his eleventh birthday, Justin reached puberty. He felt his voice changing and his body becoming stronger. It was no doubt the manifestation of his Roman blood, he concluded. The time was soon coming when he would no longer be victimized. His passage into adulthood would grant him the ability to annihilate his tormenters. He viewed it as a rebirth. The defenseless child he had been was no more.

Justin looked forward to seeing his older brother. He wanted to show Jerrod what he had become. A man in control of his life, a man who would not allow abuse or shame to rule him. A man with an inner strength that would crush his adversaries. Justin had a big surprise in store for his brother.

Jerrod had completed his education at Harvard, and Justin assumed he would be home soon. But then Justin learned Jerrod had married and would remain on the east coast with his new wife for the time being. It was a bitter defeat for Justin; he dreamt his big brother would return as a friend and maybe even fill the role of a parent.

Left alone, Justin turned increasingly inward. He began having vivid fantasies of retribution against Earl and his pedophile friends. When he masturbated for the first time, he thought of sodomizing Earl. But he soon realized that he was not sexually attracted to men. It was the thought of women, helpless and naked, that aroused him. He imagined females trembling before him, as he told them what he intended to do. The sex act itself was always secondary in his ritual. The foreplay, consisting of beating and humiliating his victims, excited him far more.

Justin's masturbatory fantasies brought him periods of tranquility and satisfaction, and he sometimes indulged himself several times a day.

But he knew it wasn't enough. His mind would always return to achieving the true resolution of his conflicts. And it needed to start with Earl.

Once he exhausted the contents of his school library, Justin often rode his bike three miles to the county library. He never checked out a book, but would spend long hours researching subjects he found interesting. From a textbook discussing 1st century Roman politics, Justin learned that hemlock was a poison favored by an assassin named Canidia. A book on California flora said it might be available in the hills surrounding Santa Clara Valley.

Three weeks later, on a bright spring morning, Justin found what he was looking for off a hiking trail on the outskirts of Cupertino. The hemlock plant grew on a creek bank in a thicket shadowed by oak trees. It had not yet begun to flower and emitted an unpleasant musty odor. The leaves were in a state of maximum toxicity. Justin carefully picked twenty leaves, sealed them in a plastic baggie, and peddled his bike home.

Locked in his room, he dried the leaves, then ground them into a powder. Content with his work, he carefully funneled the contents into a small glass vial. He kept the vial with him for three days.

On the fourth day, he woke early and watched Earl pour his morning coffee and add a heaping teaspoon of sugar. As was his habit, before taking a sip, Earl walked out the front door to get the morning paper. When his mother turned her back, Justin emptied the vial into Earl's coffee.

After finishing the coffee, Earl left the table to shower and dress. Before he was done, Marcia Palatine backed her car out of the garage and drove off to work. Once she was gone, Justin walked outside to the box in the side yard and disconnected the telephone line. Then he went back inside and waited.

Fifteen minutes later, Earl returned to the kitchen, his shirt untucked. "I feel like shit," he said, sitting heavily. His hands were trembling, and he clutched his gut.

"Your pupils are dilated," Justin said.

"What?"

"There's a flu bug going around at school."

"I must have caught it from you, you little dip."

"Maybe so. You should lie down."

Earl staggered to the family room couch. "I feel like I've been beat with a baseball bat."

"You better rest," Justin said. "I need to go to school. But I'll come home at lunch to check on you."

Earl wiped at a string of drool that had escaped his mouth. His hand was twitching. "Bring me the phone," he said. "I need to call a doctor."

"Sure thing, Earl." Justin got the phone from the kitchen. "I better go," he said, handing the handset to Earl. "I don't want to be late, you know." Then a grin formed on his face. His belly felt warm and happy in a way he couldn't quite explain.

. . .

Justin sat through his morning classes, half-listening to his teachers drone on. He was a straight-A student, and rarely took notes or paid much attention in class. The classwork seemed designed for imbeciles, and he easily aced his exams.

As the minutes ticked by, Justin felt almost deliriously jubilant. He wondered if this was how drug addicts felt after getting a fix. His cheeks were creased with a smile he couldn't stop without a deliberate effort. He couldn't wait to ride his bike home at lunchtime. He hoped Earl would still be alive when he got there.

Finally, at 11:45, Justin hopped on his bike and peddled faster than he ever had. It was as if the wind was at his back and he could fly. He rode across his lawn and left his bike on the front porch.

"Hello," he called out, walking into the sitting room. Earl was still on the couch, lying on his stomach. "You still with us, big guy?"

Earl didn't respond. His head was turned to the side, facing the room. His tongue protruded from his open mouth, and his arm hung to the ground, the wrist bent at an awkward angle. Every few seconds, his body jerked spasmodically. Justin knelt so they were at eye level, and lifted Earl's head by the hair.

"You can't talk, but I know you can hear me. I want to let you know, this is my way of saying thanks for how you treated me all these years. I wish I could prolong your suffering, but this is the best I could do. I spiked your coffee with hemlock this morning. I guess you didn't notice it was a little more bitter than usual."

Earl stared back at Justin without expression. His breath came in labored wheezes. "Hemlock was a popular poison in ancient times," Justin said. "If you're wondering why you can't move, it's because hemlock causes total paralysis. Soon enough, your respiratory function will shut down. You'll be unable to breathe, and you'll suffocate. It will be as if you drowned. The cool thing is, your mind will remain totally functional until the moment you die." Justin glanced at his watch. "I'd say you have about half an hour. Maybe you can use that time to pray you don't get sent to hell. But I wouldn't get your hopes up. Anyway, please don't die just yet. I need to make a quick lunch. Hang tight, and I'll be right back."

Justin hurriedly made himself a ham and cheese sandwich, then dragged a kitchen chair to the couch. He sat and took a bite, watching Earl's body twitch. Unexpectedly, he felt blood rushing to his crotch, and a moment later, he had a painfully stiff erection.

"Wow, I got a boner. Can you believe that, Earl? Watching you suffer is really turning me on. I'm tempted to butt ram you here and now, just like you and your friends did to me. But that might leave incriminating evidence, so I'll have to resist."

Earl gasped, and his face turned white. Then his chest jerked and his mouth opened wide, reminding Justin of a hooked fish.

"Don't die on me yet, you piece of dog shit," Justin said. "I'm not done with you."

But Earl's face was turning blue, and a minute later, he was dead.

· · ·

After reconnecting the telephone line, Justin returned to school that afternoon. He did his best to pay attention to his teachers, but he was distracted by an odd floating sensation, as if he was hovering on the edge of a new dimension. The experience of his childhood, the terror he felt as a defenseless boy, it all seemed to fade into the past, nothing more than a bad memory. He felt strong, confident, and in control.

He rode to the county library after classes ended, and didn't leave for home until 5:30. He wanted to make sure his mother would be there when he arrived. When he turned onto his street, he saw a firetruck and an ambulance in front of the house. He parked his bike in the side yard and was approaching the front door when his mother stepped outside.

"It looks like Earl had a heart attack," she said. Her face was void of expression, her eyes staring past Justin at some unknown vision.

"Will he be okay?" Justin asked.

"No, he died."

At that moment, two paramedics wheeled a gurney out the front door. A covered body lay on the bed.

Justin and Marcia Palatine watched in silence as the paramedics opened the ambulance's rear doors and maneuvered the gurney inside. They closed the doors, and one of the men waved at Justin and his mother before they climbed into the front seat. The engine started, and the driver revved the motor before pulling from the curb.

"He will be missed," Justin said, his voice flat.

Marcia looked at her son for a long moment. Then they went inside. It was dinnertime, and Justin was hungry.

· · ·

In the months after Earl's death, Justin tried to tell himself that all was good in his world. He had been moved up a year in school; he was now a high school sophomore. This made it doubly challenging for him to make friends, as he was younger than his classmates. Over time, he stopped making an effort to converse with them. But he was extremely attracted to a few girls in his classes.

In his private time, alone in his house, he would often have sexual fantasies. With increasing frequency, he imagined what it would be like to hold a girl hostage and do with her as he pleased. This involved ripping her clothes off and beating her with his fists, or perhaps a belt. The sex act itself would be equally savage; he found anal penetration particularly exciting, especially if he was strangling his victim as he thrusted into her, pushing his rock hard member into her rectum as deep as it could go.

After he satisfied himself, he would lie on his bed and sometimes enter a surreal state of detachment. It was during these moments that he could objectively appraise himself, almost as if his consciousness existed outside his body.

He knew he'd been victimized during his childhood, and he knew he'd killed the man responsible. So why did his past seem so unresolved?

The answer, he concluded, had to do with his mother. She had brought Earl into their house and let him rape Justin repeatedly. She had stood by silently while Earl invited his friends to sodomize a defenseless child. There was no doubt she knew what was happening. And she had done nothing to stop it.

It was the most heinous betrayal imaginable. A mother allowing her child to be violated by pedophiles. Justin could still recall when he loved her, when he actually considered her a mother. Those days ended shortly after Earl moved in. From that point on, Marcia Palatine had become distant and uncaring. Justin didn't know why she abandoned him. He didn't know why there was no love in her heart. Maybe she was mentally unstable, like Justin's father. Or maybe she had crossed a line at some juncture, and had become truly wicked, her heart blackened and turned to stone.

Justin doubted he'd ever truly know what went on in his mother's head. Their relationship was cold and empty, and he would have been pleased to find her dead. But he knew he needed her until he was old enough to live on his own. He would tolerate her callous aloofness out of necessity. Until the time came to leave the house for good, and then perhaps he would kill her.

During his introspective moments, Justin knew his rape fantasies were connected to his hatred of his mother. He knew he wanted to punish all females for his mother's perfidy. He knew this objectively, but also knew he could not stop it from happening. It was like a relentless thirst begging to be quenched.

Justin was fourteen years old when he committed his first rape.

. . .

When Justin turned sixteen, he began working at a pizza parlor. Although he had no friends, he could be quite charming when it served a purpose. He also understood how to use his intelligence to impress adults. The owner of the pizza joint was no doubt impressed, because he hired Justin ahead of many other teenage applicants. Within a month, Justin discovered the restaurant lacked adequate employee theft systems, and he could safely pocket an extra $30 per shift. After six months, Justin had saved enough money to afford a used car.

Mobility was a key imperative for Justin. Without an automobile, it was impossible to abduct and transport victims. His only options were far more risky. He had planned his first rape meticulously, but it involved entering a nearby home once he was sure the victim was there alone. It was a perilous endeavor, made doubly so because the girl attended Justin's high school. He had worn a mask and had a well-planned escape route, but he knew he needed to expand his territory. The rape had been reported to the police, and everyone at his school knew about it. The community was on high alert.

Limited to his bicycle, Justin could only venture so far from his home. He waited five frustrating months for the furor to subside before risking another local attack. But once a car was at his disposal, it opened up a new realm of opportunities.

By the time he was eighteen, Justin was living in an apartment and attending SJSU. His older brother was still in Massachusetts, where he'd graduated from Harvard with honors and became vice president of a medium-size software company at the young age of twenty-three. When the company's stock price skyrocketed during the dot-com boom, Jerrod Palatine sold his options for millions, then resigned and formed Digicloud.

Having become a wealthy man, Jerrod agreed to pay Justin's tuition and living expenses, and the two spoke by telephone on a weekly basis. Justin enjoyed talking to Jerrod about business and technology. On occasion, when the conversations veered to women or sex, Justin quickly shifted to other subjects. He kept his base urges locked away, secure in a sharp-edged corner of his mind.

As Justin's superior intellect became apparent to fellow students, he was asked to join study groups. It was during this time that Justin decided he needed to be more social. Being friendless would ultimately draw attention; if he was viewed as an outcast, it could cause suspicion. So he began developing a handful of superficial relationships. With his disarming smile and an uncanny ability to articulate complex matters in plain words and simple sentences, he found that certain people gravitated to him.

He was still a freshman at the university when he had his first and only girlfriend. She was a sophomore, a serious, studious, young brunette majoring in math. Her personality was very dry and matter-of-fact, and she was captivated by Justin's intelligent and emotionless manner. Justin allowed the relationship to happen and found it took little effort to keep her from suspecting his inner desires. Even in bed together, Justin performed as an actor, resisting the urge to punish and demean. But he found the sex wholly unsatisfying, and the relationship ended after just a few weeks.

Over the next six months, Justin raped three women, all students at the university. He perfected the carotid chop, rendering his victims unconscious before he loaded them into his Ford LTD sedan. After blind-folding the disabled girls, he drove to a secluded place in the mountains east of San Jose. A place where he could not be seen or heard.

During this time period, Justin coined a term for his rapes: *festival.* The word itself would make his pulse pound with anticipation. On festival days, he felt energized and unstoppable. He imagined himself as a snarling wolf eager to rip its prey apart. By the time he arrived at his spot in the mountains, his member would be fully erect and near ejaculation. His attacks grew increasingly violent.

On the third rape, the girl fought harder than the others, and left a deep scrape on Justin's cheek. Worse, she recognized his car, and although it had stolen plates, Justin realized the Ford could lead the police to him. Unwilling to accept this risk, Justin grabbed his victim by the neck and strangled her to death. Then he carried her corpse deep into the scrub and covered her with leaves and branches.

A week later, a hiker found the decaying body, and the police began suspecting a serial rapist was responsible. Justin donated his Ford to a scrap yard after learning they would strip the car of parts and crush the body. Shortly afterward, he convinced his brother to buy him a used Dodge sedan.

Jerrod Palatine moved back to California when Justin was twenty. Digicloud was growing exponentially, and Jerrod realized he needed to be in Silicon Valley to employ the world's top code writers. Within a year after relocating, Digicloud had hired over eighty people to work at its new Santa Clara headquarters.

Justin earned his bachelor's degree in computer science in three years. Upon graduating, he went to work at Digicloud. The other employees treated him warily, suspecting he was a spy for Jerrod. But Justin went out of his way to be humble and friendly, and his coworkers stopped seeing him as a threat. It was during this time that Justin learned how easy it was to blend in, to seem perfectly normal. The only awkward moments came when his male colleagues talked about women and sex. One night,

Justin agreed to meet three software engineers at a brewpub. They were swilling pints when he arrived, and the conversation turned bawdy. Justin smiled, but didn't participate in the locker room banter. He wondered if they thought he was gay. He didn't care if they drew that conclusion.

As Justin acclimated to his new career, his relationship with Jerrod evolved. They talked on a regular basis, but it was always about business; rarely did their conversations veer in other directions. Still, Justin felt a growing kinship with his older brother. In part, this was because he sensed Jerrod knew something very wrong had happened while he was away at school. Justin believed Jerrod wanted to atone for his absence during the time Justin was abused.

Regardless, Justin had no desire to discuss his childhood with Jerrod, or anyone else. But once, on his twenty-fourth birthday, their conversation took an uncomfortable turn.

"Have you spoken to mom lately?" Jerrod asked. They were having a late dinner at an upscale Santa Clara restaurant. The dining room was dark, and they were seated at a booth in the corner.

Justin felt his mouth twitch. It was strange hearing his brother utter the word "mom."

"No," he replied. "We don't talk."

"She called me yesterday to ask for money."

"That's no surprise."

"I think she struggled after our father died," Jerrod said. "No doubt she struggled when he was alive."

"I don't remember much about it."

"Sometimes I think she resented us. We reminded her of him."

Justin was silent for a long moment. "Did she dislike him?" he asked.

"I think their love died after he lost his mind. He became a burden."

And so did I, Justin thought, staring at his plate.

"Anyway, the past is the past," Jerrod continued. "I envision great things moving forward. For both of us."

"Always the optimist," Justin said.

"I always think positively. My thoughts steer my life."

"So do mine," Justin said quietly.

．．．

After they left the restaurant that night, Justin went home and changed clothes, then drove to a business class hotel in Cupertino. It was a warm summer evening, windless and still. There was no moon, and the stars were barely visible in the black sky. He parked his car in an unlit area behind the hotel. The few automobiles parked nearby all belonged to hotel employees. One of the cars was a blue Kia coupe. The owner was a woman in her early fifties who worked as a front desk clerk. Her shift ended at midnight. Justin had been watching her for weeks. She bore a close resemblance to his mother.

Justin left his car and walked to a dirt area bordering the lot. He stood in the shadows, waiting behind the trunk of an oak tree. From his position, he could reach the Kia in a few quick steps. His pulse pounded in anticipation. He had never taken a woman who looked like his mother. He tried not to think about what he would do to her. But he couldn't prevent the tent that formed in the front of his trousers.

The minutes ticked by, and Justin told himself to be patient. He could afford nothing less than flawless execution, but his breathing was ragged, and he felt a wet spot on his underwear. When she finally came out the back door, Justin watched her approach and fumble with her keys. Then he pounced, striking her neck with the meat of his fist. Before she could fall, he slung her limp body over his shoulder and ran to his car, almost as if she was weightless.

．．．

The events of that evening stayed at the forefront of Justin's mind for years. Over and over, he would think back and recreate the scene in the secluded hillside clearing. The location had served him well; he'd raped many women there, and he thought of it as his 'happy place.' But on that particular night, his performance had been truly transcendent, almost otherworldly. He still felt buoyant and exuberant when he recalled his frenzied destruction of the woman who looked like his mother. He also felt a deep, abiding sense of satisfaction.

There was a single image that he always came back to, and it never failed to excite him. It was of him holding her by the hair with both hands, lifting her so her toes barely touched the ground, while he penetrated her rectum and thrust away savagely. His climax had been the most powerful he'd ever had.

When he was done, he dragged her into the brush. She was naked and bleeding, her mouth duct-taped. He tied a rope around her neck and looped it over a stout branch. He pulled it tight, forcing her body upright, strangling her. Then he kicked her in the face as hard as he could. The impact from his steel-toed boot knocked her unconscious after the first blow, but he continued kicking until she was unrecognizable. He stayed with her for a long time afterward, basking in her death, a warm glow in his stomach. It had been his most complete and triumphant festival.

It was three A.M. when Justin returned home, and he didn't fall asleep until five. He was drowsy and numb the next day at work, and kept experiencing a weightless sensation, as if he were hovering over his desk. It seemed like it was someone else typing on his keyboard, and he took long breaks, staring trancelike at his screen.

Later in the afternoon, Jerrod walked by Justin's cube. "How goes it, brother?" Jerrod asked.

Justin smiled and shrugged his shoulders. "Couldn't be better," he said, his eyes glazed and bloodshot.

7

IT WAS FIVE P.M. when Grier called. He had run the license plates from the Story Road incident. As I expected, all three trucks were registered to Hadrian Transport in San Jose. One of the plates was the same as I'd previously provided to Grier; it was for the truck that arrived at Justin Palatine's house the night I had broken in and searched the place.

"How are things going?" Grier asked.

"Slow."

"What does that mean?"

"It means I haven't figured out how to solve the problem yet."

"What does Gibbons have to say?"

"Not much."

"Huh," Grier grunted.

"I'll call you if and when I have something to report," I said.

"If?"

"You heard me. I'll talk to you later."

Cody walked into the room and sat on his couch. "I ordered a pizza," he said, turning on the television. I started to say something, but stopped when the screen came to life.

"We have late breaking news," the newscaster said. "Last night's fire at the homeless encampment in northeast San Jose now appears to be a deliberate attack. We have numerous eyewitness reports of a drive-by firebombing, potentially with a flamethrower, by masked men in pickup trucks. The attack is similar to Monday's incident on Southwest Expressway. Two homeless people have died, and many more were injured." The scene cut to a uniformed police officer at a podium. "We don't have any suspects yet," the cop said. "It appears the two incidents are related and likely committed by the same perpetrators. For now, I think all residents of homeless encampments along roadways should relocate immediately. It never was safe, and now it's become extremely dangerous."

"Mission accomplished, I'd say," Cody said, muting the sound as a weather report started.

"How so?"

"San Jose will no longer tolerate bums living on the streets. The message has been sent."

I blinked hard. "This goes all the way to the top," I said.

"At least to the mayor and the Chief of Police. I'd say we've reached a point of critical mass."

"I bet homeless advocates will make a lot of noise," I said. "California's a very liberal state."

"Yeah, full of rich liberals."

"You think any of them will speak up for the homeless?"

Cody chuckled. "Doubt it," he said. "Oh, guess what? Hilda called me back. Digicloud made a quarter-million dollar contribution to the San Jose Police Foundation last August."

"That's a fair amount of slab."

"It was by far the Foundation's largest donation this year. Starting to draw conclusions?"

"Turn the sound back on," I said, looking at the screen. A weatherman was forecasting the first big storm of the year.

"The rain in San Jose should start around midnight, and we may see local flooding by noon," he said.

. . .

After we ate, I sat at Cody's kitchen table and began scrawling notes on a sheet of unlined paper. I'd been clinging to the belief that Justin Palatine's involvement in the firebombings could be leveraged to bring about his demise. I now conceded this was a misguided notion, and I needed to refocus my efforts.

I drew an X in the middle of the page. On top of it, I wrote *prison or dead*. Then I jotted various thoughts in the surrounding space. *Past rapes, past murders, social media shaming, tax evasion.* I stopped, out of ideas. Then I wrote *assassinate*. I froze, staring at the word.

Every killing I'd ever been involved in had been an act of self-defense. Even though self-defense can be a debatable term in a courthouse, I always knew my actions were justified. Assassination, on the other hand, was beyond my moral boundaries. I was not a hired killer, even if the target was the most vile humanity had to offer. That made my agenda in San Jose infinitely more complex. I needed to find a way to push Justin Palatine to his breaking point, to a place where his intelligence failed him and he would paint himself into a corner. Or, failing that, catch him in the act of rape.

There's one more option, I mused. If I could search his house, literally take it apart, I thought there was a decent chance I could find evidence of past rapes. I tapped my knuckles on the pad of paper. Even if I had that evidence in hand, would it be admissible in a court of law? Would a judge allow illegally obtained evidence? I sighed and rubbed my brow.

My phone buzzed and I picked it up. "Palatine's on the move again," I said. It was 6:30 P.M.

"So what?" Cody said. He was on his couch with his feet rested on the coffee table. "Let's head over to Khartoum for a few pops."

"I got another idea," I said, typing. "How about we pay a friendly visit to Ron Donaldson, Palatine's boss? His house is about fifteen minutes away, in Los Gatos."

"What do you expect he'll have to say?"

"We'll see. I want to turn the screws on him."

"Oh?" Cody replied, turning to look at me, a mischievous glint in his eye.

. . .

Ron Donaldson's address was for a house at the end of a steep, winding road. It was perched on the crest of a hill, and looked like a collection of glass-walled rectangles stacked on each other at various angles. Each window emitted light, but I couldn't see into the interior.

I hung a U-turn at the cul-de-sac turnabout and parked facing downhill, about fifty yards from a curved driveway leading to the house. As we walked toward the driveway, I could see a partial view of the city lights in the valley below.

"The ex-Digicloud guy said this pad cost five million," I said, walking up the grade.

"At least," Cody said.

"I imagine Ronald McDonald is a loyal employee."

"Five mil buys a lot of loyalty."

The driveway was steep, and it took us a minute to reach a detached six-car garage. To our left was the main house. A long, lighted path led to the front door, which was dwarfed by a thirty-foot column of glass sectioned by bronze framework.

"You could hold a convention here," Cody said.

"Imagine what a call girl would think if she arrived at this joint."

"Payday."

We began down the walkway. It was illuminated by rows of square lights set in the ground. When we reached the door, I noticed two cameras pointing down at us.

"Ring the doorbell," Cody said.

"No turning back now," I muttered.

We waited for a long minute, then a voice came through a hidden speaker.

"Hello. What can I do for you?"

"Is this Ron Donaldson?"

"Who's asking?"

"Bill Shepard, private investigator. I'd like to ask a few questions about one of your coworkers at Digicloud."

"And you show up at night, without an invitation?"

"I'm sorry, I couldn't find your phone number."

He didn't respond for a long moment, then he said, "Which employee?"

"Justin Palatine."

The silence that ensued made me sure that I'd broached a touchy subject. After a minute, the voice said, "Hold on, please."

We waited silently for two more minutes. I was certain we were on video, and probably being recorded. Finally, I heard the door locks clicking.

"Come on in."

I looked at Cody. "In for a penny, in for a pound," he muttered. I pushed the door open, and we stepped into the foyer. A massive chandelier hung from the high ceiling and cast a glittery pattern on the marble tile floor. We waited under the shimmering light until a man appeared from a hallway.

"Evening, gents," he said. He was average height and wore a white bathrobe and leather sandals. His acne-pitted neck was thin, and it made his head look too big for his body. The initials *RD* were embroidered on the sleeve of his robe.

He looked from me to Cody and froze for a moment. He was clean-shaven except for a patch of blondish hair beneath his lower lip. He adjusted the wire-rim glasses resting on his nose, and inhaled through his mouth before he spoke.

"Let's go sit. I'm happy to answer any questions you have."

We followed him out of the foyer. His hair was dark and too long on top. It looked like he had tried to comb it over his bald spot.

The room we entered made me stop and blink. There was a big, white, llama skin rug in the middle of the floor, surrounded by a beige circular couch covered with furry pillows. Opposite the couch was a bar that looked like it was made of molded plastic, the edges rounded and the dimensions irregular, as if it had been a liquid poured onto a flat surface and allowed to dry in whatever shape it took. Glass shelves behind the bar were lined with expensive liquor. On the far side, outside the floor-to-ceiling windows, was a balcony overlooking a spectacular view of Santa Clara County. I walked over and gazed down at the kaleidoscope of lights twinkling under the moonlit sky.

"Can I offer you a drink?" Donaldson said, playing the gracious host. Maybe his offer was polite and genuine. Or maybe it was something else.

"Hell, yeah," Cody said. "The name's Dick Gozenya, by the way. I work with Bill."

"Nice to meet you. May I recommend a scotch and lemonade?" He walked behind the bar.

Cody and I exchanged glances. "How about a bourbon-Coke?" I said.

"Make it two." Cody took a seat on one of three chrome barstools.

Donaldson wrinkled his nose and looked disappointed. "Will Maker's do?"

"You got Jim Beam or JD?" Cody asked.

"Sorry, no." Donaldson scooped ice into two glasses and poured measured shots onto the cubes. I sat next to Cody and watched Donaldson open a plastic cola bottle.

"Let's talk about Justin Palatine, Ron," I said. "You don't mind if I call you Ron, do you?"

"Why would I? That's my name."

"I've been told you and Justin are good buddies."

"Who told you that?"

"It doesn't matter. Is it true?"

He hesitated, then straightened and said, "I wouldn't say that. He reports to me, but so do fifty other people."

"You ever know him to have a girlfriend?" Cody asked.

"I couldn't say. It's not something we've discussed."

"I'm looking for some insight, Ron," I said. "You see, Justin is bad news, and I think you know what I'm talking about."

"What?" he said, his mouth falling open.

"Hey," Cody said. "This is one hell of a fuckpad you have here. I mean, it reminds me of somewhere you could film porno films. I'm thinking, maybe you and Justin call up some high price escorts and get your party on. And maybe slap 'em around a bit, just for kicks."

Donaldson recoiled as if raw sewage had been splashed in his face. "We never, I mean, I never did anything of the sort." Then he set his round jaw and his eyes turned defiant. "And I don't need prostitutes, I assure you."

"Yeah, I heard you're a real cocksman, Ron," I said. "But let's talk about Justin. How does a guy like him get his rocks off?"

"How am I supposed to know?"

"He's been here, right?

Donaldson looked to the side, and I knew the next words he uttered would be a lie. I reached out and grabbed his wrist, hard. "Don't bullshit me, Ron. That would seriously piss me off."

"Fine, he's been here, all right? I've had a few cocktail parties for my direct reports."

I eased my grip and let him yank his arm away. "Here's the deal, Ron," I said. "Justin likes to hurt women in a permanent way. I'm talking rape and murder. And his big brother knows about it, and so do you. Now, you got a chance to get ahead of this thing. Otherwise, you could go down with him."

"It's called accessory after the fact," Cody said. "You know what the big stripes do to rapists in the pen?"

"The what?"

"The state penitentiary. You'd probably end up in San Quentin." Cody guzzled his drink and slammed the glass onto the plastic bar top with a loud thump. Ice leapt from the rim and skittered across the surface.

Donaldson stepped back and his head banged into the shelves, causing the bottles to clink off each other. He looked at his watch, then said, "What do you mean, get ahead of this thing?"

"You got somewhere you need to be?" I said, and at that moment, I heard footfalls from the hallway. I got off the stool, and a second later, three men entered the room.

"Chat time is over," Donaldson said.

Two of the men were dressed in black jeans and polo shirts. One of them I immediately recognized as Mark Costa, the ex-Marine I'd punched out and hog-tied at Justin Palatine's house. He had small, pinched eyes, a flat forehead, and puffy cheeks with three days stubble. His nose was still swollen.

The second man was a steroid case, six feet of oversized muscles. He looked taller because he wore rust-colored snakeskin cowboy boots. His blue short-sleeved shirt was western cut, with metal snaps and fancy embroidery on the shoulders. His shirtsleeves were pushed up high to accommodate his bulging biceps, which looked ready to bust the stitching. On the flat of his arm, the words SEMPER FIDELIS were etched in dark ink. His eyes were half-lidded, as if he was bored and felt the situation was beneath him. But he kept flaring his nostrils and scowling.

Man number three was the oldest, and stout as a beer keg. He wore his hair in a flattop, the bristles like a scouring brush. His forehead looked like a landslide in the making, and his eyes were slits beneath his knotted brow. He had a boxer's nose, and when he spoke, his meaty lips creased his coarse cheeks.

"What are you doing here, Gibbons?" he said.

"Not much, Mazon. Moonlighting, I take it? You're still with the force, right?"

"What's your purpose here?"

"We were just enjoying a drink with Mr. Donaldson. Ron, why don't you pour these all-stars a round of scotch and lemonades? Wait a minute. Make Mazon's straight lemonade, he's got issues with alcohol."

"I'll ask you again, Gibbons. What are you and your shit-heel partner doing here?"

"We're looking for work," I said. "You got any openings?"

"You never know," Mazon said. "Why don't you send me your ré-sumé? You too, Gibbons. We could all use a good laugh."

To my left, Mark Costa was staring at me. I turned my head and met his eyes. "You got a problem?" I asked.

"Yeah. I'm looking at it."

I paused for a long moment, knowing that nothing good would come of my initial instinct. I took a deep breath and turned to Cody. "Time to go," I said.

"Really? It was just starting to get interesting."

The bodybuilder took a step toward Cody. "You want to see interest-ing, friend, let's take it outside."

"No problem, I was thinking of having a smoke out on the balcony."

"No," I said.

"Hey, no worries, Dirt. It's a beautiful evening." Cody walked to the sliding glass door and pulled it open. The bodybuilder exchanged glances with Mazon, who nodded toward the slider. Cody stepped outside and the bodybuilder followed, sliding the door shut behind him.

For a silent moment, everyone in the room stared out at the balcony, but the two men had walked out of our line of sight.

"You should arrest this man," Costa said, looking at Mazon and pointing at me. "For breaking and entering, trespassing, and assault."

"Based on what?" I said.

"It was you at Justin Palatine's house. Don't try to deny it."

"What's your interest in Justin Palatine?" Mazon said. His gray eyes looked like pinpricks of light against his leathery skin.

"He's a rapist and a murderer."

"And what else?" Mazon asked.

"That's not enough?"

"This is about the case in Tahoe?"

"There was no question about his guilt. They just couldn't make it stick."

"He was found innocent. End of story."

"You ever work sex crimes, Mazon?" I asked. I flexed my shoulders and blew out my breath, trying to release a growing surge of anger rising in my throat.

Before Mazon could answer, we heard a shouted curse and a thump, followed by what sounded like a splash.

"What the—," Mazon said. He and Costa ran to the sliding glass door, and I followed. Donaldson remained behind the bar, his eyes wide.

Out on the balcony, Cody was walking toward us.

"What happened?" Mazon said.

"Your boy was getting overheated. I heard 'roid rage can do that. I thought it best to cool him down. So I tossed him in the pool."

We all looked over the railing at the swimming pool two stories below. The bodybuilder was pushing himself out of the water, his triceps flexed, water sloshing from his boots, his soaked shirt clinging to his torso. His eyes were round with shock and anger, and probably embarrassment. He stood at the edge of the pool, a puddle forming under him, and looked up at us.

"Fuck you!" he yelled, clenching his fists. "Get down here and fight like a man!"

"Gee, I guess he's still fired up," Cody said. "I try to help a guy, and 'fuck you' is all I get?"

Mazon sputtered something unintelligible, but I interrupted him. "You've thrown in your lot with some bad people, Mazon. I hope they're paying you well."

"Go to hell," he said.

I walked back into the house, where Donaldson held his phone against his cheek, speaking in a whisper.

"We'll show ourselves out," I said.

"Thanks for the drink," Cody added.

. . .

As we coasted down the hill, I wondered how deep Ron Donaldson had fallen down the Palatine rat hole. Far enough to have a direct line to Hadrian Transport, which was obviously a front for a goon squad that not only provided security services for Donaldson and Justin Palatine, but also seemed intent on driving the homeless population out of Santa Clara Valley. And it didn't take much to assume Hadrian was funded by Jerrod Palatine.

"What's Mazon's story?" I asked Cody.

"He's a leftover from Lander's regime. He used to work vice. His specialty was getting his pole waxed by downtown streetwalkers. I think that was the pinnacle of his career."

"He was a drunk?"

"Big time. He used to carry around a flask on the job. Then he got caught getting a blowjob from a transvestite. Landers told him to dry out or else."

I chuckled. "That was his rock bottom, huh?"

"One would hope. Let's spin over to Otto's."

"All right," I said, steering my truck through the curves and passing a number of lesser mansions. The grade flattened and a minute later, we turned onto Los Gatos Boulevard. Cody rolled down the window and the air rushing in felt heavy and warmer than it had earlier in the night.

"What did the bodybuilder say?"

"Some bullshit about we don't know who we're fucking with. He took a swing at me after I blew smoke in his face."

"And?"

"I blocked his punch and hit him with a gut shot. Then I picked him up and gave him the old heave-ho. Take a left on Lark up here."

"He probably served in the Marines, same as Costa. You catch his tattoo?"

Cody nodded. "Cops and ex-Marines in bed together. Turn here."

"I know where the bar is."

Otto's Garden Room was a standalone building on Winchester Boulevard. It had been one of my favorite haunts in my hard-drinking days, back when I was in the process of torching my career and marriage. I had done an excellent job at both, and found myself divorced, out of a job, and broke. Cody had barged into my San Jose apartment at the tail end of my binge, and convinced me to go on the wagon. I always thought that was funny; Cody telling *me* to dry out.

Otto's squat, wood-sided structure sat in front of one of the few remaining orchards in Santa Clara County. The orchard was small, only five or six acres, but the land was worth a fortune. The owner, an old-school rancher in his nineties, had finally passed away last year, and left explicit instructions that the land not be sold to developers. He also stated that Otto's was to remain as is, in case anyone had a notion to turn it into something other than a bar. The old man was a creature of habit, and for twenty years had arrived at Otto's every day, promptly at three-thirty in the afternoon. He sat on the same stool in the corner and always drank a single bottle of Coors, no more and no less.

"Does Pronto Schneider still run the joint?" I asked, parking in the dirt lot next to a row of Harleys.

"Yeah. But he doesn't come in much. Health issues."

"That's too bad. I wanted to ask him about SJPD and the homeless problem."

"Ask some bikers if you're so interested," Cody said as we walked into the joint.

The interior of Otto's was like a time capsule. It was a square room with a painted concrete floor and a long, battered bar. On the opposite side of the room, a pool table with scarred felt sat in a pool of light cast by a stained-glass billiard lamp. Dust-coated neon signs advertising long-discontinued beer brands buzzed on the wood-paneled walls, their flickering glow illuminating ceiling tiles yellowed by cigarette smoke. A relic of a jukebox in the corner was playing an old Stones song called *Let it Bleed*. The bar was full, so I took a table in the middle of the room while Cody went to order drinks.

Most of the men at the bar wore coats and vests emblazoned with patches, but these weren't outlaw bikers. The true one-percenters had stopped coming in after ex-San Jose police lieutenant Ed Schneider took over the lease. Ever since then, Otto's had been a cop hangout. Schneider had no problem with that, as long as the cops abided by a single rule—no one was to be arrested for drunk driving on their way home from Otto's. If anyone disagreed, Schneider would bluntly tell them to find somewhere else to drink.

Cody was chatting with the bartender, a young, tattooed woman wearing a low-cut T-shirt. I turned my attention to the television in the corner. A newscaster was talking about an upcoming electronics convention in Las Vegas that would be attended by hundreds of Silicon Valley technology companies. Then I saw Ed Schneider appear from a dim doorway behind the bar. He shuffled forward and hefted his body onto a stool next to a cash register.

Schneider had a full head of white hair and his cheeks were covered with gray grizzle. He moved slowly, as if the weight of his thick gut took considerable effort to carry. Cody had nicknamed him Pronto years ago, when Schneider was also known as The Slowest Bartender in the West. Eventually Schneider conceded the point, and hired a squad of female bartenders, particularly ones who were attractive and willing to show some skin. The current bartender was braless, and when she leaned over to wash glasses, her bare breasts were plainly visible.

Cody finally ended his conversation and walked over to where I waited. He set two highball glasses on the table, but before he sat, I said, "There's Pronto."

"Really?" Cody looked toward the bar. "It's your lucky day. I'll ask him to join us."

A minute later, Schneider followed Cody to our table and sat with a groan.

"Gout still bothering you?" I asked.

"You've always been a perceptive one."

"I've made a career of it."

"What brings you to Los Gatos this fine evening?"

"I'm trying to dig up some dirt on a creep named Justin Palatine. I think he's involved in the firebomb attacks on the homeless camps."

"I saw it on the news," Schneider said. "What's the world coming to, huh?"

"Justin is the younger brother of Jerrod Palatine, CEO of Digicloud."

"And guess who recently made a quarter-million dollar donation to the San Jose Police Foundation," Cody said.

"You serious?" Schneider looked surprised for an instant, then his eyes narrowed.

"I think Jerrod Palatine has paid off SJPD to not pursue the attacks on the homeless," I said. "Do you think that's possible?"

Schneider looked down at his meaty forearms, then locked his bleak eyes on mine. "If you asked me a year ago, I would have said no chance. But today…"

"Today what?"

"Let me put it this way. What percentage of people do you think are outraged by the firebombings?"

"How would I know?"

"I read something recently that said for every ten comments condemning the homeless on social media, there's only one comment defending their rights. Draw your own conclusions."

I took a long slug from my bourbon-Coke. "Thanks for the perspective," I said.

"Something else I heard," Schneider said. "Jerrod Palatine has political aspirations."

"You're kidding, I hope."

"No, sir."

"What, he wants to run for mayor of Santa Clara? Or San Jose?"

Schneider huffed a mouthful of barroom air from his nostrils. "Mayor, hell. He wants to be governor of California. Chew on that one."

Just as Schneider pushed himself up to leave, the entry door swung open, and behind the silhouette of a large figure I could see the pavement shining with moisture. Then the person stepped into the light. It was Buck Kierdorf.

Schneider returned to his perch behind the bar while Cody and I watched Kierdorf. He didn't look our way as he took the single empty seat at the bar. Within a minute, the four bikers to his left stood and walked out into the night. A moment later, the man to Kierdorf's right did the same.

"The guy's like a walking case of crab lice," Cody said.

"He's bad for business, all right."

"I guess we ought to go say hello."

"And ruin a perfectly good evening?" I said, finishing my drink.

"What else we got to do?" Cody pushed his chair back and I followed him to the bar.

"Well, what the fuck, I'm in luck, it's Buck," Cody said loudly, standing behind Kierdorf, patting him hard on the shoulder. "I hear you've been saying nice things about me."

I pulled a stool out of the way and stood at the bar, ready to react if the situation went south.

"Fancy meeting you here, Gibbons. Nice to see you, man. How long has it been?"

"And polite, too. I must have caught you on a rare night."

"Hey, I'm just having a quick one before I head home. All good, brother." Kierdorf sipped from his drink and made an attempt at a smile, but his facial muscles wouldn't quite cooperate.

"You working any interesting cases these days?" Cody asked.

"Not really. Just routine stuff."

"Talk to your old buddy Landers lately?"

"Landers? I heard he's a P.I. in Denver. And we were never buddies."

"Well, that's a relief," Cody said. "Because he was one crooked cock-sucker."

The skin on Kierdorf's face seemed to tighten against his skull, and one eye quivered. He tried again to smile, but the best he could manage was an ugly sneer. "Whatever Landers did is none of my business," he said, his jaw clenched. "I live in the present. You ought to try it."

My cell buzzed, and I pulled it from my pocket. Justin's Mercedes was on the move.

"Let's hit it," I said.

"See you later, Buck," Cody said.

"I look forward to it."

· · ·

Mist had descended upon the parking lot and condensation coated my windshield. I handed Cody my phone and accelerated onto Winchester Boulevard, my tires slipping on the wet pavement. I headed back toward the freeway entrance.

"I want to follow Justin all night long," I said. "Maybe he's cruising for a victim."

"That's your strategy, huh?"

"It's a gut feel. You got any better ideas?"

"You catch Kierdorf's act?"

"Like he was trying his best to be friendly. But why?"

Cody rubbed a knuckle over the stubble on his jaw. "He's trying to put us at ease. But he's a lousy actor."

"Where is the Mercedes?"

"Northbound on San Tomas."

"I'll take 880 north," I said.

"Righto," Cody replied.

It was eight P.M. and the rush hour traffic had died down. I drove at freeway speed, wondering if a man like Jerrod Palatine could be elected to California's highest political office. Given the public's unhappiness with the homeless situation, the current governor was taking a lot of heat. If Palatine offered solutions, he could be very electable. He might even prove to be less corrupt than a typical career politician. Of course, the opposite could also be true.

"He got onto 101," Cody said, staring at my phone. "Going east, toward San Jose. If he stays on the freeway, we'll intersect him where 880 and 101 cross over."

"Rain's coming. Maybe the firebombers will take the night off."

"Who knows?" Cody said.

We drove in silence for another couple of minutes, until Cody said, "He's taking the Brokaw exit."

I eased off the gas. "Which way on Brokaw?"

"Toward the airport. Get over and take 87. We'll be right on his tail."

I took the 87 on-ramp and gunned it. Behind a tall fence, a runway was on my left, and I could hear the thunder of a plane taking off. "He's not going into the airport, is he?"

"Wait a sec, he's at a light. Now, he's going again. Hold on. Now he's turning…onto Airport Boulevard."

I cut across the lanes and took the Skyport off-ramp, which led directly into the airport complex. I stepped on the pedal and blew through a yellow light.

"He's passing the terminal turnoff. I think he's heading to long-term parking. Yeah, he just turned in."

It took a full minute to reach the parking area. Palatine had parked and I assumed was on foot, likely waiting for a shuttle bus. I drove to a covered area where a few people were waiting under the lights. As I passed by, I spotted Palatine approaching, pulling a roller bag.

"Stop up here," Cody said. "I'll get on the bus with him. Take your phone." Before I fully stopped, Cody swung open the door and hopped out.

I drove deeper into the parking lot and saw a shuttle bus coming toward me. I considered parking and running back to the pickup zone, but the lot was crammed full and I didn't see any open spots. So I continued forward until I turned down a row leading to the exit. As I left the lot, I spotted the bus in my rearview mirror. A minute later, I passed by the terminal and parked at a designated cell phone waiting area.

I climbed out of my rig and leaned against the fender. The sky was heavy with clouds and it began to drizzle. A quarter-mile away, the terminal lights were refracted, shimmering and flickering in the rain. I stared through the wetness and saw the shuttle bus at the curb, but I couldn't see much detail. After a minute, the bus pulled away.

The rain started coming down harder, and I got back into my truck. I stared at my cell, waiting for Cody to send a text message. Then I set the phone on my leg and tapped a cadence on the steering wheel. Where would Justin Palatine fly to on a Sunday night in October? And for what purpose, business or pleasure? Whatever the case, I wanted to follow him. Palatine's version of pleasure might well include finding a new victim. I made a mental note to ask Grier if he could access airline records for Palatine going back five or ten years. Maybe there were unsolved rape cases in states Palatine had visited.

My phone buzzed, and I saw Cody had sent a text: *Behind him in security line.*

Where's he going? I responded.

Don't know. Want me to ask him?

I laughed silently. *Whatever it takes,* I texted.

When he didn't reply, I pulled up the San Jose International Airport website on my phone. I was outside of terminal B, which serviced primarily Southwest Airlines, but also Alaska Airlines and British Airways. That meant Palatine could be going almost anywhere. But I doubted he was traveling overseas, because his suitcase looked small enough to fit in the plane's overhead bins.

I stared out my wet windshield, watching tiny rivulets race downward. At that moment I felt a pang of humiliation, for I didn't know enough about Justin Palatine to have any idea where his destination might be. "Come on, come on," I muttered, tapping my foot, trying to flip through my mental cue cards, hoping for a revelation. But I couldn't come up with anything. Despite my efforts to learn everything I could about Palatine, I didn't know if he had friends or associates outside of Northern California. There was no excuse for it; it was weak detective work on my part. I sighed and tried to swallow my frustration.

My cell buzzed with a text alert. *Come pick me up,* it read. I drove around the loop and spotted Cody standing on the departure sidewalk in front of terminal B. I cut in front of a cabbie, ignoring the blare of his horn, and Cody jumped in.

"What'd you find out?"

"He's heading to Vegas. I heard the TSA guy say it. Let's go."

"Where?"

"To my house, where else? We need to pack our bags."

"You want to fly down there?"

"Palatine's on the last flight tonight, and it's sold out. So is every flight tomorrow."

"Why?"

"A big convention. Cloud something or other."

"Cloudcon."

"Huh?"

"It's at The Las Vegas Convention Center. All the biggest tech companies will be there. Google it."

While Cody worked his phone, I considered the looming practical challenges. To start, an eight-hour night drive through the rain. If we slept in shifts and stayed on the road, we could make it to Vegas by dawn. Then we'd have to find Justin Palatine and tail him. I wasn't sure how difficult that would be during a convention with over 100,000 attendees. The crowds could help if we played it right. But I'd never been in Vegas during a massive convention, and I wasn't quite sure what to expect.

"Here's the lowdown," Cody said. "Cloudcon is a new convention—this is the first one. Every hotel on the Strip is sold out. Every rental car in the city is pre-booked. Over five hundred companies have displays at the convention center, and another couple hundred have smaller displays in hotel suites. It's gonna be a freaking zoo."

"Can we get rooms in old downtown?"

"I'll check the Golden Nugget," he said. "Hmm. They have availability, but looks like they doubled the price."

"No worries, Grier's paying for it."

"Out of his own pocket?"

"That's his problem, not mine."

"Okay, Kemosabe. Let's roll."

. . .

Half an hour later, we were packed and on the road. It was sprinkling in San Jose, but as we passed through Morgan Hill, the rain was coming down so hard I couldn't see individual raindrops hit my windshield; it was as if I was driving through a wall of water. I slowed as I felt my tires hydroplaning, and then, ten southbound minutes later, the precipitation abruptly halted.

"Looks like we drove out of the storm," I said.

"Weather forecast says it should be dry from here," Cody said.

"Have you talked to Abbey recently?" I asked.

"Sure. She's my daughter, why wouldn't I?"

I paused before replying. In all the years I'd known Cody, his relationship with women had always been temporary. Even though Abbey was his daughter, I didn't want to make any assumptions. I had been with him a year ago when he met Abbey for the first time, over lunch at the Hard Rock Cafe in Vegas. At the time, she was an intern for the Las Vegas Police Department, and since then she'd been hired as a fulltime patrolwoman.

"How are things going for her at LVPD?"

"She likes it. But she really wants to work plainclothes."

"She's still a rookie. Twenty-one years old, right?"

"Yeah, but she's already better than some of the bums on their detective squad."

When I didn't reply, Cody said, "What? You doubt it?"

"Not really. But it usually takes at least a couple years to get promoted."

"For most, maybe."

"You think Abbey's an exception?"

"She's got it in her blood, Dirt."

"A chip off the ol' block, huh?"

Cody's laugh had a nervous edge to it. "Let's hope not," he said.

"You gonna let her know you're in town?"

"Why wouldn't I?"

"Think she could do a rental car search for us? I want to see if Palatine rents a car."

"I'll text her."

We drove into the starless night, leaving the dense prosperity of Santa Clara County behind. I checked my speed in Gilroy after spotting a highway patrol car lurking on the shoulder, then exited the freeway and turned east, heading for Pacheco Pass. The road was deserted, and I steered hard into the turns, tires howling and spitting gravel. My high beams swept over the dry hills as I crested the low summit, then I bombed down the grade, making time to Highway 5. After that, it would be two and a half hours through the sprawling flatlands of the San Joaquin Valley before making a hard left into the desert.

I manned the wheel until one A.M. while Cody dozed. Then I pulled into a truck stop in the squat, dusty town of Bakersfield to get coffee and fill the tank. When I woke Cody, he climbed out of my cab and stood stretching under the harsh glow of the overhead lights. Then he pulled something from his pocket, popped a pill, and gulped it down with a sip of steaming coffee.

"Caffeine pill?" I asked.

"No. Armodafinil."

"Never heard of it."

"They prescribe it for narcolepsy. It's non-narcotic and keeps you wide awake. Give me your keys."

Five minutes later we were reeling in the miles, ignoring the speed limit and streaking across the sparse desert landscape. I tried to stay awake, but my eyes felt sandblasted. I closed them briefly, just to alleviate the burning. A moment later, I drifted off.

The dream came abruptly, not even waiting until I was fully asleep. I was in the driveway of my childhood home in San Jose, watching my father argue with a fat man in a dirty white shirt. The man, out on bail, was unhappy he was facing jail time. As an assistant district attorney, my dad could have minimized or even dropped the charges. The conversation quickly escalated into a fistfight. I jumped into the fray with all ninety pounds of my ten-year-old body, swinging with everything I had. My punches connected but had no effect. The fight ended as quickly as it started. The fat man lay on the concrete, bruised and battered, and smiled up at me, his teeth red with blood. "Your time will come," he said. I looked at my father, but he stared through me as if I wasn't there. Somehow we both knew he'd be dead soon. It felt as if he already was.

When I woke, I was parched and dazed. I swilled the remains of my lukewarm coffee and tried to shake the dream from my head. My father had died over twenty years ago, but he still sometimes visited me, his spirit hovering just outside my vision. He often showed up when I was working a case. When I was younger, it disturbed me, but more recently, I found his presence oddly reassuring, for I'd come to believe we shared certain unspoken values. At his core, he stood for principle and justice. He prosecuted criminals who both deserved and needed to be locked away. He was unerring in his convictions, and unwilling to compromise. It ultimately killed him, but even in death, he was steadfast.

I glanced at the speedometer and saw it bouncing off 100. "How long was I out?" I said.

"A while. We're almost to Barstow."

I slumped in my seat, told myself to trust Cody's driving, and tried to relax. But I felt like I was being drawn into something far more tenuous and complex than I'd anticipated. I tried not to think about why I was fleeing into the badlands to track a rapist who had avoided prosecution by his own wit and had unlimited financial resources backing his play. The more I thought about the deal I'd cut with Marcus Grier and Tim Cook, the more bizarre and farcical it seemed. Yet here I was, racing into the abyss of the Mojave as if on a rogue spacecraft chasing aliens from an unknown dimension.

I sat up straight, arched my back, and stared out at the ghostly darkness beyond the headlights. The telephone poles raced by like mythical markers pointing to the end of the earth. I continued staring, hoping answers might materialize out of the black void. Then I redirected my attention to the road and said, "Who speaks for her?"

"What?"

"I was thinking about the pictures from the case file Grier gave me. The look in the girl's eyes."

"What about it?"

"It was like she'd lost everything. Innocence, hope, happiness—all gone. She was looking into a bottomless pit of despair. Like she'd spend the rest of her life trying to reclaim her soul."

"Pretty heavy, Dirt."

"That's how it is."

"The world can be a grim place. What do you want to do about it?"

I didn't answer for a long moment, then I said, "Exactly what Grier asked me to do."

"I'll drink to that," Cody replied.

8

THE SKIES WERE STILL pitch black when we crossed the state line into Nevada. It wasn't until we reached the outskirts of Vegas that the darkness began to lift. A shard of sunlight flared over a distant eastern ridgeline, and suddenly the sky turned orange and purple. A moment later, the glass-walled towers on the Strip flashed with bursts of silver light. I put on my sunglasses, yawned, and checked the time.

"Let's check in and get breakfast," Cody said.

"I'd like to get another couple hours of sleep."

"Not me. I'm wired."

We passed Fremont Street, the main drag of downtown Las Vegas, and parked in the multilevel lot at the Golden Nugget. We lugged our bags, heavy with tools of the trade, to the elevator. After checking in, we headed for the casino diner and sat at a large table in the corner.

I opened my notebook and connected to the Internet while Cody studied the menu.

"Hmm, I don't know if I should order the *huevos rancheros,* or a breakfast burrito."

"Get both," I said.

"That's what I like about you, Dirt, you always have the right answer."

"I'm trying to figure out where Digicloud is displaying their wares."

"At the LV Convention Center, right?"

"Yeah, but the place is four point six million square feet. I don't feel like walking around hoping to get lucky."

"I thought you liked exercise."

"Shit," I said, squinting at my screen. "We can't get into the convention hall without registering and getting a badge."

I began filling out the required online registration fields. The waitress came by to take our order, and when she left I said, "What name and company do you want to go by?"

"How about Emerson Boozer from Johnny Walker Corp?"

"Apt, but let's try something more generic. You'll be Roger McDowell from Web Research Inc."

"Let me guess, you get to be Chuck U. Farley."

"Tempting, but no. I'm Brian Scott from Data Unlimited."

"I should have ordered a bloody mary," Cody said, as I typed.

"A hundred-twenty-nine bucks each just to get in," I said.

"Pricey. Grier's tab is getting up there."

"I'm sure it is, with your appetite."

"Just wait until he sees the booze bill."

The waitress returned with plates and after we finished eating, we returned to the registration lobby and left our bags with the bellhop. "We need to go get our badges," I said. "The nearest place is over at the Stratosphere."

"Let's grab a taxi," Cody said, heading to the front doors. As soon as we walked outside, a cab pulled up. There were three more waiting behind it.

"Stratosphere," I said as we sat. "We're here for the convention."

"You and everyone else," the cabbie said.

"Got a busy week, huh?"

"Shows this size are nuts. A two-mile ride on the Strip can take an hour. Just wait, you'll see."

"Every hotel on the Strip is sold out," I said. "Closest rooms we could find are downtown."

"The corporations buy up everything months in advance. A hundred-fifty-thousand rooms, sold out at double rates."

Fortunately, we were well north of the convention hall, and there wasn't much traffic at eight A.M. The taxi dropped us off at the main entrance to the Stratosphere, and we walked through the glass doors to see a line of about a hundred people. They were mostly men wearing sport coats or polo shirts. Many carried briefcases or wore backpacks. The smattering of women wore pants and low-heel shoes that prioritized comfort over fashion.

We got in line and waited silently. I noticed a few sideways glances, and I looked down at my rumpled jeans and scratched my unshaven jaw. If the conventioneers thought I looked like I spent the night in a car, I could only shrug. I looked at Cody, who wore a long-sleeved blue shirt with the logo of a Texas bar and grill printed on the chest. He definitely looked like he'd spent the night in a car. We'd need to make some changes to blend in.

The line moved forward a few paces. I checked my phone for nearby clothing stores, and found a Macy's about a mile away, in a shopping mall next to The Mirage.

While we waited, I eavesdropped on conversations taking place around us. A couple of men were discussing meeting schedules at their suite in the Venetian. Two younger guys were bemoaning their booth duty hours. A pair of women chatted about the potential for finding new customers. They worked for a firm selling alternative power sources for data centers. I listened carefully for industry jargon and heard so many terms that it almost sounded like a foreign language. I began entering the words into a text message: *scalability, colocation, packet acceleration, critical cooling load, dedicated hosting, hybrid cloud, latency, short cycling.*

In the half hour it took to reach the registration kiosk, I tapped in over a hundred words. I sent the message to Cody while we waited for a woman to print our badges, insert them into plastic sleeves, and attach them to orange lanyards. I put mine over my head so the badge rested on my chest. I motioned for Cody to do the same, but he ignored me.

"Get with the program, man." I said as we walked away.

"What the hell is this long text you sent me?"

"Cyber lingo. Study up, there'll be a test later."

"What happens if I fail?"

"No drinks tonight."

"Oh, my. You sure know how to motivate a guy."

We waited in a short line before climbing into a cab. The driver had an impatient gleam in his eye. He accelerated with a jolt and took a roundabout path, cutting through parking lots and staying off Las Vegas Boulevard. Eventually we ended up on Sammy Davis Jr. Drive. A minute later, he dropped us off at a back entrance to Macy's.

"We need to look the part," I said.

"Like a computer nerd?"

"You can go that direction if you want. But I think business apparel blends in best."

"Business apparel? Like shoes and the whole bit?"

"It wouldn't hurt you to clean up some."

"Me? What about you? I doubt you even know how to tie a necktie."

"And you do?"

"Hell, yeah. I would have brought a damn suit if I thought about it."

"You mean the one you wear to funerals?"

"I own a large collection of formal wear, I'll have you know."

"Yeah, right."

It took over an hour to shop and get out of Macy's, and it reminded me why I seldom buy new clothes. Finding a pair of pants and shirt that fit right was a hassle, but for Cody it was almost impossible. Fortunately, we found a store in the mall that specialized in big and tall sizes. Cody bought a complete outfit, sport jacket, shirt, pants, belt, and shoes, size thirteen.

When we finally left the mall, we went out the front entrance and stood looking at Las Vegas Boulevard. It was eleven A.M. and the Strip was packed bumper to bumper with cars. Horns blared and cabs were darting in and out of parking lots, searching for short cuts. For a brief moment, I considered walking to the convention center, which was only a mile and a half away. But I'd only slept for a couple of hours on the road, and I wanted to be well rested for the evening.

"Let's get a cab back to the Nugget," I said. "I need to crash for a few hours."

"Where the hell are we going to get a taxi?"

I looked up and down the Strip. "Nearest hotel," I said, pointing to our right. "Treasure Island."

We hiked for ten minutes, plastic clothes bags slung over our shoulders. Then we waited another twenty minutes in a cab line in front of the hotel. The sun was high in the sky by the time we got back to the Golden Nugget. It was in the seventies, and the morning clouds had been reduced to wisps of white against the pale blue sky.

My head was heavy when I got to my room, and I lay on the bed fully dressed and fell asleep almost immediately. My slumber was deep, and I dreamt of fireworks exploding low in the sky. I woke with a start and held up my hand against the sunlight glaring through the curtains. I swung my legs off the bed and found my cell phone on the carpet. It was 2:30 in the afternoon. I called Cody, but he didn't answer.

After brewing a cup in the room's miniature coffee maker, I showered, shaved, and dressed in my new duds. I looked in the mirror, and the man staring back wore a blue polo shirt, black slacks, and a tan, herringbone pattern, tweed blazer. I liked the jacket, but I was more interested in the shoes I'd bought. They were a hybrid design, with shiny brown leather uppers and a stout treaded sole. I had worn them out of the store, and was confident they'd be suitable for running, hiking in moderate terrain, or kicking, if need be. The toe wasn't steel-tipped, but the leather was thick and hardened.

I called Cody again, and when he didn't pick up, I texted him: *where are you, meet me in lobby.* Then I dumped my gear bag on the bed and selected items I wanted to carry for the day. My handgun, an extra eleven-round clip, a pair of binoculars, a plastic bag containing three dime-sized bugs and a transceiver, a few strap ties, and my sap, heavy with lead ball bearings. I removed the notebook computer from my black backpack and replaced it with the other items, trying to make the pack evenly weighted. I had no reason to think I'd need anything but the binoculars, because my objective for the next twelve hours or so was strictly surveillance. But as my first boss used to say, failing to plan is planning to fail. Always better to be prepared.

I took the elevator downstairs and walked into the lobby. I looked at the huge aquarium behind the reservation counter and wondered where the hell Cody was. He was probably still sleeping, I thought. If I didn't hear from him soon, I'd take off on my own.

A magazine with a Cloudcom ad on the cover lay on an end table next to a row of white leather chairs. I sat and began flipping through the publication. It was actually a convention guide, including maps showing where each company had booth displays.

Digicloud occupied 3000 square feet in the middle of the convention center's main hall. It was surrounded by other high-profile Silicon Valley companies, including Oracle, Hewlett Packard, Facebook, Google, Apple, and Intel.

I continued turning pages, and found a list of executive suites companies used for private meetings. Digicloud had a suite at the Venetian, on the 30th floor.

I stood and tried Cody's cell again. When he didn't answer, I slung my backpack over my shoulder and went out the main entrance. I assumed parking would be problematic anywhere on the Strip, so I waved for a cab. One pulled up promptly, and I jumped in.

"Convention center," I said.

The cabbie headed east, weaving through the downtown grid, until we turned south. A few minutes later, he turned again, heading toward the strip.

"You okay to walk a couple hundred yards? Save you fifteen minutes."

"No problem," I said, as he pulled over on East Desert Inn Road. I got out and walked across the street toward a tall, white building. When I got closer, I saw hundreds of people milling about in front of a long, sweeping drop-off zone at the Westgate Hotel. I continued forward and asked a woman if she could point me toward the main convention hall.

"Follow the sidewalk for ten minutes," she said, pointing.

The crowd thickened as I walked. When I reached a set of glass doors with two security guards checking badges, I figured I was in the right place. A guard checked my badge and a young woman handed me a plastic tote bag filled with glossy marketing sheets. I followed the horde, and after a minute came to another pair of security guards standing at an archway to a connected building.

"Is this the main hall?"

"Yes, sir."

Once inside, I moved out of the stream of human traffic and stood against a wall. The expanse looked large enough to hold two or three football fields. It was packed full of booth displays separated by carpeted walkways.

I took the map from my backpack and tried to ascertain which direction I should go to find Digicloud's display area. The drone of thousands of voices created a discernible vibration, the walls rumbling as if motorized.

Walking toward the center of the hall, I cut through booths to avoid the crowds and finally saw a large Digicloud sign mounted thirty feet above the floor. A minute later, I entered the booth, which had a white structure in the center, and several smaller kiosks placed in a circular pattern around the edges.

The white structure had doors, which I assumed opened to small rooms for employees or perhaps for customer meetings. People in red polo shirts with Digicloud logos were everywhere, talking among themselves or with visitors. I wandered about, pretending to study my phone while eavesdropping. Nothing caught my attention until I came upon two red-shirted guys leaning against a kiosk.

"Palatine is throwing a big Italian dinner tonight for his sycophants," one said.

"Where?"

"Carbone restaurant in the Aria."

"Good. I'll be sure to stay away."

"Ditto that."

I loitered for another few minutes, avoiding eye contact, wondering if Justin Palatine was around. I picked up a few product brochures and dropped them in my plastic bag, then left the booth and surveyed it from different perimeter points. If Justin was here, he could only be behind one of the doors in the center. After twenty minutes passed, I left the hall and stood in the cab line outside the convention center. The minutes ticked by.

Half an hour later, I climbed into a taxi. The driver took Paradise Road to Sands Avenue until we were forced onto Las Vegas Boulevard. From there it took twenty minutes to reach the rotunda at the Venetian.

I exited the cab and walked through a swarm of people into the massive, marble-floored lobby. Beyond the room reservations counter was the casino floor. It was jam packed, but most of the slot machines were unoccupied. I followed the overhead signs through the casino, dodging and sidestepping conventioneers for about a quarter-mile, until I stopped at a long line leading to a bank of elevators.

Everyone in the line was either studying their cell phones or chatting with colleagues. Most toted backpacks. With my orange lanyard and name badge resting on my chest, I fit right in.

I reached the front of the line, where two hotel employees were directing traffic and making sure the elevators were not overloaded. When

I got into an elevator, I saw that the light for floor 30 was on, and none of the twenty people aboard had chosen any other destination. The elevator ascended without pause to the 30th floor.

I stepped out of the elevator into a round lobby that served as a hub for four hallways. In the middle was a circular seating area full of people balancing notebook computers on their laps. I walked around the perimeter, reading the company names and suite numbers posted on signs in front of each hallway. Digicloud was in suite 30806.

It was five P.M. when I reached the suite. The door was closed. I moved toward the end of the hallway and leaned against the wall, mimicking a dozen nearby people. I texted Cody: *I'm at the Venetian, scoping Digicloud's suite.*

I just woke up, he responded.

Get ready to go. We got dinner plans.

Where?

Carbone at Aria. Stand by, I'll make reservations.

I called the restaurant. "Could I get a table for two tonight?"

"We're booked until ten P.M."

"Do you have bar seating?"

"Yes, but it's first come first served."

At that moment, the suite door opened, and three people appeared. I didn't recognize two of them, but the third, a man about six feet tall with thick graying hair, was Jerrod Palatine. I stared at him, and we made eye contact briefly before he turned and started down the hall toward the elevators. I watched him walk away, trying to read his body language. Sometimes I can tell things about a person by the way they walk. Whether they're aggressive or passive, easygoing or tightly wound, athletic or uncoordinated. But nothing about Jerrod Palatine's gait revealed anything about his nature. Then again, I really didn't expect a killer of homeless people or an aspiring governor to have a particular type of stride.

I stood where I was, wondering if anyone remained in the suite. No one had locked the door on the way out, but it was probably auto-locking.

I took a step toward the suite, but stopped when my phone rang. It was Cody.

"Abbey called with the car rental info," he said. "Justin rented a gray Hyundai Tucson from Hertz. License plate 067JXR9."

"All right," I said, entering the digits into my phone. "Hey, I got an idea. Why don't you invite Abbey to meet us for dinner?"

"Why?"

"We'll look less conspicuous if we have a woman with us."

The line went silent for a long moment, then Cody said, "Huh. I'll ask her."

We hung up, and I stood looking at the suite door. Then I strode hurriedly back down the hallway toward the elevators. But as I neared the hub, I could see, of course, another line.

I stood waiting, separated from Jerrod Palatine by three people. A few minutes passed, and I heard more people get in line behind me. I kept my head down, working my cell. I Googled *Venetian parking* and saw that self-parking was available, but valet service was free.

I stepped out of the line and walked to a stairwell door next to the elevators. I glanced behind me as I opened the door. The line had doubled in length since I joined it. Standing toward the back was a man of average height and medium-brown hair. I turned away before he saw me. It was Justin Palatine.

As I went down the stairs, I called the Venetian room reservations number. I descended six flights before a clerk answered.

"Justin Palatine, please."

"Yes sir, I'll ring him. Please hold."

I disconnected the call and ran down the stairs, swinging from the railing and vaulting over each landing. It took less than a minute to reach the third floor. I stepped into the casino and followed the overhead signs for another minute to the valet parking garage.

"Shit," I said, as soon as I entered the dimly lit garage. I peered down a row of cars that stretched for longer than I could see. I took off at a jog, my head swiveling back and forth as I searched for a gray Hyundai Tucson. By the time I reached the end of the row, I could feel my shirt dampen under the weight of the backpack. I peeled the blazer from my torso, folded it as neatly as I could, and wedged it into the pack. As soon as I took a step forward, a car came squealing around the bend. I kept my head down as I walked by it. Then I turned down the next row and picked up the pace, my breathing falling into a rhythm as I moved at a fast jog. I reached the end of the row and turned down the next. A valet attendant was standing against the opposite wall, smoking and talking on his cell phone, but he didn't look up as I passed.

I'd almost covered the entire valet parking area before I realized I was probably wasting my time. If Justin needed his car for any nefarious agenda in Vegas, there was no way he'd have it valet parked. The valet system would likely keep records of when cars left the garage and returned. Justin was too smart to leave that kind of trail.

I put my hands on my hips and shook my head. Here I was, running around like a dumbass, working up a sweat, when Justin's wheels were probably in the self-parking garage. I blew out my breath and began hiking back toward the casino.

The self-parking garage was on the ground level. To get there I had to navigate the Venetian's labyrinth of lobbies, retail shops, walkways, and escalators. When I found the garage, it was a quarter past six P.M.

It was cool and dark in the garage, and I was happy for that. After twenty minutes of patient searching, I spotted Justin's rental car, a midsize SUV. It was backed into a spot between two sedans. I shrugged out of my backpack and removed a baggie containing dime-sized bugs and a small rag soaked in degreasing fluid. As an afterthought, I also removed the plastic tote bag given to me when I entered the convention hall.

After a quick glance around, I set the tote bag on the concrete floor and lay on it, hoping to save my shirt from oil stains. Then I shimmied underneath the Hyundai, which fortunately sat higher off the ground than a standard passenger car. I rested my cell phone on my chest, flashlight on, and found a good spot under a lip on the frame rail. I wiped away a thin coat of sludge and pressed a magnetized bug into place.

Just as I began pushing myself out from underneath the chassis, I heard footsteps. A moment later, a beep sounded, and the driver's side door opened. The frame rocked as someone sat behind the wheel, then the engine started. I lurched toward the rear of the vehicle just in time to catch a mouthful of exhaust as the driver hit the gas.

I rolled to my feet, coughing, and retrieved my backpack from under the bumper of the car next to me. I took a moment to check the app on my phone and saw the tracking software had activated.

"All right, Justin, let's see what you're up to in Sin City," I muttered, smoothing my hair as I hoofed it back toward the main drag.

. . .

I called Cody as I walked onto South Las Vegas Boulevard.

"Abbey's gonna meet us," he said. "What time?"

"I put a tracker on Justin's rental car."

"Good work. What time for dinner?"

"I want to follow him."

"I told her we're going to a fancy restaurant. She said she's looking forward to it. I think she likes you, god knows why."

"I need to stay on Justin Palatine."

"Fine, get your ass back here and get your truck. I'll have dinner with Abbey and meet you later."

I paused in the glare of the low sun. The traffic was gridlocked in both directions for as far as I could see. When I looked toward the Venetian's drop-off zone, the cab line extended beyond the rotunda and out of sight. As for the sidewalk, it was swarming with conventioneers, but at least they were moving. I decided walking was my best option. The Aria was only a mile and a quarter away, and there was a reasonable chance that's where Justin was headed. If not, I could track his travels on my phone, so at least I'd know where he went.

"I'll meet you in the bar at the Carbone in half an hour," I said.

. . .

As I walked down the Strip, I wondered if Las Vegas's commercial development would ever cease. In the countless trips I'd made to Vegas over the last fifteen years, I'd seen no pause in the building of new casinos and hotels. Many of them I couldn't name on a bet. It seemed like the city felt it must keep growing upward and outward in an effort to divert attention from the fact that its very existence relied on slot machines that paid out a miniscule fraction of incoming dollars. Visitors usually had to learn the hard way that the oasis was an illusion; the Strip was truly the worst place to gamble in the western states. Whoever nicknamed it *Lost Wages* was right on the money.

I passed by Madam Tussauds wax museum, then resisted the lure of Fat Tuesday's sidewalk daiquiri bar. I dodged a pair of scantily clad women holding signs advertising a local sports bar, and made my way past the long, open-air entrance to Harrah's. As the chimes of the slots faded and I approached the Linq Promenade shopping mall, the sidewalk grew less crowded, but when I reached the Margaritaville restaurant and casino, I ran into a solid wall of people. I made my way forward and saw a group of about fifty tourists clogging the walkway, taking pictures of Caesar's Palace. I glanced across the street at the iconic casino, its façade resplendent in white and gold. An oversized statue of Julius Caesar beckoned from a massive marble pedestal, arm outstretched in benign goodwill, inviting the uninitiated to join the party and make a donation to the gods. I still remembered when I was twenty-one, drunk and naïve, dropping three hundred at a Caesar's video poker machine. It was money I could scarcely afford to lose.

I crossed the street on the pedestrian overpass at Flamingo Road and went past the Belagio's manmade lake just as the choreographed fountain show started. Streams of water shot skyward as Elvis Presley belted out *Viva Las Vegas*. Across the street, people watched the show from the Paris's 541-foot tall replica of the Eiffel Tower.

I checked my tracker app as I walked by the Cosmopolitan and Planet Hollywood. Justin was heading south on Koval Lane. It looked like he was avoiding the traffic and taking an alternate route to the Aria. I hustled past countless restaurants and upscale stores before finally reaching Aria Place. I turned down the quarter-mile cul-de-sac, heading to a complex of towering blue glass structures that shimmered in the last of the day's sunlight.

The Aria was one of the newer megaresorts in town. It was the centerpiece of CityCenter, a development consisting of three tall, curvilinear buildings. The three were linked together to form an S-shape, which enabled each building's mirrored exterior panels to reflect off each other. The effect was futuristic and impressive, even by Vegas's larger-than-life standards. Rather than targeting old money, like the neighboring Waldorf Astoria, I thought the Aria might cater to a younger but no less affluent clientele. Maybe it specifically targeted the tech-wealthy.

I walked through the front doors and took in the extravagant lobby for a moment, gazing at the spectacular arrangements of polished steel, glass, and marble. I walked without direction, knowing there's one sure thing in Vegas: all roads lead to the casino. It took me about ten seconds to find it, then I walked the length of the crowded floor, following the overhead signs to an escalator.

After ascending to the promenade level, I saw a neon sign hanging from the ceiling. Beneath the sign, groups of people in evening dress held drinks, talking and laughing. I walked past them and entered the Carbone. A hostess was standing at a podium in front of the bar.

"I'm with the Palatine party," I said. She looked down at her reservations book. "You're early. The reservation is for 7:30."

"Right," I said. "How many are attending?"

"The reservation is for twelve, in one of our private rooms."

"Which one?"

"The Sicily room. Would you like to wait there?"

"No, that's okay. I'll wait in the bar."

I waded into the place, which was loud with chatter and too brightly lit for my taste. The bar was long and there must have been two hundred bottles of booze on the mirrored shelves. I didn't see any unoccupied seats, and I continued into the dining room. The tables were arranged around a large cascading chandelier in the center of the space, and the perimeter was lined with curtained alcoves. To the right, way in the back, were arched glass doors. I walked closer and saw the word *Sicily* etched in gold on a small wooden inlay above the doors.

"Looking for the restrooms, sir?" a waiter asked. I walked in the direction he pointed, entered the men's room, and checked my clothes in the mirror. Not bad, considering the rigors of the day. I splashed water on my face and returned to the bar.

I stood in a corner, watching the cocktail area seating. A group of four got up to leave, and I immediately took their table. While a busboy cleared the plates and replaced the tablecloth, I started to check my phone, then saw Cody and his daughter enter the room. I stood and waved them over.

"Well, you look pretty dapper there, Dirty Dan," Abbey said, sitting across from me.

"Hey, what about me?" Cody said, following behind her. He pulled on the lapels of his blazer. Amazingly, it seemed to fit his massive torso quite well.

"I don't think dapper applies to you," Abbey said.

"Fine, you can just call me suave and debonair."

"Whatever floats your boat, Pops."

Cody's mouth fell open. "I wish you wouldn't call me that," he said.

Abbey rolled her eyes. "Okay, *Dad*. Can we get a drink around this place? All that booze behind the bar is making me thirsty."

Cody started to say something, but checked himself. Abbey smiled broadly, her lips testing the confines of her cheeks. She seemed to enjoy putting Cody on the defensive, and apparently found him an easy target. It seemed not much had changed since Cody first met her a year ago.

I felt like reminding her that Cody had saved her life back then. But I really didn't know about the dynamics of their relationship. If she harbored resentment over Cody's absence during her childhood, I guess that was justified. On the other hand, Cody had sought her out, and I knew he wanted to be part of her life moving forward.

"How's the job going?" I asked her, hoping for a safer subject.

"I love it," she said. "I think it's what I was born to do. But I really want to be in plainclothes."

"You know," I said slowly, trying to measure my words. "I've been a private investigator my entire career. Never did anything else, except tend bar now and then. And your dad is the best detective I've ever known. I'm dead serious about that."

"You're just saying that because you're his friend."

"Nope. You want to be a detective, you've got the best teacher in the world sitting next to you."

I looked at Cody, and he was blushing, which would have been funny if not for his eyes turning watery. I blinked, and his expression turned uncertain and then, to my shock, vulnerable. His typical cocksure and irreverent aura seemed to have drained through his shoes. What replaced it was a grown man trying to become something he felt deeply, but knew little about.

I waved my hand in the air. "Drinks, goddammit," I said, loud enough for people at nearby tables to hear. Fortunately, a waitress was already on her way over.

"Two Jim Beam and Cokes," I said.

"Vodka tonic for me, please."

"Anyway," Abbey continued, either unaware of or uninterested in Cody's emotional crisis, "LVPD mandates martial arts training for all female cops, and any men who care to join. I spar with guys three times a week."

"How's that going?" I asked.

"Great. I'm sure I could teach you a few things."

I laughed. "Maybe so."

"Hold on," Cody sputtered. "You actually spar with men?"

"You got it."

"And you can hold your own?"

"Damn right. Just last night, one of the guys was getting a little tough, trying to make sure I knew my place. I drilled him with a snap kick, right in the throat. He couldn't breathe and was white as a ghost. For a minute I was really worried."

"Oh, my," Cody said.

"Kicking is my strength. But my hand speed's not bad either."

I looked at Abbey silently. She was wearing a sleeveless top that showed off her wide shoulders and toned arms. Her wrists were ample and her hands were larger than most women's. She wore jeans and flats and stood about five-foot-ten.

"Well, let's hope you never have reason to punch someone," Cody said.

"For their own good," I added.

Abbey's green eyes crinkled with mirth. Her nose was smallish, and she had freckles on her cheekbones. She wasn't what anyone would consider a classic beauty, but I thought she was quite attractive, in her own way.

"So tell me about the case you're working," she said.

I looked at Cody. "Go ahead."

"All right," he said. "We're keeping tabs on a suspected serial rapist. He's in town for the convention."

"You were hired by one of his victims?"

"Something like that," I said.

"And you think he might commit another rape here?"

"Serial rapists are always thinking about their next rape," Cody said. "This guy is smart, though. He's a planner."

"That's why he's never been convicted," I said.

"You mean, he's been arrested and tried, but found not guilty?"

"Yeah," I replied. "On technicalities."

"Do you have reason to think he's planning a rape in my town?"

"Your town?" Cody asked, an eyebrow raised.

"I live here, don't I?"

"We have no specific reason to suspect he's planning a rape in Vegas," I said. "Other than his recent history. He lives in San Jose, but raped a teenager in South Lake Tahoe."

"Ah," Abbey said. "*Your* town."

"He's attacked women in San Jose, as well as other cities," Cody said. "Maybe the prospect of a new victim in a new town excites him."

"That sounds somewhat theoretical," Abbey said.

"Sometimes that's all you have to go on," I said.

Cody looked directly at Abbey. "You study a subject, study their behavior, past and present, and come up with theories. What motivates them, and why? Is it money? Lust? Revenge?"

"Simple as that, huh?"

"No," Cody said. "But it's a starting point."

We paused while the waitress set our drinks on the table.

"So, what comes next?" Abbey said.

"You test your theory," Cody replied.

"And if it doesn't hold water?"

"Then you better come up with another theory." Cody took a long sip from his highball.

"Is that how it works, Dan?"

"Pretty much. It's rarely a linear process."

"Now you sound like one of my college professors."

"Abbey," Cody said. "You spend enough time in the business, you learn never to give criminals the benefit of the doubt. Always expect the worst."

"Your dad is dead right," I said. "Which reminds me…" I took my phone from my breast pocket and checked the tracker app. I felt my brow furrow.

"What's up?" Cody asked.

"I thought Palatine was headed here. But he turned the other way on Harmon. He's over near the university."

"Palatine?" Abbey said. Cody and I looked at her in surprise.

"Justin Palatine. You ran his rental car plates for us," Cody said.

"I know. He's not related to Jerrod Palatine, is he?"

"Justin is Jerrod's kid brother," I said.

"Wow. That's interesting."

"Why?"

"Jerrod Palatine just announced he's running for governor of California."

"When?" Cody said.

"I saw it on the news right before I picked you up."

Cody and I exchanged glances. "Pronto was right," he muttered.

"Weird timing," I said. "Announcing it while he's here on business."

"Maybe he aspires to a higher calling." Cody leaned forward and tapped his chin with his knuckle.

"The only calling higher than money is power," I said.

"Words of wisdom, that. Take note, Abbey."

I again looked at my tracker. The gray Hyundai had stopped, but not at an intersection.

"Do you know where Spencer Street is?" I asked Abbey. "Near Rochelle Avenue."

"That's right around the corner from my apartment."

"Looks like Palatine is parked there."

"Why?"

Cody looked up, and we locked eyes. "He's probably on foot," I said.

"Scouting for a victim." Cody guzzled his drink, then rose from his chair. "Let's go."

"What about dinner?" Abbey said.

"We'll pick up something later."

. . .

As we hurried to the self-parking garage, I tried to sort through the possibilities. Could Justin be strolling the streets surrounding the campus at this moment, looking for a woman to abduct? It was a stretch, because I doubted he'd had time to find a suitable location to carry out an attack. This was only his second night in town, and he'd arrived late the first night, around eleven P.M.

Site selection was no doubt a key challenge he faced. If Justin were to commit a rape, he'd need to transport his victim to an isolated spot—somewhere he couldn't be seen or heard. In Tahoe he'd found a drivable fire trail that took him a short distance to a secluded area. I suspected this was his typical method of operation. But it was unlikely he'd been in Vegas long enough to find a spot that fit the criteria.

Of course, this was all conjecture on my part. He could have stayed up until two or three in the morning after arriving, and driven around searching for the right place. Or, he could have visited Las Vegas previously, and found the perfect spot to unleash his violent urges. Hell, for all I knew, he'd raped women in Vegas before.

I checked my phone again as we reached Abbey's Dodge Charger. Justin's Hyundai was still parked near the campus. Before we got in, Cody bent down and inspected a rear tire.

"Tread looks good. You probably got another year before you need new rubber."

"Thanks for the advice," Abbey said, climbing into the driver's seat. Cody sat next to her, and I got in the back.

"Bad tires cause problems. It's not if, it's when."

"Yes, dad," Abbey said, her voice tinged with exasperation.

We drove out of the Aria, and it took ten minutes to make it off the Strip and onto E. Harmon Avenue. From there it was a straight shot to the university. But while we waited at a light, the Hyundai started moving.

"Pull over," I said. I squinted at my phone, watching the vehicle head south, toward the airport. It then turned west, then south on Paradise.

"Go up and take a right on Paradise," I said.

"Where's he going?" Abbey asked.

"Maybe back to the Venetian."

"Not if he found a victim."

"We'll know soon enough."

The Hyundai stayed southbound, passing the airport complex. We were about a mile behind it. A couple of minutes later, the car got on the 215 heading west. It passed over South Las Vegas Boulevard and continued for ten minutes until the freeway turned north.

"It's almost like he's driving aimlessly," Cody said.

"I don't think so. Step on it," I said. "Let's close the gap."

Abbey hit the gas and steered to the fast lane. The V8 motor accelerated effortlessly to ninety mph. We made time for five miles and were only a hundred yards behind Palatine when he exited the freeway at West Charleston and turned left.

"There's not much out here," Abbey said a minute later. "He's heading into Red Rock."

"Where?"

"Red Rock Canyon. People come mostly to hike and check out the rock formations. I jog the trails on the weekends."

"This road is a loop," I said. "It leads all the way back to Southern Vegas. It doesn't look like there're any houses or businesses along the way."

"It's a scenic loop. The only building I know of is the visitor center. It's about five miles ahead."

We followed the Hyundai due west for a mile, then the road turned dark and deserted.

"Hang back, give him room," I said.

"He might have a woman with him," Abbey said, but she let off the throttle.

"If he does, we'll catch him in the act," Cody said.

For a long stretch, the road was straight and flat. The moon was nearly full, and I told Abbey to switch off the headlights. We let the Hyundai gain ground on us until its taillights were barely visible. Then the SUV disappeared around a corner shouldered by a rock outcropping. The road turned again after that, then straightened for as far I could see. We were the only cars on the road, and we stayed at least a quarter-mile behind Palatine.

"He turned off," I said.

"At the visitor center?" Abbey asked.

"Hold on," I said, expanding the map image. "Yeah, looks like it."

"Has he stopped?" Cody said.

"No, he's creeping along real slow. Abbey, pull over, let's give him some time."

"Time to do what?"

"I want to wait until he's parked."

Abbey slowed, then rolled onto a gravel turnout flanked by a wall of orange sandstone. My eyes were glued to the tracker. The Hyundai stopped twice, but only for brief moments.

"He's looking for a spot," I said. "Now he's coming back. He's back on the road, let's go, nice and slow, no headlights."

We drove at twenty miles an hour, keeping well behind Palatine. Then he braked and turned left.

"He's on a road that dead-ends after a quarter-mile or so," I said. "Drive past it, then drop me off."

"What are you gonna do?" Abbey asked.

"That depends on what he does."

Abbey drove past where Palatine had left the main road, then U-turned and parked on the shoulder. I removed my holstered pistol from my backpack, clipped it to my belt loop, and hopped out. Then I took off at a jog down the gravel road Palatine had taken.

The moon was bright and there were no trees to provide cover. I stayed close to a long rock wall that ran alongside the road. The desert night had turned cold, and I buttoned my coat. After a minute, I came to a small building, a restroom, off the trail to the left. Up ahead, the road widened to a broad turnabout, the gravel replaced by a gently sloping red rock plateau that stretched fifty yards or so to a series of sandstone formations, some a couple of hundred feet high. I stopped and took my binoculars from my pack.

The Hyundai had stopped in the center of the plateau, its headlights illuminating the rock formations. Justin stood aside the vehicle, looking out at the lighted terrain. Then he set out on foot in the path of his head-lights.

I waited until he neared a cluster of spires silhouetted against the moonlit sky. Hoping he wouldn't hear me, I ran, stepping as lightly as I could, cringing at the sound of gravel crunching beneath my shoes. I stepped onto the rock floor and ran faster. When I got to the Hyundai, Justin was no longer visible. He must have found a pathway into the for-mations.

I peered into the vehicle, cupping my hands on each window. I didn't expect to see an unconscious or bound female, and I was right; the SUV was empty. That meant Palatine was purely on a recon mission. I turned to run back, then a sudden thought made me freeze.

Waiting for Justin to return would be so easy. I could hide behind the vehicle and attack him before he got in the driver's seat. It would be simple to come up from behind and slap him into a chokehold. Within thirty seconds, he would lose consciousness, and three minutes later he'd be dead. Or I could opt for a quicker tactic—approach him from the front, wrap my right arm around his neck, and flip him over my hip while holding his head stationary with my left hand. The move, outlawed in mixed martial arts, is called *kubi kudaki*. It results in a tearing of the spinal column, causing either paralysis or death.

Justin was five-foot-ten and about a hundred seventy-five pounds. I outweighed him by a good thirty-five pounds, and I was a trained fighter. Killing him would take little effort, from a physical standpoint.

But mentally, it was a different story. It would be murder, plain and simple. No claim to self-defense could be made. To justify killing him, I could only say he's evil incarnate, an aberration of the gene pool, a vicious predator who has inflicted untold pain and suffering. By his actions, he has surrendered his right to exist. Morally, killing him would be defensible. But legally, forget about it.

There was also the immediate aftermath to consider. If I killed him, what would I tell Cody and his daughter? As a member of LVPD, Abbey would be in a precarious position. Once she found out Palatine was dead, whether I told her or she found out otherwise, she would have to live with the weight of the crime on her shoulders. She might even have to lie about it, putting herself at risk. Or, she might be forced to tell the truth, which could send me to prison for life.

I squeezed my eyes shut for a long moment. When I opened them, I saw Palatine emerge from an opening in the rocks.

"*Fuck,*" I whispered, crouching behind the vehicle. I moved to the passenger side and knelt near the rear tire, where he'd be least likely to spot me. If he did, I didn't know what I'd do. Probably make up a story he'd see right through. No doubt he'd recognize me—I assumed the thugs from Hadrian Security told him about Cody's and my visit to Ron Donaldson's house.

My indecision had put me in a bad spot. If Justin knew I was following me, my trip to Vegas would be a waste of time and money.

Goddammit, Marcus, I thought, momentarily blaming him for my predicament. I looked in the Hyundai's passenger side mirror and ducked lower. The seconds ticked by until I heard his footfalls on the rock, then the front door opened. I moved behind the SUV, my nose an inch from the rear bumper.

The engine started, and I watched the taillights, hoping he didn't shift into reverse. When he pulled forward, I lay flat on my stomach. He wouldn't see me unless he checked his rearview mirror, and even then, he might not see me in the dark.

The Hyundai made a wide U-turn, its tires chafing the oxidized rock. I stayed down, my jaw pressed against the rough surface, until Palatine reached the gravel path and disappeared around a corner.

I stood and called Cody. "He's heading back, get out of there, go park at the visitor center," I said.

"He was alone?" Cody asked.

"Right. I'll meet you in five minutes."

I jogged the quarter-mile back to the main road, the path easy to follow in the moonlight. Then I picked up speed on the pavement, enjoying the cold air against my face as I covered the half-mile to the visitor center. Abbey had backed into a parking spot, and flashed her headlights as I approached.

"You got rust all over your new clothes," Cody said as I got into the Dodge.

"It's iron oxide," Abbey said.

"We saw the Hyundai drive past. He's headed toward town." Cody turned in his seat and looked back at me.

"He was looking for a place to bring a victim," I said. "I think he found one. Let's go check it out."

Abbey drove us back to the gravel turnoff, and a minute later, we parked in the same place Palatine had. We all got out of the car, and I led us to the cluster of sandstone formations.

"This is where he went," I said. "There's an opening here somewhere." We turned on our cell phone flashlights and began searching.

"Here," Abbey said. Cody and I followed her into a narrow passage. After ten feet it opened into a circular space about twenty feet in diameter. It was surrounded by walls that looked like stacked rock slabs.

"It's perfect," I said, looking around and walking the perimeter. "Sheltered, no one around at night, easy to park and drag a woman here."

We stood silently. "What do you think, detective?" Cody said to Abbey.

"Install cameras," she said. "Activated by motion detectors. These walls have millions of places to hide cameras. Maybe paint them red to blend in."

"That might record the crime, but it wouldn't stop it," Cody said.

"The solution is to tail Palatine everywhere he drives," I said. "But just in case, I think it would be a good idea to stay at the closest hotel we can find. Wasn't there a hotel right where we exited the freeway?"

"It was a casino," Abbey said.

"Let's head back and check it out."

We hiked back to Abbey's car and piled in. She started the motor, but I said, "Hold on. Let's time it. Drive like a bat out of hell, Abbey."

"Wrong," Cody said. "*I'll* drive. Get out, Abbey."

"What? What makes you so special? Forget it."

"I own a car that's basically a street legal race car. I had to go to racing school to learn how to drive it. I'm an expert, so step aside, rookie."

"The hell with that," Abbey said, and hit the gas. The Dodge fishtailed on the rock, and we bounced onto the gravel path with a jolt. I started the timer and held on as the car swayed, spraying gravel and coming within inches of hitting the wall on our left.

When we reached the main road, Abbey performed a well-executed power slide, the tires howling on the asphalt. The engine revved and we jetted forward. I saw Cody turn toward Abbey, a fiendish grin on his face. "Go, go!" he said.

"Map search the hotel, Cody," I said. "Make sure we take the quickest route." I looked at the timer. It had just hit 60 seconds.

"Five miles to go," he replied as we accelerated. "No traffic lights. We'll take a right on Desert Foothills Drive in, oh…" He looked over at the speedometer, which had just passed 100 mph. "About three minutes."

"There are two curves coming up, Abbey," I said. "Don't wreck us."

"Is he always like that?" Abbey said.

"He's a worrier," Cody said, "But he may have a point. I hope your brakes are good." Abbey was running the Dodge flat out. The speedometer had hit 120.

By the time we reached where the road had been carved through a low mesa, Abbey had slowed enough to navigate the turns without skidding into a wall. We did, however, annihilate an errant tumbleweed that had strayed onto the shoulder. A half-mile later, she jammed the brakes, made a hard right, and kept the speed down as we drove through a residential area that led us to the hotel parking lot.

"Four minutes and forty seconds," I said.

"Let's head on in, find a bar," Cody said. "I'd say celebration's in order."

"Why, because you survived my driving?"

"No, because for the first time, I think we've got a grip on Justin Palatine," Cody said. "You agree, Kemosabe?"

"Maybe so," I said. "I could go for a beer right about now."

"Abbey?"

"I'll join you for one, then I need to go home."

We got out of Abbey's car and stood before the Red Rock Casino Hotel Resort. It was a big, modern building, at least twelve stories tall, and looked newly built. The parking lot out front took up many acres, but we were well away from the center of town, and undeveloped land was abundant. I checked my tracker app, and saw the Hyundai on the freeway, going toward the Strip.

As we walked to the main entrance, I saw that the building stretched for almost the length of a city block. If we stayed here, I'd want rooms on the first floor, nearest the lobby.

We went past the reservations counter and into the casino. The place wasn't crowded, and we found a bar quickly and sat at a cocktail table.

"Here's the plan," I said. "We'll make room reservations and check in here tomorrow."

"We'll need to find a store that sells surveillance gear," Cody said. "I like Abbey's idea. Let's see if we can film the son of a bitch."

"We can take care of it first thing in the morning," I said. "We'll have all day to get the cameras and set them up."

"You think he'll strike tomorrow night?" Abbey asked, stirring her vodka tonic.

"He's only here for the week. If not tomorrow, then the next night. As soon as he can find a victim."

"I want you to call me if you know he's headed to the spot," Abbey said. "I'm working day shifts. I get off at five."

"Hey," Cody said. "You want credit for a bust, it's a perfect opportunity."

"As long as he gets put away," I said.

"For life," Cody added.

"Twenty years would do." I held up my beer, and we clinked glasses.

"Here's to taking this sadist prick off the street," Cody said.

After that, Cody and Abbey started chatting, seemingly enjoying each other's company. I sat back and thought about our plan, searching for holes. The tracking bug I planted on Palatine's vehicle could fail, but the battery still had plenty of life and only drained when the car was in motion. Another potential problem was the camera installation and operation; we'd have to test the gear thoroughly and make sure we fully understood how it worked.

Getting video of Justin committing a rape should make his conviction a lock. Video evidence was becoming increasingly common in criminal trials. Even the most nuanced defense arguments had a tough time overcoming a good piece of video.

However, the goal was not only to film Justin during an attack, but to stop him from actually committing a rape. To that end, either Cody or I could be hiding near the site, ready to intervene before the act occurred.

I went to get a beer and sat in front of a video poker machine inset in the bar top. A television mounted in the corner was tuned to a local news station. The sound was muted, and I stared at the screen blankly. How sweet it would be to catch Justin in the act tomorrow night. Abbey could arrest him on the spot and take him to jail. I would provide her the video content and personally talk to the Las Vegas D.A., sharing everything I knew about Palatine. I'd warn him that Palatine was highly intelligent and adept at defending himself. With any luck, the Vegas justice department would assign their top prosecutor to the case. Hopefully, he would be more capable than Tim Cook, and make sure Palatine was held without bail. The next step would be to promptly convict him of kidnapping, assault, and attempted rape.

If all went well, I could leave Las Vegas within 48 hours. I'd buy Cody a flight back to San Jose, then drive four hundred miles up the western flank of Nevada, until I turned west at the Walker River Reservation. After that, I'd take Old Highway 395 north, then gun it up Kingsbury Grade and coast into South Lake Tahoe.

I suddenly felt remiss about not calling Candi. *But she hadn't called me either,* I thought, staring at the video poker screen. I started calling her number, then realized it was 9:30 P.M., which made it 11:30 in Texas. I put my phone down, ready to get Cody and leave for the Golden Nugget. But something on the television made me stop. Standing behind a podium was Jerrod Palatine. He was wearing a business suit and smiling. I read the closed captions on the screen as he spoke.

Yes, I'm formally entering the race for governor of California. Our state is in dire need of leadership. Nothing illustrates this more visibly than the homeless epidemic. It's a problem that is beyond the capabilities of our current governor. As governor of California, I guarantee to end the homeless problem. I will deploy California's vast financial resources to find adequate housing solutions for the mentally ill. The indigent will be provided jobs and shelter. Our streets, parks, and vacant fields will be cleared of transients. Panhandling and vagrancy will be prosecutable offences.

From off-screen a voice asked, *Do you propose making homelessness illegal?*

I will prioritize programs to provide housing for every homeless person in California. Those who prefer living on the street will be subject to jail. We will no longer tolerate filth and squalor on our streets. I will return our state to its natural beauty.

I turned to look at Cody, but he and Abbey were laughing, and I didn't want to interrupt. I fed a ten-dollar bill into the poker machine and considered Jerrod Palatine's chances of being elected to California's top post. He was a political outsider, a man who'd never held office. But he was a member of a small, elitist group of businessmen with recognizable names. He was also one of a handful of modern American industrialists with enough money to bankroll a major campaign. If he was moderately charismatic, I thought he had a decent chance. Of course, his campaign could implode if it became known that his brother was a rapist.

I lost a few hands, then froze when I looked again at the television. A lady newscaster stood, microphone in hand, on a paved trail I thought I recognized.

So far, there are thirty confirmed dead of gunshot wounds along the Los Gatos Creek Trail in San Jose. It appears they were homeless inhabitants of the tents and makeshift shelters that have sprung up along the creek over the last year. The shootings apparently happened during last night's torrential downpour.

The shot switched to a uniformed policeman surrounded by microphones. *The evidence so far indicates a coordinated mass killing. The hundreds of shell casing we found along the banks are the type most commonly used in military assault rifles. There had to have been at least three shooters, maybe more. We are still collecting evidence and interviewing witnesses. Regardless of the socioeconomic status of the victims, this case is our top priority.*

The screen cut to a commercial. I sat for a moment, the last sentence reverberating in my head. Why did the cop bother qualifying the priority of the case? Thirty people, shot dead? I couldn't recall there ever being a mass shooting that large in California. Obviously the case would be a huge priority. I wouldn't be surprised if the FBI was already onsite.

"What was that?" Cody said, coming up behind me.

"Last night, while we were driving, thirty homeless people were gunned down on the Los Gatos Creek Trail. Right near your house."

"Be serious."

"You think I'd make that up? Google it."

Cody worked his phone for a minute, then his eyes widened. "During the rain, someone shot up a bunch of homeless tents. A local reported a body in the creek this morning, and by noon every police agency in the valley was there, walking the trails along the water and checking the tents. The place looked like a war zone, bloody corpses everywhere. They think multiple shooters were involved. Talk about a shit storm. The media's calling it *The Los Gatos Creek homeless massacre.*"

"It's blowing up on social media," I said scrolling on my phone. "You should see what people are posting."

"Like what?"

"One guy says, 'It's about time,' another says, 'Hate to say this, but good riddance to bad rubbish,' and another goes on about how society finds remedies for problems our government is unwilling to solve."

I saw Abbey come out from a hallway leading to restrooms.

"Let's go," she said. "I got work tomorrow."

9

THE DOWNTOWN PARTY WAS in full swing when Abbey dropped us off at the Golden Nugget. The lighted canopy over Fremont Street pulsed with color, and the revelers paraded in a swarm, dancing and drinking from green hurricane tumblers with curlicue straws. Before Cody could suggest joining them, I said, "Come on," and led us into the hotel lobby. I stood in front of the huge aquarium and checked my tracker app.

"Justin is back at the Venetian," I said. "Looks like he's retired for the night."

"In the city that never sleeps?"

"He's here on business. I assume he's got responsibilities tomorrow morning." I looked at my watch. It was 10:30.

"I guess," Cody said. "Let's go chill out and play some keno."

"We got responsibilities too," I said.

"What do you want to do, go to your room and stare at the wall?

When I didn't respond, Cody said, "I swear, Dirt, quit trying to be in charge of the world. You look like your head's in a vise. Today was a good day, and we got a plan in place. It's time to relax."

I took a breath and rolled my shoulders. "All right," I said.

We went into the casino and found a cluster of empty tables facing a keno screen. A waitress in a short skirt came by promptly, and we filled out keno cards and ordered drinks.

"I won three hundo at Harrah's last time I was in South Lake," Cody said. "I have good luck at keno."

"Not me. I don't think I've ever won a cent."

"Try to be optimistic. Send positive waves to the gods of gambling. It works, I tell you."

"It looks like you and Abbey are getting along fine," I said.

Cody paused before replying. "She keeps me on my toes."

"How so?"

"I don't know," he said, his fingernails raking his hair. "I think she doesn't want me to forget I was absent for most of her life. But at the same time, she wants to be my daughter."

"I think she realizes your blood runs in her veins."

"Huh?"

"She's a female version of you."

"Come on," he scoffed.

"You're too close to see it."

"Give me an example."

"Okay. She's a risk taker with minimal fear. She's aggressive, not passive. Her way is to push a situation until it breaks."

Cody's eyes narrowed. "How do you reach those conclusions?"

"She wants to be in the middle of the action, not outside of it. It's all over her personality."

"You think that's a bad thing?"

I shrugged. "It's served you well."

The waitress returned with our highballs, and we handed her our $5 keno slips.

"She is a bit feisty, I'll give you that," he said.

"I'm not making judgments. People are all wired different."

"That's very diplomatic."

"Look, we all have our ways. Me, I like to keep it close to the vest, play it conservative."

Cody laughed and chugged his drink. "Yeah, I know. You're Mr. Conservative. Until you get pissed off, and then it's all gas, no brakes, balls to the wall. Ever since I first met you. You're like a ticking time bomb."

"How did this become about me?"

"I don't know, Doctor Freud."

"I'd like to think my actions are always appropriate to the situation."

Cody laughed again, his eyes crinkling with mirth. "There's a lot of busted up chumps who might disagree. Like Pablo Escobar's son. Oh yeah, he's dead, courtesy of a Dan Reno right cross."

I turned my palms upward. "He tried to stab me. And what about your track record?"

"I never claimed to be conservative, like you."

"Well," I said, "As long as it ends well."

"Fuckin' A, brother." Cody raised his glass at me and we drained our bourbon-Cokes.

For the next hour, we drank and gambled and I actually won a $220 keno jackpot. When I saw I'd won, it was as if a steam valve flicked open in my brain. The tension in my head felt like it was blowing out of my ears, and a drunken grin took hold on my face. At that moment, I stopped thinking about the Palatines, and did not worry about Candi, or anything else. My luck had turned. The evildoers in the world were somebody else's problem. Cody and I were in league with the good-hearted, and our numbers would always triumph over those with venal intentions. Like Cody said, sometimes a little positive thinking is a good thing.

Cody began flirting with the waitress, entertaining us with his irreverent charm. She was very pretty and seemed quite pleased with the attention.

"What's your story?" she asked me when Cody paused.

"Sometimes I work too much," I said. "And sometimes, not enough."

"Sounds like a nutty way to live."

"I couldn't have summed it up better."

"A little crazy helps keep you sane," Cody said. I nodded in agreement, but the waitress looked confused. "I'll see you two later," she said.

At that moment, Cody's cell rang. When he looked at it, his brow pinched.

"Who is it?" I asked.

"I don't know. Vegas area code." He tapped his screen. "Hello?"

I couldn't hear the caller's voice, but as I watched Cody, I felt a jolt of alarm. The blood left his face and his skin became the color of granite. He sat listening for a long minute, then said, "Where are you now?"

He tapped an address into his phone's map app. When he was done, he said, "Don't go anywhere. We're on our way." He dropped his cell into his shirt pocket and looked at me. I could see the color return to his face and his ears turned red, the way they always did when he was under stress or angry. I felt the boozy euphoria drain from my head and hit my stomach with a thud.

"What?" I said, as he stood. I followed him out toward the lobby.

"Abbey was struck and knocked unconscious when she was walking to her apartment. She came to in the backseat of a car, and guess where it was headed?"

I raised my phone as we walked and checked the tracker app. The Hyundai was still parked at the Venetian.

"I don't know," I said dumbly.

"Yeah, you do. We were just there."

"But the Hyundai's at the Venetian. It hasn't moved since Palatine returned there."

"She was abducted in a Chevy Impala."

I stopped. "Cody, what happened to her?"

"She kicked his ass and got away. Come on, keep moving."

"Was it Palatine?"

"He wore a mask, but his height and weight were a match."

We went through a door and into the garage. "Where's your rig?" Cody asked.

"This way," I said.

"Abbey ran on a trail, all the way back to a residential neighborhood. She knocked on someone's door, and they called 911, then let her use their phone."

We reached my truck and climbed in. "Palatine switched vehicles?"

"Looks that way. But he picked the wrong victim."

I paused for a moment, then said, "I'll say."

"Hurry up, we need to get there sometime tonight."

I squealed out of the lot and it took five minutes to navigate through downtown and get on the freeway. Then I stomped on the gas and bombed eastward for fifteen miles, passing cars at a dangerous rate.

"She said she drilled him with a kick to the solar plexus when he dragged her out of the car," Cody said, staring out the windshield. "She also kicked him in the face. Then she ran about four miles on a trail leading back to town. She saw the Impala going back that direction. She got the plate number."

"That's pretty impressive."

"It could have been a lot worse. She got lucky."

I slowed and took the ramp to 215 south. Could Justin Palatine have changed vehicles and kidnapped Abbey, all while Cody and I were blowing off steam at the casino? I had a hard time wrapping my head around it. He must have had the vehicle switch planned ahead of time. Maybe he rented two cars. Or maybe he traded vehicles with a coworker. Or he could have stolen the damn Chevy.

But did he know his Hyundai was being tracked? I doubted it. I assumed he switched cars because the Hyundai was a link back to him. In that light, it was a smart move. It was also one I didn't anticipate.

"Take the Charleston exit," Cody said.

"The bastard outsmarted us," I said.

"I know," Cody replied. The stark words hovered in the air like a noxious odor. I couldn't remember Cody ever admitting to being mentally beaten by a crook. Cody's great advantage was that because he often operated on the sidelines of the law, he had good insight into criminal thinking and was rarely surprised by their behavior. But Justin Palatine was far more intelligent than your average miscreant.

A minute later, we turned into a neighborhood of recently built tract homes. We saw the lights of a squad car at the end of a court.

I pulled up and parked behind the cruiser. Abbey was standing on the sidewalk with two patrolmen. A man and a woman watched from the lighted doorway of the nearest house. Cody walked to where Abbey stood at the fender of the squad car. The red and blue lights made her face look garish, and she was hugging herself against the cold night air. Cody put his blazer over her shoulders.

"And you are?" one of the uniforms said. He was young, tall, and looked fit, but his face was boyish, his eyes round as if permanently surprised.

"My father," Abbey said.

"Oh, the ex-cop from SJPD," his partner said. He was shorter and stockier. Maybe twenty-five years old, maybe younger.

"Justin Palatine is the man who attacked and abducted her," Cody said. "He's staying at the Venetian. Go bring him in."

"Is there enough evidence to arrest him?" the taller uniform asked.

"He's a known rapist from San Jose," I said. "We followed him earlier tonight to where he intended to rape Abbey. He had the spot picked out. Up there, about five miles, there's a gravel trail just wide enough for a single car. It's secluded and remote."

"And that's where he brought me," Abbey said.

"Yes, but how do you know it was Justin Palatine? You never got a look at his face, right, Abbey?"

She hesitated long enough to show she was considering a less than truthful answer. Then she said, "No, he was wearing a mask. I never saw his face."

"But she got the plate number. Did you run it yet?" I asked.

"That's the first thing we did. It belongs to a Ford Taurus. Plate was stolen, no doubt."

"Who's the night chief?" Cody said.

"Sergeant Barbosa," Abbey said.

"Have you contacted him?" Cody looked down at the two uniforms.

"We were just about to when you got here," the stocky patrolman replied.

"One of your own was attacked by a serial rapist. Tell this Barbosa to get his ass to the Venetian and make the arrest in person." Cody shook his head. "What's the matter with you guys?"

"We'll need to take her to the hospital. That bruise looks pretty nasty," the taller one said.

"I'm fine."

"It's mandatory, Abbey. You know that."

Cody put his arm around his daughter. "Look," he said. "Run Palatine's jacket. He was busted in San Jose for rape, and the charges were only dropped because he paid off the vic."

"And, he was arrested for rape earlier this year in South Lake Tahoe," I said. "He got off on a technicality. But he was guilty as hell."

"You know, Mr. Gibbons," the stocky cop said. "You have quite a reputation. But at Las Vegas Metro, we play by the book. So don't tell us what to do."

"Fine," Cody said, shaking his head in exasperation. "Please call Sergeant Barbosa. The crime scene needs to be secured and searched for evidence. Palatine needs to be interrogated. I hope you see it as a priority."

They got into their car without responding and began talking on the radio. The windows were rolled up, and we couldn't hear what they were saying.

"Does your neck hurt?" Cody asked.

"Yeah."

"We'll take you to the emergency clinic as soon as these halfwits get on it."

"They might be right about lack of evidence," Abbey said.

"That doesn't mean Palatine can't be interrogated. He can be brought in as a person of interest."

"Unless he declines," I said.

Cody glowered at me, but Abbey just looked sad. Standing next to her father, she looked much younger than she was.

. . .

At midnight, the Summerlin emergency clinic waiting room was half-full. Groups of two or three sat huddled in isolated clusters, their faces tired and morose, their conversations hushed. A man with one side of his face covered by white gauze waited alone in stoic silence. An obese woman moaned periodically, her grossly swollen foot propped on a chair.

We waited an hour for Abbey to be seen. She reappeared ten minutes later. The on-duty physician determined she'd suffered nothing worse than a bruised neck. We walked through the glass doors, out to where my truck waited in the parking lot. Above the glare of the lampposts, the desert sky looked abysmal and unending, the moon nothing more than an aberration in the darkness.

"My purse is gone, my driver's license, credit cards, cell phone, everything," Abbey said.

"I'll help you take care of it first thing in the morning," Cody said.

"I need to be at the station at nine A.M. to meet with whatever detectives they assign to the case."

"When we get to your apartment, I'll cancel your credit cards. I'll spend the night on your couch and while you're getting ready in the morning, I'll take care of your license. Then I'll go get you a new phone."

"You don't need to do that."

"Yeah, I do."

"It's a good idea he stays with you," I said.

"Why do you say that?" Abbey asked.

"Because Justin Palatine is unpredictable."

"You mean, you actually think he might come after me again?"

"Dan's right," Cody said. "We're dealing with someone who plays by a different set of rules."

The roads were empty as we drove back across Las Vegas. When we reached Abbey's apartment, I said, "I'm gonna go search for the Impala in the Venetian parking lots. What color did you say it was?"

"Silver," Abbey said.

"Get some sleep," I said to Cody as he climbed out of my cab.

"Yeah, right," he replied.

I pulled away and drove back toward Las Vegas Boulevard. At one in the morning, the roads were quiet and dark, until I reached the 24-hour spectacle of the Strip. I waited through a series of lights, creeping through the traffic, watching the streams of pedestrians flow down the sidewalks. When I finally entered the Venetian complex, I followed an access road to the self-parking lot. Starting at the ground level, I began slowly driving down the rows, searching for a silver Chevy Impala. I took the ramp to the second level, and then the third. It wasn't until the fifth level I saw a car that fit the description. I took a picture of its plate, which did not match the digits Abbey had seen. I stopped when I saw a gray Hyundai Tucson parked on the seventh floor, but it wasn't Palatine's. I kept crawling forward.

On the eighth level, I spotted another silver Impala, but it had an Arizona plate. And then one more with a non-matching plate on the ninth floor. By the time I'd reached the top floor of the garage, I'd seen and photographed five late model Impalas. None of the license plates matched the plate of the car that had been used to abduct Abbey. I parked and texted the plate pictures to Cody, asking that Abbey run the numbers first thing tomorrow. Then I called him and asked, "Did LVPD send anyone to the Venetian yet?"

"Abbey's been trying to get a confirmation. But I called Palatine's room and nobody answered."

Sighing, I rubbed my eyes and stared out my bug-splattered windshield. After a moment, I reached behind me, grabbed my backpack, and pulled my sport jacket from where I'd stuffed it into the main compartment. As I left my truck, I tried to shake out the wrinkles, with moderate success. I wiped at the reddish streaks on my shirt, frowning. Stained clothing is a sure way to attract attention. I found the elevator, took it down to the casino level, and ducked into the first bathroom I saw. A couple of minutes later, I was reasonably presentable; shirt blotted clean, hair combed.

I set out across the casino floor, heading for the room elevators. I weaved through banks of slot machines and went past a food court. The casino was less crowded than earlier in the day, but the card tables were full and there were still hundreds of people milling about. That would make it relatively easy to stay inconspicuous.

There was a bar across from the elevator lobby, and I sat at a cocktail table that provided a direct line of sight. My plan was to wait for the police to go to Palatine's room. At the least, LVPD should send a pair of uniforms to bring Palatine in for questioning. My goal was to follow them and learn Palatine's room number. When the cops approached the elevators, I could easily stroll on up and join them. If a plainclothesman arrived, I was pretty sure I could spot him. A bulge under the jacket, usually on the left side, is a sure giveaway.

If LVPD didn't have a graveyard detective on duty, they needed to wake one. After all, one of their own, a young female cop, had been attacked. If that wasn't enough to get an investigator out of bed, I didn't know what would be, short of a mass shooting.

I got a soft drink and sat waiting. After ten minutes passed, I wondered if I was too late. Maybe the cops had already been here, and Abbey hadn't been informed. Or, I might be too early. All I could do was wait.

From behind me, I heard someone approach. I smelled her perfume before I turned in my seat.

"Well, hello," a woman said. "Mind if I join you?"

She sat before I could reply. She had long, straight, blonde hair, and wore a blue, one-piece dress made of thin, shiny material. The hem slid high up on her thigh when she crossed her legs. The dress was cut low in the front, and she was braless, the shape of her breasts clearly visible.

"Sorry, I'm waiting for someone," I said.

"Do you have a light?" she asked, smiling. Her teeth were perfect, her lips red. She was classically pretty, but the hard-edged glint in her eyes was unmistakable. At a glance, I concluded she probably learned at an early age that her physical prowess was a means to control her world, and of course, control always involved money. The learning process was surely a hard one, stealing her innocence and replacing it with the jaded, mean-spirited realization that men could be used, as long as she was shrewd and unwilling to compromise the rules of the game.

Shaking a cigarette from her pack, she leaned forward to let her unencumbered bosom sway against the silky fabric of her dress.

"I don't smoke, and I'm not looking for company," I said, turning back toward the elevators.

"I've got a joke for you," she said. "Ready?"

I looked back at her. "Then you'll leave?"

"Sure. Here goes: Having sex on an elevator is wrong, on so many levels." She tried to smile, but looked a little embarrassed.

"That's so not funny, it's funny," I said, laughing.

She looked past my shoulder, then reached out and grabbed my hand. "See you later, cowboy," she said, sliding off her chair and strutting away.

Another five minutes passed, and no cops, uniformed or otherwise, came to the elevator lobby. I decided to wait another thirty minutes, then call it a night. Then my phone buzzed with a text message.

Whatever your interest in the Palatines, it ends now. Go back to Tahoe and bust shoplifters or whatever. You're in over your head, so consider this a goodwill warning. Just so you get it, I'm texting this picture to Candi. We know she's in Houston.

The text came from a phone number with a Nevada area code. I tapped on the attached photo and saw it had just been taken. It showed the blonde woman with her hand on mine, and I was smiling.

I immediately stood and looked around. The picture's angle meant the photographer must have been standing to my left, near a small collection of eateries. I walked that direction, scanning the swirl of people, hoping to spot someone who didn't fit. It was a tall order, because the variety of individuals in a casino at any moment was infinite—older, younger, any race, well dressed or sloppy, smiling or frowning, relaxed or tense. All I could do was rely on my gut.

Staying on the main walkways, I strode all the way to the reservation lobby. Then I doubled back on a different path, zigzagging through the casino maze.

It took ten minutes to find them. They were sitting at a bar, their backs to me, at the opposite side of the casino, near the walkway to the adjoining Palazzo Resort Hotel Casino. They were easy to recognize, because I'd met them previously. It was the ex-Marine, Mark Costa, and his bodybuilding partner in cowboy boots, the one Cody flung off a balcony into a swimming pool.

My initial instinct was to come up behind them and ask what the fuck they were doing here. But I knew I wasn't thinking clearly. I hadn't been since I saw Candi's name in their text message.

I moved back, retreating to the end of a row of slots, and sat staring at the pair. Ex-military muscle, on Jerrod Palatine's payroll. They could have been here mainly to provide security for Jerrod. Or, as I increasingly suspected, I had been spotted earlier in the day, and they'd arrived in town with the primary agenda to get me to back off. But from what? Did they think my interest was the Palatines' role in the slaughter of San Jose's homeless population? Or did they know my sole purpose was taking Justin Palatine off the board?

Either way, I couldn't say I was surprised to see them. Cody and I had put ourselves in plain view when we visited Ron Donaldson's house. We'd forgone any pretense of a covert operation. We'd even let it be known that our focal point was Justin Palatine. But they might think my true interest was not Justin's history as a rapist, but his role in the fire and ice attacks.

Whatever the situation, it was clear that Hadrian Transport was a resourceful agency. They employed both ex-Marines and current San Jose police officers, which meant they had access to police databases. They had learned that Candi was in Houston, knew I was in Las Vegas, and probably knew I was staying at the Golden Nugget. And they had located me at the Venetian and arranged for compromising photos. I would be a fool to take them lightly.

Even still, the urge to confront the two hired thugs was tugging hard at me. They had implicitly threatened Candi, and that was unforgivable. I wanted to get them out of the casino and bust them up, send them to the hospital. I took a deep breath, expanding my chest, the muscles tight against the skin. The weight of Goodnight, Irene, my lead sap, was heavy in my coat pocket. My hand moved away from it as I considered the repercussions. Injury assault could be prosecuted as a felony, and I knew they'd report it to the police, which would probably land me in local lockup for an indeterminate time. That would be playing right into their hands.

If I was leaving for California at dawn, I might have risked it. But I needed to sit down with LVPD detectives in the morning. I intended to share everything I knew about Justin Palatine, and hope they could find cause to bring him in and charge him with a crime. But I wasn't optimistic.

Watching and waiting with no plan, I called the Venetian front desk and asked for Mark Costa.

"I have no record of a guest by that name," the clerk said.

Just as I hung up, Costa and his steroid-case comrade stood and left the bar. I cut through the slots and followed them toward the front lobby. They didn't break stride and went through the revolving door out to the rotunda. I stopped and watched them through the glass windows. A minute passed before a valet attendant pulled up in a Hyundai Tucson. I recognized the license plate. The two climbed inside and drove away.

I stepped out onto the sidewalk and stood in the brisk night. Cabs were pulling up, dropping off and picking up passengers. I breathed in the cold, dry air and tried to clear my head. After a minute, I checked the tracker app on my phone. The Hyundai was heading toward the I-15 freeway.

When I walked back inside, I wanted to sit somewhere away from people and the hubbub of the casino. So I found the sports book. Sports books are always deserted in the wee hours of the morning. It was one of the few sure things in Vegas.

I sat in the middle of a long row of seats and set my cell phone on the betting desk. On the big screens were soccer games, Formula 1 auto racing, and tennis. All occurring in Europe, I assumed. I was the sole viewer at the Venetian.

Checking the tracker app again, I saw the Hyundai was traveling northbound on the freeway. I watched the red arrow move for a minute, then I texted Cody: *I saw your buddy at the Venetian*

Who? he replied.

The bodybuilder and his Marine pal. They know I'm here

Cody didn't respond for a minute, then he texted, *Shall we discourage them?*

No. What time should I meet you at PD station tomorrow?

9am

I sat slumped in my chair for a minute, watching a tennis match between two men who seemed intent on winning based on the sheer velocity of their forehand power strokes. After a heated point ended, I texted

Candi: *You may receive a text from a 775 #. If you do, please don't respond, just forward to me and call me.* I stared at my phone, then wrote a second text: *Some bad guys are trying to get me to quit an investigation. No worries.*

Hoping Candi wouldn't be overly alarmed or otherwise tweaked, I turned my attention back to the tennis match. One of the players was slamming his racquet against the clay surface, until the frame bent and the strings snapped free. Then he winged it across the court. It crashed into the wall at the base of the referee's chair, and the cameraman zoomed in on the mangled remains.

I laughed silently, but my grin faded when I checked the tracker and saw the Hyundai had exited in downtown Las Vegas. I watched the Hyundai make a few turns before it got onto South Casino Center Boulevard. A minute later, it parked at the Golden Nugget.

Leaning forward, I rested my chin on my fists. The pair from Hadrian Transport, driving Justin Palatine's rented SUV, arriving at the same out-of-the-way hotel where I was staying. Could they have traded rental cars with Justin? Or maybe they didn't have a rental car and were borrowing the Hyundai. I picked up my phone and sent another text to Cody: *Please ask Abbey to run a trace on Mark Costa car rental in Vegas*

I left the sports book and headed for the elevator to the parking garage. The only reason Costa and his partner were at the Golden Nugget was to surveil me. That had to be their agenda. But did the order come from Jerrod or Justin? And if it came from Justin, did they understand he was a serial rapist?

As a group, sexual predators occupy a unique status in criminal society. No evildoers are more despised, and more subject to violent aggression. Drug kingpins, cartel enforcers, racist thugs, outlaw bikers, grave robbers, cannibals, scam artists who target the elderly, killers who slaughter their own family—they all have one thing in common: they enjoy moral superiority over the rapist. The worst of the criminal world look down on sexual predators as the most heinous and subhuman of lawbreakers.

Once arrested, the most dangerous period for a child molester or common rapist is during the first weeks following their incarceration. Upon arrival at county jail, and lasting through their court appearances and sentencing, they are designated open game. There is complete cooperation between guards and inmates. Race ceases to be an issue. No green light is needed. Those with the unfortunate 'S' designation are constantly at risk of beatings or worse, until they are assigned to their permanent housing, where they are segregated from other convicts.

Unless they themselves were rapists, I couldn't imagine the ex-Marines would lower themselves to do Justin Palatine's bidding, assuming they knew his history. But they were probably oblivious. Justin's arrests in San Jose and South Lake Tahoe had to be closely guarded family secrets, perhaps known only by Jerrod Palatine.

But the arrests were public record. If the details were publicized, the results could be disastrous for Jerrod's political aspirations. All it would take is a few well-placed social media posts.

I stepped wide of a drunken man who looked ready to vomit, a victim of too many free casino drinks. Jerrod must have a plan in place to mitigate the risk of his brother's arrest record. The first thing Jerrod's political opponents would do is look for dirt, and they wouldn't have to look far. Maybe I could beat them to it and use Justin's arrest record as leverage, but to what end? I couldn't see how it would result in his incarceration.

As I rode the elevator to the top floor of the self-park garage, I texted Cody: *Still awake?*

Yo, he replied.

I'm coming over to pick up your room key

Why?

Costa and friend are at Nugget. I want to get your stuff and bail to new hotel

Text me when you get here

When the elevator reached the 14th floor, I walked across the dim garage and got into my truck. As soon as I started the motor, my cell rang.

"Candi?"

"Hi." She sounded groggy.

"What are you doing up so early?"

"I just woke up. Where are you?"

"Las Vegas."

"I got your text, and the other one. Who's the bimbo?"

"Someone hired by a couple of chumps who are trying to mess with me. What did the text say?"

"I just sent it to you."

My phone buzzed, and I opened the text. It was the same picture I'd been sent, but this one included the words, *Heads up, hope you're enjoying Houston, your man is definitely enjoying Vegas.*

"Why are you in Vegas?" she asked.

"Case work."

"I thought it was for Marcus Grier."

"It is. He asked me to look into a guy who committed a crime in Tahoe. The guy's in Vegas for a technology convention."

"Is Grier paying you?"

"Somewhat. How's everything with you and your folks?"

"My dad's still adjusting to his retirement. He's staying busy on the ranch, but he's driving mom a little batty."

"Have you been seeing the therapist she recommended?"

"I went once. It was good."

"Okay."

"Mom and I are thinking about driving out to Galveston, seeing the beach. Just for a change of scenery."

"How far is it?"

"About an hour and a half drive." I heard her yawn. "I'm sleepy, I'm gonna go back to bed."

"Don't worry about that text, Candi. It's nothing."

"Okay, my guy."

I set my phone in the center console and drove down the spiral exit ramp. When I left the garage and reached the main drag, I was relieved to see that, at two-thirty in the morning, the traffic on the Strip had finally receded. It only took five minutes to reach Abbey's apartment. I parked on the sidewalk in front of her unit and texted Cody. A minute later he appeared, and I climbed out to join him under a street lamp.

Cody leaned against my fender and lit a cigarette. He was still wearing his business getup. His other clothes were at the Nugget.

"Check out the text Candi got," I said, handing him my cell.

"Who's the piece of tail? You're busted, dude."

"Costa and the bodybuilder set me up. She's a pro."

"You talk to Candi?"

"Yeah. It's a non-issue."

"But they know she's in Houston. That *is* an issue. They're sending a pretty clear message." He cut his eyes at me. "Maybe we need to send one back."

"Not yet. I want to keep them guessing. Give me your room key."

He pulled his wallet from his coat pocket and handed me a card-key. "We never confirmed if LVPD sent anyone to the Venetian," he said. "My guess is they'll wait until the detectives talk to Abbey and us."

"I'll be back with your bags in half an hour or so," I said, climbing into my truck.

Before I drove off, I checked the tracker app and saw the Hyundai was still at the Nugget. I was tempted to call the Nugget and ask for Mark Costa. I wanted to know if he'd checked in, but if he had, I didn't want to wake or otherwise alert him. I wondered if he might be hanging around the lobby, hoping to spot me. Maybe he and his partner wanted to have a conversation. But I wasn't interested in whatever they had to say.

I took the deserted Maryland Parkway north and fifteen minutes later turned into the Nugget's parking garage. I found a spot near the elevator and took it to my room floor. The hallway was clear. I went to my room, packed my stuff, then went down the hall to Cody's room. Ten minutes later, I was back in the elevator with fifty pounds hanging from my shoulders. When I reached my rig, I threw the luggage into the bed and quickly exited the garage.

As I drove, I wondered what Costa and his musclebound buddy might be capable of. Their initial effort to discourage me was nothing more than a chicken shit ploy. I was actually a little offended that they would bother with such a weak ruse. It reiterated what I believed from the beginning—they were amateurs.

But Costa was ex-Marine, and I assumed the same for his nameless counterpart. That meant they should be proficient in firearm usage and hand-to-hand combat, although neither had fared well against Cody or me in the latter. That aside, I doubted their military training involved investigative work or covert operations. Simply put, I believed they were nothing more than hired muscle.

Still, I didn't want to discount the threat they represented. Given their backgrounds, they would be quite capable of the firebombing or machine gun attacks on the homeless camps. I believed it likely that they were involved in these atrocities. It meant they were not simply killers; they were murderers of defenseless victims. Did that mean they might try to kill Cody or me if they felt it expedient?

I checked my mirrors as I navigated out of the downtown area and back south. It was nearly three a.m., and I was tired. I needed to wake early in the morning and be ready for a long day. A few hours ago, while playing keno at the Nugget, I was celebrating the end of a productive workday. That notion dissolved when Abbey called Cody. Now I needed to reset my priorities, and the thought made me weary. Despite my fatigue, I kept checking my mirrors.

10

A FTER DROPPING OFF CODY's bags, I drove all the way across town, back to the Red Rock Casino. It was the closest hotel to the LV Metro Summerlin Area Command station. That was where Abbey was scheduled to meet with detectives in less than six hours.

I checked in under an assumed name. I hadn't bothered checking out of the Golden Nugget; I wanted Costa to think Cody and I were still staying there.

Finally, I lugged my gear to a room on the second floor. I barely had the energy to undress, but I forced myself to hang up my new sport coat. I liked it and planned to wear it again soon. That was my last thought before I set my alarm and fell onto the bed.

• • •

I'd slept for five solid hours before the alarm jolted me from a dreamless slumber. Half awake, I got into the shower and let hot water pound on my shoulders, then I stuck my face close to the nozzle and turned the water temperature to cold. It wasn't pleasant, but it woke me up.

After dressing in fresh jeans and a wrinkle-free T-shirt, I sat sipping coffee while watching the morning news. The San Jose shooting was the lead story.

"According to police," the newscaster said, "it's been difficult to find witnesses since almost everyone was indoors because of the rainstorm. The pounding of the rain seems to have obscured the sound of the assault rifles, as no gunshots were reported last night. Detectives continue to search for clues, while we ask, *what could be the motive behind such a horrible crime?*"

The question was left open-ended as the telecast shifted to weather. A cheery woman announced that Bay Area weather was forecasted to be dry with clear skies for the next few days.

At 8:45, I headed downstairs. I got into my rig and texted Cody that I was on my way to the police station. I wheeled out of the parking lot and drove through the desert for less than five minutes before I arrived.

The Summerlin station looked newly built—the tan paint was fresh, and the trees were planted at wide intervals, allowing them space to mature. The building was a long, single-story, contemporary design. It favored square and rectangular elements, nothing ornate or curved, no diagonal components except for the obligatory triangular rooflines. The structure looked designed to peacefully blend with the stark desert surroundings. Behind the building, about ten miles distant, the skyline of the Strip was visible under a broad layer of high clouds.

I parked in the half-full lot and walked to the main entrance, where five stout, iron-reinforced pillars, three feet tall and spaced four feet apart, barricaded the front doors. If a disgruntled citizen was tempted to ram his vehicle through the doors, he'd have to breach the pillars, which was unlikely unless he was driving a tank.

Inside, I took a seat on a folding chair against the wall and waited. Two desk cops sat behind bulletproof glass partitions with round speakers inset in the center. They ignored me while they did paperwork.

A minute later, Abbey walked in, with Cody following. Cody sat next to me as Abbey went to a door on the far side of the lobby and used a card-key to enter.

"Might as well get comfortable," Cody said, stretching his legs out before him. "This might be awhile."

"Hell, if they had a couple cots available, we could catch some Zs."

"I only got about two hours last night. You?"

"Five hours. I'm good."

Cody leaned his head back and shut his eyes. "Wake me up when Abbey comes out," he said.

I put my elbows on my knees and stared at the floor. Last night's plan to bust Justin Palatine had seemed so solid, but now it was blown to shit. His carefully selected location had been compromised, and he'd be foolish to return there. To make it worse, he was no longer driving his rented Hyundai, so I couldn't track his whereabouts. That left me without a plan. I felt like a beginner chess player who knows how the pieces move, but doesn't understand the tactics or strategy necessary to win.

My only idea was to reconvene surveillance on Palatine, and hope he did something incriminating. But he'd already done that, and the only evidence we had was circumstantial and relatively weak. He'd worn a mask, driven a car with a stolen plate, and left no DNA or fingerprints that I knew of. The more I thought about it, the more I accepted that there wasn't enough for an arrest.

I closed my eyes and tried to make my mind empty. There had to be another angle, a better angle. All I could think was, maybe Palatine *had* left fingerprints, or even better, Abbey's DNA in the Impala. I'd provided five Impala plate numbers to Abbey. If one of them matched a car rented by anyone employed by Digicloud or Hadrian Transport, then that was the car Palatine used. If it could be located quickly, it might contain the key evidence to put Justin Palatine away.

Half an hour later, Abbey came back into the lobby. She stood at the door to the back offices and waved us over.

"Detectives Perch and Gunderson are waiting," she said.

We followed her to the squad room and then into an office with a whiteboard on the wall and a file cabinet in the corner. The two detectives were standing next to a metal table surrounded by chairs.

"Gentlemen," Cody said.

"I'm Detective Perch," one said. He was average height, on the skinny side, and his hair fit his head like a helmet, apparently rock hard with hairspray. When he spoke, I saw he had a jutting yellow eyetooth. "This is Detective Gunderson," Perch said.

Gunderson was nearly as large as Cody. His complexion was like putty, his features blunt. His small blue eyes squinted under colorless eyebrows, and he had a pug nose. Several moles dotted his cheeks. His skin looked void of pigmentation.

"Please take a seat. We understand you've been investigating Justin Palatine," Gunderson said.

Cody and I sat, but the detectives and Abbey remained standing.

"He's a serial rapist," Cody said. "You should call Detectives Dunning and Hernandez at SJPD. They're familiar with him."

"You should also call Sheriff Marcus Grier in South Lake Tahoe," I said. "Palatine was arrested for a rape there, but got off on a technicality. Ask Grier to share the victim photos."

"Why do you think he would commit a crime in Las Vegas?" Perch asked. He twitched and puckered his lips, as if trying to scratch the inside of his mouth with his teeth.

"Because rape is what he does," Cody said. "It's not if, it's when."

"So," Perch said, "Your suspicion is based solely on his history?"

"No," I said. "Palatine's signature move is a carotid chop. He strikes his victim on the neck, knocking them unconscious. Take a look at the bruise on Abbey's neck. It's Palatine's calling card."

The detectives glanced at Abbey. "Is it enough for probable cause?" I asked.

"I doubt it," Perch said. "But we can talk to the D.A."

"What about the Impala license plates?" Cody said. "You run them yet?"

"We've got someone doing it now," Gunderson replied.

"Look," I said, trying to keep my tone neutral, "We followed Palatine in his Hyundai rental car, all the way to the site where he brought Abbey. The site matches his M.O. It's out in the sticks, away from buildings, where nobody can hear his victims scream."

"Yes, Abbey told us," Perch said. "You put a tracking device on his car?"

"That's right."

Perch shook his head. "I don't think any evidence linked to it would be admissible."

"Why the hell not?" Cody said.

"Because it's illegal. California made it a law a while ago. Nevada just implemented it. Let me double-check." Gunderson began tapping his phone. We waited in silence for less than thirty seconds before he said, "Here it is. Putting a tracking device on a vehicle is illegal, unless the owner or lessee of the vehicle has consented."

Cody began arguing, but I didn't hear much of what he said. My mind was suddenly in a different place, as if a ray of clarity had struck me from the heavens. I felt the wrinkles on my forehead recede and for a time I stared at nothing. When Cody paused, I waved my hand benignly.

"I have one request. If you can't arrest Palatine, at least tell him you're watching him. Like all rapists, Palatine lacks impulse control, but his intelligence overrides his urges. He doesn't want to get caught, and he'll wait until the risk is minimized. He's very calculating."

Everyone in the room looked at me curiously.

"You want to discourage Palatine from committing a crime in your city, that's the way to do it. Either that, or put him under twenty-four-hour surveillance."

"I'll sign up for that," Abbey said.

Perch and Gunderson exchanged glances. "I'm sure you would," Perch said.

At that moment, the door opened, and a woman handed Gunderson a sheet of paper. We all watched as Gunderson studied the page.

"The plates," he said.

"All rentals?" I asked.

"All but one, an Arizona plate.

"Are there company names listed?"

"Yes," he said. "Ciara Computer, AMD, Internas, and Hadrian Transport."

"Bingo," I said. "Hadrian Transport is an outfit contracted by Digicloud, where Justin Palatine works. That's the car he used to abduct Abbey."

"Find it, you got a smoking gun," Cody said. "Palatine's prints and Abbey's DNA should be all over the interior."

"Unless he cleaned the hell out of it," I said.

"It's parked at the Venetian, right, Dan?" Abbey said.

"It was at two A.M."

"We'll see if we can get a warrant," Perch said, but I could hear the doubt in his voice.

"My daughter is an LV Metro cop," Cody said, standing abruptly. His metal chair fell over and clattered loudly on the concrete floor. "Make sure whatever damn judge you go to understands that. Make sure he understands that if it wasn't for her training, she would have been raped and maybe killed."

When the detectives didn't respond, I said, "Can you share the name from Hadrian?"

"Why?" Gunderson asked.

"I might know him."

He shrugged. "Chad Sheridan. Sound familiar?"

I shook my head. "No."

"One more thing," Perch said. "This is now an official LV Metro investigation. The best way to help is to not interfere. Understood?"

I stood and stuck my hands in my back pockets. "Okay."

"Whatever you say, detective," Cody said.

. . .

We left the Las Vegas detectives to their work, whatever that would be. Standing at my truck, I said to Cody, "Grab your gear."

"What's the plan?" Abbey asked.

"Our cover in Vegas is blown. But that's not necessarily bad news."

"Why not?" Cody said.

"Because I didn't check us out of the Nugget. Mark Costa and the bodybuilder, Chad Sheridan, think we're staying here. So now's the time to haul ass back to San Jose."

"What for?"

"I want to take apart Palatine's house. My bet is Costa and Sheridan make up the bulk of Hadrian Transport. Without them to worry about, I bet I can find Palatine's souvenirs."

"You're forgetting about something," Cody said.

"What?"

"Mack Mazon and Buck Kierdorf."

"They're moonlighters. I doubt they're hooked up to Palatine's alarm system."

"Maybe, maybe not." Cody lit a cigarette and gazed past the police station, to where the hardscrabble flatlands stretched to a long escarpment on the horizon. "It's a gamble," he said.

"You want to stay here with Abbey, it's okay."

"You'll need a wingman," he conceded after a long moment. He blew a stream of smoke into the dry air, and we watched it dissipate like a mirage. Then he grabbed his bags from Abbey's Dodge, tossed them into my truck bed, and turned to Abbey.

"Listen now, you double-lock your doors and keep your pistol handy. Don't be out alone at night. Watch your back. This Palatine is a sneaky son of a bitch."

"I see him again, I'll fucking shoot him," Abbey said.

. . .

Leaving Las Vegas always feels dreamlike. I know of no other large city surrounded by such vast nothingness. For miles in every direction, the desert is unrelenting, the terrain stark and featureless. The emptiness of the land is exceeded only by its contrast to the bombastic grandeur of the casinos. It feels like the Strip could have been dropped onto the desert floor from outer space, maybe by profligate extraterrestrials seeking a clandestine getaway for vice and debauchery.

Driving southwest, we descended into the Mojave, blowing road dust from the baked pavement. We crossed the state border and entered California at thirty miles over the speed limit.

"Try to get some sleep," I said to Cody. "We'll be busy tonight."

"I assume you have some details worked out."

"Ideally, I'd like to get into Palatine's house without tripping the alarm. But even if I could get to the circuit box and shut off the electricity, the alarm likely has a battery backup."

"The breaker box is probably in the garage. But I don't know of any easy way to open a garage door from the outside."

"I do—Palatine's garage door has four window panels near the top. I can break one, and should be able to reach in and pull the release cord."

"Not bad, but what's the point if the alarm has a battery backup? Loss of power would automatically trigger the alarm."

"No way to know. That's why…"

"What?"

"I need you out front as lookout. If anyone shows, disable them until I'm done."

"I get all the glamourous jobs."

"Well, someone's got to do it."

"What happens if you can't find anything? You got a plan B?"

"Well," I said slowly. "It's more just an idea."

"Please share, the worst I can do is laugh."

"All right. Consider that Jerrod Palatine is running for governor. What's he gonna do when his opponents find out his brother, whom he employs, has an arrest record for rape?"

"Hmm," Cody said. "The first thing he should do is fire Justin's ass."

"Yeah, but that won't be enough."

"What, then?"

"If Jerrod Palatine really wants to be elected, he needs to find a way to distance himself from Justin in a serious way."

"Maybe declare Justin isn't his blood brother, either a step brother or adopted."

"He could try that, I guess."

"What else could he try?"

"Have him killed. An unfortunate and tragic accident."

"His own brother?" Cody looked at me with one eye cocked.

"Why not? Fratricide was pretty common during the Roman Empire."

"Sounds like you've done some homework. But you're stretching."

"I don't know. The Palatine patriarch was so obsessed with his heritage that he thought he was a reincarnation of Caesar."

"You're talking about the schizophrenic who walked onto the freeway?"

"Right. Maybe his sons aren't all that grounded, either."

"I wouldn't argue that point. But for a man to kill his own brother…"

"Justin is a big-time liability to Jerrod's political ambition. Jerrod will need to deal with him somehow." I let off the gas as a pair of jackrabbits darted across the road.

"So, you're thinking, maybe send Jerrod a few subtle hints. Like, hey, might be a good time for Justin to have an accident. Or else look out for Justin's outing on social media."

"It's a thought," I said. "But I've got to assume Jerrod's already working on a plan."

We made time on the deserted roadway, and Cody dozed off as we went through Baker. The sun was high in the sky when we reached Barstow, and he was still asleep. I stayed hard on the pedal until stopping for fast food in Tehachapi. Cody finally woke when I set a bag of tacos at his feet.

"Christ, I was really out," he said, rubbing his eyes.

"Eat up and you can take another nap. We're nearly to Bakersfield."

And that's what he did, as we turned north into California's heartland. The San Joaquin Valley lay before us, a 160-mile straight shot on I-5. The miles fell behind us as we sliced through the state's agricultural expanse, racing past fields that produce 13% of the United States' fruit and vegetable supply. Aside from a quick break at a truck stop in Kettleman City, we drove without pause to San Jose.

The twilight skies were conceding to the night when we reached Cody's house. We lugged our gear inside, and just as we sat at the kitchen table, Cody's cell rang.

"Hi, Abbey," he said, putting her on speaker.

"We got a warrant and found the Impala rented to Chad Sheridan," she said.

"And?"

"It had probably been steam cleaned. There wasn't a shred of forensic evidence. No Palatine fingerprints, DNA, nothing."

"Figures," I said.

"Can you check if Mark Costa and Sheridan are checked in at the Nugget?" Cody said.

"Will do. I'll text you."

Cody hung up and looked at me. "One A.M. sound about right?"

"Yeah."

"You best rest up. Your eyes look like two piss holes in the snow."

"How's your tool supply?"

"Let's go to the garage."

We walked out the back slider, past Cody's barbeque and lounge chair, to the detached structure at the rear of his property. Cody flipped a light switch when we went in, and I found myself staring at the car he called the hellfire hooptie.

"How's she running?" I asked.

"Fast and ugly as ever."

And it was indeed both. We'd once driven it from Vegas to Cedar City, Utah. We needed to cover the 170 miles in a hurry. Much of the trip was done at over 130 mph, and we exceeded 150 on the straights. The car was built with race components and accelerated with neck snapping power. It went around corners as if on rails, and could slow from 70 mph to zero in under 140 feet, which was on par with sports cars that cost well over a hundred grand.

As for appearances, the hellfire hooptie was designed to look mundane and unappealing. Cody wanted the car to be suitable for stakeouts in rough neighborhoods. It was a 1990s Toyota Camry, the burgundy paint faded, missing a hubcap, a key scratch marring a door and a fender. The only thing that gave away its performance was wider tires and a lowered stance.

I looked at a tool chest and a pegboard full of hammers, saws, and pliers. "Could use a battery-powered drill, a bolt cutter, a crowbar, and maybe a saw, too."

Cody grabbed a three foot-long dual-handled apparatus from the board. "You have a smaller one?" I asked. "I need to fit it into my backpack."

"Here," he said, finding a shorter bolt cutter in his tool chest. "Try this, too." He handed me a headlamp. I stretched the elastic band over my forehead and pushed a button. A bright, wide beam of light appeared before me.

"Nice," I said.

We went back into Cody's house. With time to kill, I started my computer and spent an hour reading about the Roman Empire. I tried to picture Jerrod Palatine as a would-be emperor, and looked for historical examples that could have influenced him. Over the centuries, the empire had no shortage of egomaniacal, blood-thirsty rulers. There existed an imperial cult that propagated the notion that emperors were deities, and some of the monarchs truly believed it. Thus, any atrocity on their part was not only justified, but sanctioned by the gods. But there were also many virtuous and pragmatic leaders, without whom the empire could never have survived for as long as it did.

If there was one common thread that linked all the emperors, it was their control over the military. The Roman Empire was nothing without its military might; Rome was a warrior state. Its armies allowed it to conquer and retain territory that included almost all of Europe and North Africa, plus much of the Middle East. Even the most peace-loving emperors prioritized the health and financial welfare of the soldiers.

When I shut down my PC, I joined Cody on the couch, where he was watching an old war movie with Clint Eastwood and Telly Savalas. I'd seen the movie before, and while I stared at the screen, I wondered if Jerrod Palatine's aspirations were much grander than simply becoming California's top politician. Maybe he wished to seize more control than a state governor was entitled to. It seemed farfetched and probably impossible, but perhaps Jerrod thought he could make the state's police forces his private army. Any rational person would think that was a crazy notion, but rational people don't usually understand that criminal behavior can be its own form of insanity.

And besides, Jerrod Palatine had already enlisted certain members of SJPD to do his bidding. Of that much, I was sure. Would he seek to expand that engagement if he became governor? The answer was obvious; of course he would.

I tried to pay attention to the movie, but I felt like I was on a mental treadmill, my thinking circular and leading nowhere. I needed to forget about Jerrod, and focus on finding evidence that I could use as leverage against Justin Palatine. That needed to be my sole directive. The problem was, even if I found evidence at his house, I didn't know exactly what to do with it. But I'd figure that out when the time came. I'd find an angle, I hoped.

At ten o'clock, I went to Cody's guest room and lay down. My alarm was set for one a.m. I closed my eyes, but doubted I'd sleep. Sighing, I told myself that simply lying on my back would provide a modicum of rest. It would have to do. My eyes opened and I stared at the ceiling. The minutes ticked by.

11

I THREW THE BLANKETS off as soon as the alarm pinged and sat straight up. Within five minutes, I was dressed in black and ready to work. When I walked into the living room. I saw Cody was still watching television.

"Abbey texted me. Costa and Chad Sheridan are checked in at the Nugget," he said.

"Good. Let's go," I said, shouldering my pack.

We went out into the still night and entered the garage. Cody ducked into his modified Toyota. From outside the car, the lowered seat allowed him to look like a man of average height. He backed out, the engine a low rumble, and we took off toward Justin Palatine's house. We didn't speak as Cody drove the dark, empty streets.

It took less than ten minutes to get there. Cody parked two houses away, and I set off on foot. Mask and gloves on, I walked straight to Palatine's garage. When the motion-activated security light came on, I jumped up and broke it with a screwdriver. Then I reached up and punched one of the rectangular windows in the garage door. The glass was thin and broke easily. Stepping on a trim piece, I pushed myself up, cleared the glass, and reached inside. My hand found a handle attached to a cord. I pulled down hard and heard a loud clunk.

I lowered myself to the concrete and pushed the door up. Crouching, I entered the garage, closed the door behind me, and flicked on my headlamp. The fuse box was mounted on the opposite wall. I opened the tin panel and flipped the main breaker. A quick series of clicks followed, and I heard a whirring sound as the climate control system shut down. Then I went through the door into the house.

The first thing I did was check the security cameras in the main room. The same two from my previous visit were still there, and they were easy to find, as each blinked with green light. I disconnected the pair, and found a small unit with antenna ears mounted behind an end table. I yanked the device from the wall and pulled the battery out.

I started in the kitchen. People like to hide things in kitchens. There is plenty of clutter and hard to reach places. I went through each drawer and cabinet, removing all the pots, pans, plates, and various cooking implements. I searched for false panels, knocking on surfaces, listening for hollow areas. Finding nothing, I moved to the refrigerator.

My headlamp illuminated the scant contents. It looked like Palatine had let his food store dwindle, probably in anticipation of his business trip. I checked everything, removing lids and looking for bottles with hidden inserts. Then I unloaded the contents of the freezer. The last thing I checked was the icemaker, but it held nothing but ice. Before moving on, I yanked on the refrigerator door seal-gaskets. I once knew a man who hid drugs inside a refrigerator door. But the gaskets were firm; I found no indication a hiding place could be accessed without a lengthy dismantling.

I checked behind a wall print, and unscrewed the wall-socket cover plates. Then I grabbed a kitchen chair and reached up to remove the florescent light covers in the ceiling. When that bore no fruit, I surveyed the linoleum floor, looking for a section that might be detachable.

Finally, I stood and checked my watch. I'd spent nearly half an hour in the kitchen, and declared it clean. Vowing patience, I moved down the hall, to Justin's bedroom. I didn't have time to search it when I was here last. I reminded myself that I was in a hurry, but not to hurry.

The most obvious hiding place would have been under the bed, maybe in a shoebox. I didn't think there was any chance Justin would have trusted his keepsakes to such an undisguised location, but I checked anyway. Next, I stripped the sheets and blankets from the mattress and looked for any tears that might reveal a hidden compartment. Then I knelt and moved along the perimeter of the room, pulling on the carpet. I was hoping to find a loose section and a removable floorboard beneath, but had no such luck.

Moving to a dresser along the wall, I opened every drawer and threw the clothes on the bed. Coming up empty, I opened a sliding closet door, and found hanging pants, light jackets, and shirts. I checked all the pockets and tossed each garment onto the bed. Once the closet was bare, I surveyed the walls, looking for a removable portion that might access a hidden space in the wall.

It was nearly two A.M. when I finished with the bedroom. I knew Cody was waiting in his car, and while I was pleased I'd not been interrupted, I hoped he was keeping a sharp eye out. *Still looking,* I texted him.

I went to the locked door to Justin's office. I picked it without trouble and began searching. I removed two potted plants from their containers and checked his desk drawers for false bottoms. After unscrewing the vents from the floor, I reached down and felt for anything that might be stashed in the ducting. I saved the closet for last, for I knew it was full and would require a significant investment in time.

I started by pulling out a box heavy with hard cover books. I opened each book, looking for cutaways. One of the books was a paperback reviewing the Roman Empire's most notable emperors. I tossed it into my bag, then went through five more boxes containing mostly paperwork. I tried not to spend time reading any of the contents, but I meticulously searched for any document that didn't belong, like a driver's license belonging to a young woman.

Finally, I stood and stretched. The boxes were clean, and I'd made a hell of a mess, scattering papers all over Justin's office. I bent to the closet again, checking the floor and walls, then I searched the pockets of a dozen coats that hung above where the boxes had been.

The only thing left in the closet was an upright vacuum cleaner. My eyes fell on it for a long, hopeful moment. I pulled it out and removed the panel holding the dirt bag. When I unzipped the bag, a plume of stale dust rose into my face. I stuck my hand inside and swirled the contents, creating a bigger cloud that caused me to cough. Cursing, I zipped it closed. The bag held nothing but dirt.

When I left the office, doubt was creeping from the edges of my mind. There are only so many accessible hiding places in a house. One of them was a longshot right above me. In the hallway ceiling was a cutout section that opened to the attic. I carried a kitchen chair to the hall, stepped up, and pushed the square open. Then I grabbed a stud and did a pull-up. The attic floors and walls were lined with pink fiberglass insulation. I could feel the glassy dust in my eyes. I got an elbow over a two-by-four and struggled up until I could sit with my legs hanging down. The attic was empty; no boxes or anything else in storage. Glad for my mask and gloves, I pulled the insulation from the floor, and uncovered a six foot radius from the opening before I quit.

Lowering myself into the hall, I shook my hands, trying to remove the fiberglass shards clinging to my gloves. I didn't check my watch, but moved straight to the bathroom. I eyed the grout work carefully, searching for removable tiles. The medicine cabinet was clean, as were the sockets, light fixtures, and vents.

It was now almost 3:30 am. I was sweating and took a moment to catch my breath. Then I went back to Justin's bedroom and searched the master bathroom. When I finished, I went out to the living room and stood with my hands on my hips. After a moment, I upended the couch and padded chair, unzipping the cushions and pulling out the stuffing. After that, I yanked a heavy, framed picture of a rainy cityscape from the wall and tore the paper off the back. When I found nothing, I threw the picture onto the couch, and when it slid off, I kicked it. My boot broke the glass and left a gaping hole in the center.

The only good news, I thought, was no one from Hadrian Transport had shown up. The bad news was, there was only one area left to search, and that was the garage. I wasn't looking forward to it, because the flash of my headlamp would be clearly visible to anyone on the street. All it would take is an early riser walking their dog and a call to the police. *Alert me if you see anyone*, I texted Cody. Then I opened the door and stepped down to the concrete surface.

The space was just large enough to hold two cars, but it was empty, as Palatine's Mercedes was parked at the airport. A bicycle leaned against a wall. It hadn't been ridden in months, based on the cobwebs. A small green box was mounted on the wall near the bike. I opened the plastic door. It was a sprinkler system timer. In the corner was a water heater mounted on a raised pedestal. I gave it a thorough inspection, but couldn't see a potential hiding place.

On the opposite wall was a large metal cabinet. I opened it and found a hodgepodge of tools, including an electric lawn mower, a long extension cord, and hedge clippers. I poked around, looking for a stash spot. Five minutes later, I conceded there was nothing there.

After checking the walls and floor surface for irregularities, I dragged a chair into the garage and climbed up to eye level with the housing unit for the electric garage door opener. I popped open the box and saw nothing but a pair of light bulbs and some circuitry and buttons.

I pulled the chair back inside the house and sat in the middle of the main room. Before me was a fireplace, and above it, a mounted television. I stuck my hand up the chimney and pulled the flue open. It would have been a good, although dirty, hiding place. The flue coated my glove in soot, but offered nothing beyond that. I rose and looked behind the TV. There wasn't room there to hide anything.

Stepping back, I looked around the room. There had to be something I'd neglected. I could feel my teeth grinding, my jaw tight. "Think," I muttered. "Goddammit, think." Then I let my jaw go slack and closed my eyes. The room seemed to grow quieter. After a minute, all I could hear was the second hand of a clock ticking. I hadn't been aware of it before, but it suddenly became louder.

When I opened my eyes, they fell onto a clock mounted on a wall perpendicular to the fireplace. I watched the second hand's staccato pulse as it ticked off the seconds. Battery powered, no doubt. It was 4:26 A.M.

I stood and walked to it. The clock was about eighteen inches in diameter. It had a black rim and sans-serif numerals. I reached up and took it from the single wall screw that supported its weight. It was plastic and weighed about two pounds, maybe less.

When I shook it, I felt a ping of anticipation in my chest. I could hear something moving about inside, something light and forgiving, like paper or cardboard. I returned to the chair and set the clock face down on my lap. A latch allowed the back plate to hinge open, probably to access the battery and time reset buttons. I pushed the latch with my thumb.

Inside the clock was a plastic baggie about twelve inches square. It contained a variety of items: driver's licenses, rings, hair clips, lipstick, mascara. The baggie was so full it barely fit in its hiding place. "Pay dirt," I whispered, clenching my fist.

I didn't spend any time studying the items. Instead, I moved to Justin's office, where I'd seen a similar clock. I yanked it from the wall and discovered a second baggie. Holding the goods in my hands, I allowed myself a moment of jubilation, although it was tempered by a sickening realization. Then my phone buzzed with a text: *Mazon here. Go out back. Meet you next block.*

I stuffed the baggies into my pack and ran to the rear slider. I pulled the frame bolt free, flung the door open, and sprinted to the rear fence. With a single motion, I pulled myself over the top and dropped into the neighbor's yard. The sprinklers were on and I ran through the spray to the side yard. The gate was unlocked and within thirty seconds of Cody's text, I was on the street.

I heard Cody's Toyota before I saw it. He squealed around the corner, motor revving, and jerked to a stop where I waited on the sidewalk.

"Get in, he's coming," he said. At that moment, I heard an engine roar, then a late model Chevy Camaro came around the corner, tires howling. I jumped into Cody's passenger seat, and before I could close the door, he dumped the clutch. The Camaro gained on us while our tires spun futilely, then we caught traction and launched forward.

We were deep in a residential grid. Cody shifted into second and took the first corner at sixty. The rear of the Toyota pitched sideways and Cody deftly counter-steered. The next corner came quickly, and we turned left, power sliding and nearly clipping a parked car. I turned in my seat and saw the Camaro skidding, then fishtailing as Mazon over-corrected. His headlights flashed crazily over the trees lining the street.

Cody shifted to third and buried the throttle. The Camaro had fallen back. We flew through an intersection, then Cody slammed the brakes and turned left. The hellfire hooptie slid sideways for a long stretch, burning the tread off the tires, until he eased off the gas and we straightened.

We turned right and headed north, accelerating to over a hundred mph, and the Camaro's lights were pinpricks. But when we slowed for the next corner, I saw he was coming hard. The Toyota slid around the turn and Cody stomped the gas. I was straining against my seatbelt to see out the rear window.

Mazon entered the corner too fast. The Camaro's rear tire banged into the curb, blowing out the tire. The car careened to the left and spun almost 360 degrees before the front end slammed into an elm tree and burst into flames.

"He's toast," I said. Cody screeched to a stop and we jumped out of the Toyota. A man in pajamas rushed out of a house holding a fire extinguisher. He ran to the Chevy and coated the hood and fenders in white foam.

"Glad to see there's some good Samaritans left in this town," Cody said. "He's still alive, I can see him moving."

"Probably busted up pretty good. A few broken bones, at least."

"He needs to work on his cornering technique."

"Let's get the hell out of here," I said.

We did so without hesitation, and didn't speak until we crossed over El Camino Real. Then he said, "What did you find?"

"Two big plastic baggies, stuffed with driver's licenses and assorted trophies. I found them less than a minute before you called."

"You always got good timing, Dirt. Any out-of-state licenses?"

I pulled one of the zip-locked baggies from my pack. Not wanting to open it and potentially taint the evidence, I shook the baggie and watched an Oregon State license fall to the bottom.

"Oregon."

"Then it just became a federal case. You want to call the FBI?"

"Are you fucking nuts?" I said.

"I was just kidding."

"If Grier wants to ring up the Feds, that's his call." I held up the baggie. "But I don't think any of this would be admissible in court."

"Then what good is it?"

"I'm thinking, give it to Grier and Tim Cook, and let them figure it out."

"Really? And you walk away, a job well done?"

We stopped at a traffic light. It was still full dark, but I could see the Diablo ridgeline etched faintly against the starless sky. A pickup with dual cabs and roof racks stopped next to us, the driver sipping from a steaming cup. When the light turned green, I said, "One way or another, it's time to head back to Tahoe."

"Fine, I'll pack my bag."

"You want to join me?"

"What, you think I want to hang out at home and wait for SJPD to come kick a two-by-four up my ass?"

"Mazon was off the clock," I said.

"Doesn't matter. All he has to do is say he saw my car, and they'll charge me with breaking and entering."

"They could never prove it."

"Since when does that matter? We need to blow Dodge."

12

THE DAWN HADN'T YET cracked when we left town, and few cars were on the roadways. Cody was following me in his diesel truck. We drove due north on 680 for 75 miles, watching the sky turn from gray to a drab, sullied blue. Just as the sun crested the horizon, the interstate veered east. I put on my sunglasses and squinted at the white glare burning through the smog. I stayed at the speed limit, for the last thing I wanted was an interaction with the CHP or any police agency.

As we passed Fairfield and Vacaville, I told myself I had reason to feel cautiously optimistic, so why not think positively? Although Justin Palatine was still alive and free, the items I'd found at his house were iron-clad proof of his guilt. It was up to our government authorities to figure out how to use it to convict him. Those authorities might include district attorneys in a variety of states. Or maybe the inevitable route was to a federal prosecutor. Maybe Cody was right: the best way to send Justin Palatine into a hole was to get the FBI involved.

But that was a decision Grier and Tim Cook would need to make. I fully intended to present them with the evidence, and tell them I'd filled my obligation. Then I could wash my hands of the Palatines and their weird obsessions. I had other things to worry about, like helping Candi get her mojo back. I had no idea what that might entail, other than simply being there for her. I tried not to frown. I wasn't good at accepting ambiguity, but lately it seemed to be a central theme in my life.

It was a little past 8:30 A.M. when we stopped at a small town in the foothills east of Sacramento. The sky was cloudless and pastel, and the air smelled of pine and moss and rushing river water. A cool breeze rippled through the pines, scattering needles across the pavement. We bought breakfast at a fast-food restaurant and sat at a plastic booth in the back.

Cody deftly cut a stack of pancakes into squares. "You ready to vote in the California elections next month?" he asked.

"Why bother?"

"Because it's the American way of life. You shouldn't take our democracy for granted."

"The last guy I voted for broke every campaign promise he made."

"Yeah, but this time you get to consider Jerrod Palatine for governor."

I laughed out loud. "Are you gonna vote for him?"

"Well, I'll have to think about it. I do like his stance on the homeless."

"You mean, sending hit teams after them?"

"He's letting the dirtbags know they better get to work and get a roof over their heads, or else. And you know what? SJPD is behind him."

"That doesn't make it right."

"Does it make it wrong?"

"Not only is it illegal as hell, it's a rogue attack on U.S. citizens. It's almost as bad as ethnic cleansing. It's a step toward a dictatorship, or maybe even anarchy."

"And you're surprised?" Cody said.

"Aren't you?" I asked, looking up over my coffee cup.

"Don't kid yourself, Dirt. Our government is capable of far worse. Most of their misdeeds never make it to the public eye. It's been going on since the days of George Washington."

"That doesn't mean we should support it."

"Consider the alternative. We have a milquetoast governor who's allowed the homeless problem to fuck over the state, big time. Something has to be done."

"Jerrod Palatine must know about Justin's rapes. And he's done nothing but show him brotherly love. Gave him a job, helped him buy a house. As far as I'm concerned, it's guilt by association."

"Well, no politician's perfect," Cody replied, a smile beginning on his mug.

"I'd settle for decent," I said.

"That's asking a lot," he said, grinning.

. . .

An hour later, we were driving along a narrow stretch of Highway 50 shadowed by columns of Ponderosa pine and white fir. Above the treetops, the sky was a stunning deep blue, as if the heavens were smiling down on the immaculate fall morning. I steered through the sweeping curves, past the lodge at Strawberry and Horsetail Falls. Then we crested Echo Summit and slowed to navigate the granite-walled corkscrew descending into Tahoe Valley.

When we arrived at my house, I parked in the driveway and watched Cody climb out of his truck.

"I didn't sleep last night," he said. "I could barely keep my eyes open for the last hour. I need to crash."

We walked inside and Cody lumbered off toward the guest room. "I'll wake you in the afternoon," I said to his back. Standing in the family room, I gave myself a minute to stretch and ready myself for the task at hand. Then I went into my office, pulled on a pair of latex gloves, and set Justin Palatine's trophy bags on my metal desk. I carefully opened the first zip-locked bag and began removing the contents.

There were nine driver's licenses, all women's. Five were from California, two from Nevada, one from Oregon, and one from Washington State. Handling them by the edges, I took pictures of each license. As for the remainder of the items, I had no way of knowing which victim they came from. I assumed Justin had that information committed to memory.

The second bag contained eight licenses. One of them belonged to the teenager he raped about a mile from where I sat. The others included two from Colorado and one from Arizona. I took pictures of each, then put them back into the baggie.

Seventeen rapes spanning six states. A chill ran through my viscera. I had no reason to be surprised, but I had to take a moment to process the scale of what I'd just learned. From a legal perspective, a single rape or murder is punishable by almost the same sentence as would be levied for multiple offenses. But when measuring the pain and suffering caused by the offender, it increases exponentially with each heinous act. In Justin's case, the multiplier was at least seventeen.

I wondered how many of these women he had killed. I wondered if all the bodies had been found. And though I tried to shove the thought from my mind, I wondered about the unfathomable misery he'd inflicted not only on his victims, but also on their families.

It was noon when I called Marcus Grier.

"Still in San Jose?" he asked.

"No, I'm at home. I have some evidence you need to see."

"Evidence? We had plenty of evidence on Justin Palatine. Lot of good it did us."

"I've got driver's licenses for seventeen victims in six states. I assume Palatine's prints are all over them. You probably need to call the Feds."

The line went silent, then Grier said, "How did you get this?"

"I broke into his house and ransacked it."

Grier made a sound deep in his throat. "I don't know if we can do anything with it."

"Talk to Tim Cook. There's got to be a way."

"We'll see."

"I want to sit down with you and Cook ASAP. You need to look at this stuff."

"I'll talk to him."

"My house, six P.M. Be here."

"I'll get back to you."

After Grier hung up, I set my phone aside and stared at the baggies. Then I went to the floor safe in my closet, opened the thick door, and placed the baggies inside. The safe had metal flanges welded to six-foot sections of square steel tube bolted to the two-by-fours inside the closet wall. If I ever sold the house, the safe would come with it.

For the next hour, I searched the Internet for legislation pertaining to the admission of evidence. The overriding legal provision that limited admissibility was known as *the exclusionary rule.* Based on constitutional law, the rule prevents evidence acquired in violation of a defendant's constitutional rights from being entered in a court of law. An extension of the Fourth Amendment, the rule sought to protect the accused from illegal search and seizure.

I read through pages of legal precedents and case law, including rulings by Supreme Court justices. I learned that in 1960, only 22 states had adopted the exclusionary rule, but in 1961, to meet the due process definition in the Fourteenth Amendment, the Supreme Court mandated it be enforced by all states.

I rapped my fingers on the edge of my desk, where the green army surplus paint had chipped away. Could the same founding principles that made the United States a free country render the evidence I'd found meaningless? I felt a band of pressure in my temples. It was a question that could have many different answers. I needed to dig deeper.

It was early afternoon when I finally found something that made my eyes widen. In a California legal brief discussing limitations of the exclusionary rule, it specifically stated that evidence illegally obtained by private persons was indeed admissible. The inadmissibility clause only applied to evidence unlawfully attained by police or government employees.

I read the section three times before I pushed myself back in my chair and shook my head. All along, I'd assumed it would take some extreme legal maneuvering to make the evidence I'd uncovered admissible. I'd figured that was a best-case scenario, and I was prepared for the alternative. But what I'd just read seemed to confirm that the contents of the baggies were fully admissible. It almost seemed too good to be true.

Of course, I was ignoring the fact I could be held criminally liable for breaking and entering, and maybe even vandalism and theft. Or, assuming Justin Palatine hired an aggressive attorney, I could be subject to a civil suit.

Regardless, I stood, lips tight, and shook my fist, the knuckles tight against the skin. "The noose is tightening, motherfucker," I said.

I called Grier, but he didn't pick up. I tried Tim Cook, but it went to voice mail. Then, a pang of guilt in my heart, I called Candi. She picked up after a single ring.

"Did you and your mom go to Galveston?" I asked.

"Yeah, we're here now."

"Oh, great. How is it?"

"It's nice and sunny today. Being here reminds me of trips when I was a little girl. It's a happy thing."

"That's really good to hear, Candi."

"We're down on the boardwalk, looking for restaurants for tonight. Are you still in Vegas?"

"No, I'm back home."

"Is your case finished?"

"Almost. One thing—did you get any more text messages from that Nevada number?"

"No. I would have told you if I did."

"Right. Listen, you enjoy your time with your mom. I'll see you, when, in a few days?"

"I think so, yeah. I'm going to another grief session when we get back to town."

"Okay. Take care of yourself. That's the most important thing."

"Thanks, Dan."

After we hung up, I walked outside, stood on my deck, and breathed in the crisp air. I wondered if all men felt incapable when dealing with distressed women. I suspected the challenge dated back to the stone age and remained constant over the eons. But that didn't make me feel any better about my own perceived inadequacies. The mere thought of it made me want to head to Whiskey Dick's.

Instead, I changed into sweats and running shoes, and drove to the gym on Lake Tahoe Boulevard. I hit the weights hard for ninety minutes while listening to rock and roll at high volume through my headphones. I hoped the music would blot out my thoughts about what I wanted to do to Justin Palatine. As I pushed my body to the brink of exhaustion, I kept reminding myself that our legal system would take care of the problem. I really wanted to believe that.

It was late afternoon when I got home. Cody was sitting on my couch, eating something and watching TV.

"I hope you don't mind me scarfing your last frozen dinner," he said, "but I was starving."

"Don't eat too much. I told Grier to be here at six. Then we can head over to Zeke's Pit."

"Right on, I'm definitely in the mood for Texas brisket."

Cody pointed the remote control, and the channel changed to a local newscast.

"Whoa," I said. On the screen, Jerrod Palatine was standing in a room, flanked on either side by men in business suits. When he spoke, his voice was calm, his tone matter-of-fact.

"Earlier today, one of my political adversaries posted claims on social media that my younger brother has a history of criminal behavior. These claims are spurious and are an attempt to undermine my campaign to be governor. More so, the claims are libelous, and I have every intention of pursuing the strongest legal recourse."

Palatine stepped aside and allowed the man on his left to take center screen.

"As legal representative for the Palatine for Governor campaign, I want to alert those seeking to defame Mr. Palatine or his family members. We will not tolerate false or misleading comments, and to those who deploy these unsavory tactics, we will bring both civil and criminal lawsuits."

"Good grief," Cody said, leaning forward and squinting at the screen. "That's Bernie Holdsworth."

"Who?"

"He's the head honcho of Holdsworth, Rubenstein, and Salle. They're the number one law firm in the Bay Area. If they come after you, you may as well jump off a bridge."

"Come on."

"I'm serious. Remember that husband and wife team that defrauded dozens of elderly people out of their life savings earlier this year?"

"Yeah, what happened with that?"

"They hired Holdsworth, that's what happened. They got off scot-free. The same thing for the son of the wealthy philanthropist who killed two of his classmates. The evidence was rock solid, but he walked."

I pinched the bridge of my nose. "How do they do it?"

"Two things. One, they employ a couple hundred attorneys who do nothing but legal research and case study. If there's an angle, they'll find it. The other way is money. They'll tie up civil cases endlessly, until the other party goes broke and gives up. They do the same in criminal cases, dragging it out for years until the D.A. agrees to a minimal plea."

"That's it?"

"Our justice system lets it happen. Holdsworth and his lawyers know all the moves. As long as their client can pay, they have infinite patience. To them, it's all just billable hours."

I felt an acidy knot in my gut, as if I'd chased a greasy cheeseburger with a pint of cheap whiskey and my stomach had declared it unacceptable.

I stood and took a deep breath. At that moment, my phone rang. My eyes narrowed when I recognized the number; it had a Nevada area code.

"Hello?"

"Don't ask who this is, because you don't need to know. Here's the deal, Reno. You broke into a house last night and took some stuff that doesn't belong to you. We want it back, and I mean all of it, today. You cooperate, you get to walk away, no harm no foul, and let me tell you, that's one hell of a deal."

Cody was eyeing me, and I knew he wanted me to turn on the speaker. But I kept the phone glued to my cheek.

"That's a very intriguing offer," I said. "And what if I'm not interested?"

"Here comes the fun part, smart guy. My partner and I are in a small town outside of Houston now, and we're keeping an eye on your girl, Candi. I got to hand it to you, for a low-rent private dick, you got a pretty hot girlfriend. We can just watch her, or we can grab her whenever it's convenient. That might be today, tomorrow, or a week from now. But know this, you cooperate or we will get her. Actually, I kind of hope we get the chance. She looks like she'd be a lot of fun."

I heard what sounded like a toilet flushing. I didn't say anything for a long moment. "You still there?" the voice said.

"Where do you want me to drop off the stuff?"

"At Justin Palatine's house. We'll have a man meet you there."

"I'm not in San Jose now. Maybe I can make it tomorrow."

"Tomorrow doesn't work, my friend. You have until midnight, then all bets are off."

"Okay. If I leave now, I think I can make it by midnight."

"We'll be waiting," he said.

I disconnected the call. Cody stared at me and said, "What now?"

"That was Chad Sheridan. He says he and Mark Costa are in Houston scoping Candi. He wants me to bring the evidence back to Justin's house and give it to one of their guys, or else."

"You sure it was Sheridan?"

"I recognized his voice. Can you call Abbey?"

"Why?"

"I want to see if she can call the airlines and find out if those two flew from Vegas to Houston today."

"And what if they did?"

"I think it's time we had another face-to-face chat with these boys."

. . .

Neither of us had had time to unpack, and that was the good news. As soon as Abbey confirmed that Costa and Sheridan had taken a direct 1:25 P.M. flight from Vegas to George Bush International Airport, we got on the road. I hurried us out of the house because I wanted to get to the bank before it closed, to secure the baggies of evidence in my safe deposit box. Even though my safe was virtually impenetrable, I didn't want to take any chances. If someone from Hadrian broke into my house, they'd be out of luck.

Once I finished at the bank, I sat in the parking lot making flight reservations on my phone. I booked two one-way, first-class seats on United, at $800 each. We didn't need to hurry to the Reno airport, because the only flight we could get was an 8:20 P.M. departure to San Francisco, with a two-hour layover before taking off to Houston. We wouldn't arrive there until 5:30 A.M.

"Sheridan must have called me right after they landed," I said. "My guess is he called me from the bathroom at the Houston airport."

"How long of a drive is it to her parent's house?"

"About half an hour. But Candi's not there. She and her mom went to visit Galveston."

"There's no way Sheridan could know that."

"Right." I started my truck and steered onto Highway 50, heading toward the state line.

"So it's only her dad, the ex-sheriff, at home."

"Yup. I better call him."

"Probably a good idea," Cody said.

I gave Cody my phone and asked him to find the number for Candi's father, whose name was Glen, but everyone called him Bud. I'd met him on the single trip I'd taken to Houston to meet Candi's parents about a year ago. His face looked carved from flint, the leathery skin the color of tarnished copper beneath his silver hair. He was slim, but his shoulders were wide, his arms all sinew and muscle. When he spoke, he would gaze off, as if his thoughts were turned inward, until he finished making a point. Then he would turn his head and his gray eyes would meet mine briefly. During those glances, I always felt like we shared some unspeakable truths. But he didn't talk much, and though I thought he was laconic by nature, I also suspected that events in his past had caused him to become guarded and taciturn, and maybe even withdrawn. Candi had basically confided as much when she told me of her older sister's rape and eventual suicide.

"Hello, Dan," he said, his voice coming through my truck's audio system.

"Hi, Bud. I'm on my way to the airport to catch a redeye to Houston."

"Oh? Seems sudden."

"Are you at home?" I asked.

"Yes, why?"

"There are two men from San Jose I've had issues with. I think they may pay you a visit tonight. They threatened to harm Candi."

The line became silent, then Bud said, "Do they know Candice is in Galveston?"

"I don't think so."

"Describe them, please.

"One is five-foot-eleven, two hundred pounds, dark hair, thirty years old. The other is six-foot, two-twenty, short blonde hair, a body builder. They landed at Houston International less than an hour ago. They'll come in a rental car."

"Armed?"

"Probably."

"Have you told Candice about this?"

"No. I was going to call her next."

"Please do. I need to hurry and prepare for our guests."

"They gave me a deadline of midnight, California time, to deliver some stuff. So if they try anything, it probably won't be until after two A.M. your time. I'll arrive in Houston at five-thirty tomorrow morning. I'll text you when I'm in my rental car."

"Do you have any suggestions what I should do if these two set foot on my property?"

"Have them arrested for trespassing. Let them cool their heels in a cell for a few days."

"Hey, Bud," Cody said. "This is Cody Gibbons, Dan's partner. Actually, we'd appreciate if you could restrain and hold them until we get there. We need to have a word with them in an environment where they can speak freely."

I muted my phone and shot a look at Cody. "What are you thinking?"

"Roll with me, I got an idea," he said.

I unmuted the phone and said, "Bud, do you think you can do what Cody asked?"

"Tell me more about these guys."

"Ex-Marines, working for a private security firm. I think they may have been actively involved in the indiscriminate killing of homeless people in San Jose."

"I read about that in the paper. Struck me as a damn cowardly thing."

"Especially watch out for Sheridan. He's got a chip on his shoulder."

"I'll make sure to greet them appropriately. Please call Candice, or let me know if you'd like me to."

"I'll do it now," I said.

· · ·

My conversation with Candi was brief. I told her I didn't think she was in danger, because there wasn't any way Costa and Sheridan could know she was in Galveston. But I asked her to keep her eyes open regardless, and to avoid dark, deserted areas. I also told her I'd be in Houston the next day, and looked forward to seeing her once we straightened the situation out.

"Who's we?" she asked.

"Cody's coming to help out."

"Oh." She didn't say anything for a moment, and I was almost ready to say goodbye when she said, "What do you plan on doing to them?"

"That depends on what they do. At the least, I'll make sure they pose no threat to you. So please relax and enjoy your time with your mom."

We hung up just as I began accelerating up Spooner Pass. The rolling hills were covered with brown field grass, and every now and then a tumbleweed would blow off a bluff and bound across the road. The sun was low and colorless in the sky, and I could feel the temperature outside turn colder.

"Care to share your idea?" I asked Cody.

"What good does putting them in jail for twenty-four hours do? I want to talk to these guys, see if we can clear up a few things."

"They threatened Candi. I'm not giving them a pass."

Cody chuckled. "I don't think Bud will either. He knows what he's doing, right?"

"Before he was a sheriff in Houston, he spent ten years leading an inner-city SWAT team."

"A real commando, huh?"

"I wouldn't mess with him."

"Especially considering he's your fiancée's father."

"Right," I said absently, then my mouth fell open. "Shit, I better call Grier and tell him to forget about tonight."

"I'll text him for you," Cody said.

The miles fell behind us as we crested the grade and coasted down the sweeping curves above Carson City. By the time we reached the valley and turned north, the skies were lavender and early stars were visible. We shot across the high-desert flats, piercing the twilight as I gunned it toward Reno. I wanted to get to the airport quickly and get our bags checked through; sometimes the firearms caused delays.

The airport was uncrowded when we arrived, and we checked in and cleared security without issue. As soon as we found our gate, I sat and opened up my notebook PC.

"Might as well get a bite," Cody said, scrutinizing a food court to our left. "I'll bring you something."

"Okay," I said, as I connected to the Internet. I logged into a site I favored and ran a search on Chad Sheridan.

He was easy to find because there was a recent photo next to his name. His public record included a divorce at age twenty-two, enlistment in the Marine Corps a year later, and a Bad Conduct Discharge at twenty-five that carried a two-year sentence in military prison. After his release, he had a sole civilian charge of assault and battery. There was no indication he served time for that offense.

I'd never heard of a Bad Conduct Discharge, but quickly learned it was imposed for crimes such as grand theft, aggravated assault, or drug use. It was less severe than a dishonorable discharge, which was reserved for rape, murder, high treason, or desertion.

Other than that, there was nothing notable about Sheridan, other than his lack of work history. His only listed employer was Hadrian Transport, and he'd only been there for six months. Excluding Hadrian, there was no indication what he did for income in the two years after he was released from the brig, or before his stint in the Marines. I assumed he was either supported by his parents, worked under the table for cash, or was involved in illegal activities. Of the three, I would have bet on the latter. His military record probably made it difficult to find work, but apparently he was perfectly qualified to work for Jerrod Palatine's private security firm. That job seemed to offer plenty of opportunity for criminal conduct.

With nothing else to do, I reached into my backpack for the paperback book I'd taken from Justin's house. The author presented his list of the ten best and ten worst Roman emperors, and devoted a chapter to each. As I held the book that had been cradled in the hands of a serial rapist, my fingers felt sullied and a twinge of revulsion began in my gut. I ignored my emotional response and told myself I might glean insight into Justin's mindset by reading the book. I doubted it, but I started reading anyway. The first chapter was about Augustus, the founder of the empire. He was portrayed as a wise and noble leader, a visionary of sorts.

An hour later, we boarded the plane. While Cody took advantage of the free cocktails offered in the first-class cabin, I continued reading. The chapters on the worst emperors described rulers who were not only narcissistic and evil, but seemed like lunatics. Most of them were eventually murdered, but only after they caused great chaos and carnage. Nero, who took the throne at age sixteen, killed both his wives, was suspected of setting Rome on fire, and nearly bankrupted the empire. He was outdone by Caligula, a sadist who enjoyed torturing and killing not only high-ranking senators, but many of his blood relatives. He also forced his sisters and wives of his friends and allies to have sex with him. *These guys make modern U.S. politicians look like saints,* I thought.

When we touched down in San Francisco, I checked my phone and saw Grier had called me. I waited until we were in the terminal to call him back.

"I thought you wanted to meet tonight," he said.

"Change in plans, I have to go to Houston."

"Why?"

"Because Candi's there, and a couple of Palatine's thugs threatened her."

"Thugs?"

"They work for a security company owned by Jerrod Palatine, Justin's brother."

"Why would they threaten her?"

"They want Palatine's souvenirs back."

"Oh," Grier said. "You're not considering it, are you?"

"No."

"Because I talked to Tim Cook, and he said that evidence is admissible."

"I know it is."

"How long until you're back?"

"Maybe tomorrow, maybe the next day. Something else you should tell Cook, Marcus. The Palatines are represented by the Bay Area's top law firm. Even with the evidence, there's no guarantee of a conviction."

I heard him sigh. "What's the name of this law firm?"

"Holdsworth, Rubenstein, and Salle. They've gotten a lot of criminals off the hook."

"I'll tell Cook."

"Talk to you later, then."

"Wait a minute. Are you with Cody?"

"Yeah, he's coming with me to Texas."

"Oh? That's good."

"Why do you say that?"

"Well, you two make a good team, right?"

13

I WAS PLANNING TO sleep for most of the three and a half hour flight, but I stayed awake for longer than I wanted, compelled to finish the book. Near the end, I read about an emperor named Elagabalus, a sex-crazed bisexual teenager who, when he wasn't fornicating with the countless men and women his scouts rounded up, enjoyed torturing and sacrificing children.

In contrast was Marcus Aurelius, a philosopher and writer whose stoic tome *Meditations* is considered brilliant by modern scholars. But I was equally interested in an emperor on the list of the ten worst: a French-born ruler named Caracalla had killed his brother after they feuded for power.

As I slumped in my leather seat and grew drowsy, I wondered which emperor Jerrod Palatine modeled himself after. The visionary Augustus or the wise Marcus Aurelius? Or perhaps he was more inspired by the sadistic Caracalla. Maybe Jerrod was truly contemplating the elimination of his problematic brother. The murder of family members seemed to be commonplace in the Roman Empire.

I nodded off over Arizona and didn't wake until the jolt of the tires hitting the runway in Texas. I'd been in the middle of a bizarre dream that bordered on a nightmare. It involved Justin Palatine as the emperor

Elagabalus. Men and women were brought to his private chambers, some willingly, some not. But the dread came not from what happened in his room, but rather from what he was planning, which involved the mutilation and burning of children. My role was to prevent it, but I didn't know when or how to do that.

I rubbed the sleep from my eyes as we departed the plane. We walked into the mostly vacant terminal, and fortunately found a vendor offering coffee. A few minutes later, we stood at the baggage carousel waiting for our luggage. Once we got our bags, we wordlessly went into the men's room and geared up, body armor strapped tight, side arms in place, coats zipped to conceal our weaponry. Before we left, I brushed my teeth. That simple act always shakes the cobwebs from my head.

I checked my phone for messages as we made our way to the rental car garage. Then I texted Candi's father that we'd be there in about thirty minutes.

It was still dark when we drove out of the rental garage in a black Ford sedan. Once we left the airport grounds, we headed due north on a toll road, away from Houston. As the dawn broke, I could see we were crossing a vast expanse of flat terrain. High-voltage transmission towers ran alongside the freeway, and beyond the towers were endless fields, the land flat and uniform, interrupted by occasional low buildings.

It was 6:30 A.M. when I exited the freeway and drove down a street parallel to railroad tracks. I spotted three or four homes set back off the road, separated by at least a quarter-mile from their neighbor. Two turns later, I slowed to a stop next to a wood rail fence. Parked in front of me was a white Nissan.

We're here, I texted.

Come on in, Bud replied.

All good? I asked.

Yes sir.

"Let's go," I said. We left the car and walked into the damp, cold morning, following the fence until we reached a dirt driveway beneath a roughhewn wooden archway. Deep tire tracks were stamped into the ground, and through the morning haze, I could see a long, single-story house about a hundred yards off the road. To the left was a barn, and to the right of the house, bales of hay sat in an open-sided metal structure. Beyond that was a corral and a few acres of flat land. A handful of horses were clustered on the near side of the corral, as if waiting for something.

We followed the tire tracks to where Bud waited for us under his porch awning. He wore blue jeans, a plaid wool shirt, and a padded vest. His face was shadowed by a wide-brim Stetson hat. When he looked up, his gray eyes looked jaded and stoic.

"They're in the barn," he said.

"What happened?" I said.

"They came at three in the morning. They triggered a motion sensor on the sycamore over there." He pointed to a single tree about midway between the house and the fence line. "They walked right up to the front door and tried the door knob. That's when I tased them."

"How'd you do that?" Cody asked.

"I've got a setup in these shrubs here," Bud said, pointing to either side of him. "From my office, I can see anybody who approaches the house on video. I control the tasers remotely."

"Pretty elaborate," Cody said.

"I made a fair amount of enemies during my career. I take my security serious."

"What happened after you tased them?" I asked.

"I took their pistols, cuffed 'em, and pulled them onto a pallet. I used my forklift to drive them to the barn. I threw a couple horse blankets on 'em so they wouldn't freeze."

"I got to hand it to you, Bud," I said, shaking my head.

"I reckon I could teach you a few things," he said, the beginnings of a smile on his lips. "What you fixin' to do with these rascals?"

"We'll have a little chat, then make sure they leave and don't come back," I said.

"Let's go," he said, stepping off the porch. "I got horses to tend to."

We followed him across the dirt yard to the barn, and he pulled open the big sliding door. It was dark and musty inside and smelled of hay and horse manure. In the gloom, I could barely make out a forklift parked in the center of the space. Bud grabbed a flashlight from a corner and shined it on the forklift. The forks were raised to maximum height and held a pallet about eight feet off the ground. He climbed onto the driver's seat and lowered the tines until the pallet hit the dirt.

Mark Costa and Chad Sheridan lay shivering under a blanket. I tossed the blanket aside and saw they were each handcuffed behind the back, with a third pair of cuffs connecting them.

"You jackasses made a big mistake coming out here," I said. "I guess you've already figured that out."

Neither replied, and I stood looking down at them, at Sheridan's cowboy boots and his partially untucked, mud-stained, long-sleeved western shirt. Costa was in better shape, wearing a heavy sweatshirt that would have kept him warmer.

"The lawful thing would be for us to call the sheriff and have you both arrested for trespassing and attempted kidnapping," Cody said. "But maybe we can avoid that."

Costa craned his neck to look up at us. His pupils looked like black pellets. "What do you want?" he croaked.

"I'll leave you boys be," Bud said, handing me a key as he walked out of the barn.

Cody paused for a long moment, then said, "You thought you were going to kidnap my buddy's old lady for ransom, but you failed miserably." Cody lowered himself to a knee so he could look directly at Costa. "So now you're gonna have to pay for the goods."

"Meaning what?" Costa said.

"Two hundred fifty grand in C-notes. Hand delivered by Justin Palatine himself. In return, he can have back his rape trophies."

"You're crazy, man."

"You tell Justin that if he wants to save his ass, he better deliver. Of course, you don't like this deal, we'll call the local sheriff and press charges. Did I tell you ole' Bud used to be a cop in Houston? He's pretty tight with the sheriff in this small town. So you figure it out."

"Hey," Sheridan said, as if he'd just woken. "I got no problem taking your offer to Justin. Just un-cuff us and we'll be on our way to the airport."

"Where do you want the exchange to take place?" Costa asked.

"My partner's house in South Lake Tahoe," Cody said quickly.

I shot a look at Cody, my brow pinched. He held up his hand in a placating gesture.

"When?" Sheridan said.

"Today's Tuesday, so we'll do it six P.M. Thursday night," Cody said. "That will give Justin plenty of time to come up with the money."

"And if he can't?" Costa said.

"Then the evidence goes to the FBI," I said. "He's committed rapes in six states. It will be national news."

Both men lay silently in the cold, their bodies pressed against the rough pallet boards.

"You know what really disappoints me?" I said. "Two ex-Marines would stoop so low to protect a serial rapist."

"We don't work for Justin Palatine," Sheridan said.

"Yeah, I know, you work for his brother, Jerrod." I kicked at the pallet, the boards vibrating against Sheridan's jaw. "What do you think it will do for Jerrod's campaign for governor if Justin goes to trial?"

"I already said we'd take your offer to Justin," Sheridan said.

"One more thing," I said, kneeling and grabbing Sheridan's head so I could look into his eyes. "You ever make threats against my woman again, I'll hunt you down and break your fucking neck." When he didn't reply, I said, "You don't think so? I'll un-cuff you and we'll do it here and now."

For a long moment his eyes glowed with defiance, then he blinked and looked away. "No need," he muttered.

"What now?" Costa asked.

"You get your asses to the airport and catch the first flight to San Jose," I said. "And in case you get any bright ideas about sticking around Houston, you should know Candi's not even in town. So your trip was a big waste of time and energy."

"Can't argue that," Costa said.

"You text me by noon tomorrow, confirming the meet, or I call the FBI. Then you can explain the situation to Jerrod Palatine."

"Let us go and we'll do it," Sheridan said. "All right?"

I bent down and released Costa first, then Sheridan. They both sat up slowly, rubbing their wrists. "Man, I got to piss," Costa said, standing.

In my career as an investigator and bounty hunter, there are certain moments that stick in my mind like photographs, almost as if time slipped a cog and motion ceased. Or perhaps I was experiencing the click of a cosmic pause button in the instant before a soul departs this earth and begins a journey downward. I always recall these moments not merely as a facial expression or a hand clutching a weapon, but as a culmination of an individual's rage, frustration, and regret, captured in a dimensional freeze frame.

Chad Sheridan remained sitting, resting his forearms on his knees. He raised his right arm toward me, as if he expected I'd reach down and help him to his feet. But his fist was clenched.

Then he splayed his fingers, and a shot rang out. The slug hit me dead center in the chest, but it was a small caliber round, and it didn't knock me down. He closed his fist and pointed his arm at Cody, but not fast enough, for I'd already pulled my Beretta. When I jerked the trigger, the sound shook the rafters and dust floated downward. The bullet pierced Sheridan's right shoulder, but before blood could gush from the wound, I heard the boom of Cody's .357 Magnum.

The bullet hit Sheridan beneath his nose and reduced his face to something resembling a ripe tomato smashed against a wall. He toppled over, no longer recognizable, the maw of his face bleeding all over the hay on the floor, half his skull missing.

We turned our weapons on Mark Costa. He flung his hands up in the air. "Don't shoot!" he cried.

"Keep him covered," I said to Cody. I walked to where Sheridan lay, careful not to step in the growing pool of blood around the remains of his head. Reaching down, I unsnapped his shirtsleeve and pulled the cloth up his forearm, revealing a sliding metal apparatus attached to a palm-size stainless steel automatic pistol. A length of fishing line ran from the trigger to a ring on his finger.

"Only place I've ever seen this is in Western movies," I said.

"Derringer?" Cody asked.

"No, it's a Seecamp. Looks like a twenty-five cal."

"Keep your arms straight up," Cody said, leveling his big revolver at Costa's head.

"I'm unarmed, that gun was Sheridan's crazy idea."

"Put your hands on the forklift," I said, and patted him down. He was unarmed.

"Look, I'm just a hired hand. I was looking for a new job." Costa stared down at his shoes, then looked up at me. "I know I fucked up, man."

"You came here to kidnap my fiancée. I could put a bullet in you and sleep well tonight."

Costa's face turned pale, then he grabbed his crotch and gritted his teeth. "I'm gonna piss my pants."

"Come on," I said, pointing outside. I followed him as he went to the side of the barn and urinated in the dirt.

"Why did Sheridan end up in military prison?"

"He was an addict," Costa said, looking over his shoulder as he zipped his pants. "It started with steroids, but then he discovered coke and meth. He couldn't stop. He got busted for stealing our drill sergeant's car, can you believe that?"

We walked back to the front of the barn, where Cody waited outside, watching Bud gallop toward us on a brown horse with a white streak running between its eyes. The horse snorted as Bud swung his leg clear of the saddle.

In his hands was a lever-action rifle. He walked into the barn, his square-toe boots thudding on the ground, and silently stood over Sheridan's body.

"A sleeve gun?" he said, shaking his head. He came back outside and looked at me as if expecting an answer.

"I took a round in my vest," I said, pulling aside my black work coat. The slug was still embedded in the Kevlar. "You didn't notice it when you cuffed him?"

"I guess not," Bud said. "My damn fault."

The three of us stood facing Costa. "What happens now?" he said.

"I'll go call the sheriff," Bud said. He climbed back into the saddle and trotted to the front of his house.

"There are two outcomes here, pal," Cody said once Bud was out of earshot. "We press charges, you're going down for trespassing, attempted kidnapping, and aiding and abetting attempted murder. You can kiss your ass goodbye."

"The second option?" Costa asked, a glimmer of hope in his bird-like eyes.

"First, tell us about Hadrian Transport and the firebombings and shooting of the homeless," I said.

"And what do I get in return?"

Cody looked at me, then said, "You make sure Justin shows up with the two-fifty, you can skate on down the road."

Costa kicked at the dirt. His eyes looked round and hollow, as if he'd teetered on the edge of a cliff and pulled back at the last moment.

"I guess I have no choice but to trust you," he said. He ran his hand through his tangled hair, and a few small leaves fluttered to the ground. "I didn't shoot anyone, and I didn't light anyone up."

"I don't care about what you did or didn't do," I said. "Tell me about Jerrod Palatine."

"All the orders came from Justin. But we all assumed Jerrod was behind it. He's the man with the bankroll."

"Why would he want to kill a bunch of down-on-their-luck homeless people?" I asked.

Costa shrugged. "Your guess is as good as mine."

"All right," Cody said. "The important thing here is the money. Six P.M. this Thursday, at Dan's house. Just Justin and the money. Then you're off the hook, and so is Justin."

"That's a lot of dough," Costa said.

"Not for Jerrod, it ain't," Cody replied.

. . .

Fifteen minutes later, a squad car, an unmarked sedan, and an ambulance rumbled into Bud's yard. We waited in front of the barn and watched as two detectives, two uniformed cops, and a paramedic slowed to a halt and got out of their vehicles.

"The body's in there," Bud said. We stood aside as the detectives went into the barn. After a minute, they motioned to the paramedic, who wheeled a gurney to where the corpse lay.

"Who did the shooting?" a squat detective with a shaved head asked. Cody and I both raised a hand. The other detective, a middle-age man wearing black jeans and a bolo tie, waved Cody over to the squad car, while the heavyset one took me to a weather-beaten picnic table near the corral, about a hundred feet away.

We sat across from each other. After jotting my name, occupation, address, and phone number on a pad of paper, he asked me to explain what I was doing here.

"I'm investigating a serial rapist from California. Chad Sheridan, the deceased, was employed by the rapist's rich brother. Sheridan knew my fiancée, Bud's daughter, was visiting here. Sheridan threatened to kidnap her to get me to stop investigating. That's why Sheridan was here. I came to intercede."

The detective raised his eyebrows and rows of wrinkles appeared on his forehead. "I'll say you interceded."

"He shot first. If it wasn't for my vest, I'd be the dead man. I pulled my coat off and pried the bullet out of my body armor. "Here you go," I said, handing him the round.

He took it in his palm and studied it. "Twenty-five cal., I'd say."

"You'll find it matches Sheridan's weapon."

The detective scribbled some notes, then said, "What about the other guy?"

"Mark Costa. He's also employed by the rapist's brother, but for now, I'm not pressing charges against him.

"Why not?"

"Because I need him in California. He's agreed to aid me in my investigation."

"A serial rapist, you say."

"As in seventeen and counting."

A thin ray of sunshine appeared between the layers of clouds on the horizon. The detective sighed and looked toward the sunlight as if it might brighten his day. Or at least ease the paperwork he was facing. Then he asked me more questions, trying to catch me in a lie, and when that failed, he asked me about Justin Palatine. Ten minutes later, he pushed himself up and I followed him back to where Cody was waiting with the other detective. Costa was sitting in the backseat of the squad car.

We all stood watching the paramedic wheel Chad Sheridan's body to the ambulance. The dirt was uneven and bumpy and he struggled to keep the gurney upright. One of the uniforms came over to help, while the two detectives and Bud walked toward the house. They stopped and spoke for a few minutes before returning.

"We can hold him overnight if you like," the taller detective said, nodding toward the squad car.

"Better he heads back to San Jose ASAP," I said. "But he needs to know charges are still pending, unless he lives up to his end of the deal."

"And what specifically is that?" the squat detective asked.

"Nothing illegal," Cody answered.

After a silent moment, the detective turned to a uniform and said, "Let him free."

When Costa climbed out of the cruiser, I took him aside.

"I'm making a judgment call on you," I said. "I think you're a decent person who got involved with the wrong guys. You got a chance to turn it around. But keep in mind, Bud there can press charges at any time. You were involved in a plot to kidnap his daughter, and I'll testify to it. Plus, a man died as a result, which puts you even deeper up shit creek."

"I know, man, I know."

"There's a three P.M. Southwest flight direct to San Jose. Make sure you're on it. We'll check with the airlines to verify. Then make sure Justin Palatine shows up on time with the money. Because if he doesn't, you got a big problem. And so do the Palatines."

"I'll lay it out for him. It's pretty straight forward."

"Let's hope so," I said. "I'll be waiting for your text tomorrow."

I watched Costa jog to his rental car and take off, hunched over the wheel. Then I returned to where Cody was chatting with Bud while the cops continued taking photographs, scribbling notes, and making phone calls. The ambulance departed after a few minutes, followed by the squad car, and fifteen minutes later, the detectives finally got into their car and drove toward the fence line. I stood with Bud and Cody in a cold haze of sunlight, watching the sedan turn onto the pavement and accelerate down the road.

"I'm sorry for bringing this mess to your house," I said.

"An occupational hazard," Bud replied. "You came here to take care of it." He nodded a single time in affirmation.

"As soon I get confirmation Costa is on a plane, I'll call Candi, tell her she's safe."

"Hey, Bud," Cody said. "Would you mind showing us your surveillance system? I'm thinking of getting something similar."

"You strike me as someone who might need it," Bud drawled, and for the first time I could remember, I saw him smile.

. . .

I went inside the house with Cody and Bud to a room that had three monitors mounted on a wall above a long desk. I soon got lost in Bud's technical description of his cameras and Taser system, and I went outside and sat on the porch. I knew I had a phone call to make, but I didn't look forward to it. If there was a good way to tell Candi about the shooting, *my* shooting, at her parent's house, I wished somebody would let me know.

Regardless, I tapped on my cell and waited to hear her voice.

"Hi, Dan," she answered.

"Oh, hi, babe."

"Where are you?"

"At your parent's house."

"Why?"

"Because that's where I expected the two guys that threatened you would go."

"And did they?"

"Yup."

"And?"

"One tried to shoot me. I mean, he did shoot me, but I was wearing my vest."

"You're okay, then?"

"Yes, I'm fine."

"What happened after you got shot?"

"I returned fire. So did Cody."

"Is he—did he survive?"

"Cody's fine, too."

"No, I mean the guy who shot you."

"He's no longer a threat."

"I asked you if he survived," she said, a hint of vexation in her voice.

"No. He's dead. Cody and I were both acting in self-defense. The local police already came and left. We're not being charged with anything."

"Was my dad involved?"

"These guys showed up at three A.M. Your dad was ready for them. He held them until we arrived at about six-thirty this morning."

"What about the second guy?"

"He was a follower, not a leader. He's flying back to San Jose today."

"So, is it safe to come home?"

"Not yet. We need to confirm he got on his three P.M. flight."

"How are you feeling?"

"Me?"

"There're only two people on this call, right?"

"I feel fine, I mean, I feel a hell of a lot better than Chad Sheridan."

"He's the guy you and Cody shot?"

"Right."

"Does it bother you?"

I took a deep breath. "It never feels good watching someone die. Even if they're the most despicable scumbag on the planet, it's never a fun thing. But in this case, we're talking about a man who told me he intended to kidnap you, and maybe rape you." I could hear my tone shift, and a voice in my head told me to ease up, but I ignored it. "He was a stupid, evil man who tried to kill me. So if you're asking if I feel any remorse or regret, the answer is no."

"Dan," Candi said.

"What?"

"You never have to apologize for protecting me, for doing the right thing."

"I'm not apologizing."

"Don't forget that I grew up with a father in law enforcement. He's killed men too, and I know it sometimes bothered him, even though they always deserved it. I'm not judging you, Dan. I love you."

"I'll always try to do the right thing. I promise you that, Candi."

"I never doubted you. Why don't you drive out to Galveston? You'd like this place. Join my mom and me for dinner."

"I'm sorry, I won't have time. I have to fly back today."

"It's okay, I'll get a flight home in a day or so."

"Uh, how about planning on Friday?"

"Why?"

"I'll be meeting with a guy Thursday night in Tahoe. You'll be safer here."

"Is this a bad guy?"

"Yes."

The line went silent for a long moment. Then she said, "I understand."

After we hung up, I sat on the porch and stared at nothing. In my gut, I felt bad about asking Candi to delay her return, I regretted involving her father in a killing, and it made me uncomfortable admitting I felt no remorse. I looked away from the barn, out past the road. No other houses interrupted the acres of flat land that stretched under the colorless sky. The fields were mostly brown, admitting only occasional splotches of drab green. There wasn't a hill or any undulation in the terrain for as far as I could see, all the way to the blurry horizon. The landscape struck me as bleak and forlorn, and I wondered if this was a place one lives when they wish to minimize their contact with the human race.

I shook the thoughts from my head, then turned my attention to my phone and began searching for flights back to Reno. There were no direct flights out of Houston, Austin, or San Antonio. The quickest way to get home was to drive over three hours to Dallas and catch a four P.M. direct flight to Reno.

I stood and stretched, feeling empty and weary. I had a sudden craving for strong drink, even though it was only 8:30 in the morning. I promised myself a couple of double whiskey-Cokes at the Dallas airport, and possibly a few more on the flight. Maybe that would sufficiently blur my memory of Sheridan's blown apart face.

A horse's whinny broke the silence, and I walked across the lot to the corral. Three of the horses came to the fence and stuck their heads over the rail as I approached. I put my hand on the nose of an Appaloosa and it snorted lightly and pushed his head into my palm. A buckskin horse nudged his way toward me and asked for attention. Then a white mare did the same.

"You guys seem pretty happy," I said, petting all three. "You like it out here, huh?"

After a minute, they meandered away, and the Appaloosa began trotting across the coral, its head held high like a show horse. They all seemed quite content and very much in their element.

I turned around to see Bud and Cody come out the front door. I walked over and said, "We need to drive to Dallas and catch a flight."

"Direct to Reno?" Cody asked.

"Yeah, Dallas is the quickest way back."

"Good, because we've got some work to do."

· · ·

We said goodbye to Bud and hit the road. Dallas was due north, a straight shot on Interstate 45. The drive would take almost four hours if we didn't stop. But since our flight wasn't until the late afternoon, we didn't need to hurry. I didn't feel inclined to, either. My head was heavy from lack of sleep and the rigors of the morning. More than anything, I wanted to relax, settle in, and drive into the plains, thinking as little as possible.

But Cody had other ideas, and started talking excitedly once the city of Conroe faded in our rearview mirror.

"I found a store in Reno that has everything we need. Cameras, monitors, sensors, all the stuff. We're going to wire your house to the max."

"Slow down. How'd you come up with two-hundred-fifty grand?"

"I want them to think we're just in it for the money."

I braked behind an eighteen-wheeler, changed lanes, and accelerated past it. "I doubt they'll believe that."

"What do we have to lose? It's a good diversion, if nothing else. Anyway, it will take us a few hours to install your new system. We'll do it tomorrow."

"I've already got a security camera on my front door."

"Yeah, I've seen your rinky-dink set up. It definitely needs an up-grade."

I rolled my eyes. "I think it's time you shared your grand plan. Because I have no intention of giving Justin his freaking souvenirs back, no matter how much money he offers."

Cody started laughing, and I looked at him with wide eyes. "Are you okay?" I asked, seriously concerned. I wondered if the pills he took, in conjunction with his booze intake, might have short-circuited his wiring.

"I'm beautiful, baby," he said.

"What's so funny?"

"Here's how this will go down. The rapist will come to your house Thursday with the cash. You invite him in, grab the dough, and tell him hit the bricks."

"That's it?"

"No, I left out the part where you're going to get his confession, which will be captured on video. Then you tell him to beat it."

"And when he protests?"

"I'll be watching the whole thing on camera from your office. If he pulls a gun, I'll come out and blow him out of his socks."

"You assume he'll come alone."

"No, I don't. I assume he'll have backup. But we'll have your front yard and back yard covered—I'll have a screen devoted to each. I'll be like the eye in the sky, man. I'll see everything."

I kept my eyes on the road, considering the uncertainties in Cody's plan. Finally, he said, "Pure genius, don't you think?"

"How do you expect this to end?"

"Just like Marcus Grier requested. With Justin Palatine either in jail or dead." Now there was no mirth in his voice, and when I looked over, his profile was stone-like, his jaw set, the crow's feet etched sharply. Then he turned toward me, his eyes sharp as razors.

As I drove, I knew I could discount Cody's scheme as disjointed or even cockamamie. It was also downright dangerous. It would put both of us at risk of being shot, not by Justin, but by whoever came with him. That could include numerous hired gunmen, if that's how Jerrod Palatine decided to play it.

To make matters worse, the event would take place in my home, a place I held sacred and detached from my career. It was where I hoped to raise a family with Candi, and the last thing I wanted to do was invite a criminal of the most heinous type into my living room.

As a lesser concern, I had no desire to fleece a quarter-million dollars from the Palatines. But I couldn't deny that my expenses probably already exceeded what Grier and Tim Cook could afford to pay, unless I was willing to wait months to be made whole.

"Give me a cigarette," I said.

"Smoking again?"

Cody handed me a Marlboro and his lighter. I lit up, took a drag, and rolled the driver's window all the way down. The cold air rushed into the car, swirling around and blowing my hair in every direction. I blew a lungful of smoke into the maelstrom, and then felt an odd sensation, as if I was throwing armfuls of fall leaves into the wind. With it came a palpable sense of release, which I slowly recognized as my rejection of the prolonged stress weighing on my shoulders. In that moment, I'd depleted my capacity to care about things beyond my control. I accepted that I didn't have any better plan than Cody's. But more so, I accepted my chosen career and its risks, and all the uncertainty that came with it, and that included my relationship with Candi and everyone else I knew. There was a short and easy way to summarize it:

"Fuck it," I said.

"What?"

"Where's the store in Reno?"

"Near the airport. If our flight's on time, we can get there before they close."

"My credit card is near its limit."

"Don't worry about it."

I smiled crookedly, as if I'd awoke drunk the morning after a night of heavy drinking. "Okay, good buddy."

. . .

There wasn't much to look at as we drove up the gut of Texas. The scenery along the interstate consisted of power poles, single-story industrial buildings, and long stretches of low trees, some evergreen, some losing their leaves. I relaxed as Cody shared funny and sometimes outrageous stories about various women he'd dated over the years. The relationships had all been temporary, except for an on-and-off-again tryst he had with a gal he called Heidi-ho. I used to feel sorry for Cody, thinking he'd surely want a more stable situation. But over the years, I'd realized that a no-madic love life worked well for him. His sole attempt at marriage, when he was still in his teens, had ended badly. The only upshot was his daughter. I knew he wanted his relationship with Abbey to be close and permanent.

Outside of Madisonville, we stopped at a Buc-ee's gas station for coffee. We stopped again up the road in Centerville, because Cody insisted on visiting Woody's Smokehouse, which claimed to be the Jerky Capital of the World. After Cody dropped a hundred bucks on various types of beef jerky, we drove without pause to Dallas, reaching the airport at 1:30. We had just enough time for lunch at Dickey's Barbeque Pit and a quick cocktail at a crowded bar before we boarded the plane.

We sat in the first-class cabin, and I fell asleep before the plane took off. When I woke, Cody was eating a cookie and drinking a white concoction in a highball glass.

"Milk?" I asked.

"Nice try. White Russian."

"It smells like a bakery in here."

"They just served hot chocolate chip cookies. You were passed out, so I ate yours."

I stretched and looked out the window. We were flying over a vast labyrinth of cliffs, canyons, and gorges. I stared down for a minute, waiting for the landscape to change, but it seemed endless.

"Are we over Arizona already?" I said.

"Southern Utah. You were out for about an hour and a half."

I rubbed my eyes. "I need coffee."

"Order up, the price is right," Cody said, waving at a stewardess.

For the next hour I watched the scenery change as we entered the air space above Nevada. Below us were four hundred unrelenting miles of uninhabited high-desert terrain, the mountain ranges, cirques, mesas, and fissures stretching for almost the entire width of the state.

An hour later we landed with a jolt in Reno, collected our bags, and drove to the store Cody wanted to visit. He already had a complete buy list prepared. The man at the counter asked which company we worked for, and it became clear that they didn't typically sell home surveillance solutions.

"Here's everything we need," Cody said, handing him a sheet of paper.

The man disappeared into a back room, and twenty minutes later my truck bed was full of boxes, which I tied down securely next to our luggage.

"Let's get over the hill and head to Zeke's," Cody said. "We need to be well fed for tomorrow."

14

THE SUN HAD JUST fallen behind the Sierra as we rolled into Carson City, and it was full dark over Spooner Pass. When we reached Lake Tahoe, the sky was inky black and the temp gauge on my dashboard read forty degrees. We crossed the border into California and arrived at my house at 7:30 P.M. I half-expected to see signs of a break-in, but all the doors and windows were locked and untampered with. Pleased and somewhat relieved, I stowed the newly purchased gear in my office, and five minutes later, Cody and I bounced into the parking lot at Zeke's.

It was a Tuesday night in the off-season, and the bar was occupied by a pair of locals sharing a pitcher of beer. We sat at a table in a dark nook next to the wood-burning stove. Shadowy and tucked under a television in the corner, it was my preferred spot for hushed conversations.

"Let's order up some brisket," Cody said.

"You had that for lunch," I said.

"So?"

I went into the kitchen and found Zak tending the open fire pit, tongs in hand, chicken sizzling on the grill. I asked him to prepare a couple of plates.

"You got it, boss," he said. When I returned to the lounge, Cody was standing at the bar, ordering drinks from Liz. Apparently, the chilly fall weather had not inspired a change in her apparel. She wore a spaghetti strap halter, and as always, she was braless.

Cody joined me at the table and put a bourbon-Coke in my hand. "Didn't you have a fling with her once?" he asked.

"I think I should tell Grier about Thursday night," I said, leaning forward and tilting the highball to my lips.

"Bad idea," Cody said.

"Why?"

"He's a lawman. If things get sketchy, we don't want him in the way."

"I see it different. I think he could help."

"How so?" Cody asked, taking a long pull from his glass.

"Look, we don't know if Justin will bring the money. He might try to jack us around. I mean, why would he trust us?"

"If he wants the evidence, he has no choice. You're holding the cards."

"So, what would you do in his shoes?" I asked.

"I'd do whatever I could to get that evidence in my hands. But after that, all bets are off."

"Meaning, take out anyone he views as a threat to either him or his brother's agenda."

Cody finished his drink. "Exactly. But we'll be ready."

"There's only two of us. We don't know how many Justin will bring."

Cody eyed me wanly. "So, what, bring Grier for extra firepower? That's your idea?"

"I can think of worse things," I said. "It might not hurt to have a man outside. Like in the vacant house across the street."

"Hmm," Cody said. "Maybe. If he's willing."

"He better be. This is his gig."

. . .

I went to bed stone sober that evening, abandoning my plans for a whiskey buzz. I simply wasn't in the mood for it. This wasn't a conscious choice, but one I automatically made out of a sense of self-preservation. When violence occurs in an investigation, it's usually sudden and leaves no time for mental preparation. But in this case, I had ample reason to expect shooting was likely, and plenty of time to prepare.

In my career, consistent hand-to-hand combat and firearms training helped me survive a number of harrowing situations. Every weekend I sparred with cage fighters at Rex's Gym in Carson City, and frequently practiced various striking techniques on the heavy bag in my garage. But in life or death situations, more important was the ability to fire a pistol quickly and accurately. I wore a shoulder holster that placed my Beretta semiautomatic against my left rib cage. During my weekly trips to the shooting range, I devoted much of my time to quick-draw practice, which meant shooting from the hip. Hitting a twelve-inch target at fifty feet was once challenging for me. Now I rarely miss.

When I woke, I dressed, made coffee, put on my ski jacket, and stepped out the front door onto the redwood deck overlooking my frost-covered front lawn. My front door was actually on the side of the house, whereas the garage faced the street, at a right angle from the front door.

I turned away from the street and looked toward the rear of my property. Beyond the back fence was a meadow roughly half a mile wide and at least two miles long. It stretched all the way from Highway 50 to Pioneer Trail. Anyone who wanted to approach my house from the rear could simply park at the gas station on the highway, step over a low fence, and walk less than a mile to my rear gate. I kept it locked, but scaling the fence would be relatively easy. It would also be easy for me to install a motion-activated light and a camera on the fence.

I walked across the deck and down the two stairs to the driveway, where Cody's red truck was parked. I'd ask him to move it by Thursday, maybe park it at a casino lot. Justin would probably expect Cody to be at my house for our meeting, but I saw no reason to make it obvious.

Across the street from my house was a cabin on a dirt lot without fencing, set back from the road and shadowed by two huge sugar pines. It became vacant shortly after I moved here. The owner had passed away, and his four middle-aged children all contested the will. For years, no one had set foot inside. The same worker came by monthly to mow the weeds and sweep the needles off the roof.

I walked over to the front of the cabin. The windows were boarded with plywood, the door secured by a deadbolt. Walking to the rear of the house, I saw all the windows were boarded up.

Standing behind one of the big pines, I had a perfect line of sight to the front of my house. This would be the spot to post Grier. I looked up the street, toward Lake Tahoe Boulevard. Justin and whoever came with him could come from that direction, or they might opt to enter my neighborhood from the opposite side, from Pioneer Trail. From where I stood, I could view cars coming from either direction.

When I returned to my house, it was 7:30. I rekindled the stove and threw some frozen hash browns into a big frying pan. Then I turned the heat down and added strips of bacon. Once the food was sizzling and crackling noisily, I heard Cody walking down the hall, his footfalls like an elephant's.

"Sleep well?" I asked, tending to the pan.

"Why wouldn't I?" he said, grabbing a coffee mug from a cabinet.

"How many eggs do you want?"

"How many you got?"

I cracked five eggs into a second pan. "I want to install a spotlight and a camera on the back fence," I said, scrambling the eggs and chopping the potatoes with a spatula.

"We got enough gear to do whatever you want." Cody sat at the kitchen table. He took the chair I usually sat in, facing away from the kitchen. To his diagonal left, about ten feet in front of him, was a large window that provided a nice view of the ten thousand foot ridgeline of the Sierras' western flank.

I loaded a plate and set it in front of Cody. "I'll be right back," I said. He eyed me curiously as I walked out the front door. I went across my yard, leaving wet footprints in the frost. When I reached the side fence separating my yard from my neighbor's, I looked at the window and walked down the fence line, trying to find a location from where I could see Cody. The best I could do was see the chair on the opposite side of the table. The angle disallowed seeing deeper into the interior.

I went back inside and forked two strips of bacon and some potatoes onto a plate. Then I sat across from Cody and pointed at the window.

"When Palatine comes, I'll operate from where you're sitting. If someone outside is trying to line up a shot, there's no way they could see me. They could see me sitting on this side of the table, but not on your side."

"Why not just close the blinds?"

"Because I'm gonna have the deck lit up. I want to see if anyone approaches the front door. Or the window."

Cody wiped his mouth with a napkin. "We'll have a camera on the deck. I'll see if anyone comes."

"Maybe not quick enough."

He nodded in agreement. "Let me finish my coffee, then we'll get to work."

. . .

As I expected, installing the security system was neither quick nor easy. By noon, we still hadn't solved a glitch in the motion sensor spotlight I'd installed on the fence next to my back gate. I thought the unit was faulty, and was ready to give up when I got a text message from a number I didn't recognize.

Meeting confirmed 6pm Thurs

Identify yourself, I replied.

MC

I'll be waiting, I texted, then looked up at Cody, who was standing in the meadow near the gate and waving his arms, trying to get the light to activate. "Costa just texted me," I said. "The meeting is confirmed."

The spotlight flashed and stayed on until Cody froze. "Good," he said. "Let's check the monitors again."

We went into my office, where a long folding table now occupied the wall perpendicular to my desk. On the table were three 15" flat screen monitors. One showed my driveway and part of the street. The second, from a camera I'd mounted to the pine tree in my yard, showed the deck and front door. And the third captured the area around my back fence.

"Call my cell and go walk around," Cody said. "I want to see if there are any blind spots."

That exercise led to another hour of work, as we tried to adjust the cameras for optimum coverage. We finally conceded that avoiding every blind spot was impossible unless we went out and bought another half-dozen cameras. But there's no way anyone approaching the house would know where the blind spots were. And that was assuming they suspected cameras were installed and were trying to avoid detection.

The sun was out, and the afternoon had turned warm enough to sit outside in a sweatshirt. I pulled my picnic table out of the shade and relaxed in the sunlight for a minute before calling Sheriff Grier.

"Dan," he answered.

"Justin Palatine will be at my house at six P.M. tomorrow," I said.

"What?"

"You heard me. I sent word to him that if he wants his trophies back, he needs to come get them."

"And he agreed?"

"Damn right, he did. Not only is his freedom at stake, but his older brother's political aspirations are on the line."

"This is the CEO of that big technology company?"

"Yeah. And he's running for governor. He's doing everything he can to keep Justin out of the spotlight, for obvious reasons."

Grier sputtered something unintelligible, then said, "What the hell are you planning, Dan?"

"I think Justin might pull a gun on me. Or he might bring people who will. I want you to be here, to arrest him for it."

"Wait. What is he giving you in return for the souvenirs?"

"It doesn't matter. I don't intend to give them to him. He'll try to criminally force me to. Then you can step in and arrest him."

"This sounds like a shootout in the making."

"Not necessarily. All I need you to do is wait behind a tree across the street from my house. If you see anyone that's not Justin approach, stop them. Then come on in and arrest Justin."

"Who thought this up?" he asked, his voice edged with incredulity. "Cody Gibbons?"

"Well, I'd hate to give him all the credit."

"Credit? For what? You're hoping Justin will carry a gun and threaten you? But you're not worried he'll pull the trigger?"

"You let me worry about that. All I need you to do is stop anyone Justin brings. And Marcus, please assume they'll be armed."

"No shit, huh?"

Grier proceeded to ask me several more questions, none of which I could answer in a definitive way. In the end, I told him there were only three potential outcomes for the meeting: One, Grier arrests Justin for felony assault, two, Justin leaves without the evidence, in which case the FBI would go after him, or three, Cody or I would shoot Justin in self-defense.

"This is crazy, number two makes the most sense. I should call the FBI right now," Grier said.

"Marcus, you're forgetting the Palatines have the best law firm in Northern California on their side. There's no guarantee Justin will wind up in jail."

The line went silent, and I almost thought we'd become disconnected when Grier said, very quietly, "I'll be in place at five-thirty tomorrow."

After we hung up, I sat for a while, staring off at the layered clouds hovering over the mountain peaks. What if Justin didn't show up, but instead sent a team of hitmen to kill Cody and me before they grabbed the souvenirs? If so, he'd have to assume I had the evidence bags in hand, and was ready and willing to exchange them for cash. This was what Cody wanted Justin to think; that we were just in it for the money. I doubted Justin believed that, but regardless, I didn't think he would risk queering the deal by not showing up. He needed to get his souvenirs back, and his best chance at that was to be here in person.

As for Cody's notion of getting Justin to make incriminating remarks on camera, I had some ideas percolating in the back of my head. At a gut level, I believe most violent criminals are products of severely dysfunctional upbringings. This doesn't mean that all people with rough childhoods become vicious predators. But for those born with an innate capacity for violence, when they grow up unloved and exposed to racial hatred, crime, drug abuse, or maybe sexual depravation, the results can be catastrophic.

In the case of serial rapists, I felt that, by default, their childhoods were almost certainly devoid of ordinary nurturing, and probably included many horrific elements that caused not only their inability to form normal relationships, but their need to punish the world for their victimhood.

If I knew anything about Justin's upbringing, I might be able to push him to the brink and goad him into making incriminating statements. It was a long shot, and a moot point unless I came across some real information about his early years.

I again thought about his mother, her mind failing from dementia. If she were lucid, I might have tried to call and ask questions. But I'd been told her symptoms were late stage, which made it doubtful she could tell me anything, even if she wanted to.

Tapping my fingers on a plank of weathered redwood, I tried to think who would know about Justin's childhood. His father was dead, his mother nearly so, and his older brother was out of the question. I'd run all the names through public record searches, and couldn't recall seeing any extended relatives.

Back inside, I saw Cody cleaning his revolver on my kitchen table. I told him I needed to do some research and went into my office. I paused for a moment, looking at the three surveillance monitors, before I sat at my desk and pulled up the saved people-finder reports on the Palatines. For half an hour, I tried to find aunts, uncles, nieces, or nephews.

The best potential contact was a niece, a daughter of Marcia Palatine's younger sister. She was forty-five years old and her last posted address was in Maine. When I called her phone number, it rang a dozen times before disconnecting. I found another Palatine who could have been a nephew on the mother's side, and when I called his number he answered, but said he was not related.

I turned away from my computer and shifted my thoughts to the seventeen driver's licenses. I scrolled through the photos I'd taken of each, wondering if there might be a common thread in the attacks that hinted at Justin's background. After a minute, I called Grier.

"Yes?"

"Of the seventeen driver's licenses, nine are in California. Can you run the names and pull up police reports?"

"I'm on patrol now."

"Doing what, busting jaywalkers?"

"Forgive me, but I'm not in the mood for your wise ass comments."

"This is important, Marcus. I'll text you the names."

"It's a highly irregular request."

I laughed. "So is everything about our arrangement."

I heard him sigh. "Give me until tomorrow morning."

. . .

That evening Cody and I headed out at twilight. We drove into Nevada and up the highway to Sam's Place, a small roadhouse with video poker machines inset in the bar top. The interior was dim, and cigarette smoke wafted upward through the yellow light into vents in the soffit. From an open room at the end of the bar, we could hear the crack of pool balls caroming off each other and thudding into the bumpers.

We sat in the middle of the empty bar and ordered highballs. I contemplated the poker machine, then glanced at Cody.

"You ever think back to your childhood?" I asked.

"Not often," he said, sipping his drink.

"A shrink once told me that my career was a subconscious choice to allow me to seek retribution against my father's murderer."

"I thought that guy is dead."

"He is. The shrink was speaking metaphorically."

"Do you buy into it?"

I took a cigarette from Cody's pack. "Maybe."

"So every time a bad guy bites the dust, it's like avenging your old man?"

"Sounds crazy, huh?"

"Not really," Cody said, lighting a smoke and handing me his lighter. "But I can't relate, because my dad was basically a mean, drunken asshole who treated my mother like dirt."

"You wouldn't care if he died?"

"I don't know. I'll cross that bridge when I come to it, because the old bastard's still alive."

I guzzled my drink, the ice cubes rattling against the glass. I caught the bartender's eye and signaled for two more.

"Do you ever think of him when you kill a man?" I asked.

Cody looked at me, his face surprised. "That's a hell of question," he said after a moment.

"You don't have to answer."

He finished his drink and took a big belt from the fresh one the bartender had just set down. Then he set his chin on his fist and said, "If I really think about it, he doesn't enter my mind. But it always makes me feel satisfied to blow away pricks who prey on the defenseless."

Because your dad preyed on your mom, I thought, but I didn't say anything.

"Is there something wrong with that, Doctor Freud?" he asked.

"Not in my book, partner," I said.

We ordered dinner and played poker into the night, nursing our drinks and avoiding discussion of what might happen tomorrow. As we ate, I tried not to contemplate what Cody had experienced while growing up with an abusive, alcoholic father. Nor did I think about the difficulty he faced after his dad kicked him out of the house at age fifteen. We all have our demons, I told myself. What mattered most was that Cody and I saw evildoers through the same lens, and our goal was always one that, despite claims otherwise by cowards and legal nitpickers, was virtuous and required no justification. That's how we saw it, and that part of our relationship was elemental and beyond discussion.

15

A T TEN-THIRTY THE NEXT morning, Grier called and said to check my mailbox. I went outside and saw it was stuffed with a manila envelope that was too full to seal shut.

"What's that?" Cody asked when I came back inside.

"I gave Grier the names of nine of Palatine's California driver's licenses and asked him to run crime reports." I held up the envelope. "In the mood for some light reading?"

I sat across from Cody at the kitchen table and pulled the reports out of the envelope. "Here you go," I said, handing him one.

The first report I read was dated twenty years ago, when Justin was still in his teens. It described an attack on a twenty-three-year-old woman in Los Gatos, an upscale suburban city south of San Jose. She had been knocked unconscious by a carotid chop and taken to a remote location in the nearby hills. Her injuries were numerous and included a broken jaw and tearing of her rectum. She said the assailant was masked and threatened to kill her. I took notes on a few details, and started reading the next report in the stack.

The report did not include a description of an attack, as the fifty-one year-old woman had been found dead. The bruising on her neck indicated a carotid chop, but that was the most modest of her injuries. Besides being penetrated vaginally and anally, the woman had been beaten to death. She was found tied to a tree, her hands bound. It appeared her attacker battered her face to the point that she suffocated on her own blood.

"You should read this one," I said to Cody.

"Why?"

"Because it confirmed my suspicion he's a murderer."

For the next hour, we read and reread the files, until I said, "This is literally making me sick to my stomach."

Cody didn't reply, but his face had taken on a granite hue and his eyebrows were pinched in a V-shape. It was a look I recognized, and one that spelled bad news.

"I need some fresh air," he said. He lurched to his feet and went out the front door. I took a deep breath, then left the reports scattered on the table and joined him outside.

Cody was leaning with his elbows on the deck railing, staring at the distant mountains.

"Four murders," I said, standing beside him. When he didn't reply, I added, "and that's only California."

We stood silently for a minute, and when Cody finally spoke, he didn't turn toward me. "A bullet in the head is too good for him," he said, as if speaking to someone else.

"My boiler is acting up," I replied, my hand on my gut. "I'm gonna take a walk." I walked to the back gate and left Cody, unmoving and statue-like, on my deck.

The skies were clouded over, and it felt colder than it was. I shoved my hands deep in my pockets and trudged down the trail to the stream. There were patches of snow in the shade, and along the banks, thickets of swamp grass were coated with frost. I watched the brownish water flow downstream, swirling with broken sticks and half-sunken pine boughs. After a minute, I began trudging down a trail toward the highway.

The reports Grier provided told a story of a man journalists might describe as a "monster." The term insinuates that the subject is not only vicious, but has a preternatural ability to survive. In the case of Justin Palatine, so far he had not only survived, but also stayed out of prison. For over twenty years, he had outsmarted our justice system while destroying both lives and families.

Did I think Justin Palatine could continue plying his grim trade for as long as he desired, with no repercussions? Maybe he could. Or maybe he was ready to run headlong into an alternate brand of justice, one that came smoking with red heat out of the barrel of a large bore pistol.

I shook those thoughts from my head and instead started mentally sifting through the details of the attacks. With few exceptions, rape is a violent crime, but the violence depicted in Justin's attacks was extreme, as if he was in a frenzy. Every incident included anal penetration, and in half the cases, he didn't even bother with vaginal sex. And in four of the cases, he had beaten his victims to death, either by blows to the face or strangulation.

His need to degrade and inflict pain must have been intense. He'd been at it since he was a teenager, seemingly insatiable. It went beyond a rapist's typical assertion of dominance. Justin seemed driven by something in his early years that caused him tremendous rage and hatred.

I paced along, watching the traffic on 50 grow closer. I'd once dealt with a rapist who wanted to pay back the female race for their rejection of his advances. A scorned and frustrated lover, his anger reached the point where he sought revenge. But his attacks never included beatings or murder. He was satisfied with the simple act of rape. Ultimately, he landed in San Quentin, where I heard he was victimized by prison yard rapists who turned the tables on him.

When I reached the low metal guardrail along the road, I stopped and kicked at one of the posts a few times. There wasn't much that Justin's victims had in common. They were mostly white women, with a few Hispanic names mixed in. About half were single, the other half married. Their ages ranged from teenagers to women in their twenties and thirties.

The only exceptions were two victims in their forties, and one in her fifties. Those three had been brutally murdered.

I kicked the post again and stared at the ground. His fourth murder victim had been in her late thirties. Would it be fair to assume Justin's rage was fixated on women older than him? I turned and started heading back toward my house. What kind of horrific thing could an older woman have done to Justin? What misdeed could be so heinous?

As I hiked back through the meadow, I had a hard time imagining a scenario that fit. Until I considered that whatever happened must have occurred when Justin was prepubescent, maybe when he was a small, defenseless child. If I allowed my mind to delve into the darkest corners of human behavior, I could come up with some theories.

Subjecting victims to anal penetration is not unusual in rape cases, but in Justin's case, I didn't know if it was solely a means to cause pain and humiliation. It might be rooted in something else. Something in Justin's childhood involving a full-grown woman. Maybe even his mother.

When I got back to the house, Cody had returned to the kitchen table and was reading one of the crime reports.

"See any trends?" I asked

"The four he killed were all much older than him."

"Yeah, I noticed."

"Maybe he has a mommy problem."

"He might have had issues with potty training when he was a toddler," I said. "Suppose his mother humiliated him over it. Like, in public."

"Give me a break," Cody said, rolling his eyes.

"You got any better ideas?"

Cody set down the report and looked at me. "Maybe his mother pimped him out to pedophiles. That would be enough to piss a kid off, don't you think?"

I grimaced. "I'll ask him tonight. I'm sure he'll be dying to talk about it."

. . .

By the time Grier called at 5:30, Cody and I had checked and double-checked our newly installed surveillance system. If anyone approached my house from the front, side, or back, they'd be detected. I wasn't concerned that there were a few small blind spots. I was more concerned with how the scenario would play out once Justin entered my house. I'd gone to the bank and picked up his souvenir bags, thinking he'd be more inclined to talk once he saw I had them.

"I'm parked in my Subaru down the street," Grier said. "As soon as it gets a little darker, I'll go wait behind the big pine across from your place. I'm in street clothes."

"Palatine won't come alone," I said. "That much we know."

"I see anyone else, I'll stop them."

After we hung up, I went and stood behind the peninsula that separated my kitchen from the main room. I set the souvenir bags on a tiled counter six inches below the laminate top. The peninsula was not quite four feet tall and overlooked the kitchen table. From this vantage, I could see out the big window facing my yard. Anyone approaching my front door from the street would have to pass right by the window. Of course, they could always duck below it, but the camera attached high on the trunk of my pine tree would spot anyone on the deck.

Satisfied my position was optimum, I went to the bedroom and strapped on my body armor and secured my holster against my ribs. Then I went into my office, where Cody was still fiddling with the system.

"In a few minutes, I'll call your cell," he said. "Just answer and keep the call live. Put it on speaker, and I'll shout if I see anyone coming."

"All right," I said.

"Hey," he said, looking up from his chair.

"Yeah?"

"I've got a drop if you need it." He pulled a snub nose revolver from his coat pocket. "Untraceable. Just in case, huh?"

"Right," I said, and went to the kitchen to wait.

· · ·

At exactly six P.M., I saw a man in a gray coat pass by my window. A moment later, he knocked on the door.

"Come in," I said loudly, standing behind the counter, my hand on the butt of my pistol.

The door opened, and in walked Justin Palatine. He wore black chinos and a gray parka with a fleece lined hood. It was a heavy, padded coat, and could have easily concealed a firearm. I watched him closely as he closed the door.

In his right hand, he held a leather satchel. When he turned to face me, he said, "I brought the money. Cash, just like you asked."

"Take off your coat, please," I said. He looked at me as he pulled his arms out of the sleeves. His wavy brown hair was parted neatly on the side. He had even features, his face neither round nor thin, his nose and chin in proportion, his eyes a dull hazel. He wasn't ugly, nor was he handsome. In person and up close, I was struck by how unremarkable and bland he appeared.

"Set your coat and the bag on the couch," I said, walking around the counter. "I need to search you. Put your hands on the door."

He cooperated without comment. I patted him down, and he was clean. He wore a brown short-sleeve shirt, and he'd buttoned the top button, which made him look nerdy. That was the sole flash of personality he emitted.

"Stay there," I said, while I checked his coat for weapons. Then I grabbed the bag and unzipped it. It was stacked with cash. I moved my hand around the interior and felt nothing but bundles of crisp bills.

I backed up slowly and returned behind the peninsula.

"Now take a seat at the table."

He sat in the chair facing me. His expression was neutral and almost serene. He seemed neither concerned nor in a hurry.

"I have a few questions before we get on with this, Justin," I said. "I've been looking through your rape souvenirs, and I'm curious about a few things."

His eyes didn't wince or even blink.

"You look like an ordinary guy. But you're an abomination, an unfortunate freak of nature. What drives you to such atrocities?" I held up one of the plastic bags.

He looked down at where his hands rested clasped on the table, then he looked up at me, a slight smile beginning on his mouth. I caught a glimmer of light in his eyes.

"We're all products of nature and nurture," he said. "It's the way of the world."

I came around the counter and stood three feet from him. "I hear you have a genius IQ. I got to hand it to you, raping and killing all these years and never landing in prison. You must be one smart dude."

"That's part of my nature."

"I'm sure it is. But let's talk about your nurture. That's where the trouble started, right?"

He looked up at me out of the corner of his eye. He appeared relaxed, almost as if he was suppressing a grin. "Oh, I don't know about that," he said.

I leaned down and put my hands on the table, my face just inches from his. "Let me tell you what I think. I think your mother fucked you over big time, submitted you to some mean, nasty shit. She must have really hated your guts."

For a moment, I could have sworn I saw the air change around his head, as if a cold wind blew through his soul. But just as I was sure his face would crack, he giggled. The sound was so unexpected and odd that I backed up a step. "Marvelous!" he exclaimed. "Please, tell me more." He was now smiling widely, his eyes bright.

I sat in the chair across from him. "I think you took it up the ass when you were a kid, and your mom arranged it all."

"Oh, you're good, you're good," he said.

"What did she do, pimp you to pedophiles for spending cash?"

"I must hand it to you," he said, leaning forward. His face was beaming, his teeth wet with saliva, his eyes shining as if he was savoring every moment. "You have excellent intuition. Excellent! So much better than most of the dimwitted policemen I've met over the years."

"So why have you raped and killed so many women?"

Justin shrugged his shoulders and seemed to shudder with pleasure. He tried to speak, but was grinning so widely his mouth wouldn't cooperate.

I sat staring dumbly at him, knowing I was beat. I considered putting my gun to his head, but at that instant, I was sure he would challenge me to pull the trigger. For a long moment, I was tempted, but I didn't have it in me; I would not stoop to cold-blooded murder.

But maybe I had another card to play, I thought, suddenly smiling myself.

"Hey, Justin, as long as we're having a good time, I wanted to ask you about your weird obsession with the Roman Empire. What the hell's that about?"

"What can I say, I'm a history buff."

"No, I think it's more than that. I heard your old man thought he was the reincarnation of Augustus Caesar, first emperor of Rome. They had to send him to the funny farm."

"Well, you seem to be well-informed, but I was very young when he died."

"And I heard your big shot brother Jerrod runs his business like he's some kind of emperor. What is it with you people?"

"If you're so interested in the Roman Empire, go read a book," he said, his smile gone. "Or get an audio version if you're not a reader. You're not, are you?"

"Actually, I like to read, and I just read a book about the different Roman emperors. And there was one I think is your favorite. Care to guess?"

He looked at me with eyes half lidded, his expression pinched.

"No problem, I'll tell you. I think you model yourself after Emperor Elagabalus. I mean, what a guy! A bisexual teenager who spent all his time smoking pole and getting his ass reamed. You remind me of him," I said, stifling a laugh. "You're weak and spoiled and fucked up in the head, and your only real accomplishment is raping and murdering defenseless women." I pounded my fist on the table, laughing from the gut. "You're the most pathetic creep I've ever laid eyes on."

"You," he said, his face reddening, "have no idea who I am, you howling imbecile."

"Then why don't you tell me?" I said.

"I'll tell you this," he said, but he never got to finish his sentence.

The next three seconds seemed to occur almost instantaneously, but when I think back, it always feels like the seconds were more like minutes.

First, I heard Cody's voice through my cell phone. "Back door!" he yelled. I jumped up just as my picture window spider-webbed and a bullet slammed into the back of Justin's skull. The round exited through his mouth and whacked into a wall stud under one of Candi's paintings. As Justin fell out of his chair, I spun toward the back door and saw Cody coming like a locomotive down the hall, his pistol in his hand. I aimed at the door just as it flew open with a loud crack. I caught a brief glimpse of Buck Kierdorf as he stepped over the threshold, and my finger was tightening on the trigger when the boom of Cody's Magnum .357 split the air. Kierdorf flew off the rear step and into the darkness.

From the street came a third shot. I looked at Cody. "He might still be alive," I said, heading for the back door. Cody went to the broken window and stood aside it, peeking out and looking for a shooter.

Buck Kierdorf lay on the cold dirt, staring up at the stars. Cody's hollow point round had blown a gaping hole in his stomach. His arms were outstretched, his right hand still clutching an automatic, a Glock .45. I stepped on his wrist and kicked the gun away.

"Why?" I said, lowering myself to a knee.

"That money was supposed to be mine," he wheezed, blood bubbling from his mouth. "I was gonna kill all you fuckers."

"For Jerrod Palatine?"

Through his pain, a tiny smile creased his cheeks. "Funny, ain't it?" he said. Then blood poured from his mouth and his body tensed. He gurgled, eyes bulging, and a second later his breath left him in a long sigh.

I heard Cody behind me. He stepped down onto the dirt, his attention focused to the right.

"Cover me," he said, and began walking along the backside of my house, toward the lawn. I followed him, knowing that once we reached the end of the wall, we'd be exposed to whoever fired the shot that broke my window.

Cody poked his head around the corner, looking over the grass and the deck and the fence that separated my lot from my neighbor's. "I don't see anything," he whispered.

"I'm gonna make a run for it," I said. "To the pine tree." I stepped around Cody, leapt up onto the deck, and ran the ten yards to the tree, expecting to hear a shot at any instant. Then I saw Marcus Grier walking up the driveway.

"He's gone," Grier said, pointing down the street. His eyes were round, and he held his .38 revolver at his side. I saw a body lying on the pavement, a few feet from my mailbox.

"What happened?" I asked, eyes darting.

"He ran up and was almost to your driveway when I told him to halt. He pointed his gun at me and I fired. Hit him in the chest."

"He's the one that fired into my house?"

"No. That was someone else. The shot came from your neighbor's yard. I saw the shooter run off."

"Clear, Cody," I yelled. He walked out from behind the house and joined us on the deck.

"Who's that?" Cody said, eyeing the body in the street. We followed Grier to the corpse. The man was lying face down, one arm twisted behind his back. I knelt and looked at his face. A single sightless eye stared back at me.

"Mark Costa," I said.

"Who?" Grier said.

"One of Jerrod Palatine's security squad."

"I always thought he was in over his head," Cody said.

"You were right."

"Where's Justin Palatine?" Grier said, looking toward my house.

"On his way to hell," I said. "Whoever shot him was quite a marksman."

"Another one of Jerrod Palatine's security men?" Grier asked.

Before I could answer, a loud bang sounded from around the corner. We all ducked and started toward my house for cover.

"What was that?" Cody said.

"Gunshot," Grier replied.

"No," I said, walking back toward the street and listening to the fading rumble of an engine. "It was a backfire."

· · ·

Two ambulances arrived shortly, followed by a pair of detectives who worked for Grier. He pulled them aside, and they talked for a few minutes while the paramedics waited. Then the detectives began taking pictures, first of Costa, and when they were done, I took them inside, where they photographed Palatine's body and tried to ascertain the trajectory of the bullet that killed him. One of the detectives crouched at the table, approximating Palatine's position when he'd been shot. He pointed a laser device at the bullet hole in the window. The other detective went outside, and I saw him walk across the yard to the fence, and then out to the sidewalk. When he returned a minute later, he said, "There's an overturned bucket on the other side of the fence. The shooter probably stood on it. That would let him balance his rifle on top of the fence. It lines up pretty well. I knocked on the door, but the house is dark."

"Are your neighbor's home?" the first detective asked me.

"Apparently not."

It took almost half an hour for the detectives to finish up. They took pictures of Kierdorf's body, along with my broken door, which had a footprint in the center that matched the tread of Kierdorf's shoe.

Standing on the sidewalk, Grier again conversed with the detectives, before finally giving the paramedics the okay to remove the bodies. Cody and I stood watching from the driveway as they body-bagged Mark Costa and loaded him into the ambulance. I shook my head at the sight. I thought Costa was the type of enlisted man who was better at taking orders than making his own decisions. After leaving the Marines, I imagined his master plan was for Jerrod Palatine to provide him a comfortable living. He may have realized he was a dupe as he lay dying in the street. Or maybe he died before it occurred to him.

Once they were done with Costa, one of the paramedics rolled a gurney through my yard and behind the house to where Buck Kierdorf, by virtue of his venality and wickedness, had surrendered his claim to life. By all accounts, Kierdorf was an immoral and evil man, and part of an unfortunate subspecies of law enforcement personnel that, despite ongoing pressures to reform, police forces can never seem to permanently rid themselves of.

While Cody helped lift Kierdorf's dead weight onto the stretcher, I led the second paramedic into the house. Justin Palatine lay crumpled next to the kitchen table, his chair on its side. His head was twisted as though he were looking over his shoulder, and his face rested in a pool of blood thickening on the linoleum. A hideous grimace was frozen on his profile, his lips pulled back, his mouth open in silent rage. His canines looked unusually long and pointed, as if he were a predator snarling before a kill. I looked at the ghastly sight, thinking that only in death was his true persona revealed. He had kept his savagery concealed to all but an unfortunate few, wreaking havoc and avoiding prosecution, the embodiment of the monster next door. I was almost tempted to take a picture, but I didn't want the sickening image on my phone.

A few minutes later, we stood outside as the ambulances drove off, followed by the detectives.

"Well, Sheriff," Cody said. "You look like you could use a stiff drink."

"Let me take a wild guess, Gibbons. You'd be happy to join me."

Cody turned his palms up. "It'd be downright impolite of me to let you drink alone."

We went inside, and while Cody grabbed my bottle of Jim Beam, I stood frowning at the bloody mess Palatine had left. As Cody poured shots, I got a bucket and mop from the garage and started swabbing the deck.

"It's good none got on your carpet," Grier said, sitting at the far end of the table.

"Will I hear from your detectives?" I asked, mopping and doing my best to absorb the blood.

"No. Cody's shooting was in self-defense. For that matter, so was mine."

"A tidy package, isn't it?"

"Not really. Whoever shot Palatine is still at large. My detectives took the bucket to the lab for prints."

"That's good," I said.

"Take a break, Dan." Cody held up a shot glass. I took it from his hand.

"Here's to old-fashioned justice, men," Cody said. Marcus and I exchanged glances before we drank. As a lawman, he had to have reservations about the events of the evening. When he asked me to take down Justin Palatine, I don't think he anticipated it would happen in his town. And I know he never fathomed it would result in three dead men, one by his gun. A shootout with three killed might be passing news in San Jose, but in South Lake Tahoe, it was a big deal, maybe even story of the year for an enterprising journalist. That was the last thing Grier wanted. Hell, it was also the last thing *I* wanted. I'd have to get out of town, maybe head down to Mexico for a week to let the furor die down.

"You knew the one out there?" Grier asked, nodding toward the back door.

"Yeah," Cody replied, gunning his shot. "He was a crooked cop from San Jose. A real piece of shit."

"He won't be mourned by many at SJPD," I added.

"I'm sure they'll call me," Grier said.

"I wouldn't worry about it," Cody said, pouring a second round. "The only reason he wasn't shit-canned years ago is the brass was worried about what horror stories he might leak. They'll be celebrating when they hear he got smoked."

"Speaking of leaks, I've got a present for you," I said. I went into my office, where Cody had locked Palatine's souvenir bags, along with the leather satchel. I picked up the baggies, handling them carefully, and brought them to the table.

"Here you go, Marcus," I said. "Every woman here, or their families, need to know Justin Palatine is dead."

"There's only one family I'm concerned with, and they live in South Lake Tahoe. I'll be calling them tonight."

"You have no interest?" I asked, the bags dangling from my fingertips.

"Someone needs to contact the FBI," Grier said. "But not me."

The room fell silent. Then Cody said, "I'll take care of it." Grier and I both stared at him, waiting for an explanation, but he just smiled and poured himself another shot.

"How?" I said.

"Oh, I'm sure I'll come up with something."

. . .

Grier headed home after that, leaving me to continue my cleanup work, while Cody nailed a piece of plywood over my busted window. The back door was probably a total loss, as Kierdorf's kick had dented the facing and splintered the jamb. I nailed it shut with a length of two-by-four.

"Let's go get some chow," Cody said.

"I need to make a phone call," I said, and went into my office. It was a little before eight o'clock on a Thursday night. I pulled up my address book and found the number for retired General Raymond Horvachek. He lived in Sacramento and hired me for a case a couple of years back. We still exchanged favors on occasion.

"Evening, Reno," he answered.

"Hello, General. How are you doing?"

"What can I do for you?" He was never big on pleasantries. Always brusque and to the point.

"An army veteran named Tim Cook. I'd like to know his service record."

"That's a common name. How old is he?"

"Mid-forties or thereabouts."

"Hold, please." I heard his fingers pound at a keyboard. A minute later, he said, "Born in Tennessee, 1975, five-ten, one-sixty."

"Sounds about right."

"He enlisted when he was eighteen. Saw action in Haiti, Liberia, then he did a three-year tour in Afghanistan. Received his honorable discharge as a corporal in 2005."

"Did he study or practice law in the army?"

"No, he wasn't in the JAG program."

"Did he have a specialty?"

"Yes, he was in Special Forces. A sniper."

When I didn't reply, he said, "Does that surprise you?"

I took a deep breath. "A little."

"Anything else?"

"No, sir."

"Goodnight, then."

I sat at my desk for a while, my thoughts turned inward, until Cody opened the door. "Candi?" he asked.

"No," I muttered, standing. "What a night, huh?"

"All's well that ends well, Kemosabe. Right?"

I picked up Justin Palatine's leather satchel and tossed it to Cody. "Let's count it," I said.

. . .

The money was all there, two hundred and fifty grand in bound packets of new hundred-dollar bills. I locked the bag in my safe, then we set out on foot for Whiskey Dick's. I wanted to grab a burrito at the taqueria next door and guzzle five or six bourbon-Cokes. That's how this case started, and I wanted to end it the same way. Maybe I was hoping to get a sense of closure. Or at least drink enough to blur the details to the point that I no longer cared. And with Cody by my side, that part was easy.

"You all right?" Cody asked, as we hiked toward the highway. When I didn't reply, he said, "We can get your place fixed up tomorrow morning."

"Who do you think shot Justin?" I said.

"One of his brother's men. Jerrod made the decision, gave the orders. Justin was too great a liability. The cold-hearted SOB had him killed."

"That's what I originally thought. But I was wrong."

"Huh?"

"It wasn't Jerrod. It was Tim Cook, the D.A."

"What the hell?" Cody said, laughing, but I heard an uncertain twitch in his voice.

"Hard to believe, isn't it?"

"How did you come to this conclusion?"

"That backfire we heard was Cook's rust bucket Chevy Blazer."

"How can you know that?"

"Because I recognized the sound. How many guys you know drive a car that backfires?"

"That doesn't mean he was the shooter."

"Cook was a U.S. Army sniper. He did three years in Afghanistan. I think Grier told him about the meeting tonight."

"But did Grier know he'd show up and shoot Palatine?"

I crossed my arms and kicked a pinecone down the street. "Maybe. But even if he didn't, Grier saw Cook run off after the shooting. He must have recognized him."

"Cook could have been wearing a mask."

"Yeah, maybe. But I think Grier still knew it was him."

We continued silently. It was dark and the pines towered around us. Through the boughs, pockets of light from house windows looked like distant campfires in the wilderness. It was so quiet and still that it was hard to imagine such carnage had just occurred.

"I got to hand it to you, Dirt."

"What?"

"Your district attorney is a hit man? In quaint South Lake Tahoe?"

I shrugged. "Whatever it takes."

Cody burst out laughing and thumped me on the shoulder. "And I thought I had it bad in San Jose."

16

Aᴛᴛᴇʀ ꜱᴛᴀʀᴛɪɴɢ ᴀ ᴘᴏᴛ of coffee the next morning, I went outside and stood on the deck. Frost coated the redwood planks, and storm clouds gray as raw iron loomed over the ridge tops. Blowing into my hands, I walked to the front of the house and looked up and down the street. Then I paced the perimeter of my yard, glancing at the plywood over my broken window, until I reached the rear of the house. I inspected the damage and shook my head. Buck Kierdorf's last act as a living soul had been to destroy my back door. Somehow that seemed fitting for a person who existed primarily to cause grief for others. There was a smear of blood in the dirt, and I obliterated it with the tread of my boot, erasing the last traces of a man I doubted anyone would miss. As for the door, I would try to get a new one installed by the afternoon. If I was lucky, I could get the window replaced at the same time.

I'd called Candi last night, shortly after Cody and I arrived at Whiskey Dick's. She sounded cheerful and eager to get home, and was scheduled to touch down in Reno at six ᴘ.ᴍ. tonight. When she asked about my case, I told her it had been wrapped up, except for a few stray details. I hadn't told her anything about the shootings at our house, or about the bag of cash sitting in my safe. When the time was right, I'd tell her what happened. I knew if I started hiding things from Candi, it would spell bad news for our relationship. My policy was full disclosure, even if the details might be hard to stomach.

I went back inside, and by nine A.M. I'd drunk almost a full pot. Along with two aspirin, that relieved my mild hangover. Then I got to work re-scrubbing the area where Justin had bled on the floor until it was fully sanitized.

Cody came into the kitchen as I was cooking breakfast. He sat at the table rubbing his eyes, and I poured him a cup.

"I've got an appointment at one P.M. in Sacramento," he said.

"I remember some drunken babble about a reporter last night."

"You were the one babbling. Me, I was on the phone making arrangements."

"With who?"

"A reporter at the *Sacramento Bee*. I'm gonna give him the evidence bags. He says he's got a contact at the California State Police he can work with. Once he confirms Justin's prints and DNA, he'll write an article and blow up Jerrod Palatine's campaign."

"Wait a minute. I don't want my name attached to this."

"Me either. I won't meet the reporter in person. He'll never know who we are. I'll be like Deep Throat in Watergate."

I brought a couple of plates to the table and sat across from him. "How long before it's published?"

"He said two or three days. It's front-page news, an exclusive. Reporters love this kind of stuff."

"Your buddies at SJPD will be thrilled their boy won't get elected."

Cody swallowed a bite of eggs and bacon and sipped from his mug. "They'll get over it. Despite his donations, they don't want a crooked governor pulling their strings."

"I thought you wanted to vote for Palatine."

"I've reconsidered," he said, leaning back in his chair. "Look, the homeless problem pisses me off, and our current governor hasn't done enough to fix it. But the answer isn't hit teams. I mean, that's a bit overboard, don't you think?"

"I think you give a man like Jerrod Palatine power, he'll abuse it however he likes. If he gets SJPD in his back pocket, who knows what might happen? He might try to become Emperor Palatine."

"I'm sure he'd try, but he won't get the chance. He doesn't know it yet, but his boat's sunk.

"What about his badass legal firm?"

"They might be able to scare off smaller internet guys, but not the *Sacramento Bee*. There's something to be said for old school media."

I chewed on a piece of toast. "It will get interesting. I'm thinking it might be good timing to get scarce. For both of us."

"Yeah, I'd say we've ruffled a few feathers. If things get too ugly, I might move to Vegas. I called Abbey last night and we talked about it. Right after I told her Justin Palatine ate a bullet."

"Really?"

"Yeah. Cash out my San Jose pad, go live near my daughter."

"For the near term," I said, "a week or two in Cabo might not be a bad idea. We can afford a little vacation, huh?"

"Fifty-fifty on the cash?"

"Like always, partner," I said, holding out my hand. Cody grabbed it and we shook until he rose to his feet like an exultant quarterback who just threw for a winning touchdown. "Bartender, fire up the margaritas," he exclaimed, grinning and pumping his fist. "Fuck 'em all and sleep 'til noon!"

17

THREE DAYS WENT BY before the Sacramento newspaper published their story on Justin Palatine and his criminal history. It provided his victim's names, and specified that at least four had died of their injuries. It also highlighted that Justin's only professional job had been at Digicloud, where his older brother was the CEO. I read the article on my computer while relaxing at a resort just outside of Cabo San Lucas. Candi was out on our suite's shaded balcony, wearing a bikini and sipping iced tea while gazing at the Sea of Cortez. It was 87 degrees at ten A.M. Typical fall weather for the southern tip of the Baja California Peninsula.

I finished reading the article, then ran a Google search and saw the story had been picked up by a number of media outlets, including major cable and network news providers. The editorial pieces were scathing in their analysis. Jerrod Palatine was painted as an immoral plutocrat who surely must have known of, or at least suspected his brother's horrible crimes.

I called Cody's cell. His suite was in a separate building at the sprawling resort. With him was his on-and-off again girlfriend, Heidi-ho. She was a small, blonde beauty with sparkling dark eyes and a temperamental tendency after a few drinks. Cody claimed she was a flat-chested gymnast before breast augmentation expanded her chest to forty-two inches. He also shared that she was really a brunette.

"Yo," he answered.

"Check your computer," I said. "The story's out. It's all over the Internet."

"Oh, yeah? Give me fifteen minutes, then meet me at the pool."

"Which one?"

"The one with the swim-up bar."

I gathered up Candi, and we went down the stairs and followed a meandering cobblestone path until we reached a collection of infinity pools built at the edge of the beach. I saw Cody standing under a big umbrella providing shade for four lounge chairs. Next to him, Heidi looked tiny.

"Look at you two big studs, strutting around with your shirts off," Heidi said. "You must be hell on the bad guys."

"He's hell on the bad girls, too," Candi said, slapping my butt.

"Easy, now," I said.

"Dan and I need to talk shop for a couple minutes," Cody said. "Would you excuse us? I brought down a pitcher of iced tea."

We walked over to an empty, untended bar on the opposite side of the pool.

"Palatine's through," Cody said. "He'll be lucky to stay on as CEO of his company. Digicloud stock is taking a dump."

"I'm sure there's a lot of pissed off investors out there."

"Not me. I shorted the stock."

"Really?"

"Yeah, it was too good to pass up." Cody leaned on the bar with both elbows and clasped his hands. "Do you think Jerrod knew about Justin's rapes?" he asked.

"Hard to say. Maybe the two weren't that close."

"If he didn't know, it's because he ignored the signs."

"Could be," I said, pulling out a barstool.

"Anyway, we know that Jerrod was behind the homeless killings."

"On its own, that disqualifies him from political office."

"Word gets out, it could land him in jail."

"Did you talk to the reporter about it?" I asked.

"Nope," Cody said, sitting. He looked at me out of the corner of his eye. "I want to keep it in my back pocket. If Palatine or any of his minions at SJPD give me any grief, I'll threaten to take fire and ice to the press. Imagine what they'd do with that story."

I looked across the pool, where Candi and Heidi reclined on lounge chairs, legs outstretched. They were laughing and chatting up a storm.

"You're always thinking one step ahead, old buddy," I said.

"Fuckin' A. How do you think I've survived so long in this business?"

"That's a question I ask myself sometimes."

"The answer is easy, Dirt," Cody said, a wry smile on his mug. "Life's a battle of good versus evil. Stay on the good side, and you'll never die."

"I'll have to remember that one."

"Damn right. Come on, let's get back to our women. Heidi promised me she wouldn't drink until the sun goes down, but I need to keep an eye on her."

I laughed. "And who's going to keep an eye on you?"

. . .

For dinner that evening, we had reservations at De Cortez, a fancy steakhouse at the far end of the resort. We planned to sit on the stone terrace and watch the waves roll in as we drank margaritas. I intended to catch a pleasant buzz and enjoy a steak while we chatted about anything but the Palatines. Candi seemed to be back to her old self, and I could feel the pressure of the previous weeks drain from my skull until it evaporated in its own heat, like a fever sweat. In its place was a sense of serenity I hadn't felt for months.

Candi was showering and I was sitting out on the balcony, enjoying the balmy afternoon weather, when my cell rang. It showed a Santa Clara County area code, but I didn't recognize the number.

"Hello?"

"Hello, this is Arthur De Carvalho, calling for Dave Edwards."

"Ah, yes, sir," I said after a second, remembering the elderly man I spoke to at Marcia Palatine's retirement home. "This is Dave. What can I do for you?"

"I have some information you may find useful for the book you're writing on Silicon Valley companies." His voice was cracking and sounded frail.

"Thank you for calling. I'm all ears."

"Marcia passed away yesterday. In her will, she left her belongings to me. In hindsight, I almost wish she hadn't."

"Why is that, sir?"

"I found an old diary of hers, buried in a box. It was locked with a metal clasp, but I managed to open it. Her last entry was five years ago."

"Did she write about her sons?"

"Indeed, she did. And I must tell you, I had a difficult time with what I learned. I don't quite have the words to describe it."

"Please try," I said.

"I'll do my best. One of Anthony Palatine's former caretakers at Agnews State Hospital raped Marcia. This occurred nearly ten years after Agnews closed, but Marcia recognized him."

When he didn't continue, I said, "That's unfortunate."

"Yes, it was," he said slowly. "She was impregnated by him. The result was her son, Justin."

"What?" I said.

"She contacted the police, but there wasn't enough evidence for an arrest."

"Wait a minute. I thought both Justin and Jerrod inherited their intelligence from their father."

"That's an incorrect assumption on your part, young man. Anthony Palatine had an average IQ. The brains came from Marcia. She had genius level intelligence."

"I'm very surprised to learn that."

"Yes, well, I haven't got to the worst part yet, so brace yourself. Marcia wrote that every time she looked at Justin, she saw the man who raped her. Her hatred for Justin became so profound that she allowed and even arranged for him to be molested, in the most horrible way, by a series of men."

I pressed my fingertips to my forehead. "That's a very disturbing story," I said.

"And to think I felt fondly of this woman. I could never have imagined."

"What about Jerrod?"

"He was away at Harvard while this was happening, but Marcia confided in him. He knew his younger brother was the son of a rapist, and he knew what his mother did to him. She wrote that Jerrod never forgave her."

"Jerrod tried to make up for it by supporting Justin," I said. "He hired him at Digicloud, kept him employed since he graduated from college."

"That's commendable in a way, I suppose."

"Yes, but…" I paused, deciding he didn't need to know what had become of Justin. At least not by my telling.

"Are you still there?"

"Yes, I'm here, Mr. De Carvalho."

"If you like, you can have her diary. I have no desire to keep it. Perhaps you'll gain more insight into Jerrod Palatine."

"Would it be possible to send it to me?"

"Provide me your address and I'll do so today."

After we hung up, I put my hands on the railing and stared out to where the sea merged with the horizon. The sun was low and hovered above a thin band of clouds. I stayed there long enough to watch the yellow rays pierce the clouds and shatter the sky into white shards. A moment later, a blinding silver streak split the water. The radiance appeared to be boiling, as if heated by the screams of tormented souls. I stood listening to the crash of the surf and didn't go inside until Candi called me.

EPILOGUE

THE EVENTS OF THAT fall stayed with me for longer than I care to admit, but like all things, its weight lightened with time. If anything, the experience left me with the sad knowledge that certain people, when subjected to the worst circumstances, may not only forego their humanity, but have the capacity to create evil so potent it can last for generations.

Whether Justin Palatine passed his bad seed to any of his unwitting victims, I didn't know. I hoped not, because his toxic genetic blend was born from the violent union of two psychopaths. I felt Marcia Palatine and her attacker were equally culpable in Justin's outcome. Marcia could have chosen a number of remedies for her unwanted pregnancy, some of which might have provided a decent upbringing for Justin. Instead, she opted to treat him in the most cruel and sadistic manner imaginable. In doing so, she created one of the most prolific rapists in U.S. history.

Nothing in Marcia's diary indicated she was aware of Justin's crimes, but even if she knew, I doubted she would have cared. The only good news was that all three in this grim trinity were dead; I had learned that the man who originally met Marcia Palatine at Agnews State Hospital and later raped her had burned to death in an automobile accident fifteen years ago.

The knowledge that Jerrod Palatine descended from Marcia's genes made me especially happy to see his campaign for governor go up in flames. He was smart enough to realize he could not repair the public relations disaster that ensued after the *Sacramento Bee* published their story. He quickly withdrew from the race and hunkered down, hoping to salvage his company's reputation. The last time I checked, Digicloud's stock price still hadn't recovered from the beating it took when Justin's crimes were publicized.

I had placed Marcia Palatine's diary, wrapped tightly in plain brown paper, in my safe deposit box, but I did not wish to open it again. As soon as I had a chance, I planned to toss it into a fire and watch it burn until there was nothing left. From Anthony's mental illness and suicide, to Marcia's rape, to Justin's subsequent abuse at the hands of multiple pedophiles, their sordid legacy was one of rotten luck compounded by misplaced hatred. And that was before factoring in Justin's rapes and murders, and Jerrod's indiscriminate killing of indigent people. All told, the Palatines were like a train packed with chemical waste, hurtling down the tracks, brakes failed, spewing pestilence and leaving misery and death in their wake.

Neither Cody nor I were contacted by any police agency after Justin's death. As we predicted, SJPD bore no grudge over the demise of Buck Kierdorf. The FBI, however, had called Marcus Grier to question him about the shootings at my home, and to inquire about the source of Justin's souvenir bags. Grier called to tell me the Feds were satisfied with his response, which meant I wouldn't be contacted. I imagined the bureau was preoccupied with following up on the victim list after the newspaper published their names.

"Hey, Marcus," I said. "Regarding my expenses for the investigation."

"How much do I owe you?"

"I haven't added it up. Probably at least five grand."

"That much? I'll have to pay you in installments."

"Installments? What do you think I am, a bank?"

"I'm a little low on cash right now."

"Ah, shit. How about I make you a deal?"

"Like what? Charge me interest?"

I laughed. "That's a thought. But I'll do you one better. You don't need to pay me anything. It's taken care of."

"Five grand, taken care of?"

"That's what I said. Just invite Candi and me over for a BBQ this spring, and we'll call it even."

"I don't like to be played, Dan," he said, his voice edged with suspicion.

"No games, I'm serious."

"Well," he sputtered. "That's a lot of money."

"Don't worry about it."

"Huh," he said. "I don't know why you'd do this, and I won't ask, but you got a deal."

"No problemo, Sheriff."

. . .

If there was an unexpected upside that fall, it was a marked improvement in San Jose's homeless problem. California's current governor delivered on a number of promises that had been stalled in bureaucratic lockdown. It seemed the fire and ice crimes, along with the rainy night shooting along Los Gatos Creek, had motivated the politicians to jump through the necessary hoops. A number of the city's largest encampments were cleaned up and vacated.

"You can really see the difference," Cody said. "All the hobos pitching tents on the freeway entrances and exits have vamoosed."

"Where to?"

"They've made hundreds of cheap or free living spaces available. Tiny homes, modular, prefabricated homes, low-rent hotels. The corporations are kicking in big bucks."

"Maybe they'll open up another insane asylum for the schizophrenics."

"I doubt they will, but they should. I read that roughly two thirds of California's homeless are mentally disabled or addicts. The other third are either physically disabled or just in a temporary bind. Of course, there're also some who are just lazy or stupid. They're my favorites, with the drunks and meth-heads a close second."

"But at least they're getting them off the streets."

"Yeah, it's not bad. I'm thinking of staying here for the time being. There's a lot of homeless douchebags in Vegas too, so it's not like the grass is much greener."

. . .

It was on a late afternoon a few days before Christmas, and I was tending bar at Zeke's Pit when Tim Cook walked in. I saw him stop at the hostess stand and ask to place a to-go order.

"Hey, Tim," I yelled, and waved him over to the bar. I grabbed a pen and a pad of paper.

"What can I get you?" I asked.

"Two chicken dinners and a side order of brisket."

"You want a draught while you wait?"

"All right," he said, climbing onto a stool.

I poured him a beer and wiped down the bar. We were the only people in the room.

"Looks like a good start to the ski season," I said, looking out the front window at banks of snow surrounding the parking lot.

"We need it. The resorts are hurting after last year's drought."

I nodded and washed a few glasses. "You want to get your muffler fixed, I got a buddy who'll give you a good deal."

He looked at me, eyebrows raised in surprise. "Actually, I just bought a new car."

"Really? What kind?"

"Another Blazer. I'm a Chevy guy."

We chatted about cars for a minute, until a group arrived and bought drinks. After they sat at a table, Zak came from the kitchen with three Styrofoam containers stacked in a plastic bag.

"What do I owe you?" Cook said, reaching for his wallet.

"It's on the house, Tim," I said.

"Thanks, but I can't accept gifts. It's against the ethics of my job."

"This has nothing to do with your job. I consider you an American hero. Your money's no good here."

We met eyes, and he winced briefly. I gave him the thumbs up and grinned. "Keep on fightin' the good fight, man," I said.

He nodded in affirmation, and in his eyes I caught a glimmer of defiant individualism that countered what I always thought was his by-the-book personality. I watched him hurry out the door, then I went to the front window to check out his new ride. It had started snowing again, and his tires spun on the ice before biting into the road. I stood there as he turned onto Highway 50 and drove off into the winter haze.

The Christmas lights spiraling upward on the big pine in the parking lot were twinkling through the snowflakes. I stepped out into the cold and gazed up at the tree, then I turned my eyes to the mountains surrounding Tahoe Valley. The sight of snow floating down from the sky and the jagged peaks coated in white reminded me that the world is a grand place. In some ways, I believe it's better than perfect.

Of course, there's always the other side of the coin to consider, if one is inclined. But not me, not today. Like a nightmare that releases its hold in the light of day, the Palatines and others as wicked would pass through my life, but their presence was always temporary. If there was anything positive about them, it was the perspective they provided. If not for their ilk, I might not appreciate the little things so much. I might take for granted my friendship with Cody Gibbons or my relationship with Candi. I might even become jaded to the natural beauty in the idyllic place I was fortunate enough to call home. And I most definitely would find it harder to make a living.

I breathed in the cold air as tiny snowflakes melted on my face. When I went back inside, I saw Liz behind the bar, starting her shift. I took off my apron and asked her to make me a drink, just one, before I headed home to where Candi waited. Sitting at the bar, I realized I was lucky in more ways than I could count.

ABOUT THE AUTHOR

BORN IN DETROIT, MICHIGAN, in 1960, Dave Stanton moved to Northern California in 1961. He attended San Jose State University and received a BA in journalism in 1983. Over the years, he worked as a bartender, newspaper advertising salesman, furniture mover, debt collector, and technology salesman. He has two children, Austin and Haley. He and his wife, Heidi, live in San Jose, California.

Stanton is the author of eight novels, all featuring private investigator Dan Reno and his ex-cop buddy, Cody Gibbons.

To learn more, visit the author's website at:

http://danrenonovels.com/

If you enjoyed THE ASYLUM THREAD, please
don't hesitate to leave a review at:

Amazon US: http://bit.ly/DaveStanton
Amazon UK: http://bit.ly/DaveStantonUK

To contact Dave Stanton or subscribe to his newsletter, go to:

http://danrenonovels.com/contact/

More Dan Reno Novels:

STATELINE

Cancel the wedding–the groom is dead.

When a tycoon's son is murdered the night before his wedding, the enraged and grief-stricken father offers investigator Dan Reno (that's *Reno,* as in *no problemo)*, a life-changing bounty to find the killer. Reno, nearly broke, figures he's finally landed in the right place at the right time. It's a nice thought, but when a band of crooked cops get involved, Reno finds himself not only earning every penny of his paycheck, but also fighting for his life.

Who committed the murder, and why? And what of the dark sexual deviations that keep surfacing? Haunted by his murdered father and a violent, hard drinking past, Reno wants no more blood on his hands. But a man's got to make a living, and backing off is not in his DNA. Traversing the snowy alpine winter in the Sierras and the lonely deserts of Nevada, Reno must revert to his old ways to survive. Because the fat bounty won't do him much good if he's dead...

Available on Amazon.com US: http://bit.ly/Stateline-Amazon

DYING FOR THE HIGHLIFE

Jimmy Homestead's glory days as a high school stud were a distant memory. His adulthood had amounted to little more than temporary jobs, petty crime, and discount whiskey. But he always felt he was special, and winning the Lotto proved it.

Flush with millions, everything is great for Jimmy—until people from his past start coming out of the woodwork, seeking payback over transgressions Jimmy thought were long forgotten.

Caught in the middle are private detective Dan Reno and his good buddy Cody Gibbons, two guys just trying to make an honest paycheck. Reno, fighting to save his home from foreclosure, thinks that's his biggest problem. But his priorities change when he's drawn into a hard-boiled mess that leaves dead bodies scattered all over northern Nevada.

Available on Amazon.com US: http://bit.ly/TheHighlife

SPEED METAL BLUES

Bounty hunter Dan Reno never thought he'd be the prey.

It's a two-for-one deal when a pair of accused rapists from a New Jersey-based gang surface in South Lake Tahoe. The first is easy to catch, but the second, a Satanist suspected of a string of murders, is an adversary unlike any Reno has faced. After escaping Reno's clutches in the desert outside of Carson City, the target vanishes. That is, until he makes it clear he intends to settle the score.

To make matters worse, the criminal takes an interest in a teenage boy and his talented sister, both friends of Reno's. Wading through a drug-dealing turf war and a deadly feud between mobsters running a local casino, Reno can't figure out how his target fits in with the new outlaws in town. He only knows he's hunting for a ghost-like adversary calling all the shots.

The more Reno learns about his target, the more he's convinced that mayhem is inevitable unless he can capture him quickly. He'd prefer to do it clean, without further bloodshed. But sometimes that ain't in the cards, especially when Reno's partner Cody Gibbons decides it's time for payback.

Available on Amazon.com US: http://bit.ly/SpeedMetalBlues

DARK ICE

Two murdered girls, and no motive…

While skiing deep in Lake Tahoe's backcountry, Private Eye Dan Reno finds the first naked body, buried under fresh snow. Reno's contacted by the grieving father, who wants to know who murdered his daughter, and why? And how could the body end up in such a remote, mountainous location? The questions become murkier when a second body is found. Is there a serial killer stalking promiscuous young women in South Lake Tahoe? Or are the murders linked to a different criminal agenda?

Searching for answers, Reno is accosted by a gang of racist bikers with a score to settle. He also must deal with his pal, Cody Gibbons, who the police consider a suspect. The clues lead to the owner of a strip club and a womanizing police captain, but is either the killer?

The bikers up the ante, but are unaware that Cody Gibbons has Reno's back at any cost. Meanwhile, the police won't tolerate Reno's continued involvement in the case. But Reno knows he's getting close. And the most critical clue comes from the last person he'd suspect…

Available on Amazon.com US: http://bit.ly/DarkIce

HARD PREJUDICE

The DNA evidence should have made the rape a slam dunk case.

But after the evidence disappeared from a police locker, the black man accused of brutally raping a popular actor's daughter walked free. Hired by the actor, private detective Dan Reno's job seemed simple enough: discover who took the DNA, and why. Problem is, from the beginning of the investigation, neither Reno, the South Lake Tahoe police, nor anyone else have any idea what the motivation could be to see ghetto thug Duante Tucker get away with the crime. Not even Reno's best friend, fellow investigator Cody Gibbons, has a clue.

When Reno and Gibbons tail Tucker, they learn the rapist is linked to various criminals and even a deserter from the U.S. Marine Corps. But they still can't tell who would want him set free, and for what reason?

The clues continue to build until Reno and Cody find themselves targeted for death. That tells Reno he's getting close, so he and Gibbons put the pedal to the metal. The forces of evil are running out of time, and the action reaches a boiling point before an explosive conclusion that reveals a sinister plot and motivations that Reno never imagined.

Available on Amazon.com US: http://bit.ly/hardprejudice

THE DOOMSDAY GIRL

Melanie Jordan's life seemed perfect.

Until masked intruders arrive at her house, demanding gold she doesn't have. A savage blow to the head puts her in a coma for four weeks.

When Melanie regains consciousness, she learns her husband has been murdered and her ten-year-old daughter is missing.

Private Eye Dan Reno begins investigating, but nothing about the case makes sense. Was there gold at the house or wasn't there? Was Melanie's husband hiding something? And what happened to Melanie's daughter?

To complicate things, the case leads to Las Vegas, where Reno's loose-cannon buddy, Cody Gibbons, is trying to repair his relationship with his college-aged daughter, an intern with Las Vegas P.D.

When clues implicate Russian mobsters and a mysterious African illegal, Reno tries to stay in the shadows, but once the crooks feel the noose tightening, they raise the stakes to a deadly level.

And then, as they say in Vegas, all bets are off.

Available on Amazon.com US: http://bit.ly/TheDoomsdayGirl

RIGHT CROSS

Dan Reno claimed self-defense, but the prosecuting attorney had other ideas.

The missing person case seemed wrong from the start. The client paid in cash, used a phony name, and his claim to be searching for his missing nephew didn't add up. It doesn't take Reno long to do the math, and once does, he tries to return the money to the client. And that's when things go awry.

The new D.A. in South Lake Tahoe has already drawn conclusions and wants to send Reno to prison. Out on bail, Reno has two weeks to uncover the client's true identity and motivations, or else. With his fiancée Candi at home pregnant, the stakes are higher than ever.

When Reno's partner Cody Gibbons hears what's going on, he suspects his and Reno's history in San Jose is at play. But the clues lead in the opposite direction, to Miami, and then to the Caribbean. Reno's in uncharted territory, and now he'll learn just how far he's willing to go to save himself. But Gibbons only know one way to play it. And that doesn't bode well for their enemies.

Available on Amazon.com US: https://amzn.to/34CoFDk

Available on Amazon.com UK: https://amzn.to/3HKx0WJ

Made in the USA
Middletown, DE
05 July 2023

34572248R00166